JOYCE CAROL OATES

Little Bird of Heaven

FOURTH ESTATE • *London*

Fourth Estate
An imprint of HarperCollins*Publishers*
77–85 Fulham Palace Road
Hammersmith
London W6 8JB

Visit our authors' blog at www.fifthestate.co.uk
Love this book? www.bookarmy.com

This Fourth Estate paperback edition published 2010
1

Originally published in the United States by Ecco in 2009

A catalogue record for this book is available from the British Library

ISBN 978-0-00-734254-9

Printed and bound in Great Britain by Clays Ltd, St Ives plc

Mixed Sources
Product group from well-managed
forests and other controlled sources
www.fsc.org   Cert no. SW-COC-001806
© 1996 Forest Stewardship Council

FSC

FSC is a non-profit international organisation established to promote the
responsible management of the world's forests. Products carrying the FSC
label are independently certified to assure consumers that they come
from forests that are managed to meet the social, economic and
ecological needs of present and future generations.

Find out more about HarperCollins and the environment at
www.harpercollins.co.uk/green

For Charlie Gross

Well love they tell me is a fragile thing
It's hard to fly on broken wings
I lost my ticket to the promised land
Little bird of heaven right here in my hand.

"Little Bird of Heaven,"
  by Martha Scanlan

Part

One

1

THE YEARNING IN MY HEART! This was a long time ago.

"Can't go inside with you, Krista. But I promise: I won't drive away until you're safe indoors."

That November evening at dusk we were driving along the river—the Black River, in southern Herkimer County, New York—west and slightly south of the city of Sparta, in this long-ago time swathed in mist and smelling of a slightly metallic damp: the river, the rain.

There are those of us—daughters—forever daughters, at any age— for whom the smells—likely to be twin, twined—of tobacco smoke and alcohol are not unpleasant but highly attractive, seductive.

Driving along the river, bringing me home. This man who was my father Edward Diehl—who'd been "Eddy Diehl" and a name of some notoriety in Sparta, in those years—"Eddy Diehl" who would be my father until the night his body was to be riddled with eighteen bullets fired within ten seconds by an improvised firing squad of local law enforcement officers.

Daddy's hoarse voice, always slightly teasing. And you love being teased if you're a daughter, you know it is a sign of love.

"Just say we got held up, Puss. No need to elaborate."

I laughed. Anything Daddy said, I was likely to laugh and say *Sure*.

Always you had to respond quickly to a remark of Daddy's, even if it wasn't a question. If you failed to respond Daddy would look sharply at you, not frowning but not smiling either. A nudge in the ribs—*Eh? Right?*

Of course Daddy was bringing me home just a little late, carelessly late. So that there was no mistaking that I'd been *brought home* and hadn't taken the school bus.

Careless, that was Eddy Diehl's way. It was never Eddy Diehl's intention.

Daddy was bringing me home on that November evening not long before his death-by-firing-squad to a house from which he'd been banished by my mother and the circumstances of his banishment had been humiliating to him. This was a two-storey white clapboard house of no special distinction but it was precious to my father, or had been: a house Daddy had partly built, with his hands; a house whose roofing and painting he'd overseen; a house like others on the river road, paint beginning to peel on its northern, exposed side, shutters and trim in need of repair; a house from which several years before *Edward Diehl* had been banished by an injunction issued by the *Herkimer County Criminal Court, Family Services Division.* (Neither my brother nor I had seen this document though we knew that it existed, hidden away somewhere in our mother's *legal files*.)

Our mother kept such documents from us out of a fear—it was an unreasonable fear, but typical of her—that one of us, presumably me, might take the *injunction* and tear it into pieces.

I wasn't that kind of daughter. I think that I wasn't. Clinging to a man's careless promise *Won't drive away until you're safely indoors, Puss.*

From what dangers might I be safe, by this action of my father's, Daddy did not say.

I was very moved, Daddy called me *Puss.* This was my little-girl name I had not heard in some time. Though I was no longer a little girl, Daddy must know.

Having sighted him once, seeing me. Two years ago when I'd been in eighth grade. Thirteen years old and shorter by an inch or two than I was at fifteen, not an adolescent girl exactly though no longer what you'd call a *little girl*, yes but clearly a child, young for her age. And crossing a street downtown, several blocks from school, with two other eighth-grade girls. And squealing, and giggling, and running, as a tow truck bore menacingly upon us, the (male, young) driver teasing us by driving fast and (recklessly) close to cause a small tidal wave of gutter water to splash onto our bare legs, and once on the sidewalk, safe but laughing, breathless, in the aftermath of a *frisson* of terror by chance I saw a man about to climb into a car parked at the curb, and how intently this man was staring at us, at our wetted legs and clothes, seeing this man—with thick rust-colored hair, in profile—fleetingly, for I didn't pause in running, none of us did—I thought *Is that Daddy? That man?*

Later, I would think *no*. Not Daddy. The car he'd been climbing into hadn't looked familiar—I'd thought.

Of course, I hadn't looked back. Stared-at in the street by an adult man, at age thirteen you don't look back.

That day, two years before, there'd been rain. So frequently in Sparta there was rain. From Lake Ontario to the north and west—from the Great Lakes, beyond—(which I knew only from maps, and loved to contemplate: these lakes like exquisite cloud-formations linked one to the other and so beautifully named *Ontario, Erie, Huron, Michigan, Superior* where our father had promised Ben and me he'd take us sometime, on a "yacht trip")—always a sky out of which rain-clouds, massive gray-black thunderheads, might emerge as if by malevolent magic.

Of that landscape, and of that parentage.

And so it was raining that evening. And on the narrow blacktop Huron Pike Road visibility was poor. Walls of pale mist like amnesia drifting in front of Daddy's car, the car's yellow-tinged headlights that had seemed so powerful were swallowed up in mist. In such driving conditions it's possible to forget where you are and where you are headed and for what purpose for the infrequent houses were obscured in mist and mailboxes loomed out of the dark like sudden raised arms. "Daddy? Here—" I said for abruptly there was our mailbox at the end of the graveled driveway emerging out of the mist before my father seemed to have expected it.

Daddy grunted to signal *Yes. I know where the hell you live.*

Now would Daddy turn into the driveway?—that long puddled lane leading back into darkness?—leading back as in a tunnel to our house that, in the encroaching dark, barely visible from the road, glowed a ghostly white? There was only a faint light in the living room windows, the upstairs was darkened. It might have been the case that no one was home except I knew that my mother would be at the rear of the house, in the kitchen where she spent much of her time. If Ben was home, very likely he'd be upstairs in his room also at the rear of the house.

Before he'd moved out—before the court injunction banished him—my father had repaired the steep shingled roof of our house, that had been leaking into the attic; he'd done some electrical rewiring, in the basement; he'd bolstered up the back steps leading into the house. By trade he'd been a carpenter, and a good one; he was a work foreman now, for a Sparta construction company.

Everywhere inside the house, upstairs and down, was evidence of Daddy's carpentry work, his attentiveness to the house. You would be led to presume, Edward Diehl's devotion to his family.

Daddy didn't turn into the driveway but braked to a stop on the road.

Almost I could hear him mutter to himself *God damn I will not.*

For if he had, he would approach too closely the place of his shame. The place of his expulsion. The place of his hurt and of his rage that was at times a murderous rage, and it was too risky for him who had been banished from these premises by an order of the county court, whose breath smelled frankly of whiskey and whose face was flushed with a deep hot furious fire.

Would you think it strange that to me, who had lived all her life on the Huron Pike Road, the daughter of a man not unlike other men who lived on the Huron Pike Road in those years, the smell of whiskey on my father's breath was not disturbing but a kind of comfort? (So long as my mother didn't know. But my mother needn't know.) A risky comfort, but a comfort nonetheless for it was familiar, it was *Daddy.*

And the stubbled jaws suddenly ticklish-scratchy against my face as Daddy leaned over to kiss the edge of my mouth, wetly. Daddy's movements were impulsive and clumsy as those of a man who has long lived by instinct yet has come at last to distrust instinct as he has come to distrust his own capacity for judgment, his sense of himself. Even as Daddy kissed me, roughly, a little too hard, a kiss he intended I would not soon forget, Daddy was pushing me away for a hot rush of blood had come between us.

"G'night, Puss."

Not *good-bye* he was saying but *good night*. This was crucial to me.

It had not seemed to be raining hard but as soon as I climbed out of Daddy's car and began to run to the house, a chill pelting rain started. A mad flurry of wet leaves rushed at me. Awkwardly I ran with my head lowered, I was breathless and wanting to laugh, so awkward, my backpack gripped in one hand slapping against my legs, almost tripping me. I hated to think that my father might be watching me. Halfway up the lane I turned to see—as somehow I knew I would see—the red taillights of my father's car fading into the mist.

"Daddy! G'night—"

YOU WOULD THINK *But he'd promised her! He'd wait until she was safely inside the house.*

You would think that I was disappointed, hurt. And that I was not even surprised, to be disappointed and hurt. But you would be mistaken for I have never been a daughter to judge my father who'd been so harshly, cruelly and wrongly judged by others; and I would not wish to recall so trivial, so petty an injury, a misunderstanding, a moment's carelessness on the part of a man with so much else to occupy his mind, a man drawn ever more rapidly and inexorably into the orbit of his death and his oblivion beyond the length of the graveled driveway glistening with puddles on that rainy night in November 1987 when I was fifteen years old and eager for my true life to begin.

2

REPROACH LIKE AN ARROW leaping from the bow, aimed at my heart.

Reproach in a voice of the lightest chiding, almost you'd mistake—if this were a TV comedy, if you were an unseasoned viewer—for playfulness, mischief.

"You were with him, Krista. Weren't you."

My mother did not emphasize *him*. In the light-chiding TV-Mom voice "him" was flat as concrete.

Nor was her query a question. It was a statement: an accusation.

"You could have called, at least. If you weren't going to take the bus. If you'd given a thought to anyone except yourself—and him. You'd have known that—"

That I was worried. Or if not worried, offended.

A mother's pride is easily hurt, don't mistake a mother's love as unconditional.

Breathless from my dash through the rain and indignant, stragglyhaired I kicked off my boots, fumbling to spike my jacket on a hook by the door half-hoping it would tear. A spiffy purple *faux*-silk jacket with cream-colored trim I'd quite liked when it was new not so very long ago but now had come to think looked cheap and too *hopeful*. I was avoiding confronting my mother for I did not want to have to respond to the accusing look in her eyes, a commingling of relief—for truly she'd been worried about me, not having known where I might be—and mounting anger. In the square-cut window above the kitchen counter, that my father had constructed, as he'd rebuilt much of the kitchen, our reflections appeared close together by a trick of perspective; yet you could not have identified either of us, even which was *mother*, which *daughter*. In a voice of deceptive calm my mother said, "Krista, at least look at me. Were you—you were, weren't you?—with *him*?"

And now it was *him*. Now, unmistakably.

A strap of my backpack had become tangled in my feet. I kicked it aside, my face was smarting. Near-inaudibly I murmured *Yes* for I could not lie to my mother who so knew my mutinous heart, and, when she asked what I'd said, guiltily I repeated, defiantly: "Yes. I was with—Daddy."

Daddy was a little-girl word. Ben had not uttered *Daddy* in years.

"And where were you, with 'Daddy'?"

"Just driving. Nowhere."

"'Nowhere.'"

"Along the river. Nowhere special."

But yes it was special. Because it was just Daddy and me.

Betrayal is the hurtful thing. Betrayal is the deepest wound. Betrayal is what remains of love, when love has gone.

My mother's name was Lucille. No one called her "Lucy." An acute consciousness of her authority—now, the vulnerability of her authority—seemed to grip her, to bedevil her, at such times, increasingly as I grew older; to the most casual of exchanges she brought a mysterious demand that seemed never to be fully satisfied. Since Lucille's husband—now her former husband—who was my father—had left us for the final time, or—this had never been clear to me, or to Ben—had been made to leave us, this demand had grown ever more insatiable.

"'Nowhere' would have to include a stop for drinks, yes? You must be forgetting that part."

"Well—" I'd disentangled the strap from my feet, I had no reason not to look at my mother standing close beside me. "That country place on route thirty-one, by the Rapids bridge. . . ."

"The County Line. He took you *there*?"

My mother's eyes shone like copper coins. For she had me now, she would not readily surrender me.

"Why didn't you call me, Krista? If you were in a place with a phone? You must have known I'd be waiting for you."

"I did call, Mom. I tried. . . ."

"No. I was here, I've been home since four-fifteen. I would have heard the phone ringing."

"Mom, when I called the line was busy. Two or three times I tried, the line was busy. . . ."

This was true: I'd tried to call my mother from the County Line. But I'd only tried twice. Both times the busy signal had rung. Then I'd given up, and I'd forgotten.

Now my mother was saying, conceding: maybe she had been on the phone, for just a few minutes. Maybe yes she'd missed my call. "I called Nancy's number"—Nancy was a classmate of mine who lived in Sparta, at whose house I sometimes stayed overnight—"to see if you were there, or if Nancy knew where you might be. She didn't."

"Mom, for Christ's sake! Why'd you call Nancy."

"Krista, don't use profanity in my presence. That's crude, and that's vulgar. Your father might say 'For Christ's sake'—and a lot worse—but I don't want to hear such words in my daughter's mouth."

Fuck, Mom. Such words are all I have.

My heart beat in resentment that in my mother's eyes I was still a child when I was certain I had not been a child in a long time.

"How badly was he drinking? Was it bad?"

"No."

"And he was driving. Was he—*drunk*?"

I turned away. I hated this. I would not inform on my father any more than, to my father, I would have informed on my mother.

We'd blundered out of the warm-lit kitchen of shiny maple wood cupboard doors on brass hinges and a countertop of pumpkin-colored Formica, into a shadowy, always musty-smelling alcove by the stairs to the second floor. As in an aggressive dance my mother seemed to be pushing close to me. Breathing into my face with a smell of something sour, frantic.

Lucille didn't drink: but Lucille had her *prescription medication* with the unpronounceable name: "Diaphra"—something.

"Where are you going so quickly, Krista? Why are you in such a hurry to get away from me?"

"Mom, I'm not. I have to use the bathroom. My clothes are wet, I want to change my clothes."

"He made you run through the rain? He didn't even bring you up to the house?"

"There's an 'injunction' against him, Mom. He'd be arrested, coming onto this property."

"He should be arrested, violating the custody agreement. Picking you up at school—I assume that's what he did—without my permission or knowledge. He should be arrested for drunk driving."

I was trying to smile, to placate her. Trying to ease past her without touching her for I feared that her touch would be scalding.

It was so frequently a surprise to me, a sick-thrilling sort of shock, that my mother was not so tall as she'd once been. For by magic I had grown taller, and more reckless. My hard little breasts were the size of a baby's fists but the nipples were growing fuller, a deep berry-color, and sensitive; I now wore these breasts tenderly cupped in a white cotton "bra" size 32A. I wore white cotton panties with double-thick crotches. Every four weeks or so I "menstruated"—a phenomenon that filled me with a commingled rage and pride, and anxiety that others—like my mother—would know what my body was doing, what red-earthen-colored seepage it was emitting through a tight little hole between my legs.

My mother was speaking to me, sharply. I wasn't able to concentrate. As I stood on one of the lower steps of the stairs, my mother stepped up to stand beside me. This was so weird! This was not right. At school, you'd be nudged away, standing so close; even a best friend.

In my confusion it seemed almost that my mother had slapped me, or—someone had slapped me. Or—had someone kissed me hard at the edge of my mouth? A man's whiskery-scratchy kiss that had stung.

What I wanted was: to get away from this woman, to contemplate that kiss. To draw strength from that kiss. To observe my heated face in a mirror, seeing if that kiss had left a mark.

Love ya, Puss! You know that eh?

Your old man has let you down, you and your brother, but your old man will make it up, sweetie. You know that eh?

Yes it was so, Daddy "drank." But what man did not drink? No man of my acquaintance in Sparta, no man among my father's relatives, did not drink except one or two who'd been forbidden alcohol since alcohol would now kill them.

Tell your mother I love her. That will never change.

"—I have now, you and your brother. Don't roll your eyes at me, Krista, it's so. You are my family—you are precious to me. *He* doesn't love you, he's just using you to get back at me. 'Vengeance is mine, saieth the Lord'—this was some old joke of your father's, he and his brothers would laugh about. The Diehls are all good haters. They're good enemies. They aren't trustworthy husbands, fathers, friends—but they're very good enemies." My mother paused, having made this familiar declaration: many times I'd heard it, from both my mother and from her (female) relatives. "He picked you up at school, yes? It's dangerous to drive with a drinker, Krista. You know he's been arrested for DUI—I wish they'd revoked his license forever. He has hurt others terribly, he will hurt you. He has hurt you, but you pretend not. Can't you understand, Krista, the man is an *adulterer*. It wasn't just me he betrayed, he betrayed all of us. And you know—he hurt that woman. He is a—"

I pushed free of her, with a little cry. I would not let her utter that terrible word *murderer*.

As I dared to push past my mother she lost control and slapped me: twice, hard, on the side of my head. It was rare that Lucille behaved like this—rare in recent years—for she wasn't "Mrs. Edward Diehl" any longer but had reverted to "Lucille Bauer" which was her prim girlhood name, a name of which she appeared to be proud; and Lucille Bauer, like all the Bauers, disapproved of displays of weakness in herself, as in others.

Yet her coppery eyes were fierce, she was trying to hug me in an iron grip, pin my arms against my sides. You hear of out-of-control children, autistic children, being "hugged" in such vises, for their own good. The sensation was terrible to me, terrifying. I could not bear it. I could not bear my mother's sour breath. A smell of her intimate flesh, her powdery-talcumy-plump body, the feeling of her large soft breasts nudging against me, her surprisingly strong fingers. . . . "Let me go! I hate you." Terrified I ran up the stairs, stumbling and near-falling; and then I did fall, and scraped my knee, pushed myself up again immediately like a panicked animal, running from a predator. It is said that a panicked animal's strength increases double- or triple-fold and so panic-strength coursed through me, an adrenaline kick to the heart.

To be touched—claimed—by my mother in one of her moods of possession! I knew that I was expected to be passive, meek and childlike in her embrace, this had once been peace between us, this had once been love, Mommy's little Krissie who has been naughty but now forgiven and safe in Mommy's arms protected from Daddy's loud voice and heavy footsteps and Daddy's unpredictable ways, all that is unknowable and unpredictable in maleness, but I was resisting her now, I would not ever be meek and childlike in this woman's arms, never again.

It was wounding to us both, lacerating. I would feel that my heart had been torn. Yet I was resolute, unyielding. I would not call back to her, not the most careless words of apology. Stumbling into my darkened room I slammed the door. Behind me on the stairs was the furious aggrieved voice:

"You disgust me, Krista! You're deceitful, you will turn out like him—betraying those who love you."

For there is nothing worse than betrayal, is there? Not even murder.

3

HE WOULD SAY *I am innocent you know that don't you?*

And I would say *Yes Daddy*.

But it was never enough of course. The fervent belief, the unquestioning love of a child for her father—this may be precious to the father but it can't ever be enough for him.

To claim—to claim repeatedly—that you are innocent of what it is claimed by others that you have done, or might have done, or are in some quarters *strongly suspected* of having done, is never enough unless others, numerous others, will say it for you.

Unless you are publicly vindicated of whatever it is you have been *strongly suspected* of doing, it can't be enough.

. . . *you know that darling don't you? You and your brother? You and your brother and your mother have got to know that don't you?*

Yes Daddy.

4

"HEY SORRY BABE, fuckin' sorry sweetheart you got in my *face*."

And they laughed, that I'd been knocked onto my skinny ass on the basketball court and tears sprang from my widened eyes like cartoon-eyes, not for the first time this afternoon.

And my nose leaking blood from a mean girl's swift elbow before the referee could blow her ear-shattering whistle.

"Poor baby. Poor li'l white-gal. Man, I am *sor*-ry!"

After-school basketball at Sparta High. To play with these girls you had to be tall, strong, tough, quick on your feet. Or reckless.

There were other girls I could have played with, if I'd wanted to. Girls my own age, my own size and not so athletic as I was so I'd have been the star player in their midst as I'd been in eighth and ninth grades at the junior high. But I wanted to play with these girls: Billie, Swansea, Kiki, Dolores. They were older, and bigger. They were sixteen, seventeen years old. Dolores may have been eighteen. She and Kiki lived on the Seneca Indian reservation a few miles north of Sparta—they had sleek black straight hair that lashed and swung about their shoulders heads like scimitars, their black eyes shone with malice and merriment. Driving out into the countryside north of the city—the foothills of the Adirondack Mountains—you were made to see the wreckage of long-ago glaciers in their slow violence causing the rocky landscape to contort like something forced through a meat grinder. You were made to see how, being given such untillable and near-uninhabitable land by the U.S. government in treaties they had no choice but to sign generations ago, the descendants of the original Six Tribes of upstate New York might wish to exact some sort of revenge upon their Caucasian benefactors whenever the opportunity arose.

My classmates thought that I was crazy to play with these older girls. I was the youngest, in tenth grade, slender-boned and wily as a snake weaving and darting unpredictably and my silky-blond ponytail flying behind me as if to provoke; more than once as I'd leapt to shoot a basket, I'd felt a sharp little tug on my ponytail to throw me off-stride. I weighed no more than one hundred six pounds and if I was hit—and often, you can be sure, I was hit—by one of the larger girls, I fell to the polished hardwood floor so stunned sometimes I couldn't get up for several seconds.

"Krista sweetie—you O.K.? C'mon girl, get *up*."

Mostly they liked me. Things they said to me—crude, funny, obscene—they said to one another. They were fluent in profanities meant to be endearments—"Out of my face, bitch"—"Fuckin' white bitch"—"Fuckin' cunt." (Most of us were in fact "white"—but there were gradations of "white." As there were gradations of what was never given a name—"social class"—"background." At Sparta High there were students, among them Dolores and Kiki, and several other girl-athletes, who had relatives, neighbors, friends, and boyfriends in or recently paroled from juvenile detention facilities and prisons; their obscenity-laced speech was prison-speech, a kind of roughshod poetry.) In their midst I was "Krissie" who didn't have to be taken seriously, like a team mascot. If I sometimes surprised them by sinking a basket unexpectedly, appropriating a wayward ball, running in my liquid-snaky way beneath their elbows and darting to the front of the court before anyone could stop me, still I was no competition for even the second-best players, I lacked the true athlete's aggressiveness, the willingness to be mean. When play on the court got rough—as it was sure to do at least once per game—I shrank away, never held on to the ball if I was in danger of being hurt. And if you'd been knocked down and fouled you might then be caressed, if a 150-pound girl collided with you like a dump truck colliding with a baby carriage, knocked you skidding on your skinny little ass on the floor, this same girl might stoop over you to help you to your feet: with a sly slit of a smile she might rub her knuckles against your scalp, or give your ponytail a tug, or pinch the nape of your neck murmuring, "Fuckin' sorry, baby. You got in my way."

Not so bad, then. Even a blood-dripping nose.

Limping to the foul line as girls lined up to watch: shooting fouls was what Krissie Diehl became damned good at, having had plenty of opportunities.

"'Way to go, Krissie! C'mon girl."

"You go, girl! Show us you' li'l *thang*."

Late-afternoon Thursday, my father appeared at basketball practice. No warning, never any warning for that wasn't Eddy Diehl's way.

Lucille would accuse me of making plans with "your father" behind her back but how could I have possibly planned to meet him, my father had made no attempt to contact me in months and I had no way of contacting him except through the Diehls who weren't very nice to me (as Lucille's daughter and a co-conspirator they believed); I wasn't even sure where he was living now—Buffalo? Batavia? Not a day, not an hour passed that I didn't think of my father and when I wasn't consciously thinking of him he was a dull throb of an ache in my throat and yet I could not have said with certainty where he might be.

Wake in the night, perspiring and anxious: that throb-ache.

My brother Ben said contemptuously it was like an infection, *he* had it, too. "Some damn fever. As long as we live here in Sparta and people know our name, we're sick with it: Eddy Diehl's kids."

AFTER BASKETBALL, unless I was staying overnight in town with a classmate, I took the 4:30 P.M. bus home, which was called the "late bus." (The "regular" bus left at 3:30 P.M.) Our house on the Huron Pike Road was about three miles from Sparta High and I would have been home just after 5 P.M. except: I never got on the bus.

Just inside the gym doors he was standing. Rare to see adults in the gym at such times. As the game ended I limped off the court wiping my sweaty face on my T-shirt and I heard a male voice—startling, in that context—a thrilling growly undertone: "Krista."

At once I looked up. Looked around. A man not twenty feet away, in a fawn-colored suede jacket, dark trousers, cap pulled low over his forehead. Was he signaling to me?

Now I heard him, more clearly: "Krista. Outside."

I felt weak. I could not reply. Staring after my father as he pushed through the doors to the corridor beyond, and was gone.

Other girls had seen him, heard him. Of course. They'd sighted him—a man—Krista Diehl's father?—before I had.

We shuffled into the locker room together. Girls who'd been laughing loudly had quieted. Girls who felt a certain tenderness for me, or, at least, some measure of tolerance, glanced at me with expressions of curiosity, concern.

Diehl? The one who . . . ?

That woman who was killed, he's the one who . . . ? Why's he out of prison so soon?

Someone—I think it was our gym teacher—was watching me. Asking me some question but I pretended not to hear. Through the excited buzzing in my ears there was little I might have heard, that I wished to hear.

Wanting to laugh in all their faces. For what did any of them know about my father Eddy Diehl, and me? Thinking *He has come for me, you can see how special I am after all.*

5

"IT'S OVER."

Or, "It's finished."

These were my mother's words. There was dignity in my mother's posture—erect, not visibly tremulous, head held high and eyes unflinching—as there was dignity in the brevity of such a reply: her response to questions put to her about her (ex)-husband Eddy Diehl. For it was not to be avoided, Lucille Bauer was asked about Eddy Diehl, this now much-talked-of and "controversial" individual to whom she'd been married for eighteen years, which was most of her adult life; and when Lucille wasn't asked in actual blunt rude pushy words she was asked by implication, indirection.

Oh Lucille! How is it with—? And so she'd taken to replying in this brief cool but perfectly polite way, with a knife-cut of a smile that suggested hurt, or the mockery thereof.

Want to see me cry? Want to see my broken heart? You won't.

In the 1980s, in Sparta, New York, the expectations of a young woman of Lucille's class—working-class/middle-class/"respectable"/"good"—were not essentially different from the expectations of Lucille's mother in the late 1950s and early 1960s: you yearned to be engaged young, married young, start to have your babies young. You yearned to attract the love of an attractive man, possibly even a sexy man, certainly a man who *made a good living*, a man who *was faithful*.

In the late 1960s, elsewhere in the country, or, at least, in the tabloid America fantasized, packaged and sold by the commercial media, there had been a *sexual revolution: a hippie take-over*. But not in Sparta, and not in Herkimer County. Not in upstate New York in this glacier-raddled region in the southern foothills of the Adirondack Mountains. Here, despite a rising divorce rate, more "single-parent" homes (i.e., Negro mothers on welfare, much talked-of, disapproved-of), and other unmistakable incursions of the 1960s fallout, the America of the 1950s yet prevailed, beneath a showy veneer like the *faux* yellow pine hardwood floors my father's construction company sold, since prospective homeowners didn't want to pay for the *real thing*.

Not publicly but to her family, repeatedly and dazedly my mother would say—not quite within my hearing, but I managed to hear—that she'd never known Eddy: she'd lived with a man for all those years, she'd had two children with him and she'd *never known his heart*.

(Was this so? Neither Ben nor I had any idea. Photographs of our young parents showed two strikingly attractive individuals: a very pretty round-faced girl with a cheerleader-smile, glamorous teased hair and a sizable bust straining against silk "designer" blouses; a tall broad-shouldered rust-red-haired young man with a jaw like a mallet, wary eyes and a sly half-smile very like the signature smile of the young Elvis Presley. Neither Ben nor I would have wished to acknowledge what seemed obvious if you studied these photos, especially a wedding photo in which the groom's husky arm is slung about the bride's shoulders all but crushing her against him, the groom's large male hand cupped about the bride's bare upper arm beneath a white lace stole, and the thumb of that hand unobtrusively pressing against, very likely rubbing against, the sweet fatty talcumed flesh of the bride's right breast. *Sex! Our parents! That was it.*)

Over those eighteen years, Lucille had gained weight. And then, during the eighteen months preceding her divorce, Lucille had lost weight. Her moon-shaped face that had been such a pretty girl's face well into her thirties became ravaged, cruelly lined; she'd lost weight too quickly for her skin to shrink, there were loose pockets and pouches of skin everywhere on her body she took pains to keep hidden. But Lucille had the sort of features that took well to make-up, still she could exude an aura of small-town glamour. She never left the house without dressing presentably: "primping." She never left the house without fresh-applied lipstick. Not long after the divorce—in September 1984, on the very Tuesday public schools began classes—Lucille had her hair cut and restyled and "lightened" and overnight those single steely hairs like nails had vanished, to her adolescent daughter's immense relief.

Naively Ben said: "Mom looks different today, you notice?"

"Maybe she was smiling."

"Ha-ha," Ben said, in a way meant to convey heavy sarcasm. In all things having to do with my mother Ben flared up quickly, he hated our father for how our father had hurt our mother, thus had to love our mother blindly, without judgment and without nuance. If I persisted in criticizing Lucille, Ben had been known to punch me.

Not that Lucille smiled, much. Not at home.

Away from home, yes Lucille smiled. Returning to church—the First Presbyterian Church of Sparta, a grim triangle-shaped limestone structure that made my heart clutch like a fist, in adolescent resistance each time I was dragged into it—and to her "old, best friends" she'd "all but lost" while married to Eddy Diehl who "hadn't any patience with nice people."

Boring people, Mom meant. Nice boring kind-Christian women whose boring husbands hadn't left them, not yet. Or anyway so far as anyone knew. Yet.

"Krista, Hilda Smith's daughter Pearl—you must know her, she's in your class at school?—belongs to Sparta Christian Youth Alliance—they have the most wonderful summer campground at Lake George, Hilda was telling me. I told her I'd speak to you. . . ."

O.K., Mom. You've spoken to me.

"We need to put this behind us, Krista. This ugliness. Like an earthquake, or a flood, you're in shock but then, you know, you *galvanize.* You *come alive.* The idea of the Gospels is—'Good news is possible.'"

Lucille spoke with a hard gritty optimism like one grinding away with her teeth at something lodged in her mouth—some careless taking-in of a substance not quite edible, grindable. But she would grind it down, she would swallow it. If you weren't careful she would make you swallow it, too.

The Herkimer County order of restraint against Edward Diehl had originally been issued in April 1984 and since that time reissued at least once. By this order Edward Diehl was forbidden to approach his (ex)-wife Lucille and his children Benjamin and Krista in any public or private place; he was forbidden to come closer than one hundred feet of any of them; he was forbidden to "trespass" on the Huron Pike Road property that he himself had purchased with a thirty-year mortgage, twelve years before. Of course he dared not approach the house, nor even make telephone calls to the house, which he'd partly remodeled and in which he'd executed so much carpentry over a period of years. (In an extravagant and reckless gesture my father had simply deeded the property over to my mother—"The least he could do," my mother said bitterly.)

In the months following the divorce, so far as we knew, Daddy lived in Sparta with friends, or relatives; Daddy may even have been taken in by a woman friend; for there were many who knew Eddy Diehl well, who'd gone to high school with him, and been drinking-friends of his, scarcely known to Lucille or to us. These people—mostly men but not exclusively men—were convinced that Eddy Diehl hadn't done what it was claimed by others that he had done, committed an act of murder: "homicide." They would not cease to believe in Eddy Diehl's innocence even after he'd been taken into Sparta police custody, even when it was leaked to the media that he'd "failed" a polygraph test; even when his picture began to appear in local papers and on local TV news in the company of the other "prime suspect" in the case, the father of a classmate of a Sparta man uncannily resembling Eddy Diehl in age, height, physical type.

SUSPECTS IN KRULLER HOMICIDE QUESTIONED BY POLICE

* * *

THOUGH MY MOTHER HAD had our telephone number changed, and removed from the directory, yet my father managed to acquire the number as if by magic, and called us. Sometimes when one of us answered he didn't speak: you listened and heard only a crackling sort of silence, like flames about to erupt. Timidly I said, "Daddy? Is that—you?" but Daddy would not answer, nor would Daddy hang up the phone; at such times I did not know what to do, for I loved my father very much, and was frightened of him; I had been made to be frightened of him; among the Bauers it was whispered that he was a *brute*, a *murderer*. And there were many in Sparta who believed yes, my father was a *brute*, a *murderer*. If Ben answered his voice went shrill, he was furious, half-sobbing: "We don't want you to call us, Dad," but Ben's voice weakened when he uttered *Dad*, though he'd steeled himself not to say *Dad*, yet *Dad* had come out. Once when I picked up the phone expecting to hear my friend Nancy's voice instead the voice was a man's, low and gravelly: "Krista? Just this, honey: I love you." On trembling legs I stood in the kitchen dazed and blinking as the voice continued, "Is your mother nearby? Is she listening?" and I could not manage to answer, my throat had closed tight, "Don't hang up yet, honey. Just want you to know *I love*—" but the look in my face was a signal to my mother, with an angry little cry Mom took the receiver from me and slammed it down without a word.

So that the phone could not ring again, Mom removed the receiver from the hook.

"How dare he! He's been warned! I should call the police. . . ."

We could not sit down to our dinner! We were too excited to eat.

My mother insisted, we must eat. We must not be upset by him, he must not have such power over us. Numbly we sat at the table, we passed platters of the food that my mother and I had prepared together, we tried not to see where my father stood brooding and smoking in a corner of the kitchen.

My mouth was too dry, I could not chew or swallow. "Maybe he just wants to . . ." Numbly I spoke, my words were barely audible.

In her cool calm voice my mother said, "No, Krista. It's over."

And there were the times, how many times we had no idea, when my father drove past the house; when my father cruised slowly past the house, pausing at the end of the driveway; when my father dared to park at the side of the road, in a stand of straggly trees, not visible from the house. Word sometimes came back to us, from relatives. One of my mother's cousins called. Virtually all of the Diehls supported Edward, their Eddy; the Bauers were less sure. (There was a split among the Bauers, in fact. Those who believed that Lucille's husband might have been unfaithful to her, but not that he'd killed that woman: not Eddy! And those who believed yes, Eddy Diehl was capable of murder, if he'd been drunk enough. And angry, and jealous enough.) I knew that my father was close by because, some nights, I could feel his presence. I could hear his voice *Krista? Krissie? Where's my Puss? I'm coming to get my little Krissie-puss.* There was a sensation inside my head like fire about to erupt, crystal glass about to be shattered. Almost unbearable excitement like the terrible thrill of a vehicle made to speed too fast for the road, the spinning basketball aimed at your unprotected face: that instant before the ball hits, and your nose spurts blood.

When I was thirteen, that Christmas when there'd been so much snowfall we were snowed in, and Herkimer County snowplows and tow trucks were on the Huron Pike Road through the night, that Christmas morning there was a vehicle parked at the end of the drive—just barely visible from my bedroom window—a pickup truck, it seemed to be—I saw a male figure climb out, and I saw this figure shoveling the end of our driveway where the snowplows had heaped up ridges of icy snow—at first I thought it must be someone from the county, though this wasn't part of the usual snowplowing service—then I realized it had to be my father, coming to shovel out the end of the driveway as he'd always done after a heavy snowfall, when he'd lived with us.

And where was my father living then? Not in Sparta, I think—he must have made the drive early Christmas morning, in treacherous weather conditions, for this purpose.

Neither my mother nor Ben ever knew, I never told them. That the end of the driveway wasn't blocked as usual must have made no distinct impression on my mother, when she drove her car out.

Another time, a more careless/desperate time he'd parked at the end of the driveway, very likely he'd been drinking and so forgot to switch off his headlights and Ben happened to notice from an upstairs window and shouted to my mother: "It's him, Mom! Damn bastard, *I hate him*!"

In a panic my mother called the number the Herkimer County sheriff had given her for such emergencies and within minutes a squad car careened along Huron Pike Road with a flashing red light like on TV— unresisting, Eddy Diehl was arrested, taken away in handcuffs and in the morning his car was towed away.

Why Lucille declined to press charges, she would not explain.

"It's over."

He was gone, then. Except: one afternoon months later again he was sighted driving slowly past the small shopping center where my mother had begun part-time work at the Second Time 'Round Shop—a "consignment" shop to which women brought no-longer-wanted clothing to be resold; he was sighted in the parking lot at the rear, just sitting in the car, smoking, possibly drinking; it would turn out, he'd told one of his Diehl cousins that he was wanting "just to see her, from a distance"—"not even to try to talk"—but Lucille didn't appear, and after an hour or so he drove away.

It was Daddy's statement made frequently to relatives, meant to be conveyed to Lucille: "She knows that I love her and the kids. That isn't going to change. However she feels about me, I can accept it."

SPARTA RESIDENT DIEHL, 42,
RELEASED FROM POLICE CUSTODY
"NO CHARGES AT THIS TIME"

Because my mother prowled in my room in my absence—I knew! I'd set devious Mom-traps in my sock-and-undies drawer and in my clothes closet—I kept my cache of clippings about my father in a school notebook, carried back and forth in my backpack. This clipping, from the Sparta *Journal* for April 29, 1983, commemorated the final time Edward Diehl's photograph would appear prominently on the front page of that paper.

For that reason, and for the reason that it so clearly stated that Edward Diehl *had been released from police custody, for lack of evidence linking him to the murder of Zoe Kruller*, this clipping was precious to me.

Not that I failed to note—no one could fail to note, who was even skimming the article—the begrudging *No Charges at This Time*.

The conspicuous omission of *Suspect Cleared*.

Edward Diehl had been in police custody more than once, more than twice, possibly more than three times. He'd been identified—numberless times!—as *one of the prime suspects*; yet he'd never been arrested. (Another man, the murdered woman's husband, had been arrested—but later released.) It was a season of misery and public humiliation for all of the Diehls, the Bauers, and their friends; for Ben and me, having to go to school where everyone seemed to know more about our father—our father and a woman named Zoe Kruller, who'd been "murdered"—"strangled in her bed"—than we did. For months the police investigation continued, very like a net being dragged in one direction and then in another, a nightmare net trapping all in its path, as virtually anyone who knew my father was "interviewed," often more than once. After a year, two years, several years this case was still open; by November 1987, no one had been definitively arrested, and the name *Zoe Kruller* had vanished from the newspaper; Edward Diehl was no longer a *prime suspect*, evidently—yet no public announcement had ever been made by Sparta police or by the county prosecutor that Edward Diehl's name had been cleared.

My mother never spoke of the case any longer. Like a woman who has endured a ravaging cancer, and managed to survive, she would not speak of what had almost killed her, and became white-faced with fury if anyone tried to bring it up. *Lucille, d'you mind my asking how is—*

Yes. I do mind. Please.

At the time, I had not been told much about what my mother and her family chose to call *the trouble*. I was believed to be an overly sensitive, excitable girl and so, more than my brother Ben, I was to be *spared*. But I knew that my father, who was no longer living with us, was a suspect in a local murder case, that he'd had to hire a lawyer, and in time he'd had to fire that lawyer and hire another lawyer; and, inevitably, he'd come to owe both lawyers thousands of dollars more than he could have hoped to pay them; for he was obliged to continue to support his family, which meant my mother, my brother, and me; and he'd lost his job at Sparta Construction, Inc. where he'd worked since the age of twenty, first as a carpenter's assistant, then as a carpenter, then he'd been promoted to foreman/manager by his employer who was also his friend or had been his friend until he'd been taken into police custody.

All these facts, I knew. Though no one had told me openly.

The trouble was as good a way as any of pointing to what had happened. *The trouble that has come into our lives* my mother would say, as Daddy would say *The trouble that has come into my life*.

Like lightning from the sky. A catastrophe from *out there*.

When he'd been released from police custody for the second and final time—in late April 1983—my father was told that he was free to leave Sparta, and so he moved to Watertown, sixty miles to the north on the St. Lawrence River, where he got a job as a roofer; then he moved to Buffalo, two hundred miles to the west, where he worked construction. There was a time he lived in the Keene Valley in the Adirondacks, working for a logging company. And later, we heard he had a job with Beechum County, which was adjacent to Herkimer—snow removal, highway construction. In our lives my father appeared, and disappeared; and again appeared, and disappeared. He sent birthday cards to Ben and me—though never quite in time for our birthdays. He sent Christmas cards to LUCILLE, BENJAMIN & KRISTA DIEHL, R.D. # 3, HURON PIKE RD., SPARTA N.Y. signed in a large childlike scrawl LOVE, DADDY. Sometimes just LOVE DADDY. (These cards I scavenged from the trash where my mother had thrown them, to hide away in my secret Daddy-notebook.)

There came months of silence. No one spoke of Eddy Diehl, no one seemed to know where he was. But one evening the phone would ring and if our mother answered it we'd hear a sharp intake of breath and then Mom's steely response: "No. It's over. It's finished. No more."

If Ben answered, quickly he'd hang up the phone. White-faced and quivering Ben slammed out of the room—"That sick, sorry bastard. Why doesn't he let us alone."

If I answered—if Mom wasn't there to hear me, and to snatch away the receiver—Daddy and I might talk, a little. Awkwardly, eagerly. My voice was tremulous and low-pitched and my heart beat hard hard hard like the wings of that little bird of heaven in the song Zoe Kruller once sang.

6

"KRISTA. CLIMB IN."

Outside, at the rear exit of the school, Daddy's car was waiting.

A vehicle unknown to me, I was sure I'd never seen before. A shiny expanse of dark-coppery metallic finish, gleaming chrome fixtures, new-looking, you might say flashy-looking, with whitewall tires and hubcaps like roulette wheels: one of Eddy Diehl's *specialty-autos*.

These were purchases of secondhand cars of some distinction which Daddy would rebuild or "customize"—drive for a while, and resell, pre-sumably at a profit. They were older-vintage cars—Caddies, Lincolns, Olds—or newer-vintage Thunderbirds, Corvettes, Stingrays, Mustangs, Barracudas; they were mysteriously acquired through a friend of a friend needing money suddenly, or bankruptcy sales, police auctions. Through my childhood these *specialty-autos* were both thrilling and fraught with peril for the purchases upset my mother even as they were wonderful surprises for my brother and me. Typical of Daddy to simply arrive home with a new car, without warning or explanation. There in the doorway stood Daddy rattling car keys, with his foxy-Daddy grin: "Look out in the driveway. Who wants a ride?"

We did! Ben and me! We adored our unpredictable Daddy!

It was like that now, this abruptness. My father showing up at school, in the gym. And now here. The demand that if you loved him you leapt unquestioning into the happiness that Eddy Diehl was offering you—otherwise the foxy-smile would cease abruptly, a hard cruel light would come into the narrowed eyes.

Without thinking—not a glimmer of caution—*Do I want this? Where will he take me? What will happen to me?*—nor recalling that my mother expected me home as usual within forty minutes, in this season in which dusk came early, before 5 P.M.—I climbed into the passenger's seat of this impressive vehicle my father was driving and dropped my backpack onto the floor.

"Jesus, Puss! It's been a hell of a long time."

My father grabbed me: rough bear-hug, wet-scratchy kiss, unshaven jaws, fumey smell of his breath.

"Sweet li'l Puss"—"Krissie-baby." Names no one had called me in a very long time.

As no one had hugged, kissed me like this in a very long time.

Daddy must have been forty-five—forty-six?—now. A large tall man—six foot four, 220 pounds—mostly solid meaty-muscle though beginning to slacken at the waist. He'd been a high school athlete (football, baseball) and in his early twenties he'd been a Private First Class in the U.S. Army (Vietnam) and he walked now with a slight limp in his right leg (shrapnel, wartime). He had declined to tell Ben and me about his Vietnam experiences, or adventures—we were certain that he'd had some—though we had never located any Vietnam snapshots, souvenirs, even Daddy's medals (Purple Heart, Distinguished Service Medal) or letters from friends—he'd had to have had friends in his platoon, Eddy Diehl was such a gregarious man—but always he'd shrug us off evasively muttering *It's over, kids. Don't go there.*

Our mother didn't encourage us to "provoke" Daddy. *He was hurt, he was in the hospital for eight weeks. His mother told me, they thought he might not live.*

And another time our mother told us, in a lowered voice *He has never talked about it with me and it's best that way.*

In scorn I'd thought: What kind of selfish wife doesn't even want to know about her husband in the war?

How easily, Daddy could have crushed me in his embrace. I would not realize until afterward—I mean years afterward—that Daddy may have been frightened of me, of the fact of me so suddenly with him, in his car; his laughter was loud, delighted. Possibly it was the laughter of disbelief, wonder, a pang of conscience—*My daughter? My daughter I am forbidden to see? She has come to me, this is—her?*

"That's my good girl. My good—*brave*—girl."

Tenderly my father's large hands framed my face. My father's large calloused hands. Once I had seen my father seize my mother's face in his hands like this—not in love but in fury, exasperation—to make my mother listen, to make my mother *see*—and the long-ago memory came to me now, with a stab of panic. And yet, how unresisting I was: like a child whose anxiety has at last been quelled, all fear banished even fear of Daddy. Such luxury to be so gripped, so kissed and so *loved*. I knew that my father would never hurt *me*. Tears stung my eyes, ran down my face that throbbed with hurt from having been struck by a carelessly thrown basketball within the past hour. I could not have recalled when my mother had last kissed or even hugged me—could not have recalled when I'd last wished to be kissed or hugged by her. Such displays of emotion would have embarrassed us both. We'd have steeled ourselves to hear my brother say—this was one of Ben's too-frequent household remarks delivered in a droll dry voice of disgust—*Cut the crap for Christ's sake. This ain't TV.*

This was not TV, I thought. This was improvised, unknown. This had not happened before. Or, if it had happened, it had not happened to me.

School buses were idling nearby, sending up sprays of exhaust. My classmates were running through the rain and there was much commotion in the parking lot as the buses were loading, preparing to leave. Headlights would have illuminated my father's and my excited faces which Eddy Diehl would not have wished.

Is that—Eddy Diehl? The one who—

Is he with his daughter? What's-her-name—

Quickly Daddy put his car in gear, drove out of the parking lot.

In the rain we drove for some confused yet exhilarant minutes. Not knowing where he was taking us—Edgehill Street, East End Avenue, Union Avenue—lower Main Street, a turn and steeply downhill to

Depot—these streets of Sparta so familiar, in truth they lacked names to me—they were but directions, impulses—taking us *away* from my school where we might be recognized but lacking a *destination* since there was no longer a common *destination* in our lives.

With something of his old pride in such showy purchases my father was telling me about the car he was driving, a 1976 Caddie he'd acquired just in time for this visit. The finish was "Red Canyon" and the interior was "cream-colored leather, genuine." This "beaut" of a car naturally came with power steering, whitewall tires, V-eight engine, air-conditioning, radio and tape deck, more mileage for the gallon than any other U.S. "luxury car."

It was so, Daddy conceded, the Caddie's chassis had had to be rebuilt after a rear-ending but the engine was in "damned good shape—you can hear it."

I listened, I could hear it. Eagerly I nodded *Yes yes! I can hear it.*

Stammering with schoolgirl emotion I told my father that this was the most beautiful car of his, ever. The most fantastic car I'd ever ridden in.

"Well. Pretty close, Puss."

Maybe what I said was true. Daddy's *specialty-autos* had all been spectacular. But each spectacular vehicle—Oldsmobile Cutlass Supreme, Lincoln Versailles, Chevy Corvair, vintage Thunderbird and vintage Studebaker—had a way of displacing its predecessor as the most vivid and seductive dreams are displaced by their predecessors, and begin at once to fade.

There was a pause, I knew that my father would have liked to ask what kind of car Lucille was driving now. By implication *Your life with your mother is pitiable. Like the love you get from your mother.* But then I thought that Eddy Diehl would probably know exactly what sort of car Lucille was driving—which of the not-new but serviceable cars sold to her by relatives, or given to her outright.

Yes, my father would surely have known what my mother was driving at this time. Before seeking me out at school Daddy would have sighted and observed my mother at the Second Time 'Round Shop—he'd have parked up the street, or in the parking lot at the rear. It was known that Eddy Diehl kept "close tabs" on his former wife Lucille by way of those several Diehl cousins with whom he remained close, conspiratorial; most of the Diehls continued to "believe in" Eddy, and detested Eddy's former wife for not having "stood by him" when he'd needed her so badly.

And so it seemed to me suddenly, my father probably knew more about my mother's private life than Ben and I knew, who would not have had the thought that our middle-aged, fretting and deeply unhappy mother could have a private life!

"—a little surprised, Krista but it's a good surprise, how you've grown. I mean—tall. You're going to be a *tall girl*. And pretty. You're going to be *damn pretty*. Not that you aren't pretty now, Puss—but—"

Daddy spoke distractedly as he drove the showy Cadillac through the rain, now beneath a railroad overpass where skeins of water lifted like wings behind us and I feared something might happen to the high-caliber engine, and we'd be stuck in a foot of water, "—and playing basketball with those girls—big tough Indian-looking girls—frankly, Puss, your Daddy was—" In a kind of genial-Daddy wonderment his voice trailed off. This was the sort of praise you might direct toward a child about whom you are thinking very different thoughts.

When my father wasn't speaking in his loud blustery in-control Daddy voice, I'd come to hear another sort of voice: one that bore a wounded sweetness. Sometimes I woke from tumultuous dreams hearing this voice, recalling no coherent words but shivering with yearning. Observing my father now I saw that—of course, this should not have been suprising—he looked older. His face had thickened at the jawline, his skin was weathered and creased with a look like hard-baked bread. The thick rust-red hair threaded with mica-gray was in fact thinning at the back of his head where he was spared having to see it as he was spared having to see, and kept hidden from the world, the mass of swirling scar tissue, of the color of lard, that disfigured much of his right leg and knee.

Never did Eddy Diehl wear shorts, on the hottest days of summer. Never had he gone swimming with us, at Wolf's Head Lake.

Though I'd glimpsed the injured leg, from time to time. I'd had to wonder if my mother saw it often, in my parents' bedroom; if my mother was suffused with love for Daddy, for having suffered in wartime combat, or whether she felt a subtle revulsion for the disfigured flesh.

If she felt a subtle revulsion for my father's maleness. His sexuality.

Daddy was saying now, how he'd been missing me. How he'd missed his "beautiful daughter"—how "God-damned depressed and in despair" he'd been missing his daughter he loved "more than anything on this earth."

Steering the car through deep puddles of rainwater with one hand and with the other groping for my hand, capturing both my hands, clasping both hands together in his single hand, hard.

I tried not to wince. I loved such sudden pain!

I said, shyly, "Daddy, I missed you, too. I don't know why Mom—"

"No 'Mom,' Krista. Not right now."

Despite his unshaven jaws and slightly disheveled hair threaded with gray, my father was looking handsome, I thought. Even with his battered face, discolored pouches of skin beneath his eyes as if he hadn't been sleeping well, or had been rubbing his fists into his eyes, and his forehead creased in thought or worry, Eddy Diehl was a handsome man. The suede coat he wore seemed to be padded with a woolly down like a large upright tongue—what comfort such a burly coat could give, if you were squeezed against it. And dark-graying hairs sprouting up from Daddy's chest visible at his throat, what comfort in pressing my face against that throat, hiding my face there.

We'd ascended from the rain-pelted dark of Depot Street, the warehouse district, the scrubby waterfront of the Black River, now turning onto the Highlands Bridge that was a beautiful suspension bridge above the river with a wire-net surface that hummed beneath our car tires. A wild happiness was loosed inside the 1976 Caddie Seville with the cream-colored leather interior, Canyon Red finish and whitewall tires—"Fasten your seat belt! Taking off!" Daddy was laughing, of sheer delight, or defiance; I heard myself laugh, excited and uneasy.

Where was Daddy taking me? Across the suspension bridge, into a now lightly falling rain, mist rising from the invisible river below and a blurred vision of lights along the river, the dim stretch of derelict riverfront brick mills and factories shut down for as long as I could remember—*Link Ladies Luxury Hosiery, Reynolds Bros. Paper Goods, Johnston Tomato Cannery.*

These familiar Sparta landmarks I'd been seeing all my life long before *the trouble* had destroyed my family.

"—damned proud, Krista. Seeing my li'l girl mixing it up with those big hulking girls."

Big hulking girls seemed to mean something other than its words. *Big hulking girls* contained something sexy, sniggering.

I asked Daddy how he'd known where I was? That I'd stayed after school, and was in the gym? Daddy tapped the side of his nose saying, "Your old man has you on his radar, Krista. Better believe it."

Was he drunk, I wondered. Growly-teasing voice, his words just perceptibly slurred.

And yet: there is no happiness like being fifteen years old and being driven by your (forbidden) father to a destination you can't—yet—guess. Your handsome (forbidden) father so clearly exulting in your presence as in his possession of you as a thief might gloat over having made away with the most precious of valuables, and no one in pursuit.

I was thinking how no one else loved me like this. No one else would wish to possess me.

Years ago before my father had moved from Sparta, in that interregnum of confusion and nightmare when Edward Diehl was being "taken into police custody"—"released from police custody"—banished from our household but living with relatives locally, it would happen that, as if by accident, Daddy would turn up at places where Ben and I were: boarding the school bus after school, at the mall while our mother was shopping for groceries, riding our bicycles along the Huron Pike Road. I was thrilled to see Daddy waving at us but Ben stiffened and turned away.

Muttering under his breath *Like some damn ghost haunting us. Wish he would die!*

It was a nasty side of Ben, I've never forgiven him, the eager way he reported back to our mother: "Daddy was following us! Daddy waved at us!" My mother was terrified—or wished to declare that she was terrified—that my father might "kidnap" us, such incidents left her semihysterical with indecision. Should she call the police, should she call my father's family, should she try to ignore Eddy Diehl's "harassment" or—*what should would a responsible mother do?*

No one knew. Many opinions were offered but no one knew. If you believed that Edward Diehl might have murdered—"strangled in her bed"—a Sparta woman who'd been his "mistress"—yes, "mistress" was the very term, boldly printed in local papers and pronounced on local radio and TV—you would naturally think that Edward Diehl should be forbidden to approach his children; if you believed that Edward Diehl was an innocent man, in fact a "good and loving" father to those children, you naturally felt otherwise.

A family splits apart just once, all that you learn will be for the first time.

" . . . but if you want to hold your own with tough girls like that, sweetie, you need to be more aggressive. You aren't actually the shortest girl I saw on the court but you're the least 'developed'—I mean that *muscularly*—and you need to be meaner, and to take more chances. A good athlete isn't thinking of herself but the team. If you're cautious thinking you might be hurt—'cause you can always be hurt, for sure, in any sport—you'll be a deficit not an asset to your teammates."

Deficit. Asset. In my father's voice was an echo of a long-ago high school coach.

I was hurt, Daddy was criticizing me! Daddy was not praising me as I'd expected he would.

"I was watching those girls. Three or four of them are pretty impressive for their age. The one with the black hair shaved up the sides like a guy, must be a Seneca Indian?—yes?—the way she was ducking, using her elbows, twisting in midair tossing the basket—she's dynamite. You can tell she's been playing with guys, out there on the rez. And that big busty gal, with the peroxide streaks, the way she got the ball from you, just whipped it out of your hands. And that six-foot girl who almost trampled you, straight black hair and face like a hatchet—"

"Dolores Stillwater."

"She's Indian, right? From the rez?"

Why are we talking about these girls! Why aren't we talking about me!

"If you want athletes like that to take you seriously, Krissie, you'll have to work a little harder. Not just shooting baskets—from a stationary position, that isn't hard. But on the run, playing defensively, holding your own, showing them you're willing to hurt them—foul *them*—if those little bitches get in your way. An athlete has to make a decision, early on—Coach told us, in junior high—'Either it's you, or it's them.' Either you spare yourself the risk, and they take the risk—or you take it, and run right over them. A player who gets fouled all the time isn't worth crap. If you don't want to take the risk, Puss, maybe you shouldn't be playing any sport at all."

I was remembering: how like our father this was. Ben's father, and mine. You thought you might be praised for something—anyway, not found lacking—but somehow, as Daddy pondered the subject, turning it this way and that in his thoughts as we'd see him turn a defective work tool in his fingers—it wasn't praise that was deserved after all but a *harsh but honest critique*.

In his work, Daddy was something of a perfectionist: his shrewd professional eye picked up mistakes invisible to other eyes. So Daddy once tore out tile in our kitchen floor he'd laid laboriously himself, cursing and red-faced he ripped out wallpaper over which he'd toiled for hours in summer heat, he repainted walls because the shade of paint he'd chosen "wasn't right" and it was "driving him crazy"; he'd built a redwood deck at the rear of our house to which he was always adding features, or subtracting features; on our property, work was "never done"—there was "always something to fix up"; but it was dangerous to offer to help Daddy, for Daddy's standards were high, and Daddy was inclined to be impatient snatching away from my brother's fumbling fingers a hammer, a screwdriver, an electric sander—when, years ago, poor Ben was eager to be Daddy's apprentice carpenter around the house.

Fucking up was what Eddy Diehl hated. *Fucking up*—his own mistakes, or others' mistakes—drove him crazy.

If you'd known my parents socially—not intimately—you'd have assumed that my mother might be difficult to please, and Eddy Diehl with his feckless smile and easy demeanor the one to let things go as they would, but in fact my father was the one whom any kind of *fuckup* enraged for it was a sign of a man losing control of his surroundings. In the confrontation of a *fuckup* anywhere in our vicinity my mother Lucille became alarmed and frightened, anxious how my father would react.

Not until the time of the court order banishing Eddy Diehl from our property and our lives would I learn the extent to which my mother was terrified of my father's quick, hot, "blind" temper.

Maybe I should give up basketball?—sulkily I asked my father.

My heart that had been swollen with elation, pride, wanting-to-impress Daddy was now shriveled as a prune.

Steering the Caddie Seville onto an exit ramp, frowning and squinting through the rain-splotched windshield, my father seemed not to have heard me at first; then he said, more tenderly, "I didn't say that, Krissie. Hell no. You're learning. You're promising. Sports is all about who you're contending with, see? Like life, maybe. You're only as good as your opponents let you be. They're only as good as you let them be."

This was so. Uncontestably, this was so. Now I had an idea of what my father might be feeling, his opponents thwarting him, blocking him, trampling on his life. And I had a sharper memory of how when we'd all lived together in the house on Huron Pike Road the very air reverberated with the swelling and shrinking, the waning and waxing of my father's mood.

"Baby, no. You don't ever give up."

Daddy wasn't staying with relatives or friends here in Sparta but, surprising to me, in the Days Inn on route 31. Maybe there was a reason for this, he'd explained. He was going to be "in the vicinity" until the following Monday—"seeing people"—"doing some business"—"tying up loose ends." I hoped that this didn't include trying to see my mother or any of her family. None of the Bauers wanted to see Eddy Diehl, ever again.

Your father is not welcome with us.

Your father is dead to us.

Some of my father's business in Sparta had to do with "litigation"—he'd been trying for years, with one lawyer or another, to sue local law enforcement officers and the Herkimer County prosecutor's office on grounds of *harassment, character assassination, criminal slander* and *misuse of authority.* So far as anyone knew, nothing had come of my father's lawsuits except legal fees.

I dreaded to hear that he might be seeing yet another lawyer. Or that he might be planning on speaking again with the police, the prosecutors, the local newspapers and media. Demanding that his name be *cleared.*

Whatever my father's specific business in Sparta, I knew better than to ask about it. For though Daddy seemed always to be speaking openly and frankly and in a tone of belligerent optimism you could not speak like this to him, in turn. I'd come to recognize a certain mode of adult speech that, seeming intimate, is a way of precluding intimacy. *I am telling you all that you need to know! What I don't tell you, you will not be told.*

We'd exited the eerily humming suspension bridge from downtown Sparta to East Sparta, a no-man's-land of small factories, gas stations, vacated warehouses, acres of asphalt parking lots creased and cracked and overgrown with gigantic thistles. In litter-strewn fields, in trash-choked gutters you saw lifeless bodies—you saw what appeared to be bodies—trussed and wrapped in twine, humanoid, part-decomposed. You saw, and looked again: only just garbage bags, more trash. East Sparta had lost most of its industries, now East Sparta was filling up with debris.

I asked my father where was he living now?—and my father said, "*Me?* Living *now?*" meant to be a joke and so I laughed nervously.

Maybe he wanted me to guess? I guessed Buffalo, Batavia, Port Oriskany, Strykersville. . . . He said, "I'm between habitats, right now. Left some things in storage in Buffalo. Mostly I'm in motion, y'know?—in this car that's my newest purchase/investment. Like it?"

Though I was listening intently to my father yet I seemed not to know what he was asking me. *This car? Do I like—this car?*

I had already told my father yes, I liked this car. This was a beautiful car. But he wasn't living in his car, was he? Was he living *in his car*?

The backseat was piled with things. Boxes, files, folders. A pair of men's shoes, what appeared to be clothing: outer garments. Suitcase. Suitcases. Duffel bag. More boxes.

Dead to us. Doesn't he know it?

Damn dumb ghost wish to hell he'd die.

"Anywhere I am, Krista. In my—y'know—soul. Like in my thoughts, except deeper. That's what a soul is. In my soul I'm here, in Sparta. Lots of times in my sleep in our house, on the Huron Road. That's where I wake up, until—I'm awake and I see hey no—*nooooo!*—that isn't where I am, after all."

To this, I had no idea how to reply. I was thinking how I loved my Daddy, and how strange it was that a girl has a Daddy, and a girl loves a Daddy, a girl does not judge a Daddy. I was thinking how I hated my brother Ben, who was free of having to love Daddy.

Ben didn't love me, either. I was sure.

"It's my birthplace here," Daddy said. "My birthright. Nights when I can't sleep I just shut my eyes, I'm here. I'm home."

"I wish . . ."

"Yes? What d'you wish, Puss?"

" . . . you could come live with us again, Daddy. That's what I wish."

Daddy laughed, kindly. Or maybe Daddy's laugh was resigned, wounded.

" . . . wish you could come back tonight. . . . It isn't the same without you, Daddy. Anywhere in the house. Anywhere . . ." I was wiping at my eyes, that ached as if I'd been staring into a blinding light. Maybe one of the guards on the opposing team had thumbed my eye, out of pure meanness.

Pissy little white girl get out of my face! "I miss you, Daddy. So does Ben. He doesn't say so, but he does."

This was a lie. Why I said it, impulsively, I don't know: to make Daddy happy, maybe. A little happier.

"Well, honey. Thank you. I miss you, too. Real bad." There was a pause, Daddy pondered. "And your brother."

I said yes, I'd tell him. I'd tell Ben.

It had been one of the shocks of my father's life, how his son had turned against him. *His* son, against *him*.

And maybe he'd loved Ben better than he'd loved me. Or he'd wanted to. Having a *son* was the card you led with, in Daddy's circle of men friends.

" . . . she's getting along, O.K.? Is she?"

She. We were talking about my mother, were we? All along, since I'd scrambled to climb into the Caddie Seville, the subject had been my mother.

" . . . to that church? The new one? How's that turning out?"

I told him it was turning out all right. My mother had joined a new church, my mother had "new friends" or claimed to have. I had not yet met these "new friends" but one of them was named Eve Hurtle or Huddle, the brassy-haired dump truck–shaped woman who owned Second Time 'Round.

I was uneasy thinking that my father might ask if my mother was "seeing" anyone—any man—and I prepared what I might say. *Daddy I don't know! I don't think so.* Hoping he wouldn't ask, this would be demeaning to him.

But Daddy didn't ask. Not that. If Eddy Diehl felt sexual jealousy, sexual rage, he had too much manly pride to ask. Though I could sense how badly he wanted to ask.

" . . . doesn't pass on much information about me, I guess? To you and Ben?"

Information? I wasn't sure what Daddy meant.

"It's like I'm dead, yes? 'Dead to me'—that's what she says?"

It's over. Finished. That's what she says.

Carefully I told Daddy I wasn't sure. I thought maybe he was right, she didn't pass on much information to Ben and me but then she didn't confide in us on "personal" things. I didn't think that she confided in anyone, there was too much shame involved.

Naked female strangled in her bed. Eddy Diehl's tramp mistress.

On the highway ahead of us was a school bus, carrot-colored, Herkimer Co. School District, red lights flashing as it braked to a stop to let several passengers out. Almost too late, Daddy braked the Caddie. He'd been distracted, cursing and gripping the steering wheel.

"Fuck! God damn school buses."

Both Daddy and I were wearing seat belts. Daddy was sharp-eyed about seat belts. Daddy had had a friend, an old high school friend, who'd been killed in some awful way like impaled on a steering wheel or his head half sheared off from his shoulders by broken glass, Daddy had always warned Ben and me about *belting in*.

"She cashes my checks, though. I hope she tells you that."

Cashes his checks? Was this so? All I knew, or was made to know by my mother and the Bauers, was that my father was *derelict in his duty. Neglects his family. Behind on alimony/child support.*

"Of course, it's the least I can do. I don't begrudge her. I mean, you are my family. What kind of crap 'salary' would she get from selling secondhand clothes? Least I can do, ruining that woman's life. . . ."

Daddy's voice trailed off, embarrassed. And angry. Clumsily he was lighting up a cigarette, sucking in a deep deep breath like the sweetest purest oxygen he'd been missing.

You could not tell if Daddy's embarrassment provoked his anger or whether the anger was always there, smoldering like burnt rubber in the rain, and embarrassment screened it fleetingly as a scrim of clouds screens a fierce glaring sun.

" . . . I never said I wasn't responsible, for that. Not . . . not the other, Krissie, but . . . that. Your mother, and you and Ben . . . ruining your lives. Jesus! If I had to do it over again. . . ."

This was new, I thought. I was uneasy, hearing such words from my father. *Ruining your lives. Ruining that woman's life.* For a moment I hadn't known which *woman* my father was speaking of, my mother or—the other woman.

My father had never once spoken of Zoe Kruller to me, or to Ben.

I was sure he had not spoken of her to Ben. In his claims of innocence and his protestations that he'd had nothing to do with *that woman's death* he had never given a name to Zoe Kruller. And he would not now, I knew.

" . . . grateful to be alive. And free. That's the miracle, Krissie—I am not in Attica, serving a life sentence. They say you go crazy in a few months in Attica, the inmates are crazy especially the older ones, the white ones, the guards are crazy—who else'd be a C.O. at Attica? You can't make it alone, I'd have had to join up with the Aryan Nation— there's some bikers in Attica, guys I knew from the army, already they'd sent word to me—if I got sent to Attica, I'd be O.K. Imagine, Krissie, my 'future' was being prepared for, this was what I had to look forward to, as some kind of *good news*." My father laughed, harshly. His laughter turned into a fit of coughing, in disgust he stubbed out the cigarette in an ashtray that opened out of the dashboard beside his knee. "What I am trying to determine, Krissie, is: maybe there is a God, but does God give a shit for justice on earth? For any of us, on earth? I was reading some science discovery, that God is a 'principle'—some kind of 'equation'—so there is a God, but what kind of a God is that? A man has got to forge his own justice. As a man has got to forgive his own soul. This justice can't spring forth too fast, it has to bide its time. So when it's least expected. Most of humankind, they don't give any more of a shit than 'God.' I guess you can't blame them, there's hurricanes, floods, every kind of terrible thing erupting out of the earth, every time you see a paper or turn on TV—how'd you keep up with it? I was a kid, I had to go to Sunday school for a while, till I was eleven when I wouldn't go any more, I remember how we were told about Jesus performing his miracles, how impressed everyone was, it was 'miracles' that impressed them not Jesus as a preacher, anyway—my point is—you are made to think that Jesus could raise the dead, Jesus could save his people, but in actual fact, how could Jesus 'save' the teeming multitudes that populate the world *now*? There's millions—maybe billions—of people alive, and they are all in peril. As for the God-damned 'authorities'—the 'leaders'—they don't give a damn.

It's all about power. It's about raking in cash, hiding it in Switzerland. Some banks where they don't reveal your identity. You don't pay taxes. The 'authorities'—they'd sell their own grandmother's soul, to put an innocent man in prison, or on death row—bottom line is, they want to 'close the case.' God-damned hypocrite fuckers . . ."

I was confused, frightened. It had seemed at first—hadn't it?—that my father was speaking of something painful with which he'd come to terms, something for which he acknowledged responsibility; he'd sounded remorseful at the outset of his speech but then abruptly the tone shifted, he'd become angry, indignant. His jaw jutted like a fist. His eyes stared straight ahead. Despite warm air from the Caddie's heater I felt a sensation of chill wash over me.

Can't trust a drinker. Krista promise me never never get in any vehicle with a drinker you will regret it.

Hadn't my mother warned me, many times! For surely her mother had warned her, too; and she had not listened.

It seemed that we were headed into the country on route 31, a two-lane state highway north of Sparta. The strip of fast-food restaurants, gas stations and motels where the Days Inn was located was behind us. I thought that, if Daddy had intended to kidnap me, he would not be driving in this direction—would he? In a more genial Daddy-voice he was saying now that for my sixteenth birthday just maybe he'd give me a car—"How's about a convertible coupe? Just right for sweet sixteen."

Was Daddy joking? A car, for *me*? I wondered if Daddy even knew when my birthday was.

From a cloverleaf ramp I could look into the fleeting rears of houses: sheds, animal pens, clotheslines drooping in the rain. A dispirited-looking trailer "village," a smoldering trash dump that smelled of burning rubber.

We were headed east on route 31, we seemed to have a destination. I had to wonder if Daddy was planning to meet up with someone, there was such urgency in his driving. Those places that Zoe Kruller had frequented were miles behind us: Tip Top Club, Chet's Keyboard Lounge,

Houlihan's, the Grotto, Swank's Go-Go, bars at the new Marriott and the Sheraton-Hilton. There was the HiLo Lounge at the Holiday Inn. There was Little Las Vegas at the traffic circle. These were neon-glamorous places by night and by day mostly deserted. In the raw light of day you were made aware of the crude unlit signs sporting semi-nude female figures like cartoon drawings and of overflowing Dumpsters, parking lots littered like acne. After Eddy Diehl had been taken into police custody it would be revealed that he had not been the only "family man" who moved in such circles, as his friends and companions were made to inform upon him and upon one another. *No one was arrested for any crime. Yet lives were ruined.*

I'd been too young then to know. I was still too young at fifteen to have a grasp of what it might be, that I didn't yet know.

Here in the country, in a township of Herkimer County known as the Rapids, we were in hilly farmland where by day we'd be seeing herds of Guernsey cows grazing placid and near-motionless in pastures on either side of the road. There were odd-shaped hills called drumlins, exposed shale and limestone like bone broken through skin. Eddy Diehl had relatives who lived in the Rapids but we were not going to visit them, I knew.

"Wish I could see where we were, Daddy. Where we're going."

My voice was little-girl wistful, I took care not to sound whiny or reproachful. I guessed we were headed for the County Line Tavern which was one of Eddy Diehl's places. I wished it was another time and Daddy was taking me for a sight-seeing drive along the Black River and into the countryside in his showy new car as he'd done when Ben and I were young children and sometimes our mother would come with us. *This car! I can't get over this car! What on earth are you going to do with this car! Oh Eddy. Oh my God.*

On Sunday drives Daddy would take us out to Uncle Sean's farm.

Uncle Sean was an uncle of my mother's, an old man with stark white fluffy hair and skin roughened as the skin of a pineapple. Ben and I were allowed to stroke the velvety noses of horses in their stalls, in the company of our cousin Ty who kept a close watch over us—"Careful! Walk on this side"—and we were allowed to brush the horses' sides with a wire brush, warm rippling shivery sides, always you are astonished at the size of a horse, the height of a horse, the ceaseless switching of the coarse mane and the coarse stinging tail, the fresh manure underfoot, horseflies hovering in the air, repulsive. Yet I had wanted a horse of my own. I loved to press my face against the horses' warm sides. My favorite was a mare named Molly-O, one of my uncle's smaller horses, pebble-gray, with liquidy dark eyes that knew me, I was certain.

I wondered what it meant: here was a *horse*, but I was a *girl*.

I wondered if it was just an accident, how we are born: *horse, girl*.

The way after my father was lost to us in defiance of my mother I would bicycle into Sparta and past the row house where Zoe Kruller was said to have been *strangled in her bed* and the thought came to me unbidden, illogical *If I'd lived here. Anyone who lived here. Death was meant to come here.*

You want to blame them, those who've been killed. Any woman *naked and strangled in her bed* you certainly want to blame.

" . . . shouldn't have shut me out like that. Your 'Uncle Sean.'"

"Uncle Sean" was uttered in a tone of contempt, hurt. Daddy seemed to have been following my thoughts.

"All of your mother's people, that I'd thought liked me. I mean, some of them. The men. Your 'Uncle Sean'—"

"He isn't my uncle, Daddy. He's Mom's uncle."

"He's your *great-uncle*. That's what he is."

I wanted to protest, that wasn't my fault!

I wanted to protest, Uncle Sean was just an old, ignorant man. Why should Daddy care what he thinks. . .

" . . . should know that I won't give up. A guilty man, he'd give up, he'd move away. By now he'd be vanished from Sparta. But I'm not a guilty man—anyway not guilty of *that*—and I mean to alter the judgment of bastards like 'Uncle Sean' that had no faith in me. You tell your mother, Krista: I am not going to slink away like a kicked dog, I am still fighting this. It's been—how long—going on five years—a guilty man would've given up by now, but not Eddy Diehl."

Moved by sudden emotion, Daddy reached out another time to grope for my arm, my hand. His fingers were strong, closing around my wrist. I felt a pang of alarm, a moment's unthinking panic. *Always you are astonished. Their size, their height. Their strength. That they could hurt you so easily without meaning to.*

7

"WELL, SAY! Thought it was *you*."

At Honeystone's Dairy the person you hoped would wait on you was Zoe Kruller.

Not heavyset Audrey with the sulky dark-purple mouth like a wound, not the steely-eyed grandma Mrs. Honeystone the owner's wife, or in the height of summer temporary hired-help, high school girls who took little interest in the names of most customers or in recalling that a finicky child might prefer one type of ice-cream cone (lighter, less crunchy) over another (darker, grainier and chewier), and want her chocolate scoop on the bottom and her strawberry on top so that, melting, the strawberry would seep into the chocolate and not the other way around which seemed to the finicky mildly repugnant, unnatural; and on sundaes no nuts, and no maraschino cherries. But Zoe Kruller knew, Zoe Kruller always remembered.

As Zoe remembered names: "Krissie, is it? H'lo there Krissie!"

Zoe was glamorous, not merely pretty. Your eye moved onto Zoe with startled interest as your eye might be drawn to a billboard face posed above the highway, you would never imagine might have the slightest consciousness of *you*.

If you were a child, that is. A girl-child intensely aware of adult women: their faces, their bodies.

Zoe was an adult woman, a wife and a mother. Yet you would not have guessed that Zoe was much older than the high school girls who worked behind the counter at Honeystone's. Her face was a girl's face, just this side of beauty: her eager smile revealed a band of pink gum and her long hungry-looking teeth overlapped just perceptibly in front. Her skin was pale, warmly freckled. Her hair was "strawberry blond"—crimped, flyaway, shoulder-length. Her eyebrows had been carefully plucked and filled in with eyebrow pencil, her pale lashes were inky with mascara. Her nose was a little too long, with a waxy tip, and wide nostrils. Her chin was a little too narrow. Yet her eyes were beautiful, exotic: shades of amber like sherry at the bottom of a glass, or a certain kind of children's marble, amber-glazed, changing its colors as you turned it in your fingers.

Zoe was a small woman, her figure was what's called *petite*. She could not have weighed more than one hundred pounds nor was she more than five feet two. Yet she exuded an air of sexy funny-girl swagger that made her appear taller, like one accustomed to the spotlight. Behind the counter at Honeystone's Zoe had a way of rising up on her toes when she locked eyes with a customer, smiling that glistening bared-gum smile and a light seemed truly to come into her face.

"Well, say! Thought it was *you*."

Most remarkable was Zoe's throaty purring voice. It was a voice so low and shivery it didn't seem as if it was issuing from Zoe Kruller's wide-lipped crimson mouth but from a radio. Here was a distinctive *voice* amid a clamor of voices of no distinction, that made you stop and stare at Zoe even more than her lit-up face might have warranted. *Here is someone special* you were made to think.

That red-embroidered *ZOE* on a tiny pocket above Zoe's left breast.

"'Zooh-ey.' Not 'Zoo-ey.' Please!"

In Chautauqua Park on summer nights local musicians and singers performed at the bandstand and Zoe Kruller belonged to the most popular group, that called itself Black River Breakdown. Zoe was the only woman among several men—guitarist, banjo player, fiddler and piano-player.

Except for the Elvis-looking guitarist, a kid in his early twenties with dyed-black hair and cowboy boots with a prominent heel, they were all in their thirties, ardent, excitable, yearning for applause. Their music ranged from country-and-western classics ("Little Maggie," "Down from Dover," "I'll Walk the Line") to bluegrass ("Little Bird of Heaven," "Her Little Footprints in the Snow") and disco ("I Will Survive," "Saturday Night Fever").

Especially on stage at the bandstand, sexy-seductive in a spangled dress that left most of her thighs exposed and her strawberry-blond hair frizzed and crimped in a wild halo around her head so it looked like an electric bolt had shot through her, Zoe Kruller did not resemble any other wife/mother in Sparta.

Yet she was Mrs. Kruller, the mother of a boy in Ben's class at school. This boy was named Aaron and he looked older than Ben by a year or more and had a stiff glaring face nothing like Zoe's.

"Zoe married young"—this was said of Mrs. Kruller, by our mother and our mother's friends.

"Zoe married 'way too young'"—this was said with satisfaction.

And, sometimes: "Zoe married 'way too young and the wrong man.'"

None of this meant anything to Ben and me. Being taken for a drive out to Honeystone's which was an actual dairy farm on the outskirts of Sparta, locally famous for its homemade ice cream and desserts, was a Sunday reward for having been good through the week, or one of Daddy's capricious treats. *Anybody interested in a ride? Honeystone's?*

Say I returned to Sparta. Say I looked up my few remaining "friends"— classmates from school—and asked what they remembered most vividly from our childhood, each would say—"Honeystone's!" Clutching at one another's hands, eyes misting with tears of sentiment, the sweetest sort of tears, recalling Honeystone's Dairy as you'd recall a lost paradise.

Recalling even the drive to Honeystone's, fraught with the happiest sort of anticipation.

Out East Huron Pike Road, past the water treatment tower. Past the railroad yard. Across the Black River Bridge and beyond East Sparta Memorial Park and a short mile or so to the Sparta town limits and there was the sparkling-white stucco building set back from the road in a neatly tended graveled parking lot bounded, in summer, by bright red geraniums in clay pots, and in the autumn by chrysanthemums of all hues; there was the smiling-cow sign thirty feet high, on a pole illuminated at night like a stage set—HONEYSTONE'S DAIRY. Inside Honeystone's the air was immediately distinctive: milky-cool, marble-cool, like the foyer of the Midland Sparta Bank, except here there was an odor of bakery, so sweet your mouth watered like a baby's. On the floor of Honeystone's was what appeared to be actual marble, black-and-white checked, worn but still elegant; there were ornately designed white wrought-iron tables and chairs and there were vinyl booths that resembled leather, sleek and black. Descending from the ceiling were a half-dozen slow-moving fans with blades like the propellers of small planes, both languorous and vaguely threatening. If you were to dream of Honeystone's interior, the slow-moving fans would take on an ominous note.

A dream of Honeystone's might be edgy as well because you would not clearly see who'd brought you. For invariably in these dreams you are a young child in the company of an adult and you are essentially helpless.

"What can I do you for, sweetie?"

This was Zoe's snappy way of greeting. Glamorous Zoe Kruller leaning forward onto the high counter, on her elbows, on her toes, smiling that crimson long-lipped hungry smile, baring her gums. Her eyes so exotic in black mascara, silvery-blue eye shadow and eyeliner, you gaped not knowing how to respond.

And there were other fascinating things about Aaron Kruller's mother: the way she wore the sleeves of her white Honeystone's smock pushed up past her elbows so that her slender arms were exposed, covered in dark little moles and freckles like tiny ants! Oh there was something ticklish—shivery—about Zoe Kruller! This giggly throaty-voiced woman about the size of a thirteen-year-old girl who made you want to sink your teeth into ice cream, bite down hard so your teeth ached, and your jaws, and you shuddered at the cold.

Honeystone's help had to wear white smocks over white cord trousers and both smock and trousers had to be kept spotless. Honeystone's help had to wear hairnets which made them—except for Zoe Kruller—look silly, dowdy. But on Zoe, her thick strawberry-blond hair just barely contained by the gossamer net, the effect was strangely alluring.

Zoe's pert question—"What can I do you for, sweetie?"—was like a riddle for there was something wrong with it, words were scrambled, you had to think—and blink—and think hard to figure out what was wrong.

Do you for. Not *Do for you.* This was so funny!

Even Ben, who disliked being teased, especially by people he didn't know well, laughed when Zoe Kruller leaned on her elbows to peer down at him over the counter asking what could she *Do him for* and calling him *Daddy's big boy.*

Well, if Mommy had brought us, Zoe would call Ben *Mommy's big boy.* But it wasn't so thrilling somehow, then: Zoe wouldn't pay much attention to us, then.

Our mother knew Zoe Kruller when she'd had a different last name. When she'd been a high school girl, the younger sister of a classmate of Lucille Bauer's at Sparta High.

In a small city like Sparta, everyone knows everyone else. It's a matter of age, generation. Everyone knows everyone's family background, to a degree. There are commingled histories, intense friendships and intense feuds that, having gone underground decades before, continue to smolder and pollute the air.

You can smell the pollution, but you can't see it. You could not ever guess its history.

Tangled roots, beneath the surface of the earth. How astonishing to discover these roots, so hidden. How my mother began working obsessively outdoors that spring, digging in the clayey soil beside the driveway determined to plant what she called *snow-on-the-mountains*—a hardy fast-growing perennial—and the shovel struck a tangle of roots like something ugly knotted in the brain.

When *the trouble* began in my parents' lives—except Ben and I had not known that there was anything like *the trouble*, at the start—our mother became strange to us, spending time outdoors as she'd never done in the past, sweaty and her forearms ropey-veined in a way frightening to see, and the set of her mouth grim like something zipped-up seen from the wrong side. And Mom would try to sink the shovel into the ground, using her weight as leverage, and the sole of her sneakered foot struck hard against the rim of the shovel and she cried out in pain *Oh God! God-damn.*

Beneath, those tangled roots. Severed, their insides glared a terrible white like bone marrow.

However our mother knew Zoe Kruller who was so glamorous at Honeystone's, our father knew Zoe Kruller some other way.

Say I was on comfortable speaking terms with my brother Ben—from whom I am not estranged, exactly—and I called him impulsively and asked *Do you remember us going to Honeystone's? When Daddy took us? How different was that, from when Mom took us?*

And say Ben didn't hang up the phone. But in a mood of not-bitter reminiscence he would speak sincerely to me, thoughtfully. He would say:

Sure, you could tell. For sure.

At the time?

No. Not at the time.

But later?

Right. Later.

That quickness in Daddy. Playing the car radio loud, humming loudly with it. Driving just a little too fast on Huron Pike Road and the careful way he parked in Honeystone's graveled lot, very likely it was one of Eddy Diehl's showy cars he was driving, that very morning washing, waxing, polishing in our driveway and here in Honeystone's graveled parking lot Eddy Diehl was positioning the car in such a way that, if anyone inside cared to glance out—Honeystone's front window was horizontal, long, plate-glass spanning nearly the width of the building—she would see the stately 1973 Lincoln Continental with two-tone beige-and-black finish, or maybe it was the cream-colored 1977 Oldsmobile Deluxe with its glittering chrome grille—possibly the cherry-red vintage Thunderbird like the sleekest of rockets yearning to be launched—and she would stop dead in her tracks, and stare. And smile.

Eddy Diehl's *specialty-autos* were to make observers smile.

Certain observers, that is. Others, the intention was to intimidate, provoke envy.

Jesus! Who owns that?

Seeing this vehicle in the lot, guessing the driver was probably Eddy Diehl, quickly she would turn away to check her reflection in the mirror at her back, or in the mirror of the little plastic compact she kept in a pocket of her white cord smock for just such semi-emergency occasions; there was just time for her to dab some scented ivory powder on her nose, check her eye makeup, shape a pouting smile to see if the crimson lipstick was still fresh. And adjust her hair in the damned hairnet they made you wear in this damned prissy place.

"Well say, Eddy Diehl! Thought it was *you*."

Zoe Kruller's sexy-throaty voice that was like sandpaper rubbed against sandpaper to make you shiver. Zoe Kruller's voice that was close and warm and teasing like a voice murmured in your ear as you lay in bed, head on your pillow and bedclothes clutched to your chin.

With what eagerness Daddy entered Honeystone's—pushing the door open with such force that the little bell attached overhead tinkled loudly, ushering his young children—what were their names—Ben? Krissie?— into the milky-cool, marble-cool air of Honeystone's Dairy which was so wonderful.

And there in that instant was Zoe Kruller catching sight of Eddy Diehl, and Eddy Diehl catching sight of Zoe Kruller. Almost, you could feel the rush of blood that ran through them, like an electric current.

"How're you doing, Zoe-y. Looking good."

In a casual voice my father called out a greeting. Sunday afternoons, Honeystone's was likely to be busy.

Zoe Kruller was such a favorite at the dairy, as she was a favorite at Chautauqua Park on summer-music nights, there were customers who waited in line to be waited on by her: though heavyset Audrey and white-haired Mrs. Honeystone might both be available behind the counter, scowling.

Not wanting to meet Mrs. Honeystone's eye—the white-haired older woman was Marv Honeystone's wife, and Eddy knew Marv Honeystone from having worked for him—Eddy lingered before one of the refrigerated dessert cases, hands on his hips, brooding. As if he'd come to Honeystone's with the intention of buying a strawberry whipped-cream pie, a chocolate *mousse*, a three-tiered birthday cake, a luscious glazed fruit tart or a platter of fudge, chocolate-chip cookies, *macaroons*. "O.K. Ben, Krissie—say what looks good to you. What'd you like best."

Earnestly Ben and I debated: the strawberry whipped-cream pie, banana cream pie, cherry pie with strips of golden crust like a pinwheel instead of the usual boring solid upper crust. . . .

An entire display case of birthday cakes!

This debate could occupy minutes. While Eddy Diehl glanced at Zoe Kruller in the mirror behind the display case, took in his own reflection with a critical frown and slicked back his tufted rust-red hair like a rooster's comb with a quick movement of both his hands.

Eddy Diehl's big carpenter's hands. Eddy Diehl's big thumbs. Eddy Diehl's heavy-lidded eyes behind flat sea-green "aviator" sunglasses with the metallic rims. Eddy Diehl's wordless appeal to the pert petite strawberry-blond woman with the glamorous made-up face like a Dolly Parton doll, white sleeves pushed back to bare her pale freckled forearms.

After some Sundays of this, Ben began to object: "You always ask us what we want, Dad, but you never buy anything. So why ask us?"

I didn't want to hear this. I'd made my choices to tell Daddy: banana cream pie, caramel custard pie, triple-layer chocolate cake with HAPPY BIRTHDAY scrolled in pink frosting on the top. Once I'd watched Zoe Kruller squirting a coil of pink frosting like toothpaste over a duplicate of this very cake, completing the message HAPPY BIRTHDAY ROBIN!

At the time, I'd thought how lucky Robin was.

Whoever Robin was: girl, boy.

Daddy said, just this side of annoyed: "Might be I'm making a mental note, Ben. Your Daddy has a mind like a steel trap. Filing facts, that will one day come in handy."

Mental note? I was curious about this. Asked Daddy what was a *mental note* but Daddy was casting a sidelong look over at Zoe Kruller who was casting a sidelong smile at him past a customer's frizz-permed head.

"Daddy? What's a 'mental note'—"

"You tell her, Zoe." Affably Daddy raised his voice, to draw Zoe into the conversation. A few feet away Zoe was preparing sundaes for a family of fretting young children. "What's a 'mental note.'"

This presumed that Zoe had been listening to us from a distance of ten, twelve feet. That, since Eddy Diehl had first entered Honeystone's, Zoe Kruller had been keenly aware of him and his two young children who took after the mother's side of the family, it seemed—*A gosh-darn pity since Eddy Diehl is the good-looking one and not chubby moon-faced Lucy Bauer.*

Zoe tilted her head to indicate that she was thinking hard.

"'Mental note' is—a memory. You make a special memory inside your head, to remind yourself of something at a later date. 'Mental note' is for the future, to refer back to *now.*"

Zoe spoke in a low mysterious throaty murmur. I had no idea what she and my father were talking about but any succession of words Zoe Kruller spoke no matter how ordinary or banal were freighted with significance like words blazoned on a billboard or in a bright-lit TV commercial.

Eddy Diehl wore work caps, baseball caps. Always outdoors and often indoors. He'd removed his cap—grungy dark-blue with bronze letters SPARTA CONSTRUCTION, he'd worn for years—to swipe at his hair but he'd quickly replaced it tugging the rim low over his forehead. There was something shy about him, or anyway self-conscious: here was a man who knows he is looked-at by both women and men, and wants to be looked-at, yet on his own terms exclusively.

At work—at Sparta Construction, Inc.—Daddy wore white shirts: short-sleeved in summer, long-sleeved in winter. These shirts my mother ironed, for Daddy insisted upon white cotton shirts, not wash-and-wear. Daddy wore neatly pressed trousers on the job, sport coats or jackets in cold weather, never an overcoat. You would never see a carpenter—any man who works with his hands—wearing an overcoat on the job. Summers, away from work Daddy wore T-shirts and khaki pants likely to be rumpled and stained, running shoes on his size-twelve feet.

It never ceased to amaze me, Daddy was so *big*. Daddy loomed above me, a tall muscled man with broad shoulders, long arms and powerful wrists. In spite of his *bad knee* (as my mother called it, though not in Daddy's presence) Daddy walked without wincing, or at least visibly wincing; never did he wish to allude to his *bad knee*, his *injury*; he flushed with indignation if anyone—usually female relatives of my mother's—questioned him too pointedly about his health. (So too my father coolly disdained questions from relatives both male and female about how the construction business was going, smiling and shrugging *Can't complain. Holding our own. You?*)

There was something loose and impulsive in my father's movements, a quicksilver excitement hinting almost of threat except he was teasing, smiling—wasn't he? *Don't come too close! Don't mistake my seeming friendly for my being your friend.*

On my father's tanned arms thick hairs grew in bristling swirls and eddies, dark-rust-red shading to black, springy and intransigent as wires to the touch. As a little girl I'd been intimidated by Daddy's muscled arms covered in hair and the hint of a dark wiry animal pelt covering his chest, parts of his back, beneath his white T-shirt, springing into view at his throat. Seeing the look in my face Daddy laughed: "Don't worry, Puss. Turning into a mean hairy ape won't happen to *you*."

This was Daddy joking. I like to remember Daddy joking. It is important to remember that men like my father—so very American, small-city-coming-of-age-in-the-Vietnam War-era—were given to joking, teasing, what they called *kidding around*, there was nothing more wonderful than a man like Eddy Diehl in this mood, maybe he's had a few beers, maybe he's with his buddies, guys like himself who are the only people he can trust since he can't trust any woman even his wife, not even his mother—*If you have to ask why, forget it.*

If you have to ask, go to hell.

Go fuck yourself, see? If you have to ask.

Nothing more wonderful than the smiles of these American daddies causing their hard faces to soften like boys' faces and the edges of their wary eyes to crease and yet—nothing more frightening than when these daddies cease to smile.

Suddenly, and without warning.

As in Honeystone's that day, when my father snapped at Ben: "Hey. Get the hell over here."

What had Ben been doing? Poking at a platter of fresh-baked brownies covered in cellophane, displayed on one of the glass-topped cases.

Ben at the age of ten, a lanky sweet-faced boy with fair-coppery-red-brown hair in a silky swirl that made him look like a girl, startled fair-brown eyes, a rabbity unease. Daddy's voice came much too harsh, furious for the occasion.

"God damn you what're you *doing*. Keep your hands off what doesn't belong to you."

Daddy was getting *pissed*, as he'd say. Waiting for Zoe Kruller to pay attention to him. Waiting, and Eddy Diehl isn't accustomed to waiting for women to pay attention to him.

I felt a shivery little *frisson* of satisfaction, that my older brother was being publicly scolded by our father. So funny—the way Ben jerked back from the display case as if he'd touched a snake. Yet it scared me, that Daddy might suddenly lapse into one of his moods, and little Krista would be scolded harshly, too.

But there came Zoe's sweet-honeyed voice directed toward us at last.

"Eddy? That's some swanky car out there."

Daddy laughed, pleased. Daddy assented, yes that was his car, he'd acquired just a few days ago.

"Soon as you pulled into the lot, I knew it had to be *you*."

Now words flew between our father and Zoe Kruller swift as Ping-Pong balls. Whatever these words meant—talk of Daddy's newly acquired car, or Black River Breakdown's next "gig" in a week or two—talk of respective spouses, families—on their surface these words were innocuous and banal like the smiles of adults as they gaze at you thinking their own faraway private thoughts.

Zoe was teasing but beneath you could see that Zoe was dead-serious.

Fixing Eddy Diehl with her crazed-amber eyes, calculating and ardent; stroking her bared forearm that was freckled and stippled with tiny moles.

I saw how Zoe Kruller's fingernails flashed crimson. I saw how Daddy would see, and felt my blood quicken.

After what seemed like a long time—though it must have been no more than two or three minutes—Zoe turned her wide-eyed gaze upon Ben and me: "So—Ben? And—Krissie? Daddy's little guy, and Daddy's little gal—what can I do you for today?"

We laughed, this was so curious a way of speaking, like a riddle, like tickling. I wasn't sure that I liked it, words scrambled in such a way. As a little child I'd been anxious about misspeaking, and provoking adult laughter. Saying words in the wrong sequence like wetting my panties, wetting the bed, spilling a glass of milk at supper, dropping a fork laden with mashed potatoes, what a child most dreads is the exasperated laughter of adults when you have done a *wrong thing*.

Now Zoe Kruller was mouthing funny words *Do you for. What can I. Ben? Krissie?*

I loved Zoe Kruller, I think. The way Zoe Kruller fixed her eyes on me, and called me by name.

Why was I so frightened of Zoe Kruller!

There was an interlude of teasing-Krissie—Daddy told Zoe that I wanted a coffee ice-cream cone—I protested no, I hated coffee ice cream—and Zoe laughed and said yes, she knew: what I wanted was a double-scoop cone, chocolate on the bottom and strawberry on top.

"Your daddy's a tease, sweetie. Don't think I pay your damn ol' daddy much mind."

Damn was one of those words adults could use. Depending on the tone and on who was saying it to whom it was soft-sounding as a caress, or it was harsh.

Anything that passed between Zoe Kruller and Eddy Diehl, in Honeystone's Dairy, was soft-sounding as a caress, and not harsh.

Daddy never bought ice-cream cones or sundaes for himself. Not ever. Daddy hadn't much taste for sweet things, preferred salty things like pretzels, peanuts, potato chips however stale, eating them by the mouthful as he drank beer, Sundays. And Daddy liked coffee, Daddy was "hooked" on black coffee, so pungent-smelling it made my nostrils shut up, tight. Especially Daddy liked coffee you could get at Honeystone's which smelled like a different kind of coffee than at home.

Zoe made a show of pouring the steaming liquid into a tall Styrofoam cup. "There you go, Eddy. Hope it's what you like."

"Yes. It's what I like."

One day, Zoe Kruller would be vanished from Honeystone's. One day soon and it would be a shock to me, a cruel surprise—my mother was the one to drive Ben and me to the dairy and eagerly we'd run inside looking for Zoe Kruller but there was just old Mrs. Honeystone and fat scowling Audrey and another girl who was a stranger to us and we asked Mrs. Honeystone where was Zoe? Where was Zoe? and Mrs. Honeystone said only that she'd quit, Mrs. Honeystone did not utter the name *Zoe* but only just *she*. You could see how Mrs. Honeystone would not smile and did not care to say anything further about Zoe Kruller nor would our mother inquire.

Where is she, she's gone. Gave notice, and gone.

THAT DAY, that Sunday I am thinking of. When I was eight years old and going into third grade in the fall. And Daddy and Zoe Kruller talked together in their swift Ping-Pong banter as Zoe scooped out ice cream for Ben and me and poured coffee for Daddy, rang up the order and made change and Daddy said in a lowered voice taking the change from Zoe's slender fingers with the startling crimson nails that Zoe should say hello to Del for him—someone named "Del"—and Zoe laughed and said, "Sure! When I see him." Which was an answer that possibly took Daddy by surprise, he fumbled the change, dropped a quarter that rolled across the marble-tile floor and Ben swooped to snatch it up; and Zoe said, still with that laugh in her voice like nothing could hurt her, airy and light as any little bird fluttering overhead, "And you say hi to Lucy, will you?"

Outside in the parking lot, in muggy-hot air, oppressive after the milky cool of the dairy, as we approached Daddy's car parked imprudently in the glaring sun, discovered that the tip of my ice-cream cone was caved in, broken—and then I discovered, horribly, that something was inside the tip of the cone: squirmy black weevils.

I screamed. I dropped the cone onto the ground.

Daddy heard, and came to investigate.

"What the hell, Krissie? What's wrong?"

Two scoops of ice cream—strawberry, chocolate—on the hot gravel, melting. Looking so silly, there on the ground. Something that was meant to be a treat—something special, delicious—on the ground like garbage. I told Daddy that there were weevils inside the cone, I couldn't eat it. I was gagging, close to vomiting. Daddy cursed under his breath poking at the cone with the tip of his shoe, as if he could see from his height the half-dozen black insects squirming inside the tip; his manner was skeptical, impatient; he didn't seem very sympathetic, as if the defiled cone was my fault. Or maybe, a clumsy child, I'd simply dropped it, and was trying to pass on the blame to someone else.

"Well. You're not getting another one, we're late and we're leaving."

Not another cone? When this wasn't my fault? I drew breath to protest, to cry, stricken with a child's sense of injustice, and with the loss of something I'd so craved, but Daddy was heedless, Daddy had made up his mind he wasn't going back inside the dairy, he wasn't going to complain to Zoe Kruller or to anyone about his daughter's ice-cream cone.

When I balked at leaving Daddy took my arm roughly, my thin bare arm, at the elbow, and gave me the kind of tug you don't resist. "Fuck it Krista, I said come *on.*"

Ben, smirking, licking his ice-cream cone, showed little sympathy, too. In the front seat of the car beside Daddy where, being a boy, he insisted upon sitting. In the backseat riding home—the car was an Oldsmobile, I think—some kind of special "Deluxe" model—mauve interior—the leather seat hot from the sun, searing my bare legs—I was whimpering, crying under my breath stunned with the unfairness of what had just happened, if I'd run back inside the dairy of course Zoe Kruller would have given me another ice-cream cone, if Mommy and not Daddy had brought me that day, of course Mommy would have seen to it that I'd gotten another ice-cream cone, inside Honeystone's the clerks would have been sympathetic, apologetic. But Daddy was driving away, and Daddy was flushed with anger. Daddy was cursing beneath his breath, you wouldn't want to annoy him. If he'd thought of it, Daddy would have ordered Ben to share his ice-cream cone with me but Daddy wasn't thinking about any ice-cream cone, or about his stricken daughter, his thoughts were elsewhere. I huddled in the backseat sniffing and panting thinking *Not my fault. Not my fault. Why is Daddy mad at me!* My eight-year-old heart was broken, it would not be for the first time.

A week or so later when we were taken to Honeystone's by our mother, on our way home from visiting one of Mommy's cousins outside East Sparta, Ben was eager for an ice-cream cone but I was not. Instead, I asked for a sundae, in small plastic bowl where you could see what you were eating. Though Zoe Kruller was at the counter, and remembered exactly the kind of ice-cream cone I'd always wanted, winked and called me "Krissie" in the sweetest way, and tried to get me to smile at her, I wouldn't smile, I was sulky-sullen and not the sweet little Daddy's girl and I would not lift my eyes to Zoe's shining face, I would not.

8

Two YEARS, seven months later on a snow-glaring Sunday morning in February 1983 Zoe Kruller was *found dead* in a brownstone rental on West Ferry Street, downtown Sparta.

On the front page of the Sparta *Journal* it was reported that Zoe Kruller had suffered *blunt force trauma to the head* as well as *manual strangulation* and so it was a case of *foul play, homicide.*

It was revealed that the murdered woman had been *separated from her husband, no longer living with her family.* It was revealed that the murdered woman had been *discovered in her bed, by—*

"Krista. Give that to me."

"No! I'm reading this."

"I *said—*"

She snatched the pages from me. Such agitation in her face, I surrendered the pages to prevent their being torn.

Such agitation in her face, I turned away frightened. But I'd seen—

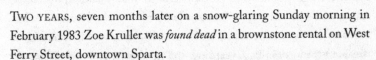

Discovered in her bed by her fourteen-year-old son Aaron
Kruller who ran into the street to summon help.

At this time, I was eleven years old. No longer a small child to be protected from what my mother called "ugly"—"nasty"—"disgusting" things. No longer a small child to tolerate such protection and so somehow I knew—I came to know—that the glamorous freckled friendly woman who'd waited on us at Honeystone's was this very woman who'd been *found strangled in her bed* by her own son; I came to know, with a thrill of horror, and of fascination, that at the time of her death Zoe Kruller had not been living with her family, as other wives and mothers lived with their families; at the time of her death Zoe Kruller had been *separated from, estranged from* her husband Delray Kruller and her son Aaron who was in my brother Ben's class at the middle school: *separated from, estranged from, broken off communication with.* Such delicious facts I came to know, that caused a sensation of numbness to pump through me, as if I were wading into a dream; a dream that resembled the Novocain injected into my tender gums, when I went to the dentist; a dream that left me short of breath, dazed and strangely aroused, headachey; a dream of the most intense yearning, and the most intense revulsion. For to these facts were added, in what was invariably an altered tone of voice, like the shifting of a radio station on the verge of dissolving into static, the fact that Zoe Kruller was *sharing quarters with another woman, at 349 West Ferry.*

Sharing quarters with a woman! Not living with her husband and son but with a woman! And the woman's name too seemed exotic: *De-Lucca.*

West Ferry Street was miles away from Huron Pike Road. West Ferry Street was not a street familiar to me. I thought it might be near the railroad yard. Off Depot Street, a block or two before the bridge. At the edge of the warehouse district, the waterfront. That part of Sparta. There were taverns there, late-night diners and restaurants. There was XXX-Rated Adult Books & Videos. There were rubble-strewn vacant lots, and there was a raw-looking windswept stretch along the river advertising itself as Sparta Renaissance Park where "high-rise condominiums" were being built.

And somehow too I knew that men came to visit Zoe Kruller in that brownstone, *male visitors.*

These *male visitors* were to be *interviewed by Sparta police.*

Why these facts so agitated my mother, I had no idea. Why my mother slammed and locked the door against me, against both Ben and me, refusing to answer our frightened queries—*Mom? Mommy? What's wrong?*—I had no idea.

It was a very cold February. There were joke-cartoons in the local paper about the Ice Age returning. Comical drawings of glaciers, mastodons and woolly mammoths with curving ice-encrusted tusks. I was in sixth grade at Harpwell Elementary and my brother Ben was in ninth grade at Sparta Middle School which was also Aaron Kruller's school. When my mother asked Ben if he knew Aaron Kruller quickly Ben said no: "He's a year behind me at school."

Adding, with a look of disdain: "He's part-Indian, Kruller. He doesn't like people like us."

"He's your age, isn't he, Ben? In the paper it says 'fourteen.'"

Irritably Ben said, "What's that got to do with it, Mom? I told you, he's a year behind me. I don't know him."

"But he isn't from the reservation, is he? He isn't a full-blooded Indian, is he? 'Delray Kruller'—he isn't an Indian."

"Jesus, Mom! What difference does it make? What are we talking about?" Ben was becoming frantic, furious. This doggedness in our mother—this persistence, in the most trivial details—had a way of upsetting Ben even more than it upset me.

Let it go, Mom. Please let it go would be my silent plea.

Still our mother persisted: "That poor boy. That's who I feel sorry for, in all this. Just a child, to discover—*her*." Even now, our mother could not bring herself to utter the name *Zoe Kruller*, only just *her* in a tone of disgust.

Ben turned away with a shrug. He hadn't looked at me at all.

Of course, Ben knew Aaron Kruller. He'd known Aaron Kruller since grade school.

But it was like Ben, not to talk about things that upset him. The fact that Zoe Kruller had died, that someone we'd known had died, seemed to embarrass him. My brother was of an age when, if you couldn't shrug and make a wisecrack about something, you turned away with a pained smirk.

To me he said, out of the corner of his mouth, "Kruller's mom—that 'Zoe'—know what she was? A slut."

Slut? I felt the word sharp and cracking like a slap across my silly-girl face.

"A *slut* is a female that *fucks.* Aaron Kruller's mom was a *slut,* and a *junkie,* too. That was why she left the dairy. That was why she left off singing. And Aaron didn't go running out to 'summon help'—they found him with her, where she was dead, and"— Ben's voice lowered even further, creased and cracked with hilarity—"he'd shit his pants. *That* news you won't find in the paper."

In the paper—in the succession of newspapers that would come into my hands—some of them hidden from us by our mother, in a drawer of her cedar bureau, others shared with me by my girlfriends at school—I would see Zoe Kruller's smiling face gazing up at me, on the verge of winking at me *Krissie! What can I do you for today?*

That riddle to which there was no answer.

As she'd turn to Daddy lifting her fevered glamour-face like a flower taunting you to pick it *Mis-ter Diehl! And what can I do you for—today?*

The most commonly printed photograph of Zoe Kruller—which in time would find its way into state-wide newspapers though never into national publications nor syndicated by the Associated Press, so far as I knew—was the one in which Zoe posed with fellow musicians from Black River Breakdown, in her spangled low-cut girl-singer attire, and with her hair crimped and springy and electric-looking cascading over one semi-bare shoulder. Another more casual photo showed a younger Zoe smiling at the camera at a sly angle as if she'd been teasing the photographer, with the exuberant ease of a high school cheerleader or prom queen. How many times these and other likenesses of *Zoe Kruller, Sparta murder victim* would be reprinted, how many times I would stare at them in wonderment that I had ever known her—that of course I knew her, still—never in my life would Krista Diehl not-know Zoe Kruller from Honeystone's—and each time it seemed to me a wrongful thing, a night-mare-thing, a cruel taunting joke that in these photographs Zoe had been smiling with such trust, never imagining that, one day, her picture would be printed—reprinted—in newspapers—shown on local TV news—with the identification *Zoe Kruller, Sparta Murder Victim*.

Though I was young for eleven, young in the ways of the (adult, even the adolescent) world yet the admonition came to me *She should not have been smiling like that.*

The early headlines were enormous banner heads running the width of the Sparta *Journal*.

SPARTA WOMAN, 34, FOUND BEATEN, STRANGLED
Death of Local Bluegrass Singer Investigated by Police
Focus on "Men Friends"—"Visitors"

Later, headlines would diminish, and their tone would subtly alter in tone:

BLUEGRASS SINGER'S PRIVATE LIFE YIELDS "SURPRISES"
Sparta Detectives Continue Investigation Following "Leads"

In our household, no one spoke of Zoe Kruller. It was a time—I guess it wasn't the first time—when Daddy was often working late, or had to stay away overnight "on business"—and Mommy was edgy and impatient with Ben and me if we asked about him—"He's *away*. He's *working*. How do I know where he is, ask him yourself!"

Which was so illogical, even Ben couldn't think how to reply.

The phone, which had not often rung, rang often now. And Mom, who hadn't often used the phone, was using it often now. At a distance from us, upstairs in the big bedroom into which we were not welcome except by invitation—when I helped my mother houseclean and vacuum, for instance—or in the kitchen with the door so oddly, unnaturally closed—the maple wood cedar door which Daddy had installed in the kitchen was *never closed*.

Except now, sometimes it was. When Ben and I returned from school on the school bus and tramped into the mudroom at the rear with our snow-wetted boots, there was the kitchen door closed over, and we could hear our mother speaking on the phone in her low urgent accusing panicky voice that was a warning to us, not to approach her *But what—? What will—happen? What does this mean? Will there be an—arrest? How can there be an arrest, if— A lawyer? Why would he need a lawyer? Oh God a lawyer—we can't afford a—*

Ben was stony-faced, kicking off his boots and stomping away upstairs loud enough so that Mom might hear. Ben ignored my entreaties as he ignored my stricken look, my wounded thumb shoved to my mouth so that I could gnaw at the nail and cause the cuticle to bleed a little more.

What does he say, you know what he says! Well he won't talk to me—maybe he'll talk to you— But no lawyer, that's— No that's crazy—

This excited voice of my mother's—this tone of reproach, bewilderment, humiliation, anger—suggested that she was speaking with her older brother, or with one of her sisters. I didn't want to hear!—quickly I pressed my hands over my ears and stomped upstairs after my brother.

Well, say! Thought it was you.

What can I do you for, Krissie?

Tried to make myself cry staring at my reflection in the bathroom mirror and speaking in Zoe Kruller's throaty-scratchy voice but I didn't cry, not one tear.

9

DADDY, we could not ask.

Not Krista, not Ben. Not our mother.

Not about Mrs. Kruller-whose-picture-was-in-the-paper. Not about the *homicide*.

There were no words for me to speak of such a thing to my father. As at any age I could not have spoken frankly to him about the physical life, or about sex; I would never have dared ask my father how much money he made, how much our house had cost, if he was insured and how much was he insured for. I could not have asked him about God: *Is there a God, and what has God to do with us?* These were taboo subjects, though the word *taboo* did not exist in our vocabulary and if it ever came to be known in Sparta, by way of advertisements and popular culture, it would be the perfume Taboo.

In any case children did not ask about death. Children could watch death on TV, gunfire, explosions, planes shot wantonly from the sky to fall in a filigree of flame, but children could not ask about death. Only very young children who would quickly learn their mistake.

When Grandpa Diehl had died, and I was four years old and too little for school. When Daddy wasn't at work he'd kept to himself in the basement of our house in his workshop where we would hear his power tools wailing through the floorboards and in the days, weeks following Grandpa's funeral Daddy did not speak to us about Grandpa Diehl except evasively to say that Grandpa had "gone away." By the look in Daddy's face, my brother and I had known not to ask where Grandpa Diehl had gone.

Mom had warned us: don't ask Daddy about Grandpa, Daddy is *upset*. On the phone Mom said *Eddy's taking it pretty hard. You know how he is, it's all inside.*

The words struck me: *It's all inside.*

Taking it pretty hard. All inside.

At school, people were talking about Zoe Kruller, who was Aaron Kruller's mother, or had been Aaron Kruller's mother. Now Mrs. Kruller too had *gone away*.

How strange it seemed to us, who'd known Zoe Kruller from both Honeystone's Dairy and from the Chautauqua Park music-nights, that a woman so friendly, so pretty and glamorous would be *strangled in her bed, murdered*. How wrong it seemed to us that you could be the girl-singer for Black River Breakdown and applauded and whistled at and made to sing encores, yet someone could still hate you enough to *beat, strangle* you in your bed.

Some worse things were done to Aaron's mother than just killing her, know why?—'cause she was a slut.

We were made to come home immediately from school. Our mothers would not allow us to stay for after-school activities nor did school authorities encourage such activities, in the months following Zoe Kruller's death. Patrol cars swung by the schools, cruising through the parking lots like friendly sharks. Bus drivers counted heads before shutting the bus doors and leaving the school property, determining that we were all *present and accounted for*. The older boys objected, they weren't *damn girls*.

Ben said: "Some things I heard, about Aaron's mother, it was just her he was after, the 'strangler.' He wouldn't be after any of *us*."

I asked Ben who'd told him this. I asked Ben what else he'd heard at his school and Ben shrugged evasively and said just some things—"Not for you to know."

In Sparta—unlike the rest of the world where people were dying and being killed in terrible ways all the time—it seemed rare that anyone died and yet more rare that anyone died in a way to cause such upset, dread, wonder. Of course the "natural" deaths were sad and people cried, especially women. Women were adept at crying, as men were humbled and stymied by crying. Women were cleansed by crying, as men were smudged and stained by crying. But the person who'd died was usually elderly, or had died *after a long illness*, or both; or had died in a car crash on the highway, or a *boating accident* on the river or one of the numerous lakes surrounding Sparta. These were sad deaths but not frightening deaths. Because you knew, if you were a child, that nothing like those deaths would ever happen to you.

Except now, people were frightened. Adults were frightened. There is such a profound difference between *dying* and *being killed*.

At Honeystone's Dairy it wasn't so much fun any longer. Without Zoe Kruller leaning on her elbows on the counter, smiling.

The ice cream was still delicious, greedily we devoured it.

The smell of the fresh-brewed coffee was pungent, disagreeable. To my sensitive nostrils, disagreeable. Since my ice-cream cone infested with nasty weevils Daddy hadn't taken Ben and me back to the dairy all summer, I had to wonder if there was some connection.

At Honeystone's I hadn't much wanted to overhear my mother speaking with old grumpy-grandma Mrs. Honeystone. The two shaking their heads in disapproval, bonded in that moment by a swell of indignation like dirty water swishing about their ankles. *And leaving her family, too! How could she.*

The mysteries you live with, as a child. Never solved, never resolved. Utterly trivial, petty. Like a tiny pebble in your shoe, that causes you to walk crookedly.

ZOE KRULLER. Zoe Kruller. Zoe Kruller.

Now in late February and early March of 1983 the white clapboard house on the Huron Pike Road quivered with this name, unspoken. In the household upstairs and down and in my father's workshop in the basement in which he spent much of the truncated time he now spent at home there was the taut tense silence that follows a lightning-flash when you wait for the thunder to roar in.

Across Lake Ontario, great armadas of winter-storm clouds. Blown eastward and south out of Canada, the air too bitter-cold for snow. The silence-before-the-storm where you wait not knowing what you are waiting for.

In their bedroom at the end of the upstairs hall—the door shut tight, only a meager band of light beneath—our parents spoke together in their low urgent alarmed voices. For hours.

We sank into sleep, Ben and me, to the sound of those voices. We were wakened from sleep, to the sound of those voices. I think this was how it was. I am trying not to mis-remember, and most of all I am trying not to invent.

Zoe Kruller. How could you! How many times! Oh why.

Those hours, middle-of-the-night. Those vibrations in the air as when the old furnace clicked on, heaving itself into life like an enlarged and failing heart.

Or maybe: my parents' bedroom door opening, and my father's footsteps in the hall, on the stairs to the first floor. So I was wakened dry-mouthed and frightened.

"Daddy? Where are you going?"

Calling down the stairs to him, and he'd tell me to get back to bed, back to sleep. And if I followed him to the stairs, and halfway down the stairs he'd speak more sharply to me: "Go back to sleep, Krista. This is not for you."

EARLIER THAT WINTER, WHAT we hadn't wanted to remember. What would be blurred and smudged in our memories—Ben's, and mine—like a blackboard across which a fist has been dragged, carelessly.

Later we would realize that these were the days *before*.

Days, nights *before* Zoe Kruller's death.

After Thanksgiving, through the long siege of Christmas and through snow-dazzled January those days we had no idea were *before*.

Those days when Daddy seemed to be away much of the time. He'd been hours late for Thanksgiving dinner—"dinner" was at 4:00 P.M.—at my aunt Sharon's house and he had not shown up at all for a birthday dinner at another relative's house. Weekdays he'd call home to say he'd be late for supper or maybe he wouldn't be having supper with us at all. And those nights when he didn't call home. And when he didn't come home.

And Ben and I persisted *Where's Daddy?* though seeing in our mother's hurt and furious eyes *Don't ask! Shut up and go away* but of course we asked, we could not stop ourselves from asking. No one so pitiless as children sensing something wrong, smelling blood and eager for someone to blame.

Where Daddy was: *at work*. Or, *meeting with a customer*. Or, *at the construction site*.

I worried that Daddy wouldn't have any supper, Daddy would be hungry. Where would Daddy eat?

Ben said not to worry, there's plenty of taverns between here and wherever Daddy might be. And Daddy knew them all.

Our mother said: "Your father is taking on more work. 'Managerial' work. Paul Cassano"—(our father's employer at Sparta Construction)—"is semi-retired, you know he'd had a minor heart attack last winter. So your father has more responsibilities."

Still I set Daddy's place at the table. Dark green "woven" plastic place mats, paper napkins neatly folded and fork, knife, spoon positioned properly.

And I helped Mom prepare dinner. When I'd been a little girl, this was such a special time! Being entrusted with stirring macaroni as it boiled in a pot on the stove, cleaning carrots and potatoes at the sink, regulating the Mixmaster at its various magical speeds—not too fast, so that mashed potatoes or frosting splattered out of the bowl; setting the oven, usually at 375° F, for casseroles and cakes. What I liked was, at such times, nudging against my mother's warm fleshy thighs, as if accidentally in our small kitchen. My mother had a crisp biscuity smell unlike the harsher perfume-smell of some of the mothers of my classmates, who lived in Sparta and in whose homes I sometimes stayed overnight, as my mother dressed more casually than these mothers did—in Kmart stretch slacks, pullover shirts and sweaters, wool socks (in cold weather), sneakers. For *just at home* my mother never wore makeup but before Daddy returned from work, late afternoons on weekdays, she took care to put on lipstick—the same shade of Revlon pink-frosted-plum she'd been wearing since high school—and to fluff out her flattened hair, pinch at her sallow cheeks.

It was a time when my mother boasted of my father, to anyone who came into our house: "These maple wood cupboards, this counter and floor—all this Eddy did by himself. Isn't it beautiful?"

And: "Eddy put in the deck by himself. That built-in grill—Eddy did that. Saved us thousands of dollars he says. Isn't it beautiful?"

No longer did my mother speak of my father in this way, when *the trouble* began. Rarely did my mother speak of my father at all except in blunt flat statements of fact *Your father won't be back tonight, don't set a place for him.*

During the lengthy, confused and unsettling Christmas season—how endless it seemed, being "recessed" from the safe, secure routines of school—the serious arguments began. These were eruptions of words not strictly confined to my parents' bedroom and therefore particularly alarming to Ben and me as the sight of, for instance, our parents' unclothed bodies would have been to us. Or, these were voices rising through furnace vents and into my room, from the kitchen; sometimes, late at night, from the living room where, a single lamp burning, TV turned low, my mother would be awaiting my father on the sofa, alone, like a sick woman curled up beneath an afghan.

Those nights when Mom insisted upon my going to bed by 9:30 P.M. and Ben by 10:30 P.M. but did not come upstairs to bed herself. Instead she was waiting for headlights to turn into our lane, from the river road. She was smoking—though Lucille Diehl *did not smoke*—and she might have been drinking—though Lucille Diehl certainly *did not drink*. She seemed to be watching television but no channel engaged her interest for long not even the Classic Movie Channel, and the sound was *muted*. Several times Ben came downstairs barefoot in his T-shirt and boxer shorts—Ben emulated Daddy, in nightwear—to say how "weird" she was getting, for God's sake why didn't she go to bed!

Mom ignored Ben. Smoking in the darkened living room with just the TV screen glimmering and glowing like something phosphorescent at the bottom of the sea, a simulacrum of life that was not life. The acrid smell of her cigarette smoke wafted upstairs to my bedroom, I dreamt that the house was on fire, my legs were tangled in bedclothes and I could not escape.

Sometimes sensing my mother's mounting desperation—unless it was my own—I would sit at the top of the stairs. In pajamas, barefoot and shivering. It was midnight: so late. And then it was 1 A.M., 2:35 A.M., alarmingly late. I was waiting with Mommy, in secret.

To see Mommy in the living room, on the sofa with her back to me, I had to slide down two or three stair steps. I had to be very quiet, hugging my knees. For if Mommy knew that I was there she would have been very angry. *Can't I have any privacy in this God-damned house for God's sake! Go away and leave me alone you God-damned kids, having babies was the end of me, lost my figure, lost my looks, God damn you go away, just leave me alone.*

This was not our daytime mother, I understood. This was Mommy-at-night in the darkened living room and with the TV set turned to *mute*. And sometimes I would fall asleep on the stairs, and one of them—it might be Mommy, it might be Daddy—would discover me, and not be angry with me, but half-carry me back to my bed and tuck me into my bed and so it was part of my dream, and a happy part of my dream, or maybe it had not happened, at all.

Krissie you naughty girl! Shut your eyes tight and sleep.

10

"YOUR FATHER WILL be staying with your uncle Earl for a while. No—don't ask me about it, he will tell you himself."

No longer *Daddy* but *your father*. This subtle change. This abrupt change. Our mother speaking to us of *your father* as she might have been speaking of *your teacher*, *your bus driver*.

This was three days after the news of Zoe Kruller was first released. Three days after the banner headlines in the Sparta *Journal* which my mother had snatched from my fingers.

Three days, during which time Daddy had not been home very much, or had been home and gone away again, and had returned late at night when Ben and I were in bed and supposedly asleep.

"Tell us—what?"

We'd just returned from school. Ben let his backpack fall onto the floor. Since the news of Zoe Kruller had entered our lives Ben had been behaving strangely, loud-laughing, crude as the older boys on the school bus who tormented younger children.

Ben's face flushed with anger. "Bullshit."

Ben pushed past our mother, ran upstairs thudding his heels on the stairs and slammed the door to his room. Looking as if she'd been struck in the face our mother stared after him but didn't call his name—didn't scold him—so I knew that something was very wrong.

"Mom? What is . . ."

"I *said*. He will tell you, Krista. Your father. Soon."

I was stunned. I could not comprehend why Ben was so angry, and what it meant that *your father* was staying with a relative. I seemed to know that this must have something to do with Zoe Kruller but could not imagine what.

The phone began ringing. We were in the kitchen and something, too, was wrong with the kitchen: there were dishes in the sink, soaking. There was a discolored sponge on the counter that looked as if it had been used to mop up coffee. There was an ashtray filled with butts, and the air stank of cigarette smoke and butts. And this was a *wrong smell*, for this house. And my mother's face looked shiny and swollen and her mouth was greasy with fresh smears of Revlon lipstick as if she'd been expecting company or possibly company had come and departed and that was why there were dishes in the sink and cigarette butts smoldering in the ashtray and an air of frantic unease that felt like a churning in the guts. I was young enough then to react as a child would react—trying to push into my mother's arms. But my mother was distracted, upset; she had no time for a needy daughter; the ringing phone seemed to stymie her as if she couldn't recognize its sound. When I moved to pick up the receiver my mother gave a little slap at me: "No, Krista. Not for you. I'll take it, *you go away*."

SO ABRUPTLY MY FATHER was staying with my uncle Earl Diehl who lived in East Sparta. But Daddy's things remained at home, most of Daddy's clothes and Daddy's tools in his basement workshop and Daddy's 1975 Willys Jeep he'd been thinking about selling, in the garage.

Each time the phone rang naturally the thought was *This is Daddy!*

But Daddy didn't call until the next evening when we were just sitting down—late—to a meal already delayed and interrupted by phone calls. In a guarded voice my mother answered and waved for Ben and me to leave the kitchen, which we did, hovering nervously in the living room, and after a few minutes my mother called Ben back—"Your father wants to speak with you, Ben! Hurry up"—and Ben took the receiver from her hand shyly and reluctantly; his face flushed red, all he could murmur was

O.K., Dad, yeah I guess so in a voice close to tears. Then it was my turn, I was dry-mouthed and anxious and like Ben stricken with shyness for how strange it was, how wrong-seeming, to be speaking with Daddy on the phone! I don't think that either Ben or I had ever spoken on the phone before with our father; I was unprepared for my father's voice so close in my ear—"Is that Puss? That's my li'l Puss? Is it? My sweet Puss—is it?" I was unable to say anything more than *Yes Daddy! Yes Daddy* for something seemed to be wrong, there was something wrong with Daddy I could not have identified *He's drunk. Couldn't get up the courage to call his family except drunk.* Unexpectedly I began to cry, I was confused and frightened and out of nowhere began to cry, and Daddy said sharply, "Damn, don't *cry.* Krista, don't you *cry.* No fucking *crying*, what the fuck's your mother been telling you, put your mother on the phone, Krista—"

What happened after that, I don't remember. My mother must have taken the receiver from me, the rest of the evening is a blank.

Hadn't heard my father's voice very clearly over the phone and so it came to be a time when I couldn't hear anyone's voice very clearly. At school I had difficulty hearing Mrs. Bender. A roaring in my ears like distant thunder. Or in the distance, the roar of one of Daddy's cars on the Huron Pike Road coming home. On the blackboard—in fact, at our school it was a green board—where chalk-words and numerals melted into one another. My eyes swam in tears. My nose ran. Hunched over my desk desperately wiping my nose with my fingers, shiny wet mucus on my fingers I had to let dry in the air, I'd used up the wad of Kleenex my mother had given me. "Krista? Are you crying? You can tell me, dear."

Mrs. Bender stooped to peer at me. Mrs. Bender provided me with fresh tissues. Mrs. Bender asked if I would like to step outside into the hall to speak with her—if I had something to say, I might want to say in private—but I shook my head *no.* My mother had cautioned me *Don't say anything about Daddy. Never say anything about our lives at home. Never anything to be repeated Krista do you understand?*

Faint and reproachful in my ears were my father's admonitory words *Don't cry! Krista, don't you cry! No fucking crying.*

I was shivering so hard, my teeth were chattering. Like a stark-wet-eyed little doll set to shaking. Somehow it had happened that a daughter of Lucille Diehl—Lucille, who took such pride in her household and in her children!—had been allowed to leave the house on a freezing February morning in just a cotton pullover and slacks beneath a winter jacket, my fine limp pale-blond hair badly snarled at the nape of my neck and my skin hot.

Tenderly Mrs. Bender pressed the back of her cool hand against my forehead.

"Oh, dear! You're running a fever."

Shivering turned to giggling. *Running a fever*—how could this be?

In the school infirmary the nurse took my temperature with a thermometer thrust beneath my tongue, making me gag. She examined the scummy interior of my mouth and my throat that throbbed with soreness. She and Mrs. Bender conferred in whispers *This girl, you know who she is—Diehl?*

It took much of an hour for the nurse to contact my mother on the phone to tell her please come immediately, take your child home she has a temperature of 102° F and seems to be coming down with the flu.

Coming down with the flu! This expression was used so frequently in Sparta in the winter, it had acquired something of the lilt and innocence of a popular song. *Coming down with the flu* explained this sick sad collapsing sensation so it wasn't scary any longer but a hopeful sign, you were just like everyone else.

"BULLSHIT."

This was what Ben said. Sometimes in disgust, sometimes laughingly. Sometimes in a mutter not meant to be overheard and sometimes rudely loud so that my mother and I had no choice but to hear.

When Mom wouldn't let us see the newspaper, watch the six o'clock local news or any TV unless she was in the room with us clutching the remote control.

When Mom took telephone calls upstairs in the bedroom with the door shut against us. When Mom no longer summoned us to the phone, to speak with Daddy. In desperation I appealed to Ben to say why, why was this happening, and Ben had no answer except a shrug—"Bull*shit*. That's all it is."

I asked Ben what this had to do with Mrs. Kruller being killed and Ben only just repeated in maddening idiocy—"Bull*shit*. I told you."

"What do you mean—'bullshit'?"

"I told you, stupid. 'Bull*shit*.'"

I followed Ben around. I pulled at Ben's arm. Ben slapped at me, shoved me. I was white-faced in desperation, indignation. I repeated my question and finally Ben relented as if taking pity on me.

"What they're saying in the news. That Dad is a 'suspect.'"

"'Suspect'—what's that?"

"The police are 'questioning' Dad about Mrs. Kruller. He's 'in custody'— Eddy Diehl is a 'suspect.'"

"But—why?"

Of course I knew what a *suspect* was. I knew what it meant when a *suspect* was *in police custody*. Yet I could not seem to comprehend what this had to do with our father, or with us. I was feeling anxious, vaguely nauseated. I could not comprehend why my brother suddenly hated me.

"Why? Because they're assholes, that's why. These men she was seeing, one of them did it, 'strangled' her—'murdered' her—and they're trying to say that Daddy was one of these men, but everybody knows Aaron's father is the killer, it's God-damned fucking bullshit, taking Dad *into custody*."

Ben's face contorted as if he were about to cry and I was frightened that Ben would cry for if Ben cried and I was a witness, Ben would be furious with me, Ben would never forgive me and would hate me even worse than he hated me now. So I said, in a silly-girl voice, like a girl on a TV comedy whose mere presence evokes expectant titters of laughter in the invisible audience: "Oh, say—know what?—Mrs. Kruller was here, once."

Ben stared at me. Ben's eyes glittered dangerously with tears.

"Here? Where?"

"Here. In this house."

"Bullshit she was! When?"

I tried to think. It must have been last year, last spring. At the start of warm weather. But we were still in school—it would have been May, early June. The memory returned to me like a TV scene that, at first, seems unfamiliar but gradually then reveals itself as familiar, comforting. The school bus from Harpwell Elementary had brought me home unexpectedly early—12:30 P.M. It was a half-day Wednesday for a teachers' meeting had been called for that afternoon. Mom was away, Mom had not known about the meeting and the half-day Wednesday. Mom was away in Chautauqua Falls visiting a relative hospitalized for surgery.

The back door was unlocked, Mom had told me—Mom had told Ben and me—just to come inside if she wasn't home by the time we got home, she was sure to be home by 5:00 P.M., she promised.

It was not unusual, to leave a house unlocked. On the Huron Pike Road in the countryside west of Sparta it was not unusual to leave a house unlocked all day, all night.

Nor was it unusual that a mother—a "devoted" mother, like Lucille Diehl—might leave her children unattended for an hour or two, in such circumstances.

And so I walked into the kitchen humming to myself, and there was Mom at the sink—no: not Mom—there was Zoe Kruller at the sink!—pretty Zoe Kruller from Honeystone's Dairy except Zoe wasn't wearing her white cord smock and trousers but silky purple slacks and a snug-fitting lavender sweater, no hairnet on her springy hair, Zoe was whistling as she rinsed coffee mugs at the sink and turning Zoe blinked at me with startled widened eyes and after the merest heartbeat of a pause Zoe said in a low throaty smooth voice like honey, "Why it's—Krissie! Well, say—Krissie! Thought that was you! What brings you home at this time of day, Krissie?"

Zoe's voice was pitched to be heard. Not just by little Krissie but by someone else, in an adjacent room perhaps. At the time I did not quite grasp this fact. At the time I was surprised—I was very surprised—but it was a pleasant surprise, wasn't it?—to see Zoe Kruller in our kitchen, at our sink? Zoe was smiling so hard at me, her cheeks were all dimpled. Her smile was wide and lustrous baring her pink gums. Against her milky skin freckles and tiny moles quivered. In the other room I heard a man's voice—a muffled voice—but of course it was Daddy's voice—I knew it was Daddy of course, I'd seen Daddy's Jeep in the driveway. I told Zoe that it was a half-day at school, I told Zoe about the teachers' meeting, and how my mother had driven to Chautauqua Falls to visit a relative in the hospital, and how my mother would be home in a few hours. At the mention of my mother Zoe seemed to brighten even more, Zoe said, "That's who I dropped by to see, Krissie—your mom. Just wanted to say hello to Lucy but Lucy isn't home—I guess? Where'd you say she went, Chautauqua Falls?"

There came Daddy into the kitchen combing his hair—it was strange to see Daddy combing his hair, in the kitchen—Daddy's bristly red-brown hair that looked newly wetted as if he'd just had a shower; Daddy was combing his hair back from his forehead in a single sweeping movement; Daddy was wearing one of his fresh-ironed short-sleeved white cotton shirts, and in the breast pocket was a plastic ballpoint pen, the kind given out at SPARTA CONSTRUCTION; and Daddy's face looked ruddy and handsome and Daddy stared at me for a long moment as if he didn't know who I was, then said, "Krissie. You're home."

Quickly Zoe intervened explaining that I had just a "half-day" at school since there was a teachers' meeting. Zoe explained that she'd told me she had dropped by to see Lucy—Lucille—"But now I guess I'll be going, since Lucille isn't here right now."

By this time Zoe had dried both coffee mugs and put them away in the maple wood cabinet in exactly the places where Mom kept them.

"You don't have to tell your mother that I was here to visit her," Zoe said. Zoe stooped to smile at me even harder, and to brush her lips against my forehead. Zoe smelled perfumy and musky and nothing at all like Honeystone's Dairy. In the hollow of her neck there was a faint glisten of moisture, I'd have liked to touch with my tongue. Around her neck Zoe was wearing a small golden bird—a dove?—on a thin golden chain. "It can be a surprise, Krissie. I'll come back tomorrow and surprise your mom so don't spoil the surprise, Krissie, all right? We'll keep it a secret between you and me, that I was here today."

Yes, I said. I liked it that there might be a secret between Zoe Kruller and me; and that Daddy was part of it, too.

"Well, Puss!—your dad has to leave, too." Awkwardly Daddy leaned over me and kissed me on the forehead, a wet embarrassed swipe of a kiss at my hairline. "See, I'm going out to a construction site—I just dropped back here to change my shirt. Well—O.K.! See you later, Krissie."

If it seemed strange that Zoe Kruller and my father scarcely acknowledged each other—scarcely glanced at each other—somehow it didn't register on me, at the time. Strange too that Zoe left the kitchen carrying her shoulder bag slung over her shoulder by a strap, with an airy growl "G'bye, you two"— and almost immediately afterward Daddy left the kitchen by the same door; within seconds there came the sound of the Willys Jeep pulling out of the driveway, and surely Zoe Kruller had to be riding with Daddy, in the passenger's seat—but already by that time I was distracted peering into the refrigerator for a snack, leftover tapioca pudding from the previous evening's dessert neatly covered in Saran Wrap.

Never did it occur to me to think at that time *Mrs. Kruller was here with Daddy! Mrs. Kruller came to visit Daddy.*

Still less would I have thought *Daddy brought Mrs. Kruller here, to be alone with her. While Mommy was away.*

"Mrs. Kruller was here," I told Ben. "Last year. When the teachers had their meeting, and we were let out of school at noon."

"We weren't! That never happened."

"*You* weren't. It wasn't your school."

"Bullshit Mrs. Kruller was here. She wasn't any friend of Mom's."

"She dropped by to see Mom, she said. She called Mom 'Lucy.' But Mom wasn't home so she went away again."

Ben said doubtfully, "Why'd she come here? Mom and Mrs. Kruller were not friends."

There was something sad and flat in the way Ben spoke the words *Mom and Mrs. Kruller were not friends.*

"Daddy was here, too. At the same time."

"He was not! You're making this up."

"No. I'm not."

"Zoe Kruller wouldn't have come here, Krista. That is such bullshit."

"Will you stop saying that! She was, too. And Daddy was here, too."

"Krista, he was *not.*"

"They went away in Daddy's Jeep. I had a half-day at school and came home early and they were here."

"Bullshit."

"They *did.*"

Ben struck me in the shoulder, hard. "That never happened, you're a God-damned liar. You tell anyone about that, I'll break your scrawny neck."

Ben pushed past me and out of the room. I felt a flame of pure hatred ripple over me for my brother who was so crude, and so cruel. *Scrawny neck!*—I would never forget these words.

Later, I would come to wonder; maybe Ben was right, and I was wrong. That might be better to think, than the other.

Had Zoe Kruller really been in our kitchen, rinsing coffee mugs at the sink? Had Zoe Kruller really been here, whistling? And Daddy had come into the kitchen combing his hair back from his face, his left arm bent and part-cradling his head, his right hand gripping the black plastic comb he carried in his rear pants pocket, and Daddy had been limping just slightly, you would have to know that Daddy had a *bad knee* to register this limp. Maybe I was remembering all of this wrongly?—the way I hadn't been hearing Mrs. Bender at school, or hadn't been able to see the smaller chalk markings on the blackboard at school.

Here was another possibility: Zoe Kruller had come to our house and Mommy *had been waiting for her.* Maybe it hadn't been the half-day at my school but another day. Mommy had invited Zoe Kruller to the house because Lucille Diehl and Zoe Kruller were friends, and it wasn't Daddy who was Zoe Kruller's friend after all.

Which would mean: Daddy had not been here. Daddy had not driven Mrs. Kruller away in the black Willys Jeep.

Daddy hadn't been here at all. Not at that time.

11

BUT I CAN LOVE YOU BEST, Daddy! I can forgive you.

That would be my secret, not even Daddy would know.

In the County Line Tavern, in our booth in a farther corner of the barroom Daddy tossed change onto the sticky tabletop—quarters, dimes, wild rolling pennies.

"Here's change for the phone, Krista. Call your mother and let her know where you are. Let her know that you are *safe*"—Daddy twisted his mouth into a sneer of a smile—"and you're having dinner with me and why doesn't she come join us?—we'd like that."

Would we like that? I wasn't so sure.

Daddy winked at me as obediently I slid out of the booth. I laughed uncertain what Daddy's wink meant.

As if my mother would want to meet *us*—in all places, the noisy County Line Tavern which was a country place on the highway five miles north of Sparta and about that far from my home, in another direction. Here the air was dense with men's uplifted voices, laughter. Loud rock music, country-and-western, blaring from a jukebox. That smell that is so poignant to me—that smell that indicates *my father, my father's world*—of beer, tobacco smoke, a just barely perceptible odor of male sweat, maybe male anxiety, anguish. There were a few women in the County Line—young women—some very young-looking girls who had to be at least twenty-one to be served alcohol, seated together in a festive knot at the bar—but predominantly the place was men: local working men, farmers, truckers who left the motors of their enormous rigs running in the parking lot—why, I never knew—wouldn't they be burning up gasoline, needlessly?—causing the fresh chill air outside to burn blue with exhaust.

At this hour of early-evening, nearing 6:00 P.M., past dusk and dark as night, the County Line was very popular. Men in no hurry to get to their homes, or men like Eddy Diehl somehow lacking a home, invisibly disfigured and yet determined to be festive, hearty. In my Sparta High jacket which was made of a synthetic fabric that resembled silk, eye-catching deep-purple glancingly-glamorous silk, in my much-laundered jeans and with my luminous-blond ponytail flaring at the back of my head and halfway down my back, I caught the eye of men the way an upright flame drifting through murky shadow would catch the eye. In a gesture of vague paternal protectiveness my father had led me to a booth in the "family" section of the tavern when we'd first entered—he'd seated me with my back to the bar—but seemed heedless now, that to call my mother on the pay phone I would have to make my way through the bustle of the barroom, by myself.

In my flurry of excitement—the daughter-enchantment of being with the forbidden Daddy—it would not have occurred to me to think *Why would Daddy bring me to such a place!* Nor was I willing to think *Is it to show me off—Eddy Diehl's daughter, who still adores him?—has faith in him?*

In the cramped corridor outside the restrooms a thick-bodied man with bristling hair stood at the pay phone cursing into the receiver— "Expect me to b'lieve that, fuck *you.*" It was a furious and yet intimate exchange, I had to wonder at the person—a woman, surely—at the other end: wife? Ex-wife? Girlfriend? Already at fifteen I seemed to know that there would not be, in my life, anything like this sort of blunt matter-of-fact intimacy; anything like such vulnerability.

The heavyset man fumbled to hang up the receiver, turned and blundered into me, muttered *Hey sor-ry!* His breath stank like diesel fuel. In exaggerated surprise his bloodshot eyes blinked at me. "Debbie, is it? Debbie Hansen? You lookin for company, Deb-bie?"

I told him *no.* I wasn't Debbie and I wasn't looking for company.

"No? Not Debbie? Shit—you're too young, what're you—a kid? High school? You callin' a boyfriend, honey? You don't need to call no boyfriend if—like—you need a ride home? You need a ride home? My name's Brent, I'm like your daddy's age—you need any help, honey."

Again I told him *no*. Told him I only just wanted to make a telephone call.

"You need some—change for the phone? I got a pocketful—see—"

He was teetering over me. I told him please leave me alone.

"—lots of change, see—help y'self—"

On his sweaty palm coins glinted. I had a sudden impulse to slap his hand, send the coins flying. With a nervous little laugh I ducked beneath the bristly-haired man's elbow as I ducked beneath the older girls' upraised elbows on the basketball court, and before he knew it I'd escaped him into the women's restroom. Laughing to show that I wasn't frightened, I knew he meant me no harm. "Now go away! I don't need anything from you."

There came a bark of laughter and the rap of knuckles on the door.

It wasn't a restroom door you could lock. I would have to run to hide inside one of the toilet stalls, to lock a door.

If I did, he'd have me trapped.

Still it was just a joke, playful-drunk joking that would not escalate into anything serious as through the ill-fitting door the bristling man with the bloodshot eyes called me *honey, baby-girl* and went on to speak of something more complicated, something I could not follow and so I cupped my hands to my mouth to say: "I'm not alone here! My father is here! My father is in the barroom! My father is Eddy Diehl, he's in the barroom, you'd better leave me alone or—"

Desperately I counted to ten, counted to twenty, now thinking *Why here, will something happen here, will my father hurt someone here* recalling how when we'd first entered the barroom from the parking lot my father had led me inside with his arm around my shoulders, fluffing my ponytail with his fingers, proudly he was showing me off, God-damned proud of his pretty blond daughter who was nothing like the wife who'd cast him aside, nothing like Lucille Bauer who had come to know Eddy Diehl too well. Entering the smoky barroom where much of the light was a lurid-neon rippling cast from beer and liquor advertisements and from the squat color TV above the bar, entering this clamorous place immediately we'd attracted attention, we'd attracted glances, and more than glances. The bartender, doughy-faced guy with Elvis sideburns, swiping at the sticky bar top with a rag, calling out, "Jesus! Is that—Ed Diehl?" It wasn't clear immediately if the greeting was a friendly one—a warily friendly one, perhaps—but the men shook hands, they were of a height, and of a certain stature, and in their early forties; near enough in kind to be brothers.

At the bar, as Daddy and the bartender spoke together, other men paused in their conversations to observe, and to listen: and these too were wary, friendly-wary, as if recognizing my father but uncertain how to address him.

Daddy said happily, excitedly: "This is my daughter Krista, my little girl Krista, she's older than she looks, she plays basketball at the high school, say *H'lo* to my buddies, Krista."

Buddies! This was pathetic, I thought.

This was not like Daddy, I thought.

Still like a three-year-old on display I smiled and said *H'lo*. My face beat with a pleasurable sort of pain and I saw that Daddy was pleased with me, I had not let him down.

Now it seemed that Brent had departed. Cautiously I pushed open the restroom door—he'd gone. Quickly I went then to the pay phone and faced the wall making myself as unobtrusive as possible. Men were trailing in and out of the men's room a few feet away, and I did not want them to take note of me. Dropped in one of Daddy's quarters and prayed for Mom to answer when I dialed the number but in immediate rebuke there came a busy signal.

"Mom, pick up! Please, Mom. It's me."

Though I had no idea what I would say to my mother if she answered the phone. That I'd been complicit with my father, who'd violated the court order forbidding him to approach me? forbidding him even to speak with me? That I had violated my mother's trust by going with her enemy, willingly? By wanting to be with him, and not wanting—at least at this moment—to be with her? By loving him—at least at this moment—more than I loved her?

Or maybe none of this was so. Maybe it was a desperate story that I was telling myself, at fifteen. I loved my father not because he was a good father or a good man—how could I have judged him, that he was a "good" man or otherwise—but because he was my father, he was my only father.

And maybe he'd been showing me off, a little—and why was that so terrible? Why couldn't that be forgiven?

Daddy hadn't truly expected Mom to take him up on his invitation, to come out to the County Line for dinner—had he? He'd spoken wistfully, an edge of hurt in his voice. He'd winked at me, he'd been joking.

Your daddy's a tease, sweetie. Don't think that I pay your damn ol' daddy much mind.

I was becoming excited, nervous hearing the busy signal at the other end of the line. Hung up the phone and waited for the coin to drop into the return slot and another time I tried my mother's number, and this time a stranger, a man, answered the phone—"Yeh? Who's this?"—and it turned out that I had misdialed, I'd dialed a wrong number. And all this while the door to the men's room was being pushed open, allowed to swing closed. I tried not to inhale odors of spilled beer, spilled urine. And a powerful stench of disinfectant beneath. *How men are their bodies, there is no escaping men's bodies* came to me as a dismal epiphany. I was hiding from men who whistled at me in passing, called me *Honey-babe* in passing, fluffed my ponytail with rude playful fingers; I was hiding from them pressing my forehead against the smudged black-plastic surface of the pay phone. Another time I dialed my mother's number—that is, our home number— and another time the busy signal came like jeering.

Of course, my mother was likely to be on the phone. Relatives were always calling her. She spoke with her mother and her sisters several times a day. She spoke with "new friends" at her church and with the minister and the minister's wife. She spoke with individuals at the county family court and she may have spoken with a lawyer. Yet it seemed to me that my mother was being deliberately irresponsible, indifferent to me, keeping the phone in use at a time when I might have tried to call her.

I don't need you! I hate you. Daddy has come to take me with him away from you.

Where there must be a choice, a girl will choose Daddy. Even if you are Mommy, you concede that this must be so: you remember when you were a girl, too.

I snatched up the coin from the return slot and went back to the booth where Daddy was waiting for me, drinking. By this time most of the barroom was filled. I had to make my way through a maze of tables. I had to make my way through the crowd at the bar, which was a horseshoe-shaped bar, long, curving, fraught with obstacles. I saw just one woman at the bar—the laughing young women had left, together—and she was a woman in her late thirties with springy curly flyaway hair in the style worn by Zoe Kruller which was a style from the popular TV show of an earlier era, *Charlie's Angels*; it was a young glamorous style but the woman at the bar was not young and glamorous but thick-jowled, with lipstick so dark it appeared black. As I approached she glanced up at me with sudden stricken attention. And others at the bar glanced up at me. Self-consciously I smiled, it was my instinct to smile, as perhaps an animal will cringe, bare its teeth in a simulacrum of a smile, to forestall harm. I pulled at my pony tail to straighten it. Loose damp tendrils of hair were stuck to my forehead. There was a way of walking I envied in some of the older girls at the high school, a kind of self-exhibiting, heads lifted high and eyes bemused *Don't interfere with me!* but this way of walking was beyond me, I lacked the sexual assurance. And there was a man stepping out to block my way. He was no one known to me—was he? He had a straggly goatee, his mouth a wide wet scar. "You're his daughter? Diehl? Why'd he come here? Why'd he bring you here? What's he doing here? The fucker."

I was stunned. Too surprised to react other than to stammer foolishly—"I'm s-sorry. . . ."

This man, this angry goatee-man whom I'd never seen before, dared to take hold of my arm. Asking again in a righteous drunken voice why had my father come here? Why'd he come back to Sparta where he sure as hell wasn't wanted? And I tried to say, stammering and apologetic, that my father was "visiting."

"Visiting who?"

I said I didn't know.

Wanting to throw off the man's hand. For my fear was, Daddy would see us. And something terrible would happen, and possibly to Daddy. I hoped that Daddy wasn't seeing this confrontation.

"Your old man never did time, did he? For what he did to Delray Kruller's wife? Y'know who that was—Zoe? How old are you? Why'd he bring a kid like you here? How'd he get away with what he did? Why's he back here? 'Visiting'—who? God-damned murderer motherfucker."

I tried to protest. I was being jostled, pulled-at by someone else—the big doughy-faced bartender who had shaken my father's hand. And there was another man, a friend of the goatee-man. Saying, "Shit, Mack, let the girl go. She's got nothing to do with it. Come on."

"Son of a bitch killed Delray's wife, and never paid shit for it. Is that him over there, in the booth? That's Diehl?"

I tried to protest, my father had not murdered anyone. My father had not been arrested, even. My father had not been indicted. . . .

Spittle-mouthed Mack was pulled aside. There came someone shoving at the bartender, who grabbed him by the shirt collar as in a cartoon, shook and unsettled him and shoved him back. There were raised vehement voices. The bartender—his name was Deke—said "Chill out. C'mon chill out. Settle down"—as now the woman with the springy flyaway hair and a creased-monkey made-up face intervened: "Don't listen to these assholes, honey! Your father has every right to drink any damn place he wants, this is the United States of America for Christ's sake." I was grateful to think that this woman was my friend, she wore a hot-pink satin designer blouse and tight-fitting jeans, she teetered on ridiculous high heels of a kind Zoe Kruller might have worn on the bandstand at Chautauqua Park. Her breath reeked of cheap whiskey, she was leaning into my face aggressively. "That Kruller woman what's her name—God-damned Zoe—hot-shit 'Zoe'—she was asking for it. Everybody knew what Zoe was. It hadn't been one man it'd been another. 'Get the bed you lay down in'—the bed you deserve, see?—who the fuck fault's that?"

I escaped back to my father in the booth. It was amazing to me, Daddy had not been aware of the commotion at the bar.

In fact Daddy was sitting with his shoulders hunched, like a bear that has been wounded and is trying to summon back his strength. A few minutes alone without the pretty blond ponytail daughter, a man like Eddy Diehl can sink into a mood. A man like Eddy Diehl is a sucker for such a mood. Elbows on the scarred tabletop and his heavy jaw brooding on his fists, eyes half-shut as if he was very tired suddenly, so fucking tired. He had ordered another Coke for me and a shot glass of whiskey and a tall glass of foaming dark ale for himself. Glancing up at me with the quick Daddy-smile, as I half-fell back into the booth.

I was dazed, but I was smiling. Another Daddy might have noted the daze beneath the smile but not this Daddy who finished off half his shot glass in a single swallow. "Listen to the song I'm playing for you—know what it is?"

I tried to listen. I thought this might be important. So much commotion in the barroom, more men at the bar staring in our direction, I couldn't concentrate very well.

> *Delia's gone, one more round!*
> *Delia's gone*

A man's deep baritone voice—a country-and-western drawl—was this Johnny Cash? I tried, but could scarcely hear.

Strange how my father lowered his head, as if it was urgent to hear the words of the song, as if the song conveyed some special meaning to him; as if Eddy Diehl had recently been in some place (but what place could that have been?) where he hadn't been allowed to hear such music. Or hadn't been allowed to sit like this drinking whiskey, drinking beer, smoking a cigarette, in a luxury of sensuousness, solitude; the peculiar solitude of the drinker-in-public.

> *Delia oh Delia*
> *Where you been so long?*
>
> *One more round, Delia's gone,*
> *One more round.*

Still at the bar we were under scrutiny. I could not bring myself to look but in the corner of my eye I was aware of the angry goatee-man—and others—observing Daddy and me. (But why wasn't Daddy aware? Was Daddy drunk, or was Daddy deliberately not seeing?) I felt an absurd leap of hope, that the drunk woman in the shiny hot-pink blouse would come to our defense; she would enlist others, in support of my father.

Of course I knew that the name *Diehl* carried certain associations now, in Sparta. In all of Herkimer County. Maybe in all of the Adirondacks. As *Zoe Kruller* would be known, and the bluegrass group Black River Breakdown. Cassettes and CDs of the band's music were passed about locally; Daddy had several in the glove compartment of the Willys Jeep, which I'd often asked him to play, when I was riding with him in that vehicle.

"Mister? Here y'are."

A waitress brought a platter of French fries to our table, and another bottle of ale. Daddy roused himself from his music-trance to offer some fries to me—"I ordered these for just now. This isn't our dinner yet—we'll go somewhere special for dinner—only right now, I'm so God-damned hungry."

He began to eat with his fingers. He'd removed his baseball cap, his hair was disheveled, dark with feathery streaks of gray, alternately thick and sparse, receding at his temples which appeared flushed and lightly beaded with sweat. It made me uneasy, that Daddy was beginning to resemble his father—Grandpa Diehl who'd always been so *old*—whom Daddy and his brothers had called *the old man* with an exasperated sort of affection—*the old bastard*—*can't put anything over on the old bastard*. A man begins to lose his hair, his skull takes on a different shape, he begins to assume a different identity. I felt such tenderness for Daddy, I wanted to stroke Daddy's face, that was looking so battered and leathery as if windburnt; clearly he'd been working outside. In his early forties Eddy Diehl was no longer a man for whom a fresh-laundered white cotton shirt was appropriate work-attire.

No longer a husband/father of whom his wife said boastfully he was of the *managerial class*.

"Krista? Have some. C'mon eat with your old man."

"No thanks, Daddy! I don't like fries."

"Must be hungry, Puss, the way you were running around on that basketball court. C'mon."

I was hungry. I was very hungry. But could not bring myself to eat the thick greasy-salty fries, reheated in a microwave oven behind the bar, doused with ketchup, the kind of food my mother was quick to perceive was likely to be leftovers from other meals, scraped off other customers' plates.

Daddy shoved the platter of fries in my direction. I thought *Ben would eat these!* and so I picked up one or two fries, to break into smaller pieces and pretend to eat.

I saw that my father's knuckles were freshly scratched, bruised. And maybe scarred, beneath. I knew he'd done treework at one time recently—working with chainsaws—I knew that there were men at Sparta Construction who'd had terrible accidents with chainsaws—I wanted to take up my father's big, scarred hand in mine—to tell him that I loved him, and I did not believe what some people said about him, *I knew it could not be true.*

Yet with his unshaven jaws and something heavy-lidded, sulky, about his eyes Daddy exuded a sharkish air; here was a man of pride, to whom you did not condescend; the voice on the jukebox, penetrating the smoky interior of the crowded County Line Tavern on a weekday evening, was the very voice of this man's soul, and you did not condescend to such a soul. I felt a warning shiver of the kind a swimmer might feel as something not-quite-visible—dark, finned, silent—passes close beneath him, he can't quite see.

The jukebox song was ending. There was a deep-baritone masculine robustness that seemed inappropriate to its subject:

> *So if your woman's devilish*
> *You can let her run,*
> *Or you can bring her down and*
> *Do her like Delia got done.*
> *Delia's gone, one more round!*
> *Delia's gone*

Daddy was nodding with grave satisfaction, chewing French fries. Big lardy-greasy fries the size of his big fingers lavishly doused with ketchup. Whatever the Johnny Cash song meant to him, it had struck a powerful chord. He'd finished his shot of whiskey and signaled for another. Took a hearty swig from the bottle of ale. Fixed me with a squinting wink and a terse Daddy-smile to finally ask what he'd been putting off asking, since I'd returned to the booth. "Well, Krista: what did your mom say?"

Mom! I had not heard this word in my father's mouth for a very long time. I saw that he'd been hopeful that my mother would be joining us, his eyes shone with a crazy hope.

12

MARCH 1983

THE TROUBLE corroding our lives like deep pockets of rust in the hulks of abandoned vehicles. *The trouble* sucking all the joy out of our lives. And the very awareness *the trouble* slow to be absorbed by us, who wished each day to think that this! this would surely be the day when *the trouble is cleared up*.

In retrospect it appears inevitable, and awful. At the time it seems just haphazard.

How Daddy was gone from our household and living with his brother in East Sparta and one day Ben said meanly, "If he's gone thirteen days he's *gone*. He won't be coming back."

Zoe Kruller was not a name to be uttered in our household. Yet *Zoe Kruller* was a name uttered everywhere in Sparta.

On the Sparta radio station local DJ's were playing songs by Black River Breakdown. Zoe Kruller's unmistakable voice—throaty, intimate, just-this-side-of-teasing—was suddenly everywhere. The most popular Zoe Kruller songs were "Footprints in the Snow"—the words of which had an eerie prescience, describing what appears to be the mysterious death of a beautiful young woman—

> *I traced her little footprints in the snow*
> *I found her little footprints in the snow*

Now she's up in heaven she's with the angel band
I know I'm going to meet her in that promised land
I found her little footprints in the snow

and "Little Bird of Heaven" which was my favorite, and I guess it was Daddy's favorite too since it was the one Daddy played most often when he was driving one of his vehicles. Zoe Kruller's voice was airy and playful in this song but melancholy too, you'd find yourself drawing in a breath and biting back a little cry, these words were so beautiful—

Well love they tell me is a fragile thing
It's hard to fly on broken wings
I lost my ticket to the promised land
Little bird of heaven right here in my hand.

So toss it up or pass it round
Pay mind to what you're carryin' round
Or keep it close, hold it while you can
There's a little bird of heaven right here in your hand.

In Sparta it came to be thought that Zoe Kruller had left a message— "a nest of clues"—in this song. Especially by girls and women it was thought that Zoe had "named her murderer" in the song and if you listened closely, or wrote the lyrics down and took note of the first letters, or the last letters, of each line, you would know who the man was.

Fallen hearts and fallen leaves
Starlings light on the broken trees
I find we all need a place to land
There's a little bird of heaven right here in your hand.

In Mom's car we were driving and there came breathy and urgent in our ears amid gushing heat from the heater—for it was a vicious-windy

March morning—the murdered woman's voice *Little bird of heaven right here in your hand*—and with a cry my mother switched off the radio.

"Her! That terrible woman."

Why is Zoe Kruller a terrible woman?

Is it because Zoe Kruller is a slut?

And does a terrible-slut woman deserve to die?

No one could understand why Black River Breakdown had never made a commercial record, never had a contract with a New York City or Los Angeles recording agency, or been invited to perform outside the Adirondack region. Now their girl-singer had been murdered, the dazed little band of musicians found themselves touched with a kind of lurid tabloid glamour like a spotlight beamed into their faces. The fiddler, who was the group's oldest musician, at forty-six, had gone into hiding and refused to be interviewed by the media except to say he'd known Zoe Kruller "since she'd been the prettiest baby you could imagine"—while the young guitarist with his Elvis sideburns and shoulder-length hair turned up anywhere you'd look—on late-afternoon local TV, in the "entertainment features" pages of the Sparta *Journal* facing the comic strips, baring his soul saying he hadn't slept a night since Zoe was murdered, he hoped to God the police would find whoever did this, and fast; he was composing a ballad in memory of Zoe he hoped he and the group could perform sometime soon. . . .

This newspaper article, and others, I would keep in my notebook, in secret. Seeming to know *This will be with me all my life. This will change my life.*

No one had been murdered in Sparta, or in all of Herkimer County, for a long time: nine years. If you didn't count—as the media did not—several killings at the Seneca Indian reservation designated *manslaughter* which had been settled without trials and publicity. And rarely had anyone in Herkimer County been murdered in such a way: in the victim's residence, in her bed, to be discovered on a Sunday morning by her own son.

The previous murder, in Sparta, had been during a robbery at the Sunoco station on route 31; before that, a homeless man had been hammered to death by another homeless man, in a Sparta shelter. Both killers had been identified and arrested by police within a day or two.

How different this was—*The murderer of Zoe Kruller remains at large.*

And—*Suspects but no arrests yet, Sparta detectives decline to comment.*

We were frightened but we were thrilled, too. We were made to come home directly from school and our mothers drove us places where just recently we'd had to walk or, in warmer weather, to ride our bicycles. We could not know it—perhaps in a way we did know it, we sensed it—and this was part of the thrill—that this interlude would mark a turn in our lives as in the small-city life of Sparta, a sense that *We will not be safe again, there is no one to protect us always.*

Boys were allowed more freedom than girls, of course. This was always the case but now more than ever for whoever had killed Zoe Kruller had to be a man and this man would not wish to kill a boy or another man, only a woman or a girl. Even a child of eleven understood this logic.

Girls were warned always to be wary of strangers. Never be talked into climbing into a stranger's car, never reply to a stranger, never make eye contact with a stranger, if a stranger approaches you, *run!*

Or: it might be someone you know. Not a stranger but an acquaintance. An adult man.

For whoever had killed Zoe Kruller, it was believed that he had known her and that she had let him into her residence willingly. One of Zoe Kruller's *male companions.*

Or, Mrs. Kruller's *husband Delray.*

Sometimes identified as her *estranged husband Delray.*

In a dictionary in our school library I looked up *estranged.* There was an exotic sound to this word, that contained the more familiar *strange* inside it like something blunt and commonplace—a pebble, say—inside a colored Easter egg.

Separated, divided, hostile, alienated, indifferent, severed, sunder: estranged.

"Is Daddy 'estranged' from us?"—with the cruel simulated naivete of the very young I dared to ask my mother this question one evening when

Daddy had been gone from the house for a week; I saw the wincing hurt in my mother's face; how I escaped being slapped across the mouth, I don't know.

How exciting our lives had become, so quickly! Breathless and unpredictable and yet the excitement left behind a sick sensation like that you felt on a roller coaster when you were a young child: you'd thought you had wanted this, you had clamored and begged for this, but maybe you had not wanted it, not *this*. You'd wanted to be frightened, and you'd wanted to be thrilled; you'd wanted something to rush through you like an electric current; you'd wanted to scream in an ecstasy of panic but maybe—maybe you had not really wanted this.

And maybe by the time you realized, it was too late.

"Krista? Come here, I have something to tell you."

Already my mother had spoken with Ben, when he'd come home from school. I'd heard his sharp raised voice and then he slammed out of the house and Mom called after him just once, a sharp little cry like a shot bird,

"Benjamin!"

From a window I saw Ben running stooped over, in the slanted sunshine of late afternoon, without his jacket. My stricken brother stomping through foot-high snow to the old barn, a short distance behind the two-car garage my father had built adjoining our house; the barn was used for storage and as a second garage for my father's succession of vehicles. I saw Ben's breath turn to vapor as he ran. I thought that I might not have recognized Ben running in that way, like something wounded, looking younger than his age, smaller.

From the upstairs hallway, I saw this. I'd hurried upstairs as soon as I came home from school, I'd brought my after-school snack with me—a bowl of cereal, with milk and raisins—so that I could begin my homework while I ate. The cereal was bite-sized shredded wheat; it had to be eaten quickly or it would become soggy, sodden like mush, and the milk would become discolored, and what should have been delicious would become faintly nauseating, an effort to eat.

I was beginning to realize that all that I loved to eat—my special childhood treats like Honeystone's ice-cream cones—could very easily turn nauseating, disgusting.

Since my father had moved out of the house I'd become susceptible to wild bouts of hunger. Especially in the afternoons, after the strain of school. I would devour a bowl of cereal like a starving animal. A childish elation came over me as if nothing else mattered except this: eating.

By which I meant solitary eating. Not at mealtimes. Not with my mother and Ben. With Daddy missing from his place at the end of the table, I'd come to hate mealtimes. I would eat standing in front of the opened refrigerator, I would eat sitting on the lower steps of the stairs, I would eat in my room or even in the bathroom, my mouth flooding with saliva. As quickly now at the little desk in my room—a desk Daddy had built for me from smooth whorled oak wood, left over from a construction site—I tried to spoon the shredded wheat into my mouth, before my mother called me as I knew she would.

First Ben, then Krista. There had to be some logic in our mother's cruelty.

Half-choking I swallowed chunks of shredded wheat, milk. Thinking *I don't know yet. What Ben knows, I don't know.*

"Krista? Come here, I have something to tell you."

My mother stood at the foot of the stairs calling to me. Her voice was sharp as a knife-blade, I could see it glittering, I wanted to run away, to hide! But I was not a small child any longer, I was eleven years old.

I could not have said if I was mature for my age, or immature. I may have looked younger than eleven but I felt older. I was the girl on the school bus who when the other, older girls shivered and shuddered whispering of *That awful thing that was done to Zoe Kruller worse than being strangled* sat very still and silent and seemed not to hear.

When I came downstairs, my mother had returned to the dining room where she'd been seated at the drop-leaf cherrywood table which was a "family heirloom" always covered by a tablecloth. The dining room was a room rarely used, and then mostly on holidays. For privacy Mom had brought the kitchen phone into this room, on an extension. These were days before portable phones and cell phones and you were bound to a socket outlet and an extension cord. It was startling to see on the dining room table so many manila folders: financial statements, insurance policies, receipts and income tax forms, scattered official-looking letters, papers.

"Mom? What's all these things?"

"Sit down, Krista. Never mind these things."

"But—"

"Wipe your mouth, Krista, for heaven's sake! It looks like you've been lapping milk. I said, sit *down*."

I hated the dining room chairs, that were so *special*. Hard cushions and wicker backs that weren't comfortable, nothing like the worn vinyl kitchen chairs. Our family meals were always in the kitchen and the dining room was used only for special occasions, occasions of forced festivity arranged by my mother and her family to celebrate birthdays, holidays. There was an inflexible schedule by which Christmas eve, Christmas day, Thanksgiving, and Easter were rotated among my mother and her relatives.

Daddy had used to tease Mom about the tablecloth: What's the point of cherrywood if no one can see it?—and Mom had said what if someone left a glass ring, a stain or a burn on the table, this was a risk she couldn't take.

Since Daddy had gone to live with his brother Earl, Mom had become busy as we'd never seen her before. Always she was bustling about the house, up and down stairs; always she was on the phone. Bauer relatives came to see her every day, in the dining room with doors slid shut. There were several women friends who smiled grimly at me and looked as if they'd like to hug me against their droopy bosoms except I ducked away.

A hawk-faced man in a suit and necktie Mom introduced to Ben and me as "my accountant." Another man in a suit and tie—"Mr. Nagel, my lawyer."

Lawyer. I didn't want to think what this might mean.

Estranged. Separated. Divorced. . . .

"Krista? I want you to listen carefully—"

With an awkward sort of tenderness my mother took hold of my chill squirmy hands. She was speaking in a quiet voice which was unsettling to me, a wrong-sounding voice, a forced voice, a voice in which something pleading quivered, though less than an hour ago I'd heard her on the phone speaking sharply, punctuating her words with bursts of what sounded like laughter. I wanted to shut my ears against her, thinking with childish stubbornness *Daddy will come back and change all this. Anything that is being done, Daddy will change back to what it should be.* Both Ben and I had noticed that our mother's eyes had a weird glassy sheen for lately she'd been taking prescription medications to help her sleep and to settle her nerves. Not wanting to see Mom's eyes I stared at our hands, locked so strangely together. As if we were in some dangerous place, on a rocky height for instance, it was our instinct to clutch at each other, in fear. And yet the fear I felt was for my mother. For those glassy red-rimmed eyes and for the smeared-lipstick mouth that might tell me something very ugly I would not wish to hear.

Here was a surprising thing: my mother had removed her rings.

The "white gold" engagement ring with the single square-cut small diamond, and the matching wedding band she said she didn't think she could force off her finger any longer, she'd gained so much weight. These were gone, I had never seen my mother's fingers without rings before.

Something was trying to make me remember it: a smile tugged at my lips.

A long-ago Daddy-game when I'd been a little girl. Daddy had hidden my hands inside his big-Daddy hands pretending they were lost, he couldn't find them.

Where are Puss's little paws? Who's seen Puss's paws? Anybody seen two lost paws?

"Why are you smiling, Krista? Is something funny?"

Quickly I told my mother *no.* Nothing was funny.

"I'm glad that someone thinks something is funny. Yes, that's good to know."

When my mother was angry she pretended to be hurt. If you didn't apologize immediately, and repeat your apology several times, my mother would become angry.

I told her *no* nothing was funny. I wasn't smiling. But I was sorry that I was smiling, if I was smiling.

My mother drew a deep breath. My mother squeezed my chill squirmy hands as if to keep me from running away.

"Well, Krista! You know that your father has been staying with your uncle Earl. And maybe you know that your father has been 'cooperating' with the Sparta police detectives who are investigating"—my mother's brave voice began to falter, I couldn't raise my eyes to her face—"the death of—that woman—the one who was hurt—Mrs. Kruller—you know who she is. Who she *was*. The one who was—killed." My mother paused, and drew another deep breath. A vein pulsed in her throat like a frantic little blue worm. "They—the police—haven't caught him yet—the one who hurt her—Mrs. Kruller—but they will. But, Krista, I wanted to tell you—and Ben—that your father has been—he has 'cooperated' with the police—he has told the police—first, he told *me*—that he had been a— a 'close friend' of that woman's. And he had visited her where she was living . . . sometimes." Now my mother was speaking in rapid little bursts and pauses, like one who is running, whose breath comes in pants; like one whose heartbeat has become erratic. She was squeezing my hands to make me wince. "He—your father—had told police at first that he hadn't visited her—not for a long time—and that they weren't friends—they had not been friends for a long time—a few years ago yes, but not recently—this is what he'd told the police—and he had told me—but that was wrong of him because it wasn't true—and it was wrong of him because the police would find out—because he should have known the police would find out—the police are questioning everyone who knew that woman and her family and everyone who worked with her or lived by her or any of the Krullers—any of that family—they are questioning them all, and so it was a mistake for your father to lie to them. Your father lied to the police, Krista, and your father lied to *me*. He was afraid, he said. He wanted to protect his family, he said. But the mistake was he has made some people think—he has made the police think—that he might have had something to do with . . ."

My mother paused, breathing rapidly. The little blue vein fluttered in her throat. Something oily glistened at her hairline. She was wearing her shapeless black stretch-band jersey slacks, a shirt with a twisted collar and a cardigan sweater buttoned crookedly to her neck. Her hair looked matted on one side as if she'd been sleeping on that side of her head and had not checked her reflection in the mirror.

The glassy eyes stung with tears. Yet these were glass-tears, that could not gather and fall.

"Well, Krista! You should be told: your father was there, at that woman's house, on *that day*. I mean—it was a night, your father has confessed that he was *there*. He had denied it previously, he had 'sworn'. . . . But now, he has confessed he was there in her 'residence' on West Ferry Street and I need to tell you and Ben because it will be revealed, on tonight's news and in tomorrow's papers it will be revealed, and everyone will know. So your father wants you to know, Krista. From me. He can't talk to you now, he is in 'police custody.' He wants me to tell you. You and Ben. How sorry he is. How ashamed he is. Your father was at that woman's house where he'd been to see her some other times, too, he is confessing now. But he says he was not there *then*—when she was hurt. She was hurt in a terrible way, Krista. She was hurt in a terrible way she did not deserve, Krista, because no one deserves to be hurt like that, not even a woman like Zoe Kruller. Your father says he doesn't know who hurt her, he has no idea who hurt her, but it was not *him*. He had seen her, but this was hours before—it happened. He says it was four or five hours before, at least. He has said, he has sworn, this time he is telling the truth—that someone came to Mrs. Kruller's residence after he'd left, and what happened to her—what was done to her—happened then." My mother paused, wiping at her eyes. "Oh Krista, your father has sworn. He did not hurt that woman, he has sworn. And I believe him. . . ."

In a haze of incomprehension I'd been listening to my mother's words in faltering little rushes. Like a person unsteady on his legs—one whose legs are about to give out—my mother was capable of sudden little rushes, an air of desperation underlaid by a determination not to collapse. By this time her fingers were so tightly gripping mine, I'd had to pull away from her. She scarcely noticed. She was trying not to—cry?—not to laugh? Her face was mottled with heat and the glassy sheen in her eyes, that appeared lashless, naked, was painful to see.

Bitterly now she said, "Oh—how do I know? What can I know? Why am I telling my daughter such things, when I don't *know*? There are things I do know: he wasn't home with his family that night. The night that woman died, in the early hours of Sunday morning, it's said— my husband Edward Diehl *was not home*. He'd asked me to lie for him, to say that he was home, and *he was in our bed*, but that was not—that is not—true, Krista! I refuse to lie to the police, as he'd asked me to. I refuse to lie because I won't lie for *him*, an adulterer. D'you know what an *adulterer* is, Krista? One who betrays. One who betrays his vows to his wife and to his family and is not then to be trusted. Not ever to be trusted. He had been lying to me for years about that woman, first he'd lied denying there was anything between them, he was 'mostly just friends' with the husband Delray, but that was a lie, he's been lying to all of us for years knowing how he could get away with it, Eddy Diehl can get away with anything, through his life from high school he'd got- ten away with—with *murder*. Why should I lie for him? Because I am his wife—Lucille? Because I am the left-behind wife he'd betrayed, I should lie for *him*? Why should anyone lie for such a man, or love him? You and Ben, Krista—*why*?"

Why?—because he is my father. Because I love him, more than I love you. Because all that he tells me, I will believe.

We were in school when, in early March, Daddy came to the house to take away the rest of his things.

For much of a frenzied day my mother had enlisted our aid, Ben's and mine, in packing Daddy's things—clothes, shoes, manual and power tools from his basement workshop—into cardboard boxes which were then dragged out onto the back porch so that Daddy would have no need to come inside the house.

"It's trash, let him haul away his trash. It's the trash of that man's life, I want nothing to do with it."

So like a county sanitation worker my father was made by my mother to come to our house and take away his things without coming inside.

So we knew that Daddy would not be coming back to live with us for a long time. And maybe never.

In my heartsick daze, I didn't cry. I don't think I cried.

Ben said, sneering, "Why's he need his big-deal 'power tools' where he's going?" and I asked where was Daddy going?—and Ben said with his new hateful laugh, "To hell, stupid. Where'd you think."

13

Four years later my father's chiding words echoed in my thoughts like loose sharp gravel flung against something soft.

If you don't want to take the risk. Maybe you shouldn't be playing at all.

14

349 WEST FERRY STREET. Where Zoe Kruller was found.

It was a brownstone row house at the corner of West Ferry and a one-way street called Mercy. It had a dull-brown soft-crumbling façade and stark staring windows and its bleak snow-cratered front yard was hardly more than the size of a card table, trod upon by myriad feet and pissed-upon by myriad neighborhood dogs. Though it was approximately two and a half miles from our house on Huron Pike Road, you could not get there directly.

There were circuitous ways. Ways I would learn in secret, in the late winter/early spring of that year.

You could hike along the railroad tracks through marshy woodlands and fields in which, in early April, the eerie high-pitched cries of peepers assailed the ear from all sides; you could avoid roads and being seen by anyone driving on roads, and make your way into the city limits of Sparta across the Black River on a plank footbridge that ran close beside the railroad bridge hoping that no locomotive would rush by, shaking and rattling the footbridge, while you were on it.

You could pause on the bridge leaning against the railing feeling a touch of vertigo, giddiness. You could stare down at the swift thinly rippling water flowing north and west in the direction of Lake Ontario with the relentless unyielding suction of water down a bathtub drain. You could note where the river was relatively shallow near shore and there were protrusions of shale strata like ribs of ancient beasts and your fear—an instinctive animal-fear engendered by this place—was that it might be the footbridge that was moving, and the thin-rippling water that was still. And the thought might come to you *This is a place and a time I can always come back to. This will always remain.*

On the farther side of the rippling-dark river there came a powerful stench of fertilizer from the Chautauqua & Buffalo railroad yard. Loud jarring noises that made the air shudder, of freight cars being coupled together by force. Men's uplifted voices sounding both angry and jocular.

Even the laughter of men working outdoors has an air of anger about it.

Beyond the railroad yard—which was massive, sprawling on several acres of fenced-off riverfront land—there was the old train depot on Denver Street, that had not been used for a decade; a derelict crumbling-brick structure of about the size of a single freight car, with boarded-up windows covered in a lacy filigree of graffiti in which even obscene words— *fuck cunt shithole*—bore the air of a mysterious secret code. Close about this abandoned Denver Street depot there was broken glass scattered on the pavement and there was a smell of stale urine and sometimes the mysterious figures—usually solitary, huddled on benches or sprawled comatose on the pavement—of vagrants, homeless men in layers of clothing, wrapped in makeshift blankets; at times there were younger men, in their twenties, high school–aged boys, likely to be swarthy-skinned, *Indian-looking*, gathered in the evenings to sell and buy drugs and to *get high* on pot, speed, "crystal meth"—so Ben told me. Ben sneered at "dopers"—"druggies"— "junkies." Ben had higher plans for himself that involved leaving Sparta as soon as he graduated from high school, entering an engineering school like Rensselaer Polytech.

Yet to me, an air of perverse romance clung to the abandoned depot, raw and overexposed in daylight, as an air of perverse romance clung to the ruins of rotting woodframe bungalows and dilapidated buildings in the old riverfront neighborhood beneath the Black River suspension bridge. I wondered if Zoe Kruller's son Aaron was one of the teenaged boys who hung out at the depot. And if, after Zoe's death, Aaron continued to return to the depot, that could not have been more than a half-mile from the brownstone on West Ferry Street.

That poor boy! Imagine! My mother spoke of Mrs. Kruller's son with an air of vehement concern as if what had happened to him, what he'd happened upon, was Zoe Kruller's fault.

This trouble that came into all our lives.

It was an afternoon in April 1983, two months after Mrs. Kruller's body had been found. The air was sunny and warm enough to rouse the peepers to their frantic din in the wetlands near our house, I felt a powerful yearning to leave the house, to slip away without telling my mother where I was going; to hike along the railroad tracks taking care to step on the railroad ties and not on the coarse gravel between the ties that hurt my feet through the soles of my boots; bravely I crossed the footbridge hoping that no train would rush up behind me and overhead and cause the footbridge to tremble convulsively; and within the Sparta city limits I descended from the footbridge to a no-man's-land bordering the railroad yard, I passed the abandoned depot with its zigzag slashes of graffiti and a rear door agape—was anyone inside? I could not see—and so across unpaved Denver Street and to West Ferry Street breathless and excited. This was forbidden territory! This was a terrible thing that I was doing! And yet, how ordinary the brownstone at 349 was, almost I could not believe that this rundown residence with its mutilated-looking front yard and blank blind windows, a scattering of advertising flyers on the front walk, was the place in which Zoe Kruller had been murdered in an upstairs room.

At one time decades ago these brownstones had been millworkers' homes. The West Ferry neighborhood had been what my mother would have identified as a "not-bad" neighborhood, "not run-down" like so much of inner Sparta. But the riverside mills—cotton goods, hosiery—had shut down in the late 1960s, before I was born.

It was something of a shock to me, to see people on West Ferry Street. A run-down house being repaired, on Mercy Street. There was street traffic, there were mothers pushing small children in strollers, boys on bicycles shouting companionably to one another. I had been envisioning the house in which Zoe Kruller had been murdered as stark and isolated as a nightmare house in a horror movie but in fact the brownstone at 349 resembled other brownstones in the block: two floors, two narrow windows on each floor, a cramped front stoop, the cramped front yard bordered by cracked and uneven sidewalks. Some of the front yards on West Ferry Street looked as if they'd been tended, winter debris had been raked away, but at 349 there were only waterlogged and rotted flyers and dog-shit-littered grassless earth. In each of the four windows facing the street blinds had been drawn to different lengths as if to suggest an air of drunken revelry. There were glimpses of grayish curtains, like underwear.

On the front door, the remains of a Christmas wreath of silvery tinsel and red plastic berries.

A Christmas wreath! I wondered if Zoe Kruller had put the wreath up, I thought yes, that would be like Zoe. (But why hadn't the wreath been taken down, after Zoe Kruller's body had been carried through that doorway? This seemed wrong to me.)

Slowly I walked past the brownstone. It was said that Zoe Kruller had left her family to live in a terrible inner-city neighborhood but this block of West Ferry wasn't so very different from stretches of the Huron Pike Road where there were run-down old houses, trailers tilting on cement blocks and the hulks of abandoned vehicles in front yards.

Next-door at 347 a family with young children must have been living for there were children's toys on the front walk, an overturned tricycle. In the backyard, laundry hung on clotheslines.

Dazzling-white sheets flapping in the wind.

"Hey: you."

A thick-bodied girl of about twelve with sharp-chiseled Indian features, coarse dark hair, a mouth twisted in a grimace of a smile—friendly? mocking?— passed me on the sidewalk pushing a small child in a stroller, so close she brushed my leg with one of the stroller wheels. "Sor-*ry*!" I shrank away, wanting to think this was just accidental. I did not want to see the girl grinning at me.

White girl! White bitch! What're you doing here, pissy little white girl!

Nervously I walked on. I did not think that the Indian-looking girl would turn the stroller around to follow me, and she did not. But I was conscious of older boys on bicycles, whooping and yelling in the street, not knowing if they were mocking me, or whether they were utterly indifferent to me. . . . After a while, the boys disappeared.

As if casually then I turned, and walked back to Zoe Kruller's former residence. My heart was pounding with anticipation—for exactly what, I could not imagine. I'd assumed that the brownstone was empty and yet: in one of the first-floor windows of the brownstone there was a sudden blurred movement as if someone inside was drawing back the blind to peer out.

A woman's hand, was it?—red-lacquered fingernails.

Quickly I walked on. I began to run. I was not thinking *That is the ghost of Zoe Kruller* for I did not believe in ghosts, I was not a silly child at the age of eleven yet my heart thumped in my chest and the hairs at the nape of my neck stirred. Blindly I ran along West Ferry and to unpaved Denver and back along the railroad yard reeking of airborne toxins and to the footbridge above the river and I was thinking how Zoe Kruller's fingernails had always been so beautifully manicured, always so perfectly polished, when she'd waited on us at Honeystone's and sung for us in the blinding-hot lights of the bandstand stage: no matter the Sparta summer air was heavy with moisture, the temperature in the park still in the nineties how Zoe Kruller craved our attention, our love, our applause. . . . Every girl in the audience wished to be Zoe Kruller up there on the stage shaking and writhing her slim little body, hips and surprisingly sizable pointy breasts, tossing her strawberry blond crimped mane of hair and flashing those red-painted nails that had to be twice as long as the ordinary plain nails of Lucille Diehl, to match the luscious red-gleaming lipstick on Zoe's widened mouth.

Sayyyy there Krissie thought it was you

And that car of your Daddy's for sure
What can I do you-all for today?

And had Ben bicycled over to West Ferry Street, yes I was sure that Ben had. Long before I'd gone to West Ferry Street. I knew this, I had to know this, though I would not have asked Ben and if I'd asked him, he would have shrugged me off. *Bullshit!* was Ben's way of coping with all of his life he could not now control. Laughing-shrugging *Bullshit!* like a jab in my ribs.

Unable to hurt the person—or persons—who'd hurt him, Ben knew that he could always hurt me.

"You, girl! You looking for—who?"

The woman's voice was mildly teasing, chiding: a Zoe Kruller kind of voice. There was an eagerness to it like a fishhook in flesh, in an instant of weakness you hesitate and the hook is *in*.

It was another afternoon, later in spring. In the spring of that year—that interminable, terrible year—in which Zoe Kruller was murdered. Several times now I had hiked in secret along the railroad tracks and across the footbridge and back to West Ferry Street and each time I went alone and each time I was struck by the ordinariness of the neighborhood which was what Caucasians like my mother called *mixed*, a neighborhood of *mixed races*. There were numerous white-skinned people here, though not so many as what my mother would call *those others*, and if I felt some uneasiness it wasn't because of the color of my skin, or theirs, but because on West Ferry and on surrounding roadways there were many trucks, there were many truck drivers and of these it was likely to suppose that some knew my father Eddy Diehl and, if they'd ever seen me, or knew me, they might recognize me and report back to my father, or to my mother, that the eleven-year-old Krista Diehl had been sighted in a Sparta neighborhood miles from her home where clearly she did not belong.

As this woman had sighted me, and was calling to me. Recognizing me not as Eddy Diehl's daughter but as a stranger who'd been walking—walking and staring—in the unpaved alley that ran behind the brownstones on West Ferry, pausing behind 349.

How ramshackle the brownstone looked, from the rear! Shabby, run-down, rotting planks in the backyard, in mud puddles black-feathered birds—ravens, grackles—with long tails splashing and bathing like manic children.

"Sweetie, hey: c'mon say hello. Nobody's gonna bite you, *promise*."

Like an apparition the woman had appeared on the back porch of Zoe Kruller's former residence. Maybe she'd been watching me through a window.

At eleven I was still young enough, or appeared young enough, to be addressed as if I were a small child, by adults. I had not an adolescent's presence of mind to simply turn away. I smiled, uneasily—I murmured *Hello*. The woman beckoned me to come forward, and so I did.

And how strange this woman was! At first glance you would think that she was beautiful, glamorous—but no, she was neither beautiful nor glamorous so much as a mockery of "feminine" beauty, glamour—a cosmetic mask that has been disfigured. Her face was large, round, moon-shaped like my mother's, but it appeared to be shiny as if rubbed with a greasy rag, and swollen. Her shoulder-length hair was a dyed-beet color that looked frizzy and matted as if she'd just gotten out of bed. Over her ample body she was wearing something lacy and black and slinky—a nightgown? "negligee"?—and over this a man's flannel shirt carelessly buttoned so that you could see, without wishing to see, a swath of black lace and large heavy lard-colored breasts. Like her face the woman's body appeared swollen, goiterous. Yet she exuded a weird sexual assurance with an elaborately painted crimson mouth, plucked and pencil-thin eyebrows, doll-like features squashed together inside the fatty face. Here was a woman—a female—whose attraction for men would be powerful, I thought. Like certain of the older and more mature high school girls whom I knew, she seemed to belong to another species of being.

Wanting to run from her but—I could not! So earnestly, so hopefully and so seductively she smiled at me.

"Well, say—my name is *Jacky*. What's yours?"

Again, the uncanny echo of Zoe Kruller. *Well, say!*

In an article in the Sparta paper about Zoe Kruller it had been noted that at the time of her death Zoe had been staying with a "woman friend" on West Ferry Street; and that this friend had been away, overnight, when Zoe was killed; yet police had reason to believe that the woman was one of the last people to have seen Zoe alive. Her name was Jacqueline DeLucca—I had memorized that name—and she'd been identified as a "cocktail waitress, unemployed."

Somehow it happened, I told "Jacky" DeLucca my name.

"'Krista'—what a pretty name. An unusual name, isn't it!"

How to answer this? I laughed, embarrassed.

"You're the first 'Krista' I ever met. That's good!"

Jacky's speech was, like her appearance, exuberant, over-animated. Spilling out of her black-lace nightgown and her flannel shirt, her frizzed dyed-beet hair stirring in the wind like a mad halo about her head, this woman-friend of Zoe Kruller looked as if she were about to clap her hands in childish delight. Though I wanted very badly not to come inside Jacky DeLucca's house with her somehow I had no way of politely saying *no*.

No warning came to me, of the countless warnings of my mother regarding the danger of being spoken-to, beguiled-by, strangers.

Inside the cluttered kitchen that smelled of something sweetish like wine, whiskey, cooking odors and scorched food Jacky was saying in her drawling-Zoe voice that I was a "pretty girl" but would have to "smile more" so that people felt good in my company, and not "heavy-hearted": "What life is, is people want to be happy, not unhappy. Men, most of all. All-age-men. It's a man's world and if you make a man unhappy, he will sure as hell unvoid you. Don't matter if you are beautiful as—what's-her-name—now she's fat and old, but—'Liz Taylor'—don't matter if you look like her, if you cause a man to be heavy-hearted, guilty and ponderous like some weight hanging around his neck, you will be left *alone*."

Jacky gripped her fleshy arms with her hands and shuddered at the prospect, or the memory, of being *alone*.

Unvoid was a word new to me. I guessed that Jacky meant to say *avoid*.

How horrified my mother would have been at the condition of this kitchen: so small, so cramped, with ugly discolored walls, cupboards lacking doors so you could see stacked plates, cups, cereal boxes, cans on shelves, a torn and sticky linoleum floor. Food-encrusted dishes not even soaking in the sink—which my mother abhorred as a lazy habit— but strewn about on every available surface. Though it wasn't yet warm weather flies were buzzing lazily about as if this was their breeding ground. Chattering happily and nervously Jacky cleared a space for us to sit at a table, she reheated hot chocolate in a pan on the stove, and served it to us in heavy chipped mugs with red valentine hearts on them. The rim of my cup was just visibly stained with lipstick, I tried inconspicuously to rub off. It seemed important not to insult or upset this friendly woman, whose mood might abruptly turn to its opposite. "Damn! Guess it was boiling." There was a scummy film on the surface of the hot chocolate, but the hot chocolate was delicious. And stale chocolate chip cookies, eagerly dumped out of a package and onto the chipped-pebbles Formica tabletop, delicious too.

"See, Krista—'Krissie'—is that what people call you, who love you?— 'Krissie'—I saw you out there in the alley, and I thought *That little girl is a friend of Zoe's. I just know it.*"

A kind of pinching sensation came into my face. My eyes shifted down, I could not meet Jacky's shining eyes.

"Am I right? Am I? I am! From when Zoe worked at the dairy, was it? I thought so."

Jacky asked me how old I was, what grade I was at school, and where I lived. Her voice rattled on like a runaway locomotive while her eyes fixed on me in that eager hungry-Zoe way that was disconcerting. Her manner was furtive, flirtatious. On her neck and right forearm—what I could see of her forearm—there were faint purplish bruises like fading clouds, which, unconsciously, Jacky stroked tenderly. I was made to remember how Zoe had stroked her freckled arms, at the dairy. Zoe's arms that were slender and milky-pale and stippled with freckles and moles like tiny ants. . . .

"D'you miss her, Krissie? D'you miss Zoe? I guess she wasn't a friend of your mom's, was she. But she was a damn good friend to her friends."

Jacky spoke vehemently. I could think of no reply. I had not told Jacky my last name—had I?—but this question seemed to suggest that she knew who I was. After a moment Jacky lurched from her chair and groped about in a cupboard and retrieved a bottle of Jamaican rum and poured an inch or two of dark liquid into her mug and drank thirstily. She smiled, with relief. She smiled and winked at me. Close up I saw now that her crimson lipstick was chipped. Her nails were broken and uneven and nothing like Zoe Kruller's perfect nails.

Out on West Ferry a dump truck lumbered past. The house vibrated like something alive, shivering. Somewhere up the street boys were shouting. It was a neighborhood of continuous noise, noises: a *mixed neighborhood* as my mother would say carefully. Not a *safe neighborhood*.

Jacky was glancing past my head now, distracted. It seemed urgent to her to keep speaking: "—eleven, you said? Or—twelve? And you live out—by the river? Huron Road?"

I was hurt to realize that Jacky DeLucca wasn't really so interested in me, only in my presence. As if she wanted badly not to be alone.

"'Mrs. Kruller'—the lady who lived here, who died—she was a friend of my mother's." I spoke suddenly, defiantly. Why these words came to me I have no idea. "Yes. She was."

"Oh—she was? Well—good."

"My mother's name is Lucille. Lucille Diehl."

"'Diehl.' Oh."

Jacky regarded me with widened eyes. Startled and distrustful eyes. As you would look at someone who has just surprised you by saying something wholly unexpected, and unlikely.

"You're their daughter, are you. 'Diehl.'"

"My father's name is Eddy Diehl."

"Yes. 'Eddy.' I knew—I know—'Eddy,' too."

Clumsily Jacky poured more rum into her mug, and drank. I was waiting for her to offer rum to me, but she did not. Her face was so amazing in its smeared smudged clownish glamour, her eyes so glassy-bright, it was painful to look at her, as at a picture too close to your eyes, but impossible to look away. She reminded me of one of my mother's older, widowed aunts—a woman made permanently bereaved by the loss of her husband, whom I scarcely knew; a woman in continuous need of attention, affection. It was not enough to be hugged by Aunt Marlene once, you must be hugged by her twice, three times. You must be kissed numerous times. There was no way to fill the hole in Aunt Marlene's heart, you wanted finally to push away from her, run away from her, call back to her *Leave me alone, I hate you* except you were not so cruel, and you did not hate Aunt Marlene only just Aunt Marlene's terrible need. And here was Jacky DeLucca breathing heavily, pressing the edge of her hand against her bosom like an aggrieved woman in a late-night TV film. Despite the kitchen odors I could smell the perfumy-sweaty odor of Jacky's flesh, her clothes that needed laundering; I could smell the rum. A sweet cloying delicious smell it seemed to me. I thought *She is a friend of Daddy's, too. Daddy has been here where I am now.*

All this while I was drinking the scummy hot chocolate Jacky had prepared from a mix on the stove. Afterward for hours my mouth would throb with a pleasurable hurt.

"Zoe was my closest friend, see. Zoe was my sister, like. Zoe and I had known each other from—oh Christ years ago. Before she was married, even. Ohhh that Delray Kruller! The way Delray is now, you'd never know how Delray was then, him and Zoe, she was just a kid fifteen-sixteen years old when they met, and crazy for him, and Delray was crazy for her except—you know—these 'mixed-blood' guys—it's said they get the worst of the Seneca blood, that can be blind crazy scary as hell, and the worst of the Caucasians—the 'whites'—that's *us*—the white race is pretty damn crazy too, y'know—like—Nazis? Germans? Vikings—is it? They'd as soon hang you upside-down and light a 'pire'—fire—in the name of religion, or whatever"—Jacky floundered, uncertain what she was talking about; then recalled—"that Delray! He was damn good-looking, that Indian-hatchet face, and that Indian-black hair that's so sexy, you'd be surprised to learn that he was—he is—only one-fourth Indian—that's what Zoe said—Delray's actual father was some kind of—Aust-ian?—like, German?—'Kruller' is some kind of—I forget what it is, but that side of Delray is not Seneca Indian, for sure. And Zoe, she was always so beautiful, at least she was to me, some fat pig like me, Jesus!—there's Zoe like some kind of—what's it—fairy—with wings—just kind of flitting around—you wouldn't be able to catch anything like that in your hands—I mean, you'd have to grab it, and squeeze hard, or it would get away. There were people—still are—who never thought that Zoe was anything special, with those freckles. The two of them, on Delray's Harley-Davidson. Zoe is a little younger than me. She was real young when they hooked up, could be Delray 'violated' some statute—some law—like it is called 'statue-tory rape'—meaning under-age girl—'jail bait'—but Zoe was sure willing, and Zoe was hot to get married, she got pregnant with Delray's baby that was like, for her, finding Christ in your heart—y'know? Like for other people finding their savior in their heart, that's how it was for Zoe. Why she got married so young, dropped out of school, and had her baby—Aaron—so young—you'd see the two of them, like a few years ago, you'd think for sure they were a sister and kid brother, not mother and son. I mean, you'd never think that Zoe had a kid that old, and that size, as Aaron!" Jacky paused, smiling. Jacky poured more rum into her mug and drank slowly.

Another time there was a sound of shouts in the street, but Jacky didn't seem to hear. "Hell it's true, Zoe and I were not always friends. Zoe and Jacky were not always 'sisters.' Men will come between you, in certain circumstances. Once Zoe left Delray, and it didn't work out with—y'know—Eddy Diehl—once that did not work out as she'd thought—there was tension between us having to do with men. Because there was always a man—there was always men—interested in Zoe. She had a wild streak, nobody can blame *me*. Once she got onstage and singing and the audiences loved her, it got too hard to say *no*. Ask who turned Zoe onto drugs, it wasn't *me*. Nor heavy drinking, either. I mean, we were drinking back in high school, guys supplied us. Guys supplied us with pot, speed, 'coke.' Not 'crack cocaine'—that came later. Now, high school kids are into that shit, but not us. We'd drink beer, and pass out. We'd smoke pot, and pass out. We were like—'flower children'! We were kind of innocent, back then. I grew up a half-mile from Zoe, on North Fork Road. We'd walk to the school bus stop together. Later, we got rides with guys together. Zoe could be the sweetest thing, but kind of devious. She'd never say what she wanted but she'd get her way. A kind of corkscrew way. Her family was the Hawksons. They could've taken her in—when she kind of collapsed, and came here to live with me—but they wouldn't. 'Washed their hands' of Zoe was the word. The fuckers! Call themselves Christians—'Presbatyrians'—the worst kind of prigs. Well, things I would not have done, ever—guys I wouldn't have broken promises to, ever—Zoe did. She had a dangerous way of thinking that, sexy as she was, good-looking and a girl country-and-western singer with a band, she'd be forgiven for doing things that others of us, not so good-looking, with maybe not so sexy a figure and not so great a voice, would not." Jacky paused, shaking her jowly face with a look of bulldog satisfaction. Then she continued, in a higher-pitched voice as if confronting her accusers: "There's people blame me, Zoe's God-damn family blames me, that I was the one turned her onto hard drugs—heroin—Jesus!—that's a joke. God damn hyper-crites—hypocrites?—saying such things about me to the police, quoted in the damn newspaper, coming right out and saying—this 'woman friend' of Zoe Kruller—this 'Jacqueline DeLucca'—she is to be held re-sponsible for Zoe 'going bad.' Bullshit! That is such crude, cruel bullshit! Between her and Del, whatever it was, how'd I have anything to do with that?—or Zoe quitting her dairy job 'cause she was God-damned bored there she said, the smell of milk was making her puke, not to mention you never get tips in a job like that having to wait half the time on God-damn fucking *kids*. And if there's no liquor license in a place, forget it. 'Cause you are not going to get fucking tips. You are not. Especially around here, in the Adirondacks where there's a scarcity of jobs. So, out on the strip, Zoe could make serious money. At the Tip Top, at Chet's Keyboard, Zoe was real popular, made more tips than any of the cocktail waitresses, but she was hoping to get a gig there singing, and there was the hope that her band—Black River Breakdown—would get a recording contract, one of these days. That never happened, but it could have. And on the Strip, guys were tripping over one another's feet to get to Zoe to buy her a drink, or dinner, or take her to Montreal, or Atlantic City, or Vegas—which was where she was going, to Vegas, with some new man friend she'd only just met. At least that was Zoe's belief, when"—Jacky paused as if a bad taste had come into her mouth, she had no choice but to swallow it down—"it happened. But see, Zoe never needed *me*. Sure I introduced her to a few guys, guys I knew like Csaba, who owns Chet's Keyboard Lounge, and some other guys out on the Strip, 'cause I know them, and they know me, and they wanted to meet Zoe. And these guys, out on the Strip, that frequent the clubs, and have money, they're not guys from Sparta, weren't born here and didn't know Delray Kruller, never heard of him. 'Kruller Cycle Shop'—'Kruller Auto Repair'—nothing they ever heard of, or gave a damn about. Things that are such a big deal in Sparta—in some circles in Sparta—people don't know anything about nor give a damn about elsewhere. Sure some of the guys must've known that Zoe was married, or used to be married, but—so what? She'd tell them she was 'separated,' she was filing for 'divorce.' No way anybody could guess her husband was a kind of dangerous hothead—part-Seneca Indian, and a drinker—or if they knew, they didn't take it seriously or give a damn, like I said none of them would've known *Delray Kruller*, who he was. Zoe was hoping this trip she was going on—to Vegas—might lead to something more permanent, not that Zoe wanted to get married again—she did not—but, say, if a man wanted to invest in Zoe's singing career, and kind of take care of her—that, she'd have liked. There was a way of Zoe being so hopeful, like a young girl sometimes. Could've been your age! 'I need a change of scene, Jacky,' Zoe told me, 'I feel like there is another world somewhere else, waiting for me. Ohhh I feel like I will suffocate here.'" In mimicry of her friend Jacky spoke in a low throaty girlish voice. A look of slow-delayed horror came into her face. "I just can't believe that Zoe is—gone. There was nobody more alive than Zoe, of anybody I knew. And now—to think—that"—Tears came into Jacky's eyes, compulsively she caressed her bruised, soft-raddled throat. "It was my belief that Delray was making trouble for Zoe again. 'Cause he was still in love with her—he'd always been crazy for her, and Zoe was crazy for him—except, you know, how things get in the way—'intervene'—he'd go through a spell he was agreed they could get divorced, then he'd change his mind, and stall, and Delray, or one of Delray's friends, would turn up where Zoe was, like 'stalking' her. Zoe told me, 'Anything bad happens to me, Jacky, it will be Delray.' I told the police this but so far as I know they have not arrested him, or anybody, only just questioned him and let him go—took him into 'custody' then let him go—it's been how long now, since February? How many weeks? My God! Poor Zoe! You can know a thing like your friend is gone but—you can't believe it, somehow. I keep thinking that Zoe will come down the stairs there—right through there, see?—the stairs—sleepy and yawning or maybe all dressed up, in her high heels, looking good, and some guy is coming in a few minutes to pick her up, and I'm asking when is she going to be back, does she have any idea, and Zoe laughs and says, 'When I'm good and ready to be back, Jacky. Just like you.' That night, Krista, it was my fault maybe, I was away. That night and half the next day. This guy, this friend of mine from Watertown, just showed up and wanted to see me, wanted to party, I was with him when Zoe was killed here, at that very hour I was miles away. I have given the police my statement about this. I didn't get back to Sparta until around noon and by that time this place was all opened up like there'd been a fire and police were here and poor Zoe—her body—had been taken away to—I guess—the county morgue. Just like that! I come up the walk here and there's this big barrel-chested guy looking at me—'Jacqueline De-Lucca, is that your name?' with a look in his face like he's smelling something bad. Because they'd been looking through this house, in all the rooms, that wasn't so clean, I guess, and talking to neighbors. Because they judge you, sons of bitches just looking at you, thinking they know you. Thinking they can put a name to you—'hooker,' 'whore.' This detective is saying to me, 'Jacqueline DeLucca, you will come with us' not even giving me time to take in what had happened to my friend, no time to cry for Zoe, I was in such shock they were telling me she'd been murdered, 'There's been a homicide here, this is a homicide scene' they were saying, nobody gave a damn how I was crying, I was close to fainting with the shock of it, and them not letting me go upstairs—not letting me into my own house—my health is not so good—I have had 'complications' after some surgery—my blood pressure is high—there is diabetes in my family I am so afraid of getting—shaking and crying and the Sparta PD bastards did not give a damn like I was not sincere in my grief for Zoe—'Chill it, Jacky. Tone it down'—like they knew me, and had a right to call me Jacky. I had to stay with friends, couldn't even return to my own house for days, and then I had to—nobody warned me—*I had to clean Zoe's bedroom.* You would think the police or somebody would do that awful work but no, you must do it yourself no matter how exhausted and grief-stricken. And now, I can't even go upstairs. I sleep downstairs on a couch. I can't sleep anyway, it's like whoever came in here and hurt Zoe the way he did has hurt me, my heart pounds sometimes so hard I think it will burst. I keep thinking—what if he comes back, to kill me? What if he does the terrible things to me, he did to Zoe? The police say that I have to tell them everything I know, all the men's names, they've had me looking at photographs, till I am exhausted. I was begging them, 'I don't want to die, officers! You can't protect me every hour of my life.' I told them that, and I told them that I knew of 'police witnesses' who were killed, and they looked at me like I was scum, and they said, 'If you don't tell us all that you know you can be arrested, Jacky,'—'cause they'd found some drugs in the house, only just painkillers, and a nickel bag of coke. There's a law, they said, about 'controlled substances' on the premises, saying I am going to be charged with narcotics possession with intention to distribute if I don't cooperate. A charge like that, you can be incarcerated for twenty years! Right then I near-about broke down. I could hardly get to a bathroom in time. They were more disgusted than I was, like I was sick to my stomach on purpose. What disgusts me is—if there is less than one hundred dollars' narcotics in this house—that came in with Zoe, and not with me—it is any kind of big deal compared to all the thousands of dollars these guys sell every day, all across the state, that the cops know about, and are getting a percentage of? Like they need to go after Jacky De-Lucca, to tell them what they already know! As if I would give them the names of my friends. And the ones who are not my friends, I would be crazy to give them. I had the shakes so bad! Damn cops have no sympathy for a person like me, a woman who is not a wife or a mother, saying, 'You need to go into rehab, Jacky. You're a drunk and a junkie'—saying such insults, to my face. 'You're going to wind up like your friend Zoe, unless you cooperate with us.' I told them that I didn't know every single thing about Zoe's private life, and this is so. I didn't know who the man was, Zoe's new friend she was so hopeful about, or even if he was a 'new' friend or some guy she'd been seeing in the past. Because Zoe was like that, if she broke up with a guy he wouldn't go away, exactly. Like Delray did not ever go away, he was always trying to get back together with her. And Zoe had another man friend—I won't say his name, Krista—he was a married man and crazy for her, she said, but there was 'no future' with him, he would not ever leave his family. His wife he might leave, but not his children, he just could not. So Zoe said it was hopeless and didn't want to see him, but he'd call her, and he'd come around, they were like each other's bad habit, that couldn't be shaken. This man's name, I had to give to the police—they'd have found out anyway, and make trouble for me. I was so scared, they would arrest me on 'obstruction of justice'—'interfering with a police investigation.' They never did believe me that I didn't know the man's name—the one who was taking her to Vegas, that Zoe was so hopeful about. One night at Chet's she was invited to sing with the jazz players there—just three of them—and Zoe was asked to sing—'Both Sides Now' was one of her best songs—and this guy is at the bar listening, he's impressed he says, really impressed—he can arrange for an audition for her in Vegas at one of the casinos he says, where he has contacts. So I think it was the next day, they were headed for Vegas. I think that's what Zoe told me. She was saying, 'Maybe I won't ever come back, Jacky!'— kind of excited, kissing my cheek and hugging me and too nervous to sit still, 'Tell Aaron good-bye from his mom, and for sure I will be calling him, maybe in a few months I will be a headliner there, at one of the casinos, I can send a plane ticket for Aaron and he can come join me.' So I said sure Zoe, I would do that. And Zoe says, 'And you too, Jacky—you can come visit me in Vegas' like it's going to happen, the way people talk when they're high. When you are high you are *hopeful*. Take away the high and you take away *hope*. And that night . . . Jesus!" Jacky paused, wiping at her mascara-smeared eyes with a paper napkin. On her cheeks were streaks of something ashy-dark like muddy tears. "I don't know what is worse—to think that, if I'd been here, and I wasn't, Zoe would not have been killed; or, if I'd been here, and this guy came for Zoe, he'd have killed me, too. I tried to tell the police this, but they just kept asking me the same questions. Like I *did not know* the man from Vegas's name, or if I did, it didn't sink in. And this guy I was with that night, we drove over to the Oneida casino where he got drunk and lost big at blackjack— staked me to five hundred dollars which I wish to hell I'd saved some out of instead of losing it all—like I said when you get *high* you get *hopeful* and that fucks you up. The thing was, the name he gave me was a fake name it turned out, 'Cornell George Hardy' he called himself like he was from a classy family but the police found out that wasn't his name, naturally they act like I was the one who made it up—'Cornell George Hardy.' Says he was some kind of 'investment banker' in Syracuse—he'd turn up some-times, weekends—stayed at a big suite at the Marriott, he'd have parties— lots of coke, he was generous with—how'd I know that 'Cornell George Hardy' wasn't his name? First thing, I'd thought he was saying 'Colo-nel'—like in the army. Or is it navy? But it wasn't 'Colonel' it was 'Cor-nell.' Anyway it was a fake. But we had good times together. He treated me O.K. He wasn't a mean drunk but got funny-sad and sleepy. Police checked with the desk clerk at the motel we stayed in to see if I was tell-ing them the truth and it turns out I am, so why'd they need to even know the name of the guy I was with, if 'Cornell George Hardy' was with me all night and I was with him? No matter his name he couldn't be the one who'd hurt Zoe—could he? No more than I could be! So, finally they let

me go. 'We ain't gonna bust you, Jacky. We're homicide not vice.' Ha-*ha*.
How'd I get back here that day?—had to call some guy I knew, woke him
in the middle of the day and asked him to get me. Bastards wouldn't even
drive me. Because I didn't know where else to go. Because if I went home,
my mother would say, 'Jacqueline, Jesus can help you if you give Him
room in your heart.' This is scary to me, I believe that my mother is probably right but it isn't the time for Jesus in my heart right now—there is too
much else there. I am not worthy. Most days I feel just so sick about Zoe.
Oh God, I mean losing Zoe. My closest friend and my sister Zoe. And
there was poor Zoe's blood smeared on the wall. Soaked into the bed. All
the bedclothes, she'd borrowed from me. There was a nice pink comforter.
And he'd strangled her, too—with a towel, they said. Some people would
say with his hands but that was not correct, it was with a towel. And he'd
hit her head so bad, he cracked the skull. That caused all the blood. A
head wound bleeds like hell, the detective said. He said whoever did it
used the towel like a 'garrote'—you can tighten, and loosen, and tighten
again. He'd hit her with something like a claw hammer, they said. They
did not find this hammer on the premises. The killer took it with him,
threw it into the river probably and it will never be found. Who'd ever
find it? They were asking did I keep a hammer in the house and I told
them no, I didn't think so, but the house is rented, it might've been in the
cellar or some closet somewhere. But if he'd brought it with him into the
house it would mean that he'd meant to kill her ahead of time and this
really scared me—maybe he'd come back, and kill *me*? This guy opened
a window, they said, so snow was blown into the bedroom so the air was
real cold and Zoe's body got to be part-frozen they said, and he'd pulled
some covers up over her, and some of her clothes he covered her with,
and—this makes me shiver—he took talcum powder of mine, white talcum powder—'White Shoulders'—he sprinkled on Zoe, and on the
bed—all over. On the walls where the blood was wet and sticky, and it
froze there. And all over the floor. He'd tracked his footprints in it on the
floor. So it looked like a 'frost' the cops said. First thing they thought it
had to be coke, cocaine—but no, 'White Shoulders'—that smells like lily

of the valley—talcum powder Zoe shared with me. And this powder everywhere mixed in with blood, I had to clean up, too. I was sobbing, and trembling, this was so awful! I couldn't just vacuum up the powder— the blood would've gotten inside the vacuum and ruined it. Had to use paper towels, a sponge mop, till I got sick, and now I am not going up- stairs anymore . . . not anywhere near that room, not ever. 'Why'd he do that, with the talcum powder,' I asked the detective, the one who's always looking at me like there's a bad smell on me, but he's kind of teasing and smirking, too, and calls me 'Jacky' like we are old friends—his name is Egloff—I never heard of any 'Egloff' and wonder what nationality it is—I don't like him, and I don't trust him—and he says, 'Why'd any of them do anything, there's no logic to what an animal will do.' A sneer in his face like he's thinking *Friends of yours, aren't they?*

Or, *Hell Jacky, you're an animal too, right?* Once he laid his big meat- hand on my arm like it was an accident but I pretended not to notice. The worst thing, Krista, I try not to think about—Zoe's son Aaron was the one who found her. He's a sad kid anyway, takes after his father with that look of Indian melancholy—'heavy-heartedness'—a kind of blunt hatchet-face like mixed-blood guys have—first look you have of them they're ugly and hurtful just to see, next look you have they are kind of— well, good-looking, sexy. I mean even this kid, who's just a kid. 'Cause he's tall already, like a man. Or almost. They said Aaron came over here around nine that morning—it's a Sunday—kids get up early, I guess—he hadn't seen his mother in a while he said so he came over here, he's not old enough to drive so he walked, two-three miles it must be, the front door is unlocked so he pushes it open, walks inside and—he says—right away he 'knew something was wrong'—'could smell something bad'—he stood downstairs and called for Zoe and there was no answer—he thought she might be asleep, if she was there at all, so he went upstairs . . . Dear God, imagine finding her! Imagine, if you were Zoe's son! A few hours later it would've been me, walking into Zoe's room . . . She used to say how guilty she felt about Aaron, it wasn't really meant for her to be a mother so young, she'd dropped out of high school and married Delray who was older than her by six or seven years but still a hotheaded kid himself. Not that Zoe didn't love her baby but she never felt she'd been meant to be a mother just then. Like Delray wasn't meant to be a father. Del had these two Seneca Indian cousins he got in tight with and spent time in the juvie facility up at Black River, that Zoe said she didn't know anything about except what he told her, that wasn't the entire truth, see—one of Del's cousins was in for *manslaughter second degree* which off the rez might've been *murder second degree* but they don't give much of a shit for what a drunk Indian will do to another drunk Indian, it would be a different story if one of them stomped a white man to death, right?—so Zoe was always kind of wondering about that, to what degree Del was involved in that *manslaughter* and it scared her, for sure—when a guy drinks and has that background, you don't know what direction it will take him in. 'If I'd had a singing career first, then I could have a baby, right about now when I'm in my thirties I'd be fine with that,' Zoe used to say, 'but being a mother when you're just a kid yourself gets in the way of your life, you know?' and I said, 'Well, Zoe—I wouldn't know.' I laughed to show that I wasn't hurt, hell I wasn't hurt, I said, 'Maybe if my baby had lived, my life would've turned out better,' and Zoe grabbed me and kissed me saying, 'Oh Jacky, I am so sorry. I didn't mean to say such a thing. But Jacky, who knows?— maybe your life would've suffocated you. No baby ever saved anybody's life that I ever heard of.' I'd known Aaron when he was just a baby—dark-skinned and kind of fierce-looking with this coarse dark hair like some little rat—he'd cry so hard and get purple-faced but without actual tears just bellowing like a baby calf and kicking and you'd think *If that baby had teeth, he'd bite*. And Zoe laughed saying Aaron sucked so hard when he was nursing, he'd near-about knock her over, and it *hurt*. Almost any baby you see it's a beautiful baby in some way but not Aaron until he was older—four or five—his face wasn't so squished-together as he got older and his eyes not so crossed-looking. I didn't know Zoe too well then but I think there was some trouble about Aaron starting school—he had some 'reading disability'—*dixlia*? Took after his father with that short temper and thin skin like *he's* the one insulted or hurt, not you. 'It's the Krullers,'

Zoe said. 'Not just Del's mixed-blood relatives but all of them. Like a clan. Don't give a damn for how they trod over your feelings but the least thing you say to them, like *Excuse me! I hope I am not bleeding on your new clothes!* they take offense and flare up. Or they are hurt, their damn heart is broken and they need to break your heart, to even the score. They need to punish you.' It was a surprise to me to see Aaron Kruller in February, when he was at the police station same time I was, Jesus!—he'd grown so tall, and looked a lot older than his age. That's like the Senecas—you see a girl who could be eighteen, turns out she's ten or eleven. It isn't breasts they grow but muscles, and they're built like fire hydrants. Aaron isn't an easy boy to like, I have to say. I feel damn sorry for him and offered to make him some supper but he said no thanks not even looking at me. I'm kind of scared, this big kid hating me. Like all the Krullers hate me, like I am to blame for Zoe leaving home. Because Zoe and me, we'd go places together, in my car. When Zoe was desperate about Del, and this married man she'd been seeing kind of shook her off, or she shook him off, that was a bad time for Zoe and she came to me and what would I do, turn Zoe away? Zoe was my heart, I would *never*."

In a rush of words Jacky DeLucca spoke, so agitated she seemed almost to have forgotten me. And now she wiped her smudged eyes and stared at me. "'Krista'—'Krissie'—you said—you are his daughter—Eddy Diehl, I mean—yes? It must be a sign, you're here—you came here, to see me—"

Quickly I said that I had to leave. The florid-faced woman with the dyed-beet hair frizzed about her head was exhausting to me as if she'd sucked all the oxygen out of the air between us.

"No, sweetie—wait! Not just yet."

Jacky heaved herself to her feet, teetering. She smiled a sweet-goofy-lopsided smile at me as if about to swoop over me and kiss me but with panicked dexterity I eluded her. The man's flannel shirt gaped open, Jacky's enormous milky-white blue-veined left breast nearly swung free like an extra appendage, alarming to see at close range. I did not want Jacky to hug me, to feel those big breasts like foam rubber. "Krissie, stay still. You're the sweetest kid, you are polite and you *listen*. There is somebody coming today—I think—he might be here at any time—you could help me, Krissie, you could tell him 'Jacky is not here right now,' you could tell him 'Jacky is staying with her sister now, in Port Oriskany.' Can you do that for me, Krissie? Sweetie? He won't try to come inside, he'll just be at the back door here, if he sees you inside, what you can tell him is you are my niece—and your mother is upstairs—can you do this for me, Krissie? Please!—for Zoe's sake, too."

I was frightened, the urgency in Jacky's voice. So all this time she'd been waiting for someone—that was why she'd wanted me with her—her hot damp skin beaded with oily sweat, her pleading eyes. The smell of rum was powerful, heady. I wanted to flee Jacky yet at the same time had an urge to press into her arms, press into the foam-rubber body. I stammered again that I had to leave, my mother would miss me and worry about where I'd gone. "Thank you for the hot chocolate, it was delicious," I said, "—and the cookies!—the cookies were delicious. Good-bye." Running for the door as in clumsy haste, surprisingly agile once she was able to get to her feet, Jacky tried to embrace me. "Krissie! Just a little hug, sweetie! We're friends now, aren't we? Sure." At the door Jacky managed to grab hold of my arm, my skinny upper arm, I had not been quick enough. Her fingers were strong as a man's fingers, I thought. I did not try to wrest away, I knew she would hurt me, in the flesh of my skinny upper arm there would be the imprint of Jacky DeLucca's fingers. With a loud laugh—a sad, reproachful laugh—Jacky kissed the top of my head, and released me.

"Promise you'll come back to see me, Krissie? Your friend Jacky De-Lucca."

Somehow, I promised *yes*.

In the alley, half-running. And then running! Through mud puddles where black-feathered birds had been splashing and bathing, along the alley littered with trash, in the fresh damp air of spring where even tossed-out garbage rotting underfoot smelled good.

* * *

"KRISTA? What is that stain on your sweater?"

Guiltily I looked down—was it a hot chocolate stain? Or a smear—a smudge—from something greasy in Jacky DeLucca's kitchen? Something like a dirty flower, my mother pointed at with a look of disgust.

"I hope it isn't blood. Did you cut yourself somehow?"

"No! I—"

"It looks like blood. Oh, Krista! I can't trust you, old as you are. Come here."

Forcibly my mother led me to the kitchen sink where she dabbed frantically at the front of my sweater with a wetted towel, fussing and scolding. I saw how the part in her hair was crooked, how there were gray hairs especially near her scalp, nothing like Jacky DeLucca's dark-dyed glamour-hair. And Mom's smell—a harsh prim Dutch Cleanser–smell—was nothing like Jacky DeLucca's. In these weeks following my father's moving out of our house and the disruption of our lives my mother often behaved unpredictably with Ben and me, flaring up in anger and disgust, weeping over our flaws, or, unaccountably, clutching at us as if we were precious to her, and vulnerable. "Well—I guess it isn't blood, it's coming out. At least you didn't hurt yourself, Krista, wherever you were all afternoon." With exasperated tenderness my mother hugged me—stooped over me, and hugged me—lightly kissed the top of my head—in the very place that Jacky DeLucca had kissed me, less than an hour before—and for a long moment held me tight in her tremulous arms.

Friends now aren't we Krissie.

Promise you'll come back to see me, Krissie. Your friend Jacky DeLucca.

15

"EDWARD DIEHL? We need to speak with you."

These grim-uttered words that would change my father's life forever.

The ruin of my father's life that was a wholly ordinary American-male life of its time and place, indistinguishable in its externals from how many hundreds of thousands of other American-male lives, none of us who loved him would have wished to think.

The time was early: 7:15 A.M. The morning of February 13, 1983.

The place, a terribly public place: Eddy Diehl's office at Sparta Construction, 991 Reservoir Street, Sparta.

God had spared him Sunday, at least.

He'd known, certainly. He had known that Sparta police would come looking for him. As soon as he'd heard the news about Zoe, he'd known.

Such stunning news—awful news—such a shock to Eddy Diehl he hadn't been able to comprehend it fully, at first. Like a drunk man, staggering. A drunk man hit over the head with a sledgehammer.

Zoe is dead? But—when? Why?

Repeating as if it were a riddle *Zoe is dead! Zoe is—dead!*

No, he could not comprehend it. He had to have a drink, two drinks—he could not have functioned otherwise.

Driving along the Black River. Driving reckless as a blind man. The driver's window was partway lowered despite the cold, freezing wind whipping at his tear-streaked face he'd somehow needed, to shock him into comprehension.

A part of his brain had been stunned but another, shrewder part of his brain understood that since Eddy Diehl had been "involved with" Zoe Kruller, and others had known of it, for it was impossible that others should not know of it despite the lovers' attempts at secrecy, homicide detectives would want to question him; but he couldn't know when.

If he'd been able to think a little more clearly, he might have gone voluntarily to the police. This would have established Eddy Diehl's wish to aid in the police investigation and this would have suggested Eddy Diehl's innocence.

This would have suggested Eddy Diehl's shock and grief, at the loss of Zoe Kruller.

But Zoe was a married woman, or had been; and Eddy Diehl was a married man. Eddy had a young son, a younger daughter. He felt such sympathy for his wife, commingled with guilt like the taste of something rotted and poisonous in his mouth, oh how Lucille would be humiliated!— shamed! Lucille would never survive this, the public nature of her husband's betrayal.

For Eddy Diehl did feel, yes he'd betrayed his wife. His family. He was an adulterous man, he'd had other sexual liaisons with other women, of a more ephemeral nature, some of them single-occasion incidents, it was not the fact of *adultery* that distressed him but the fact that others would know, and Lucille would be exposed, broken.

And his children: Ben, Krista. He had not wanted to leave Lucille to live with Zoe Kruller though he'd been in love with Zoe Kruller, he hadn't been able to think of leaving his children. He was an adulterer, a heavy drinker, a *hard man* as others saw him disapprovingly or admiringly, but in his deepest self he was a *father*, he took *fatherhood* seriously as his own father had taken it, a sacred trust, an inviolable bond. Thinking when the call came and he'd hung up the phone at early midday of that Sunday she'd been found by her son Aaron *God spare me just today, then tomorrow will be . . .*

If he was spared being taken into police custody on Sunday, at his home on the Huron Pike Road, in the presence of his wife and children, then he would come willingly with police on Monday morning. Though he wasn't a believer in God yet in his desperation he seemed to believe this bargain. As in Vietnam in times of terror he'd postulated similar bargains with the far-away and improbable Father-God he had ceased to take seriously as an adolescent.

On the door of his small office at Sparta Construction was a plaque of some synthetic substance meant to suggest walnut: EDWARD DIEHL, MANAGER. How proud Lucille had been of this promotion, this office, the plaque, frequently at first she'd visited him in his office, she'd brought the children, it had been an occasion. *This is Daddy's office, this is Daddy's desk. See, this is Daddy's name on the door. . . .*

This pride, Eddy Diehl would surrender. If he had but the Sunday of Zoe Kruller's actual death to remain a free man.

"I can never forgive him. Letting me find out the way he did. *That* was betrayal."

Of the many bitter accusations my mother would make against my father one was that, though evidently he'd learned about Zoe's death by one-thirty of that Sunday afternoon, he left the house without telling her.

Abruptly and with no explanation he walked out of the house without saying where he was going or when he'd be back though he'd had to have known that "Edward Diehl" was sure to be involved in the police investigation.

And so, through most of that day we hadn't known. My mother, Ben, me. We had no idea of how news of Zoe Kruller's murder was spreading through Sparta swift as wildfire in some quarters, before even local radio and TV bulletins began to be broadcast; a network of friends, relatives, former high school classmates of Zoe and Delray, telephoning one another with the astonishing news. Not *A woman murdered on West Ferry Street* but *Zoe Kruller murdered in that place she'd been living away from her family.*

And in tones of shock tinctured with reproach *The life Zoe had been living, something like this was bound to happen. . . .*

By late Sunday afternoon it was beginning to be known that Delray

Kruller, the "estranged" husband, had been brought to Sparta PD headquarters to be questioned about his wife's death and by Sunday night it was beginning to be said that Delray had "confessed' to the murder.

Not to the murder, but to "hurting" Zoe.

This would not be reported in the media except as a rumor and would turn out to be false. But Eddy Diehl believed it, at the time. He'd reacted with shock, fury, guilt—if Delray had killed Zoe, it was because of *him*.

Delray! That son of a bitch he'd had to be drunk . . .

The shit he'd been taking from her God damn fucker . . .

Now he's fucked, what'd he think this would solve . . .

Eddy Diehl had had to leave the house, he'd been so upset. Taking with him in the Jeep a six-pack of Molson's ale. He'd given his wife the impression that something had gone wrong at one of the home construction sites, his boss was calling on him to check it out, it was like Paul Cassano to call Eddy Diehl at such times—"emergencies"—and if Eddy didn't get back in time for Sunday dinner, Lucille would understand.

Lucille wouldn't like it, but Lucille would understand.

For in construction, something is always *hitting a snag*. More than one thing at a time can be *hitting a snag*. Especially when the electricians have begun to be involved, when the building is nearing completion. Plumbers, roofers, electricians. The more men involved, the more likelihood of problems. Lucille had grown resigned to this, to a degree. She was wary of her husband's mood, his temper when his boss Cassano called him on weekends, she didn't question his having to leave the house on short notice as she did not question—usually—where he'd gone after visiting the work site, and why he'd stayed away so late. Sometimes, Eddy had drinks with clients, going out for a few drinks was "business" and wholly justified, even Sundays. As the night before—that Saturday night, before Zoe's death early Sunday morning—Eddy Diehl had been out, he'd returned around midnight it was claimed, stumbling upstairs to bed.

With who, can't remember.

Just some guys. Different places.

Go back to sleep, Lucille. Where I've been is my own God-damned business.

"How can I forgive him! He hadn't the courage to tell me. He let me discover it for myself, the big headlines in the paper, Zoe's picture all over, 'male visitors' . . ."

My father had the idea that Zoe Kruller had been killed at around midnight but in fact, as the Herkimer County medical examiner was to determine, Zoe had died sometime between 1 A.M. and 4 A.M. early Sunday morning. It was difficult to estimate a more precise time of death since a window had been left open in the dead woman's bedroom and her body had been partly frozen. In his benumbed and despairing state Eddy Diehl would endure Sunday. Driving the Jeep along the river without knowing where he was going, or why—turning abruptly onto blacktop roads leading into the countryside, north into the foothills of the Adirondacks following such roads blindly and with an air of desperation until he realized that no, this was not what he wanted, here was a false direction, pavement disintegrating into gravel, and gravel disintegrating into rutted frozen mud. He was drinking as he drove—six cans of Molson's ale—feeling then an acute need to stop at one or another of those country taverns where in twilit interiors not unlike lighted caves men sat at bars and drank, talked together, or did not wish to talk, staring at TV sports through the long bleak winter day.

"Diehl? Hey."

At the County Line Tavern, Deke Jones he'd known since high school tending bar and staring at Eddy Diehl who'd had to know—hadn't he?— that Delray Kruller had confessed to killing his wife Zoe?—the men talked together in low urgent tones as Deke poured Eddy a drink and with a shaking hand Eddy lifted the glass to his mouth and drank. It was known—others in the County Line, at the bar, who knew Eddy Diehl would know this, and might have been talking of it before he'd come into the bar—from his edgy agitated state Eddy Diehl assumed this, that others were observing him, knew of him and Zoe and the likelihood that, if Delray had killed Zoe, it was the consequence of an action that had begun with Eddy Diehl. "Jesus, Eddy! Some shitty news." Deke poured the grieving man another shot of Jim Beam.

He drank. At the County Line, and at the Riverview Inn, and at the Grotto in East Sparta. He drank without becoming drunk nor even, he was sure, mildly intoxicated, distracted; he could not drink enough to stop his thoughts *This can't have happened! Fuck Zoe this is some damn trick of hers. Don't believe this, this is bullshit.*

In this way Sunday passed. A turbulent dream of such vivid wakefulness Eddy Diehl might have believed that he himself had died. His stubbled jaws ached with the strain of all that he wanted to protest but could not. There was a ringing in his ears and he'd been sweating inside his clothes and winded like a horse that has been whipped and made to run nearly to death. His lungs ached, his sides heaved. He was running/ stumbling through a snowy parking lot, to the Jeep. His breath was steaming, a trickle of sweat like blood ran down his face from his left temple. Maybe Zoe was in the Jeep: curled up in the passenger's seat her stockinged feet beneath her, small warm squirmy little feet he'd loved to hold in his hands, tickle the soles of those feet with his big deft thumbs *Ohhh Eddy don't that drives me crazy oh oh oh! Ed-dy!* shuddering as if he'd made her come with just stroking her feet, unless she was only teasing, touching her warm moist tongue to the tip of his tongue, breathing her fumy breath into his mouth except: the cab of the Jeep was empty, no one in the passenger's seat, Zoe Kruller hadn't been in Eddy Diehl's Jeep since December, when they'd broken up.

Through that long Sunday he had not eaten. It wasn't that he had no appetite for food nor that food would have nauseated him but that he had no thought for food at all. He was heedless that Lucille might be waiting for him back at the house, expecting him to return and eat an evening meal with his family. Thinking of Zoe, he could not think of anyone else. He thought *Next news I hear, Zoe will be O.K. And Delray arrested for beating on her. That's all. That's not so bad. I can live with that.*

Wakened by his footsteps on the stairs. Two nights in succession: Saturday, Sunday. Only in retrospect would I know what these nights were. What these nights meant. *It's Daddy. He's home. Now I am safe, I can sleep.*

A child's sense of time is airy, insubstantial. A child can be convinced that something that has happened has happened at a certain time, and not another time, though the child has in fact *lived through that time and is a witness to that time.* A child will believe what he/she is told if he/she is told in the right way and by the right adult.

Now you know there are things that happen inside a house and inside a family that are secret and must never be revealed to anyone outside the family d'you know this, Krista?—yes. *You know.*

So my mother would caution me. Putting her forefinger to my lips to press them shut.

It was a confused time!—like dead leaves blowing in a windstorm, swirling and crazy-seeming so you wanted to shut your eyes, shut your ears and scream *Go away!*

A confused time, and a child's memory is not to be trusted because no child thinks in terms of calendar days, dates. No child thinks in terms of years. No child thinks in logical terms *before, after.* In causal terms *This, following this. This, a consequence of this.* A child may think *This is here, now. This is what is happening, now.*

That Sunday night when my father returned home late—must've been after 11 P.M. when the house was darkened except for a light in the kitchen above the stove and the back porch light which my mother had left on for my father's return, unthinkable at that time it would have been for my mother not to leave a porch light on for my father's return—she was lying in bed uneasy—anxious—not yet distraught for she hadn't seen the local TV news—the "breaking news" of a Sparta woman's murder in the early morning of that Sunday and none of the Bauers had called her for what could have been the pretext for such a call?—an assumption that Lucille would understand what the connection was between Zoe Kruller and herself?—no one would have dared. Even those female relatives of my mother's for whom the task of delivering upsetting news would have been pleasurable had not dared, this was too cruel a matter.

In the dark he stumbled undressing. Cursing under his breath, panting and winded like a great wounded beast: bison, bear. Wounded, and dangerous. Pulling back the covers and falling into bed, his side of the bed, of course he'd been drinking—Eddy Diehl was beyond drunk. In a terse voice Lucille dared to ask where he'd been? and he said nowhere, go back to sleep, and Lucille protested she hadn't been asleep! She'd been lying there waiting for him and he said fuck Lucille, nobody'd asked her to lay there waiting for him, had they?

He was rude, dismissive. He was not apologetic as sometimes, at such drunk-times, out of a memory of the logic of guilt, he was. Too drunk to get completely undressed, in soiled T-shirt and shorts, light wool socks, it had been an enormous effort for him to pull off his damn boots, kick them aside and now on his back on his side of the bed unable to remain still, his leg-muscles beginning to twitch, a sensation as of swarming red ants in his armpits, in his groin, in the sweaty pelt of hair on his chest and his stubbled jaws were clenched tight and his panting breath so labored and erratic it was like trying to sleep with someone whose insides were being torn out. And so Lucille dared to ask again where he'd been? Was something wrong at work?—had there been an accident at a construction site? Was that it?— someone had been hurt, someone had died, at a construction site?

Lucille understood, *someone had died.* In that instant she knew.

He would not reply. He lay with his back to her, the sweat-soaked T-shirt through which tufts of animal-hair protruded, repulsive to the woman who felt at such moments that she was confronting the male body, the very body of *male otherness*, for the first time.

And so, Lucille recoiled in hurt. In resentment, and the beginning of fear. Knowing that what had happened, it was an event that would come between them. For when she turned aside, moving as far from his overheated body in the queen-sized bed as she could, when she recoiled in hurt, and said nothing more, he took no heed, scarcely was he aware of her, she knew *There is nothing in this man's heart for me. I am not even in his thoughts.*

Twenty-two years he'd worked at Sparta Construction, Inc. A single-storey redwood-shingled building on Garrison Road, sprawling lumber-yard/brickyard beyond. Here he was known—"Ed Diehl"—the man you talked to when the owner wasn't around or wasn't answering his phone—

a man much liked by other men, and trusted. And he had his own office now, accessible from the parking lot. By 7 A.M. unlocking this door taking note—objectively, like a scientist—how his God-damn hands shook, a bad sign. Yet with a modicum of calm telling himself *Maybe it won't happen. Or it will happen to someone else. Has happened.*

He'd had a rough night. He'd given up trying to sleep, gone downstairs at about 3 A.M. and sat in the darkened kitchen smoking the last of his Camels and drinking the last of his Molson's ales out of the refrigerator and his throat shut with the wish to sob, there was Zoe Kruller before him smiling her teasing-sweet smile *Well—say! This is a real pretty kitchen you built for your wife, in't it? What've I got to do, Ed-dy darlin, to get you to build such a pretty kitchen for me? Just tell me, dear friend, and I'll do it.*

He'd told her. Laughing he'd told her. And there in Lucille's pretty-pretty kitchen, she'd done it.

Several times he'd brought her to the house on the Huron Pike Road. Knowing that Lucille would be away, and the children at school. Wanting to show the woman his fine-carpentry touches, maple wood cabinets, the high-quality linoleum tile, redwood deck at the rear. Wanting her to see this side of him: husband, father. And the house he'd built for his family, a damn sight nicer house than the one Delray Kruller provided for her.

Just tell me Ed-dy what've I got to do, and I'll do it.

Every time.

This was Zoe in her bluegrass mode. Maybe she meant such words as she uttered them, but only at the moment of utterance.

That day, Jesus!—Krista had walked in.

Krista, home from school at noon, unexpected. And there was Zoe at the kitchen sink rinsing cups, singing to herself, whistling, and he'd been on the stairs, and he'd heard voices in the kitchen and entered in astonishment seeing his young daughter staring at him with a pleading smile—*Daddy? Am I home at the wrong time?*

This was what she'd said, that Eddy recalled. He had no idea how he'd replied.

In his office, he had calls to make. Every day, calls to suppliers, clients, workmen on the payroll. Every day and today would be no different from any other day, he wanted to think.

Except: a quick swallow from the quart of Jim Beam he kept in the lower drawer of his desk—"Just to clear my head."

Feeling the need to explain. To Lucille, or whoever.

Strange need to speak aloud, give himself instructions. Was he drunk?—not hungover but still drunk?—hadn't slept off the drunk, puked or pissed off yesterday's long haul of a drunk.

And so he was having a basic problem: comprehension.

For what did it mean *Zoe Kruller is dead, has died, has been killed*.

Yet more baffling *Zoe Kruller is gone, you will never see her again*.

It was fucking him up having to think of Zoe Kruller dead who'd been so alive in her life, and in his arms. No more thrumming-warm *livingness* than Zoe Kruller. It wasn't just his kitchen she'd be haunting but his very bed upstairs. His bed he'd had to sleep in, or try to, with his wife. Shut his eyes and he'd see the woman's hungry damp mouth, the bared gums when she smiled her happy wide smile, a sight he'd sometimes look away from it seemed too intimate, exposed. The warm freckled arms around his neck, snaky arms pulling him down to her, laughing, tongue-kissing, her hot little belly pressed against his belly, groin against his groin, he could not bear it. *Did you miss fucking me? Did you? How much did you miss fucking me? Show me.*

Or pushing him from her sulky and pouty and he'd had a moment's panic not knowing if she was sincere or teasing *Well say! You don't love me go back to your smug fat wife you bastard*.

He was on the phone, talking with the roofing supplier. Clumsily lighting a cigarette—had to be his second, there was a butt already smoldering in the black plastic ash tray with the red letters SPARTA CONSTRUCTION, INC. To his horror like a man in a film when the music comes up jagged and percussive he broke off the conversation seeing through his window two vehicles turn into the cinder-lot: a Sparta PD cruiser and a heavy new-model Olds the color of steel filings, had to be an unmarked police car.

Quickly then kicking the desk drawer closed. He'd had only a small swallow of the whiskey, nothing they could detect.

His hands trembling. Sick-gut sensation. Frankly he didn't know, could not in that instant have claimed, that he had not been the one to strangle the woman. Him, or the other guy—the husband Delray. Could not have said.

Don't tempt me Zoe! Just don't go too far.

In the outer office the receptionist Myrtle who'd only just arrived breathless and carrying a cardboard container bearing two large Styrofoam cups of coffee—one for her, one for Eddy Diehl—would be the first to greet the police officers. No time to alert Eddy, damn cops opened the door to his office and walked right in.

Four men: two youngish uniformed officers, two plainclothed detectives. In that instant it came to him *They expect me to resist. They expect to kill me. They'd sent four of them!*

"Edward Diehl? We need to speak with you."

Need. He caught that, not *want.* And not asking.

Sitting at his desk, staring at them. How would an innocent man behave?—unsmiling, taken by surprise? Polite but—unyielding? He'd hung up the phone, his hands were flat on the desktop before him. No sudden moves, he knew better. He was feeling some relief, the cops they'd sent were not men he knew. In the Sparta PD and in the Herkimer County sheriff's department there were men he knew, and it would have been embarrassing if one of them had come for him. But these men were strangers.

"Yes? Why?"

In a flash it came to him, maybe Delray hadn't confessed. Maybe that was just a rumor. On the 6 A.M. local news there'd been no mention of the husband confessing.

"No idea why, Mr. Diehl?" The older of the detectives spoke casually, with a little fishhook of a smile.

"It's maybe—about—"

His voice faltered, he fell silent. In his face was a heat-flush from the whiskey, he was sure the detectives could see.

And the whiskey felt, in his gut, like a plug of searing-hot phlegm, indigestible, horrible. He could not think why he'd done something so impulsive at 7 A.M. of a Monday morning.

The senior detective introduced himself and his partner—"Martineau"—"Brescia"—but not the younger uniformed officers. He was saying how it "might be a good idea" for Mr. Diehl to accompany them to police headquarters, downtown; they had a few questions for him in their investigation into the homicide of Zoe Kruller early Sunday morning. This, Eddy heard through a roaring in his ears like an earthmover in the near-distance. Martineau assured him that the interview wouldn't take long and in his desperation Eddy clung to these words *won't take long* as if this were a promise made to a frightened child *won't take long, won't take long!* the most blatant and transparent of falsehoods yet Eddy Diehl would cling to the words *won't take long Mr. Diehl* as shakily he arose from the swivel chair behind his desk, fumbled for his heavy down sheepskin jacket he'd tossed onto a nearby table, his leather gloves. He could not help but see in even his agitated state how the two younger police officers were poised to rush at him, to overpower him, if he "resisted"; if he made a sudden unwise movement yanking open a desk drawer to grab a weapon, or shoving his hand into a pocket of the down jacket. He'd been a soldier at one time: he'd been an excitable young man in uniform, armed, trained and poised for action. Especially, poised for action when he believed himself in the presence of danger. It was sobering to think how within seconds these young men would have grabbed his arms, yanked them behind his back and forced him onto the floor, on his face, all the while shouting at him loudly, furiously. *On the floor! On the floor! Face down, on the floor!*

Afterward he would recall how, when Martineau had introduced himself and the other detective, neither had made any offer to shake Eddy Diehl's hand. This hurt! This was insulting! He'd always been a man whom other men liked, on sight; a man whom others trusted. And now in these strangers' coolly assessing eyes he was made to know how they distrusted him, and they disliked him; they were more than willing to believe that he'd murdered a woman, in her bed; he was not a man whose hand they would wish to shake.

My punishment is beginning he thought. A strange pained smile distorted his face, his lower jaw that was stinging from—what?—a shaving cut of hours ago, when he'd scraped his skin in the downstairs bathroom shaving with a drunk's shaky hand.

This too—the sullen clot of blood beneath his lower lip, the fine-trembling fingers—he believed the detectives saw, and filed away as the symptoms of a guilty man.

In the outer office, Myrtle stared. She was fifty years old, divorced, and her ex-husband had died so she thought of herself as a widow, afflicted and aggrieved and for eight years in love with Eddy Diehl; dyed-black hair and white-bread skin, orangy-red lips never lacking a smile for good-looking Eddy Diehl except now, this Monday morning, Myrtle wasn't smiling but staring, abashed and astonished as unmistakably Eddy was being led away by Sparta police officers, without explanation. And outside in the brisk cold air of a gray-wet February morning, there was blunt-bald-headed Paul Cassano, Eddy's boss, just climbing out of his Scout pickup, staring and blinking at Eddy Diehl as if he'd never seen him before, and Eddy lifted his hand in a wan greeting: "Paul, something has come up. I'll be back in maybe an hour."

Men loading lumber onto a truck paused to watch in silence as Eddy Diehl was led to the unmarked Olds the color of steel filings, made to climb humbly, humiliated, into the backseat, behind a plastic partition.

Like an inmate in a holding cell, except he wasn't handcuffed.

These were men who'd known Ed Diehl for years. Some of them had worked with him when he'd been a carpenter, one of the work-crew. Now he'd been promoted to an office job he was still one of them, his natural sympathies were with them and not with their boss Cassano. And these men liked Ed Diehl a hell of a lot better than they liked Paul Cassano who paid their wages.

They knew of Eddy's "relationship" with Delray Kruller's wife— maybe. Some of them knew. It was not a secret, exactly.

Eddy Diehl, Jesus!—he's arrested?

He killed that woman Zoe? Him?

One hour! How mistaken he'd been.

They would keep Edward Diehl—"a person of interest"—for seven hours and forty minutes. That first day at Sparta police headquarters.

Like a man in a trance—neither fully awake, nor unconscious—he'd allowed himself to be led with uncharacteristic docility into a window-less fluorescent-lit room on the second floor of the shabby-brick building on South Main Street at Iroquois, adjacent to the Herkimer County Courthouse and the Herkimer County House of Detention. This part of Sparta was part municipal buildings and high-rise parking structures and conspicuously open "public spaces" and part inner-city slum: in the interstices of county buildings were pawnshops, bail bondsmen's shops, liquor stores with iron grillwork over their windows like grimaces. There were stores with signs in their windows—CHECKS CASHED. There were store-front establishments—HERKIMER COUNTY CHRISTIAN FAMILY COUNSELING. On Iroquois were discount outlets, hairdressers' salons, a Rite Aid pharmacy, small restaurants and pizzerias with scummy front windows, taverns. Of these Eddy Diehl knew only the Iroquois Bar & Grill where off-duty cops and courthouse workers hung out and where the bartender was a guy he'd gone to high school with: a loser back from Vietnam with a steel plate in his head whose greeting *Hey there Diehl how's it going* was welcoming to Eddy Diehl like the greeting of some sick sad left-behind brother.

"No need for a lawyer, Mr. Diehl. Not yet."

Liking it that Martineau continued to call him "Mr. Diehl." Not many people called Eddy "Mr. Diehl"—the last he recalled, one of his son's teachers he'd run into on the street.

He didn't want a lawyer of course. God damn *no*. All of the Diehls distrusted lawyers, had only disparaging things to say about lawyers, and calling one now, in the wake of Zoe's murder, would be the action of a guilty man.

Repeatedly during the seven-hour-and-forty-minute siege that followed, Eddy was assured that he had not been arrested, he was only just being "interviewed." This was a "conversation"—not an "interrogation" —though for accuracy's sake it would be taped. Eddy saw how this was an advantage of course. He was an innocent man—though he would not utter the word *innocent*—shying away from the word *innocent*—a ridiculous word, *innocent*!—for he would tell these police officers everything he knew, all that he knew, he would hold nothing back—he swore, he would hold nothing back—willing to cooperate in any way he could, to help them in their investigation into the homicide of Zoe Kruller.

This woman, Mrs. Delray Kruller, with whom Eddy Diehl had been "acquainted," wasn't that so?

Yes. That was so.

Licking his lips, frowning. He'd been scratching at his chin and his fingers came away with faint blood smears—the shaving cut. Wondering what he could say that the detectives might not already know. It was their strategy to ask questions and never to answer questions. It was their strategy to ask questions repeatedly, from slightly different perspectives. He began to hear his voice over-loud and hoarse in the windowless room, the voice of a guilty man, a very confused man. Strange to think—as an insect caught in the sticky tendrils of a spider's web might think—the more he struggled to free himself, in the exertions and agitations of the guileless, the more he was caught.

Yet it was true: he didn't know who might have hurt Zoe Kruller, really. There were those who believed—so Eddy explained, as if the detectives might not know this fact though it had been aired publicly for more than twenty-four hours—that Zoe's husband Delray was the most likely person to have "hurt" her—there was even a rumor—"Don't know if it's true"—that Delray had confessed to hurting her but of course Eddy Diehl had no idea if this was so, no firsthand knowledge of his own.

They asked him how he knew the Krullers and he told them: Kruller Auto Repair. Kruller Cycle Shop. In certain quarters in Sparta, Delray Kruller was well known. If you needed a good auto mechanic, Kruller was your man. If you liked specialty cars, Kruller was your man. Eddy spoke with admiration of how Delray had rebuilt a Pontiac GTO for him some years back—"Y'know, a 'Goat'? Nineteen seventy-five model." He'd taken a 1980 Stingray for Delray to customize for him, plus a Mustang, a 'Cuda, and the Willys Jeep he was still driving. So hot! As he spoke he was conscious of not-saying something that should be said, not-saying the name *Zoe Kruller* which was what the detectives were waiting patiently to hear. So hot! It was like a joke—it was a joke—he'd have wanted to wink at them, to acknowledge the joke—his enemies were making him sweat: *sweating it out of him.*

Except: there was nothing to *sweat out.*

There was nothing he could tell them, that would lead them to Zoe Kruller's murderer.

(Or—murderers? How'd anyone know for certain, there weren't more than one?)

(If Zoe had been involved with drugs as everyone knew she'd been, it might've been more than one. But Eddy didn't want to tell the detectives this, to insult Zoe.)

He'd taken off his corduroy sport coat, that was worn at the elbows, his favorite coat he'd been wearing for years, with his long-sleeved white-cotton shirts for the office. Damn his forehead was beaded with sweat, his skin felt flushed, his head lowered between his shoulders and in his face the look of a goaded bull.

Fuckers can't make me say the wrong thing. Incriminate myself.

How can I? I can't, I am innocent.

Finally as the questions continued he acknowledged yes, he'd known Zoe also. Delray was his friend and his wife Zoe—well, Zoe was Delray's wife—that was how Eddy knew her. Yes he'd heard that the Krullers were "estranged"—that wasn't a word people used exactly, you'd have said the Krullers were "living apart"—"separated"—"having trouble"—but Eddy Diehl didn't know particulars, he wasn't the type. Except he'd heard from friends that Zoe had left Delray and was living on her own, Zoe was seeing other men, Zoe was frustrated with living just in Sparta and her career—her "singing career"—not getting anywhere; guys who were Del's friends were likely to be harsh about Zoe saying she'd left Delray with their son, left her own household, *the shit Del had to take from that woman you wouldn't blame him, he lost control.*

Covering his face with his hands, rubbing his knuckles against his eyes. So hot! He understood that he should leave, he should tell the detectives that he'd had enough, he had said all that he knew, and yet the wish had lodged deep inside him *I will make them like me, trust me. These are men no different from me.*

Strange how, like a man on a river, in some sort of small rudderless boat on a turbulent river, he'd ceased thinking of where he might be, if he wasn't where he was: he'd ceased thinking of his office at Sparta Construction, and of the work crews he'd be instructing, at this moment; he'd ceased thinking of his house, his home on the Huron Pike Road where by this time only his wife Lucille was likely to be, the kids were at school, he was grateful none of them knew where he was, the shame would have been unbearable. *Daddy questioned by police? Daddy in the police station, like a man on TV? Questioned by police—why?*

Martineau was asking, Brescia was asking, calmly asking the most intimate of questions, words you could not ever imagine being uttered in your face except when they are uttered, and with such astonishing calm, even a kind of logic, bemused, patient, seeing the angry flush in his face and meaning to diffuse it, rephrasing the question—had he had "intimate relations"—"sexual relations"—with Zoe Kruller—rephrasing it had he ever "had a relationship" with Zoe Kruller that was "more than just friends" and Eddy Diehl heard himself say *God damn no, he had not.*

Calmly then they asked him again. Asked him again, and again. Calmly if edgily, the look in Brescia's eyes behind tinted glasses, the look in Martineau's eyes, they knew he was lying did they, if they knew he was lying why the fuck did they ask him. But they asked, and again he said *No* cleared his throat to say more forcibly *No! God damn I told you.*

These words were pebbles in his mouth, barely he could speak with pebbles in his mouth in danger of swallowing, choking. Barely he could speak. Rivulets of sweat ran down his heated face. His heart was a fist banging slowly against his ribs. His gut, where the hot phlegm-plug of un-digested Jim Beam whiskey was defined solid as a pebble. They were dar-ing to ask him if he'd been "involved" with Zoe Kruller—"having sexual relations" with Zoe Kruller—for a long time, or just the past year; was that why Zoe had moved out of her husband's house, or had Zoe moved out first; did Delray Kruller know about him, Eddy Diehl, "having sex with" his wife; and Eddy was shaking his head *No! None of this is true*.

With their calm bemused eyes they regarded him. As hunters keep a little distance regarding the shot bison, the shot bear, a thrashing wounded creature dangerous at such times so you let him bleed out in the grass, you are the victor and time is on your side.

Repeatedly asking was he sure? Was Mr. Diehl sure? Was this Eddy Diehl's statement, he was sure he wanted to sign?

He told them *yes*. This was his statement, he wanted to sign.

And had he visited Zoe Kruller at the West Ferry address he was asked and blindly, quickly said *No*. And asked if he'd seen her there, on Saturday of the previous week, just two nights ago had he seen her, had he driven there, parked on the street, gone in and seen her, and when had this been, and how long had he been there, and had he had sexual relations with her then, and had he been angry with her then, and had he struck her, strangled her, killed her and left her body in her bed, had this happened, Mr. Diehl?—was this what had happened?—and he was coughing now, sweating and miserable and unable to think except wanting to get out of this room, out of these fluorescent lights, away somewhere he could be alone, get a drink to steady his nerves, sink into sleep for he was so very tired.

No he said *no I did not. Not ever*.

GOD DAMN WHY SHOULD I hire a lawyer. Spend money on a God-damned law-yer you can't trust. I'm not the one, I didn't hurt Zoe. Never hurt Zoe oh Christ. Why'd I hurt Zoe. I did not touch Zoe not ever to harm her. I was the one who'd told her she's got to go into rehab. In December I told her. Before Christmas I told her. *Driving me crazy the way she was living so careless of herself saying Go to hell Eddy, you don't love me you can go to hell then there's others who will love me if not you. Sick-worried about Zoe but fuck her she wants to kill herself, track marks on her arms and inside her thighs she'd tried to say were from a cat's claws but the fact is she was shooting heroin, I'd all but caught her that one time. Shooting death into her veins, why'd she do it? Zoe's beautiful arms, freckled and soft. Zoe's beautiful legs not fleshy like a woman's legs can be but slender, muscled. Jesus she'd been shooting that shit into a vein at her ankle. Saying it's just so good, just try it Eddy c'mon just once, it won't kill you. Except she'd had some bad scares. Shooting up with a guy she'd been seeing, or maybe more than one guy, who supplied her all the drugs she needed, this guy from Port Oriskany and nobody known to me, nobody I wanted to know, saying she'd passed out for forty minutes and he's shouting at her and slapping her face trying to revive her, running cold water into the tub, carries her to the tub and drops her into the water, wouldn't call an ambulance he'd have let her die, a guy like that avoids cops at all costs, one look at him and a cop knows, a cop can see, ex-con, junkie-dealer a cop can identify, I told her Zoe for Christ's sake that's crazy, living like that's crazy, so close to the edge, a beautiful woman like you what is wrong with you, and Zoe says Yes you're right Eddy, I know you're right Eddy, say know what, Eddy—I love you!—leaning over to kiss me, Zoe's warm wet mouth on my mouth, tongue like a snake darting, Kiss-kiss Eddy, c'mon Eddy kiss-kiss c'mon fuck me Eddy if you love me fuck me and make me forget other things and Zoe's arms around my neck bearing me down, and Zoe's tight-muscled legs around my waist, ankles crossed behind my buttocks, I'm trying to keep my head clear but can't, trying to believe her but I can't, if the woman would not lie to me if she would not disrespect me as she'd been disrespecting her husband Delray, she starts to laugh, she's laughing and there's a sob catching in her throat, Eddy I promise, oh Eddy I promise, no more damn needles if you love me, not ever.*

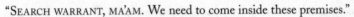

16

"SEARCH WARRANT, MA'AM. We need to come inside these premises."

Out of nowhere they'd come like tanks in wartime. Sparta PD vehicles driven up our lane and a violent rapping at the front door and no one but Eddy Diehl's left-behind wife Lucille to open the door, white-faced and astonished.

My mother in a flannel shirt, slacks, woolen socks—hair disheveled and one side of her sleep-dazed face creased from where she'd been napping—in the wake of an insomniac night—her face against the coarse-woven fabric of a sofa. My mother hoarsely stammering, "W-what? *What—?*"

This was soon after my father had been "brought in for questioning"—"taken into police custody." This new shame!—my mother would never outlive.

Never forgive my father, for bringing this upon the family.

She would say afterward—we would hear her, on the phone—the tone of her voice varying from plaintive and stunned to indignant, incensed—angry, resigned, stricken—her words frequently incoherent, interrupted by sobs—that it was as if her very body was being invaded, searched by strangers. The privacy of the home she'd taken such pride in, and such care. And none of this was her fault! How was this her fault! How did the Sparta police dare to invade Lucille's home like this! Pleading with the officers whom she followed into the rooms of the house even as they ignored her—for only the senior plainclothes detective Martineau who bore the search warrant was authorized to speak with Eddy Diehl's wife—she protested, "Stop! Go away! You have no right! I'll tell my—"

But there was no *husband* to tell. *Husband* was no longer a word in my mother's vocabulary.

My mother was being shown the search warrant which in her rattled state she could barely read. The senior officer—this was Martineau—explained to her that nothing would be damaged in the search and nothing removed from the premises without a receipt and whatever was taken would be returned in time if it wasn't found to be "evidence" crucial to their investigation and my mother heard only the term "evidence" and became further upset asking, "Evidence for what, officer? Evidence for *what*?" and with blunt politeness Martineau said: "This is a homicide investigation, ma'am. You've been informed."

But Lucille had not been informed. She didn't think so. In the strange calm of terror as in the wake of a violent thunderclap she heard herself demanding of this man—a stocky gray-haired man of no distinction except that he'd shown her his shiny Sparta PD badge like a TV cop—what the "homicide" was—and what had it to do with *her*?

Though Lucille knew. Should have known. Yes, Lucille surely knew. These many days that *Zoe Kruller* had been a name not to be uttered in this household.

Knew to ask Martineau in a pleading voice if her husband had been arrested?—and Martineau said no ma'am, not yet.

"Not *yet*? Not arrested *yet*? But—"

"Not yet, ma'am. That's all that I am authorized to say."

"Where is he? Is he—with you? At police headquarters?"

This was where Eddy Diehl was, yes. This was information Lucille already knew.

"And the husband of that woman who—the one who—who'd been killed—is he—is he arrested?"

No. Neither was Delray Kruller arrested, yet.

Police officers had already searched my father's Willys Jeep which was still parked in the lot at Sparta Construction and now in the driveway of our house they searched the family car which was a turtle-colored 1981 Plymouth sedan in reasonably good condition, by default now my mother's, that Daddy had left her. With grim frowning thoroughness they searched the back seat of the Plymouth and beneath the seats and inside the trunk as with equal thoroughness they searched the basement—every corner of the basement including the furnace and hot-water tank room—and Mom's laundry room—taking away from Daddy's workbench many of Daddy's tools for the police officers were looking for the "murder-weapon"—nothing is more crucial to a homicide investigation than the *murder weapon*—and among my father's tools which were precious to him, always kept neatly arranged, hanging from hooks in the wall or placed side by side on the top of the workbench, were several hammers of varying sizes including a newly purchased twelve-inch claw hammer; and all these hammers the police officers took away with them in their neatly labeled cardboard boxes.

Did my mother ask herself *Is one of them what he used? Should I have thrown it away oh God what should I have done?*

Or did my mother think *Good! If one of them is the hammer they want, now they have it. Now it's too late.*

This search of our house—"Basement to attic, every room"—over which my mother would be grievously upset for hours, days, weeks took place in the late morning of a weekday while Ben and I were in school. When we returned home we knew at once that something had happened—strangers had been on our property—the snow in the drive-way was raddled with tire marks and inside the house my mother was feverishly vacuuming the living room. She'd opened several windows, the air was cold. Ben called, "Mom? Hey Mom is something wrong?" for my mother's eyes were swollen and red-rimmed and her face flushed but my mother didn't seem to hear him until Ben pulled the plug from the wall socket—and the roaring vacuum abruptly ceased—and Mom began to scream at him, tried to throw the cleaner's wand at him but the hose was too short.

Later, when she was calmer, Mom told us what had happened: the Sparta police, no warning, the "search." Things they'd carried away in their cardboard boxes taken from closets, bureau drawers, the spare room where he kept financial records, even from the family laundry hamper, even his near-flattened tube of toothpaste, spray-shaving cream, wadded-up tissues and such in the pockets of his work trousers—she was laughing now, and Ben laughed with her, and with a queer twist of his mouth as if these were words meant to entertain both of us—his Mom and his kid-sister—he said, "Shit if they found some damn hammer of his how'd they know it hadn't been washed clean? You could boil water and wash away blood with detergent or bleach, I bet. *He'd* know that, wouldn't he? And if a hammer was missing, Daddy has so many damn hammers down there how'd they even know one was gone?" Ben laughed. Lately my brother's laughter had been raw, harsh and jeering like something part-alive being squeezed through a grinder, horrible to hear.

"Might've taken it myself. They gave us enough time. Threw it into the river. Maybe I was the one who cracked her head. 'Brained' her—her brains had got to be all over the floor, I heard. See, I know how to use a hammer, too. Any asshole does."

My mother stared at Ben. For a moment I thought that she would slap him—I could see that Ben was expecting to be slapped—a twitch in his right eye—the jeering smile fixed in place—but she only stared at him, and shuddered in the cold draft from the opened windows, and turned away.

Upstairs in her bedroom Mom slept for the rest of the day. Slept and slept and next morning we fixed our own cold-cereal breakfasts and tramped out the driveway to the school bus through a new-fallen snow that covered most of the tire tracks so you wouldn't have known.

Ben said with a nasty laugh we'd ought to've woken her, maybe she was passed out or dead.

But it was too late. Neither of us was going back. We waited for the school bus as always. There was a curve in the Huron Pike Road, you could see the carrot-colored bus on its way, a quarter-mile to the east approaching us. A curve in the road along the glittery river where ice was broken along the shore like ravaged teeth.

Somewhere close by a bird was singing. It was a bright liquidy persistent song, beautiful to hear. So beautiful my heart felt pierced. In the snowy boughs of an evergreen I could see a red cardinal—bright red feathers and a black cap—a male cardinal, this was—and the female was there also, olive-green feathers, identical black cap and chunky orange beak and the two of them were singing and I said, "Think that's the 'little bird of heaven'—right here? In our tree?"

Ben said, laughing, "No."

17

I think that I should say bluntly *This was the time in my life, I fell in love with Aaron Kruller.*

There would be a way of composing this that would allow the reader to understand *She is in love with that boy. She will be so humiliated, she will make such a fool of herself, can't anyone stop her!*—a way of indirection and ellipsis, suggestion and not blunt statement; but I want to speak frankly, I want say something that can't be retracted *Yes I was in love with Zoe Kruller's son, the first time in my life I was in love. And there is no time like the first.*

Even before his mother was killed in that terrible savage way, and all of Sparta talking about it, yes and dirty-minded boys laughing about it, Aaron Kruller was trouble.

He was *troubled*, and he was *trouble*.

One of the *Indian-looking kids* at my brother's school, straight dark coarse hair and glaring-dark eyes, a hard ridge of bone above his eyes and his eyebrows heavy and tufted like an adult man's, his young face scarred from lacrosse. Already in ninth grade at the age of fifteen Aaron Kruller was five feet eleven inches tall and weighed 150 pounds looming over his younger—mostly Caucasian—classmates with the gleaming menace of a switchblade among bread knives. He was a boy to avoid, you would never push near him on the stairs or in the cafeteria line or make eye contact with him, in his movements Aaron Kruller was both guarded and yet impulsive, coolly remote and yet short-tempered, unpredictable. Because he had a mixed-blood father and a Caucasian mother it wasn't clear what

Aaron Kruller was—only what he was *not*—a white kid, or a full-blooded Seneca from the reservation.

Yet: "Aaron." A beautiful and mysterious name out of the Bible, I thought. Like "Zoe" this name had acquired a special meaning in my ears, tenderly I spoke these names aloud—"Aaron"—"Zoe."

Poor kid! His father killed his mother, he was the one to discover the body.

Or *Poor kid! His mother was a heroin addict and a hooker and one of her men friends killed her, Aaron found the body.*

Or *Poor bastard that Kruller kid, the way his mother was killed and nobody arrested yet, Aaron found the body which has to have fucked the kid up totally but it's damn hard to like him, that look in his face. And the size of him . . .*

In his classes at school Aaron Kruller was a distracting presence. Often he was restless, bored. Moods shifted in him visibly like clouds in the Adirondack sky. At the rear of the classroom where he was allowed to sit—the preference of most *Indian-looking kids* in Sparta public schools was the rear of the classroom—he fixed his steely eyes upon the teacher at the front of the classroom in the way of a hunter sighting his target. He had a way of lifting his desk with his muscled thighs, forcing the back of his seat (which was attached to the desk) against the wall behind him where it was made to scratch and injure the wall in a *thump-thump-thump* rhythm that seemed calculated to annoy others, to infuriate and exasperate the teacher, yet was probably unconscious, unpremeditated. Aaron did not give the impression of being a fully conscious, premeditated being. As if his thoughts were elsewhere, and drew his fullest attention. Frequently he came to school with bruise-like shadows beneath his eyes, as if he'd been up all night; he was glaze-eyed, dreamy; he slept with his spiky-haired head lowered onto his crossed arms, and no teacher would have wished to awaken him.

Frequently too, Aaron Kruller was absent from school.

Returning then with a battered face, fresh scabs on his face and arms and if asked what had happened, by one or another concerned adult, he'd shrug and mutter what sounded like *L'croz*.

(Lacrosse wasn't a Sparta school sport. Lacrosse was some kind of wild dangerous field hockey played exclusively by the *Indian-looking kids*, no white kid would have dared to play with them for fear of getting his teeth or his brains knocked out.)

L'croz. Aaron Kruller's homeroom teacher came to interpret this as a kind of code meaning *Something to do with being who I am, the family I am from, don't ask anything more it's none of your God-damn business.*

Most days Aaron Kruller wore black T-shirts, black jeans or work pants, grease-stained. He wore flannel shirts that were laundered—when they were laundered—without being ironed. He wore a dingy green-lizard-skin vest, that looked as if it had been plundered from a biker's trash. He wore a leather belt with a brass cobra-head buckle, braided leather thongs and chain-bracelets around his wrists of the kind adult bikers wore. He wore man-sized work-boots with reinforced toes, grease-stained from working at Kruller Auto Repair out on the Quarry Road which his father Delray Kruller owned for it was said that Delray needed his son to work for him, couldn't afford full-time mechanics, Delray was close to going bankrupt from loans he owed, local lawyers he'd had to hire in this season of bad luck for him as for Eddy Diehl.

Go easy on the Indian kids was the consensus among the Sparta public school teachers *most of them will quit at sixteen, disappear out in the rez or in the U.S. Army, or in Attica.* Because he was mixed-blood Aaron Kruller was something of an exception, known to be the son of Zoe Kruller who'd been for years—before the notoriety of her death—a locally popular "girl singer" with a popular bluegrass group—so teachers made more of an effort with Aaron even as they were uneasy in his presence, and wary of his short temper; here was the kind of difficult student of whom a teacher inclined to youthful optimism would say *You know, that Kruller boy is really intelligent, if you're patient with him he catches on.*

Or *Aaron is shy, insecure. He's scared someone will laugh at him that's what makes him dangerous.*

After his mother's death it was understood that Aaron was seriously disturbed and his absences from school were rarely investigated; his empty desk at the rear of the room was a welcome sight, to teachers and classmates alike. Yet long before Zoe Kruller's death, Aaron had been a difficult presence at school, for you could not tell, if you were an adult in authority, if the tall gangling Indian-looking boy was being polite in his awkward way muttering in monosyllables *Yes ma'am—no ma'am—yessir!—nossir!*—or if he was being rude, mocking. Often Aaron would lurch to his feet, when approached, if he was seated; his reaction seemed deferential, yet it gave him the advantage of looming over the shorter, usually female teachers. Adults who knew Zoe believed that they could detect in the son some of the friendly-drawling cadences of Zoe's speech but in Aaron's face, shut up like a fist, there was never Zoe's warm flash of a smile, that flash of bared and vulnerable pink gums.

Only the glaring-dark eyes, irises like pinpricks. Uncanny how he made you feel you were being sighted in the crosshairs of a rifle scope.

More than once in grammar school and in middle school Aaron Kruller had been suspended from classes—for fighting on school grounds, threatening his classmates, "insolence" toward adults-in-authority—but always he'd been allowed to return on probation. Even those youthful optimistic teachers who claimed to see the "real" Aaron Kruller in his eyes took for granted that, the following year, when Aaron was sixteen, and no longer legally required to attend school in New York State, like his father Delray before him, he'd quit.

"That loser. You have to feel sorry for him."

Though in his sour-mocking voice Ben didn't sound at all sorry for Aaron Kruller.

Frequently now—since our father had moved out of our house, since *the trouble* had swept into our lives like a flash flood bearing filthy water, debris—my brother spoke with this air of angry hurt, sarcasm. Ben had never been a very forceful child, he'd been shy in our father's presence, eager to be noticed by Daddy and eager to be loved but shy about putting himself forward as—as Daddy's little girl—I was not; and now, as if overnight, Ben seemed to have drawn into himself something of our father's furious disdain, even Daddy's facial expressions—creased forehead, narrowed eyes, a cobra-look in those eyes of almost gleeful malevolence.

My mother was becoming frightened of Ben, I thought. The two of us stung by the ugly words springing from his mouth after the Sparta police had searched the house *Cracked her head! Brained her! I know how to use a hammer, any asshole does.*

Just joking! Sure.

These days—late February, March—it was just our mother, Ben, and me at the house on the Huron Pike Road. Ben and me returning home from school in a state of dread. We were waiting for something to happen—waiting for the news *Edward Diehl has been arrested in the homicide of*—or waiting for the news *Edward Diehl has been cleared of suspicion in the homicide of*—waiting for our mother to call out to us, as we entered the house at the rear *Daddy is coming home! It's all over.*

There was a rumor circulating at school and on the school bus that Aaron Kruller had approached Ben, in the boys' locker room at their school. Aaron Kruller at five feet eleven inches who loomed over Ben Diehl at five feet six inches as an adult man would loom over a child intimidating him by his very presence. According to this rumor which had been relayed to me—separately—gleefully—by several girl-classmates of whom one was a Bauer cousin-twice-removed—a girl who should have been protective of my brother—the Kruller boy had shoved Ben against a row of lockers without explanation or warning, when Ben tried to shove him back, struck at him with his fists, Aaron Kruller calmly slapped his face—not punched but slapped his face, with an open palm—bloodied Ben's nose—while other boys fearful of Aaron Kruller drew away staring, keeping their distance; nor would anyone report the assault to the boys' gym coach, even poor Ben.

"I fell. I fell on the ice. Hit my face, made my nose bleed. It's nothing. Never mind."

So Ben explained his battered face to our mother that evening. Overwhelmed by whatever had happened that day—of which Ben and I had little idea though guessing it involved phone calls, drives into town on "errands" and visits from Bauer relatives, a consultation with her lawyer—our mother seemed scarcely to hear.

Another incident, reported to me: Aaron Kruller had followed Ben onto the footbridge above the river threatening to push him off and laughing when Ben burst into tears.

I saw that Ben was edgy, upset. I saw the chipped tooth, the bruised face. I was frightened of angering my brother and yet I had to ask him if it was true, that Aaron Kruller was following him, had threatened him, and Ben said no, it was not true—"Bullshit."

I must have looked disbelieving. Ben said sneering no no *no* it was not true, *not fucking true*—"Don't you say anything to Mom, Krista. First thing Mom will do is call school, see? Call the principal, and get me in worse trouble. Or worse, call the cops. Keep your mouth shut."

I asked Ben if Aaron Kruller wanted to hurt him because Aaron believed that Daddy had hurt his mother and Ben said excitedly, "Are you crazy, Krista? What d'you mean saying a thing like that? That's bullshit," and I asked why, why was this bullshit, and Ben said, pushing me away— we were alone in the house, our mother had driven out on one of her desperate errands to the grocery store, drug store—seemed that Lucille Diehl was always at Walgreens getting a prescription filled—"You have to feel sorry for Kruller, he's such a loser. His drunk old man killed his mother who'd been a junkie-whore, how's it get more pathetic than that?"

The way Ben's mouth twisted on *junkie-whore*, you could see that he'd come to hate Zoe Kruller, too.

But we'd always liked Zoe, didn't we?

At Honeystone's we'd wanted to be waited on by Zoe hadn't we?

How does it happen, you like someone so much—love someone, maybe— then later, not so long later, what you feel is hate? Terrible hurtful hate? Wanting-to-kill hate?

Why?

Already when I was in eighth grade, aged thirteen, thrown together in the company of older kids on the school bus, I'd begun to hear such words as *whore, hooker, prostitute* and to have an idea what these words might mean. Without needing to inquire I understood that these were ugly words that applied exclusively to females.

Junkie was an ugly word that applied to males, also. To be a *junkie* you could be either female or male and it meant you were a *druggie, drug addict, doper.*

Turning tricks I'd begun to hear. This had an appealing sound: you could imagine showy tricks of some kind—card tricks, magic tricks, teaching a dog to teeter about on its hind legs—to arouse envy and admiration in others.

To provoke applause. Whistles of approval.

As in Chautauqua Park at the bandstand. Zoe Kruller in her shiny spangle-dress clinging to her feverish little body like liquid mercury and bowing to the crowd—the crowd that adored her—tossing her streaked-strawberry-blond hair over her head in a gesture of swift utter abjection.

Bowing low and then straightening again, arching her back. Smiling so happily at the applauding whistling crowd you'd think her heart would burst.

I think it was my brother who'd said of Zoe that she'd been *turning tricks* but maybe it had been someone else, another, older boy on our school bus. Crude loud-laughing boys you avoided looking at, pretended not to hear. Even when they called your name *Kris-ta! Krissss-taaa! Kissy-kissy-Krisss-taaa!* you pretended not to hear.

Cruel things were said of Zoe Kruller *turning tricks.* You would have thought that now Zoe was dead, and had been buried in the Lutheran cemetery on Howell Road—we hadn't gone to the funeral of course, but a girl I knew from school had gone—most people would feel sorry for her and for the Krullers but this didn't seem to be the case, not with everyone.

(Like Ben. Like my mother. Like most of our Bauer relatives.)

Adultery was a word I'd come to know, also. *Adulterer.*

There was consolation in this you would have to be an *adult* to commit *adultery,* wouldn't you?

"Your father is an adulterer, Krista. You may as well be told. Your father betrayed his marriage vows, that he'd pledged in church, before God. He betrayed the sanctity of this family. He betrayed all of us. Whatever his relations were with that woman—I feel sorry for her because I guess he betrayed her, too."

Waiting for Mom to add *But your father did not kill her.*

She didn't, though. It was a somber moment between us—we were in the kitchen just the two of us—Ben had started working after school part-time, at about this time—shortly before Daddy moved to Port Oriskany—and often it was just Mom and me in the kitchen preparing supper which we would eat promptly at 6:00 P.M.—Mom, Ben and me—and solemnly now Mom leaned over me to press her lips that looked chewed-at, dry and chapped, against the top of my head, the wavering part in my hair, as if blessing me.

"AARON."

Secretly I spoke his name. This beautiful mysterious name out of the Bible, I had never dared speak aloud to anyone.

In the fall when I was a student at Sparta Middle School which ad-joined the older, red-brick Sparta High School sometimes I was able to catch sight of Aaron Kruller at a distance. He was in tenth grade, a sopho-more; he'd been kept back a year. Now Ben who was Aaron's age—going on sixteen—was a year ahead of Aaron, in the junior class. I thought it must be humiliating to Aaron, to be kept back with younger kids. (Each year there were three or four *Indian-looking kids* who were kept back, girls as well as boys. They would keep one another company at the rear of classrooms and in tight little clusters in the cafeteria. Though it was forbidden, they would smoke cigarettes at the rear of the school waiting for the special Herkimer County bus that took them out to the reservation.) I had to wonder if Aaron Kruller knew that I existed: Ben Diehl's younger sister. If he hated me, the way he hated Ben.

Did I dare to follow Aaron Kruller? I did not.

Yet somehow it happened, there was Krista Diehl in the 7-Eleven on Chambers Street where Aaron Kruller sometimes dropped by after school. There was Krista Diehl pretending to be on an errand for her mother frowning at milk cartons displayed in the refrigerator—trying to read the labels, the expiration dates. There was Aaron Kruller opening a Coke, devouring something doughy and mashed in a cellophane wrapper, out of his hand. In the 7-Eleven there was likely to be an air of frantic festivity—kids from the high school crowding the aisles—calling out loudly to one another, flirting, exchanging mock-obscenities—while quietly, shyly blond Krista decided against buying a carton of milk, slipped out the front door without being noticed.

He saw me! He knows who I am.

Those afternoons I didn't take the school bus home. I walked home. Avoided my friends with whom I'd have been sitting on the bus who would have said *Krista are you crazy?* and might have guessed it was a boy, an older boy, in whom I was interested.

Those terrible years, your happiness can only be *He saw me! He knows who I am.*

The rubble-strewn alley where Aaron Kruller sometimes rode his bicycle, out to the Quarry Road. The asphalt pavement in front of the train depot where older boys and a few girls, loud-laughing, excitable, hung out together after school to drink beer out of cans carelessly tossed into the weeds, to smoke cigarettes, or "pot."

I knew what "pot" was: marijuana. I knew the sweet-acrid smell, that clung to the clothes and hair of certain of the older girls.

Aaron stayed only a brief while with these friends of his. Aaron smoked with them, drank with them, laughed with them. You could see that Aaron Kruller was one of them but Aaron never stayed long, he had to get home to work at his father's auto shop out on the Quarry Road.

Pot was common, at Sparta High. *Weed. Getting high.*

I thought it must be nice: *getting high.* Like a helium balloon rising above the rooftops, treetops where no one could hurt you.

Ben spoke disdainfully of kids at the high school who were *dopers.*

Dopers, stoners, druggies. Losers. Ben scorned drugs, drinking.

Ben would never be one of those kids expelled from school for bringing beer onto school property, drinking out of his locker, smoking dope in the lavatories. Ben scorned any kind of weakness. This year he meant to work hard in all his classes. The spring before, with our father gone, and *the trouble* fucking up our lives, Ben's concentration had been shattered and he hadn't done so well on final exams and for this he blamed our father, he would never forgive our father and so he'd decided he would not be a God-damned carpenter like Eddy Diehl, not a cabinet-maker, fuck working with his hands, fuck home-building and construction, Ben signed up for mechanical drawing and college-entrance math. He'd stopped hanging out with his old friends—not that these were doper-kids, they were not—but they were not college-entrance kids—and he didn't make new friends. He didn't have time for friends. He worked after school at Laird's Groceries. He would impress his teachers. He would impress the Sparta High principal, the guidance counselor. He would overcome their curiosity about him—their pity—possibly, their mild aversion—for the name *Diehl* accrued to him like an obscene scrawl across his back.

Already in his junior year of high school Ben was plotting where he'd go after graduating, not Herkimer County Community College where most of his classmates would go, if they went to "college" at all, but somewhere away from Sparta: Rensselaer Polytech in Troy, and if not Rensselaer the State University of New York at Canton where there was a good technical school.

Where the name *Diehl* would not evoke any disagreeable association, like a bad smell.

I WAS SAD—sometimes, I was angry—mostly I was bewildered—how had it happened, I'd once had an older brother who had been my friend—who had seemed to like me—to "be on my side"—but now I had not.

"Are you mad at me, Ben? Why are you mad at me?"—it did no good to ask, such questions only embarrassed my brother, and annoyed him. More and more during his high school years Ben stayed away from home, working at the grocery store or at another part-time job; hoping to avoid his lonely sister and his mother, as much as he could; saving money for his escape from Sparta.

In my dreams—that felt, sometimes, too large for my head as if my head might burst—my brother Ben and Aaron Kruller were strangely confused. The hot-pulsing dream would seem to be insisting *This is Ben* but the person I saw was Aaron Kruller as if by some authority beyond my control Aaron Kruller was meant to be my brother, and not Ben.

The uncanny authority of dreams! It has always astonished me, how we surrender ourselves to these nocturnal presences, so trusting and vulnerable as if the outermost layer of our skin has been peeled away! In sleep there is no protection, nowhere to flee, to hide; there can be no solace, if the dream is not a solace.

In eighth grade, at age thirteen when with increasing boldness—recklessness?—I followed Aaron Kruller after school, if I happened to sight him. And if at the 7-Eleven he glanced toward me quizzically, frowning or blank-faced—quickly I looked away, a hot blush rising in my face.

He saw me! Maybe he saw me! I was a shy girl, or gave that impression. I was a very young girl, in eighth grade. I had silky-pale blond hair and doll-like features, a "pretty" girl—a "good" girl—if Aaron Kruller noticed me at all, he'd have dismissed me in the same instant. I was both relieved and disappointed telling myself *He doesn't know, whose daughter I am. He doesn't know me as he knows Ben.*

Then again thinking, with a thrill of dread *Does he?*

In Sparta in those days, no matter your age, unless you were really young, you were likely to think that, if Delray Kruller had not murdered his wife in "a fit of jealous rage" you were likely to think that Eddy Diehl had murdered her for more or less that reason. There were other "persons of interest"—"suspects"—"leads"—but essentially it was Kruller, or it was Diehl. As with sports teams, people chose sides. It was a matter of family loyalties, neighborhoods, friends: allegiance to one man, or to the other. Both Delray Kruller and Eddy Diehl had a wide circle of friends and acquaintances known to them from high school—they'd both gone to Sparta High at about the same time in the late 1950s—and from their work; both men had large, sprawling families in Herkimer County; Delray Kruller had even his Seneca-Indian relatives, from whom it was said he'd long been estranged. (Maybe it was the Caucasian wife Zoe, who'd caused the rift? If there'd been a rift?) Lacking what's called "hard evidence" linking either Kruller or Diehl to the murder, the Sparta PD was said to more strongly suspect Eddy Diehl because he'd "made enemies" of them at the start of their investigation, by lying to them: like a fool he'd tried to deny being Zoe Kruller's lover, visiting her in the duplex on West Ferry Street. . . . Whereas Delray Kruller had seemed to cooperate with the police. Or maybe Delray Kruller had a friend or two in the Sparta PD who spoke of him sympathetically as a man badly treated by his wife— treated like shit by his wife! And there was Delray's fourteen-year-old son Aaron who swore to police in a formal statement that his father had been with him "all that night"—the night of Zoe Kruller's death—providing an alibi for his father while for some of that same time, for several crucial hours, my father Eddy Diehl had no one to provide an alibi for him.

Seeing Aaron Kruller I thought *He is lying.* I thought *He wants to destroy my father.* Yet I was helpless to seek him out.

WON'T LIE FOR HIM why should I! All I can tell the police is I don't know. I can't say. I was asleep. I don't know when he came home. He did come home yes sometime in the night but I don't know when, I was asleep.

And so I can't say. . . .

Ben and I would never know if it was true as our mother claimed, that our father had asked her to "lie" for him. To tell police he'd been home by at least midnight on the night that Zoe Kruller was murdered, some hours later. Ben himself said he'd been asleep—"Like Mom, I can't say"—and whatever I seemed to remember, whatever I'd have been willing to tell police, to swear to police—that yes, I thought Daddy had been home by midnight at least—no one took seriously.

One glance at Eddy Diehl's daughter, you'd see that here was a girl desperate to lie for her daddy. Here was a girl who'd say anything for her Daddy. Here was a girl whose testimony you could not rely upon, even Eddy Diehl's defense attorney doubted the worth of such an "alibi witness."

For much of that night, Eddy Diehl claimed he'd been alone. He had not been "conscious" of the time. In his Jeep driving out into the country and feeling so bad—about Zoe—at one point possibly he'd been passed out in the Jeep in a parking lot—or by the roadside—where he'd pulled over to shut his eyes, a half-hour, forty minutes, motor still running—maybe someone had seen him but probably not—earlier that evening he'd been at the County Line, he'd been at the Iroquois—maybe at the River Tree Inn—drinking alone at the bar in his black depressed/anxious mood but there'd been guys who knew him—guys he knew—had to be—maybe a woman—women—Eddy Diehl was likely to know both women and men in any tavern he'd step into, in Herkimer County, on a Saturday night—but it was suspicious, how vague Eddy was about providing names—nor could bartenders recall exactly when he'd been drinking in their presence—and so Eddy Diehl couldn't provide an "alibi" that the detectives could corroborate.

And he'd lied to them, initially. Like a fool, yes he'd lied. His hungover drunk, that quick ill-advised swallow of Jim Beam in his office before they'd come for him, makes you think you can say anything, get away with anything, if he'd been stone cold sober he would have known better, Eddy Diehl wasn't a stupid man. Well, he'd wanted to "protect" his family—there was that. Out of embarrassment and shame—shame for what Lucille would be feeling, if so exposed—he'd lied to the detectives. In that way making enemies of them and of their superior officer at the precinct, all the way up to the Sparta chief of police.

Delray, on the other hand, had not lied. From the first, Delray's story was exactly his son's story: the two had been together all that night, in the house on Quarry Road from which, months previously, Zoe Kruller had departed.

Saying, what?—*I just need to get somewhere to breathe. I just need to live my own life while I can, please don't try to stop me and please don't follow after me I am not coming back until it's time.*

This you would believe, if you believed Delray Kruller and his son Aaron. More or less, this is what you'd believe Zoe had told them.

Finally, my father Eddy Diehl had hired a lawyer. Days after he'd been interviewed by the Sparta detectives, when it was almost too late. And then, following his lawyer's advice, my father had changed his statement to police: yes he had been "involved with" Zoe Kruller, for several years; yes he had "visited with" Zoe Kruller in the West Ferry residence on a number of occasions; yes he'd "had sex with her" on the night of February 11.

On that night! On the eve of Zoe's death but no later than 11 P.M. he was sure.

Maybe 9 P.M. Maybe 10 P.M. It had not been late. She had not wanted him to stay. He had not stayed. This, Edward Diehl would swear.

All this would be revealed in large lurid headlines in the Sparta *Journal*. All this, to the horror, humiliation, disgust of Lucille Diehl who took comfort at least in the fact that she hadn't lied for her adulterer husband. Another time the glamour-photo of Zoe Kruller on the front page of the paper, beside the darkish brooding photo of Edward Diehl.

SUSPECT IN KRULLER HOMICIDE CONFESSES TO AFFAIR
Diehl Changes Story: "I Was With Zoe That Night"

Each time Aaron Kruller and I saw each other, we were made to recall such facts.

18

Aaron Kruller's beat-up mountain bike.

It was large, ungainly, ugly. Its frame looked like nothing so much as soldered-together pipes, lead-colored and graceless, with tires attached. The chrome handlebars, lowered to resemble the horns of a charging bull, were dim with rust; you could barely make out the name *Schwinn Flyer* engraved on a sort of medallion above the front wheel. The fenders had fallen off or been removed. The seat was made of black rubber and so hard it felt like rock, unyielding. *How'd anyone sit on this?*—I dared to touch the seat.

Dared to take hold of both handlebar grips, also of black rubber, worn thin. The crossbar came to approximately my mid-chest, the bike had to be twice the size of my own.

No one ever saw me there, behind Sparta High. Where Aaron Kruller left his battered old bike leaning against a wall. (Most students' bikes left behind the school were neatly arrayed in bike racks, their wheels prudently locked. The oldest, most battered bikes, which no one would wish to steal, or would have dared to steal, were just left leaning against the wall as if they'd been abandoned there for the time being, unlocked.) More than once I slipped from class in the middle school and made my way through connecting corridors into the high school and so outside to the rear of the school where Aaron left his bike with all the others. Yet I never had to search for Aaron's bike, lead-colored among so many shiny bikes, I found it immediately. Just to touch the freezing rust-stippled chrome, to stroke the hard-rubber seat with my fingers . . .

"'Aaron Kruller.'"

He wasn't yet old enough to drive a vehicle on a public street. Though he was old enough to drive vehicles on his father's property, and had been old enough for years. Except in severe winter weather Aaron Kruller bicycled to school from his house on the Quarry Road which was approximately three miles from school. Along the two-lane state highway and into the city of Sparta on potholed streets, through alleys, onto sidewalks and across the cracked and glass-littered lot of the abandoned Sears mall, unmistakable in his biker's gear, leather jacket, or vest, sometimes bareheaded and sometimes wearing a baseball cap (reversed), never protective headgear: grimly and expediently Aaron pedaled the stripped-down old *Schwinn Flyer* without the slightest interest in his surroundings except as he approached an intersection or moved into traffic. Unlike most bicyclists in Sparta you were likely to see, Aaron bent far over the handlebars of his bike so you'd have thought his spine must ache, there was something both adult and self-punishing in his posture.

It was thrilling to see him, and to be unseen by him! Aaron Kruller on his ugly lead-colored bike hurtling through stalled traffic on Union Street, his singed-looking face impassive as a clay mask.

"Who is that?"—once, on Union Street, about to turn into the Walgreens parking lot my mother saw Aaron Kruller on his bicycle as if she'd been startled out of a reverie; and I said—seated beside my mother in the passenger's seat, her only passenger that day since Ben was elsewhere—that the bicyclist was a boy from Ben's class at the high school, no one we knew, hoping that my mother wouldn't have recognized Aaron, for often my mother surprised us by knowing more than we believed she could know; but my mother said only, "In Ben's class? They're the same age? That doesn't seem possible, that's a *grown man*."

The intonation my mother gave to *grown man*, you'd have thought she was speaking of some kind of monster.

And a moment later in the parking lot, adding a remark I'd been expecting from her, that I could have supplied myself in Lucille's primly chiding slightly reproachful maternal voice: "He looked Indian. That boy.

They grow up fast, in their way of life. So you should know, Krista, and Ben too, to *keep your distance*."

Now, I did laugh. Mom looked sharply at me.

"I was just thinking, the trouble Dad is in—and you so mad at him—that's got nothing to do with anyone being Indian, does it?"

"All right, Krista! Enough of your smart mouth."

"Mom, I was just *thinking*. Any trouble Dad is in—he's what's called 'Caucasian'—"

"Yes. And if he'd been mixed-blood, like that woman's husband Kruller, it'd be a damn lot worse."

Flush-faced and indignant my mother slammed out of the car, to hurry into Walgreens before the pharmacy closed.

Such was my mother's logic. Such was Caucasian logic. Laugh at her! This was the air of Sparta we had no choice but to breathe, to exist.

A second time in the car with my mother—the turtle-colored Plymouth sedan my father had left for my mother's use, when he'd been made to move away—we were driving along Front Street by the river, we'd just turned off Huron Pike Road and were approaching the busy intersection with Chadd Boulevard—warehouse district, Mayflower moving vans—when I had time only to glimpse a boy on a bicycle approaching rapidly from our right, on Chadd, where there was a traffic light—red—and vehicles were waiting for the light to change—before I saw that the cyclist was Aaron Kruller and that he had no intention to stop with traffic but to continue through the intersection at full speed—unless it was accelerating his speed, his muscled legs pedaling rapidly, his gloved hands tight-gripping the handlebars—and in a horror of paralysis I could not warn my mother—so quickly had Aaron appeared, so swiftly his bent-over figure on the bicycle was moving—I could not warn my mother as Aaron sped into the path of our car heedless of our existence as my mother—distracted by her thoughts like the mad droning of a hive that never ceased—and this had been a bad day for Lucille, I seemed to know—poor Mom!—as my mother continued forward heedless of the cyclist's existence, placing her faith—in this case, it was blind faith—stubborn-blind faith—in the green light above the intersection upon which she'd fixed her gaze—Mom in her typical driver's posture leaning forward frowning and pursed-lipped gripping the steering wheel as if she feared it might wrench away from her and so her visual range was likely to be limited to a tunnel-space directly in front of her—and suddenly there passed before her, within a foot or two of the Plymouth's front fender, the reckless boy-cyclist—the arrogant, insolent, oblivious cyclist who had to be Aaron Kruller in leather jacket, revered baseball cap—causing my poor mother to slam her foot against the brake, to make us both cry out in surprise and alarm—

"Oh! My God! That bicycle—where did it come from—"

Often to her chagrin Lucille had accidents, around the house. In fact all of us—Ben, Mom, me—had grown clumsy and uncoordinated in recent months. Like individuals afflicted with an unknown neurological impairment we dropped things, banged into things, bruised and cut and burned ourselves; most of the time our mishaps were minor and might be construed as comical—overturning a box of Cheerios to send miniature wheat O's scattering across the floor, misjudging distances and tripping on the stairs—but there had begun to appear on my mother's car mysterious dents, scrapes, bruises and I knew that Mom had been "ticketed" for one or another traffic violation, having found the receipt misplaced with flattened paper bags in a kitchen drawer.

In the car, my mother had grown unusually cautious, anxious. She took pills "for my nerves" and she took pills "to help me sleep" and the combination of such medications could not have been good for her capacity to see, think, and react quickly. Shaken now, Mom braked the car to a shuddering stop. We were on a busy street and other drivers were sounding their horns at us angrily but no matter, my mother had to stop. So upset she didn't even think to blame me for not having warned her which was her usual reaction in such situations. "Oh, Krista! If I'd run into that man! God help me, if I'd hit—if I'd killed—"

Fortunately, Lucille didn't know that the cyclist she'd narrowly missed hitting was the son of Zoe Kruller.

My heart was pounding painfully. Not that we'd nearly run into

Aaron Kruller with our car but if Aaron had glanced around, and seen *me*—I'd have been overcome with embarrassment.

"Mom, it's all right. You didn't hit him."

I spoke with forced vehemence. I felt sorry for my mother, who had become so hard to love.

"But my God, Krista—if I had! With so much else gone wrong in our lives . . ."

"It wouldn't have been your fault, Mom. It would have been his—you were in the right."

"That makes no difference, Krista." Bitterly my mother laughed, wiping at her eyes with a tissue. "'Right'—'wrong'—when trouble comes to you, everyone is punished."

It was November 1983. My father Edward Diehl was now living in Buffalo where he'd found work "in construction" and my mother had begun "divorce proceedings" and was working at the consignment shop and had much on her mind that left her excited and hopeful at times and at other times irritable, despairing, depressed. I was not a child any longer but a canny young girl—eleven going on twelve!—whose awareness of the complexities and nuances of adult life had been sharply honed in the past nine months and whose capacity for irony had been yet more sharply honed, like a taste for bitter chocolate or dark bitter ale. It was no secret to me that my mother was still in love with my father, always my mother would be in love with my father who had so ravaged her, that was Lucille's fate.

"No. That's wrong. Mom hates him."

So Ben spoke, smugly. In our household it was my mother and Ben who were close, Ben was my mother's favorite though I was the one more frequently at home and much nicer to my mother than Ben was.

"She wants people to think she hates him. She wants him to think she hates him. But she doesn't."

"She *does*."

"She wouldn't be so hurt, then. She'd have divorced him by now. She can't let go of him, that's her problem."

"Fuck you, Krista: that's *your problem*."

In public, meaning outside our house and in the company of people other than Ben and me, or her closer Bauer relatives, my mother managed to maintain an air of dignity, even hauteur. Mostly.

In public, Lucille wasn't the sort of woman to shrink timidly away from others' eyes. Her face was no longer the face of a woman who might, in certain lights, be mistaken as young, nor was her body—solid, stolidly, fleshy-without-being-fat—a young woman's body. Being girlish, being very pretty, "sexy"—the Lucille Bauer of old snapshots posed with her handsome fiancé Eddy Diehl—all that was finished now, vanished.

Except at the Sparta Hills Mall where almost you could hear the murmurs in our wake not-unfriendly, matter-of-fact and terrible *See that woman? That's Lucille Diehl. Her husband is Eddy Diehl who murdered that woman over on West Ferry Street—he was having an affair with her, they say he killed her—look at the poor wife, Eddy Diehl's wife trying to be brave.*

19

"THAT WOMAN! Has she no *shame*."

My mother's voice was flat as the slap of a hand. Though you could hear the hurt, rage, indignation in it.

My mother was staring at an item in the Sparta *Journal*. Not on the front page but on an inside page, a single column of newsprint beneath the headline:

SPARTA WOMAN FOUND BADLY BEATEN
Towaga Street Resident Hospitalized

The accompanying photograph depicted a glamorous woman with a heavy jaw, unconvincing doll-like features, thin-plucked eyebrows and a cupid's bow mouth: Jacky DeLucca?

I knew not to betray much interest, or my mother would become suspicious. Together we read of how in the early morning of March 2, 1985—this would have been mornings ago—Ms. Jacqueline DeLucca, thirty-nine, a resident of 32 Towaga Street, East Sparta, had been found semi-conscious on a service road intersecting with route 31, a quarter-mile from Chet's Keyboard Lounge where she worked as a cocktail waitress.

Sparta police cruising the Strip—as this section of route 31 was called—discovered her and called an ambulance that brought her to Sparta General Hospital where Ms. DeLucca was admitted with injuries to her face and head, several cracked ribs, a sprained wrist and a "high level of alcohol" in her bloodstream. Her condition was listed as "stable."

Jacqueline DeLucca had told police that she had not seen her attacker
or attackers and had no idea what had provoked the attack and could not
remember circumstances leading up to it. She had left Chet's Keyboard
Lounge shortly after 2 A.M. "in the company of friends" but could not recall what happened in the interim between leaving the Lounge and being
wakened in the speeding ambulance in critical condition. The article
concluded:

> Ms. DeLucca is a former resident of 349 West Ferry Street
> where in February 1983 Ms. Zoe Kruller, with whom Ms. De-
> Lucca shared the residence, was found murdered.
>
> No arrests have been made in the Kruller case which Sparta
> detectives will describe only as "on-going."

Briskly my mother folded up the newspaper and slapped it down on
the kitchen chair by the back door, where we placed flat things like newspapers, magazines, advertising flyers and junk mail to be removed to the
trash each day. How strangely shaken and disapproving she seemed, out
of all proportion to the sordid little incident. "A woman like that! Just like
the other. 'Cocktail waitress.' 'The Strip.' You'd think they would learn,
wouldn't you. God help them!"

I thought *It isn't God you want to help them is it Mom!*

I said, "She just seems sad, Mom. Maybe you should feel sorry for
her—'cocktail waitress' is the best she can do."

"Feel sorry for *her*? For *either of them*?"

My mother stared at me as if she'd have liked to slap my face. Her eyes
welled with tears of indignation, insult.

Them, she'd said. I went away thinking it wasn't poor Jacky DeLucca
who'd so incensed my mother, but *the other*.

20

"THAT LOSER. You heard?"

Ben slammed into the house, his boy's voice lifted happily.

It was a weekday evening, near 6:30 P.M. Ben had caught a ride home with a neighbor after work, after school. Our mealtimes were now closer to 7:00 P.M. and sometimes later, if my mother was busy. Sometimes, we didn't have "mealtimes" at all but ate—if we ate—separately, leftovers from the refrigerator or Campbell's soup—or, in my case, cereal, upstairs in my room while I did homework.

It was a matter of shame to me, I would not have wanted my friends at school to know, or my girl-cousins: that when Daddy left, he'd taken so much with him. Preparing meals with my mother, all those years— mostly, that had ended, I hadn't quite understood when.

And eating together, at the kitchen table—the four of us. All that, ended.

Krista grow up! He isn't coming back, fuck him. Fuck all of them you don't need them, why do you need them you DO NOT NEED THEM.

Rare for Ben to call out in such a tone, I steeled myself to hear his news.

In fact, I'd heard rumors earlier, at school: Aaron Kruller had been "permanently expelled" from Sparta High.

I hadn't been one of those who'd crowded against windows in the school, to see a Sparta police vehicle pull up the drive followed closely by a second vehicle, this memorable event that would long be told and retold by witnesses both first- and second-hand—thrilled, gleeful, awed that one of their own classmates would not only merit the summoning of uniformed police officers but offer enough "resistance" to their efforts to warrant being handcuffed and taken forcibly away, in the rear of one of the vehicles.

I had to think that Aaron had been provoked. His short temper, his quick hard fists lashing out—he'd been wounded, it was natural for him to wish to wound others.

I felt sorry for Aaron and for myself—the bleak thought came to me, I might never see Aaron Kruller again.

"Like his drunk old man, he could kill someone. He's dangerous. He knocked Mr. Farolino down. He's a *psycho*."

Ben spoke eagerly, gloatingly. It was Ben's belief that Aaron's father Delray had killed Zoe Kruller and that Aaron had lied to protect him, about Delray being home with him that night.

I asked why didn't he feel sorry for Aaron, after all Aaron's mother had been killed. "Isn't that enough, why hate him too?"

"Why?" Ben looked at me with a quizzical sort of attention, as if a very young or slow-witted child had spoken. "Because he lied about his father, stupid. Why'd you think?"

"How do you know he lied, Ben? How can you be so sure?"

"Because it's what I didn't do, and Mom didn't do, for Dad."

Dad was not a word Ben had uttered in a long time. Whether he was conscious of uttering it now, embarrassed at having uttered it, I could not tell for Ben was looking away. A faint flush like a rash had come into his face, he began to scratch as if it itched him.

"That's weird logic, Ben." I laughed, uncomfortably. "That's actually *illogic*."

In math we'd been learning about "logic"—the deductive logic of theorems. There was another kind of logic—inductive. Yet you could not always trust either, for in life most rules didn't seem to apply.

"Know what, Krista? I hate them all, I wish they'd die. Krullers."

Krullers. Ben pronounced the name like an obscenity.

I ran away upstairs to my room. Often it was to my room—that was small, with a slanted ceiling and just a single dormer window Daddy had built overlooking an overgrown pasture beside the barn—that I ran, to hide.

I didn't want to think that, if what Ben said was true about Aaron Kruller lying to protect his father, Ben's judgment of the Krullers was more logical than my own.

There were girls in my class whom I might have called that evening, to ask what they'd heard, what was the news of a boy in the high school who'd been arrested that day and taken away by police—a boy whose name I didn't know; but I didn't dare, I couldn't risk anyone guessing that I was in love with Aaron Kruller.

Nor could I risk my mother or my brother overhearing me on the phone, asking such questions.

Downstairs I could hear Ben telling my mother the thrilling news. A half-dozen times Ben must have told and retold all that he knew. His voice and my mother's voice murmurous and rising together in a single tide of elation, spite. I threw myself onto my bed. I stuck my fingers in my ears. I didn't want to hear them so united in hatred, maybe I envied them.

At least, they had that to share.

21

NEVER RETURNED TO 349 West Ferry Street except in memory, never saw Jacky DeLucca again in those years of my growing-up in Sparta and my growing-away from Sparta though frequently in moments of weakness—in moments of loneliness—I felt the woman's warm fleshy arms folding me against her, the foam-rubber resilience of her big breasts, the sweet-stale fragrance of her unwashed body which I'd found repugnant at the time and yet in memory not at all repugnant but pleasurable—the shock of her lips against the top of my head. The gesture had seemed to me utterly spontaneous and unwilled as the sudden kiss of a dog, or a cat—pure instinct, one warm being for another. And there came the breathy childlike plea with its undercurrent of adult coercion *Friends now aren't we Krissie?*

Promise you'll come back to see me.

I had never gone back of course. And very likely, Jacky DeLucca had moved away from West Ferry Street, soon after.

To live, among other addresses perhaps, on a street called Towaga in gritty East Sparta.

My fascination with the run-down row house in which Zoe Kruller had died was a fascination too with a place—forbidden, never acknowledged within the family—to which my father had gone, by his own belated, reluctant admission. *Yes he'd visited the murder victim there. Yes he'd had sexual relations with the murder victim there. Yes within hours of her death. Yes he had lied. Yes he insisted he was innocent, he was not lying now.*

Abruptly then my fascination with this house ceased for as the weather turned more mild, and I was able to bicycle out to the Quarry Road, it became the Kruller house where Zoe had once lived, and where Aaron and his father Delray still lived, that drew me to it. *Here, Aaron lives! He is alive and living and knows nothing of you.*

How mysterious it is, to be *in love*. For you can be *in love* with one who knows nothing of you. Perhaps our greatest happinesses spring from such longings—being *in love* with one who is oblivious of you.

Shut my eyes now, years later and yet how vivid to me that long loop-ing bicycle ride along the Huron Pike Road to the cobblestone overpass that carried railroad tracks high above my head—pushing my bike up a steep dirt path to the tracks—pedaling along the bumpy cinder-strewn shoulder of the tracks to the river a quarter-mile away—and there onto the footbridge above the river where in the wake of recent storm damage there was a newly posted warning PEDESTRIAN BRIDGE CLOSED FOR REPAIR CROSS AT YOUR OWN RISK. Below was the fast-rushing Black River which began high in the Adirondacks, a confluence of numberless small creeks and rivers, and would empty into vast Lake Ontario to the west, to which we'd taken some day trips when Daddy had been in a mood for such family trips to the wide sandy beach at (oddly named! Ben and I laughed at this) Mexico Bay, very near the tiny settlement of Texas. Though I knew these facts, I could not imagine how such a wide treacherous-seeming snaky-glittering river could *begin* anywhere, as I could not imagine how anything so vividly real to me as my own life could *begin*: for *beginning* implies a time and a point before which a thing or a being *does not yet exist*—and how is this possible?

Like my feeling for Aaron Kruller. I could not have said when pre-cisely it *began*, it seemed to have been with me always.

Rationally I know, and surely I knew then: my feeling for Aaron had only to do with Zoe Kruller, and with my father. A mysterious conjunc-tion of these persons. Yet how could that explain the depth of my feeling, and its obsessiveness?—gripping me tight as in the coils of a massive boa constrictor.

Cautiously I pedaled across the bridge. You were supposed to walk not ride bicycles across such pedestrian bridges but no adult was present to reprimand me. I tried not to glance down—tried not to be distracted by glimpses of the river below—fleetingly visible through cracks between the loosely-fitted planks as a sensation of terrible dizziness rose in me—until I was safely across—and clumsily descending another steep dirt path to a service road beside the Chautauqua & Buffalo railroad yard—past the graffiti-defaced train depot and then to Front Street, and to Chadd, and a mile or so to the two-lane state highway where enormous trucks bearing trailers careened by me in a haze of exhaust and heat and sometimes sounded their horns at me, their sharp terrible braying horns at a lone girl-bicyclist on this dangerous stretch of highway where vehicles routinely sped beyond the fifty-five-mile-per-hour limit into the seventies if not higher and now came the angry adult reprimand *Get the hell out of here girl, this is no place for you.*

Following the highway into an area of industrial sites, warehouses and small factories, Atlas Van Lines, Herkimer County Animal Control where Daddy had once taken a wounded stray dog we'd found on the Huron Pike Road, no hope for the dog Daddy said *No we can't take him in, that isn't going to happen so don't push it you kids.* And there beyond Sparta Salvage was the blacktop Quarry Road where heavy dump trucks rattled through the days on their way to and from the gypsum quarry a mile or so beyond a neighborhood of small clapboard and asphalt-sided houses and tin-colored mobile homes decorated with American flags—there was Kruller's Auto Repair & Cycle Shop

There were two garages, adjoining. In a sprawl of secondhand motorcycles and other vehicles for sale, in a wide mostly grassless front yard. And at the rear of the lot at the end of a long gravel driveway was the Kruller house, a renovated old-style clapboard farmhouse of the kind common to Herkimer County painted a pale peach color with lime-green shutters, you could see Zoe Kruller's touch in these startling colors now fading. How strange it seemed to me that Zoe Kruller had lived in that house, the smiling freckle-faced woman from Honeystone's Dairy who had once appeared—unless I'd imagined it—in the kitchen of our house and had spoken to me with a feverish sort of intensity calling me *Krissie* and smiling at me assuring me there was no need to tell my mother about the visit, she would tell my mother herself; how strange to think that the same woman was the girl-singer up on the stage at Chautauqua Park, for whom people had clapped so wildly; a woman who'd been a man's wife, a boy's mother, living out on Quarry Road in the sort of neighborhood my mother called *poor white* which was a different kind of poor from *colored* and *Indian*, maybe worse.

How strange, Zoe who'd been alive was now *dead*.

More than dead, *murdered*.

Zoe had been most alive at Chautauqua Park, summer nights singing with Black River Breakdown. Summer nights I'd been allowed to stay up past my usual bedtime of 9:00 P.M. There on the stage was Zoe Kruller looking so different from how she'd looked at the dairy, glamorous-sexy like a woman on TV singing "Are You Lonesome Tonight" in her low throaty voice—"Up the Ladder and Through the Roof"—"Footprints in the Snow"—"Little Bird of Heaven." Circling her head like a quivering deranged halo were gnats and moths, Zoe did her best to ignore. She wore sparkly dresses with very short skirts unless the skirts were long, and slit at the sides to mid-thigh. Her legs shone in pale stockings or were netted in black lace stockings and her shoes were high-heeled unless—I don't think that I was imagining this—Zoe once performed in her stocking feet, or barefoot. On a very hot Sparta summer night long ago.

Yes: Zoe had kicked off her shoes. Zoe had loosened her wild-streaked hair that had been caught back from her face in some sort of headband, shook her hair free now as the audience whistled and clapped.

You knew it was the end of a performance when the performer bowed. There was Zoe Kruller bowing—smiling her wide glistening hopeful smile—lifting a hand to shade her eyes squinting past the stage lights as a more experienced singer would not have done—thanking the audience for being "the very best audience, ever—I love you—"

The lights went down. With terrible abruptness, like a heavy curtain falling.

That woman.

Yes? What woman?

You know what woman.

Del Kruller's wife? What?

Is there something between the two of you?

Something—what? Like what, Lucille?

I asked, is there something between the two of you.

Based on—what?

Based on you. And her.

About as much as there's between you and Del.

I hardly know Delray Kruller! He doesn't know me.

There you are, Lucille. We're even.

Damn that's a low thing to say. Damn you.

In the car, driving home. Daddy driving and Mommy in the passenger's seat and Ben and me in the backseat drifting into sleep.

Thinking of such things, pedaling past the driveway to the Kruller house. It was a gauzy summer day, overcast sky and white-hot sunlight reflected everywhere. I was fourteen years old lanky-limbed and skinny and looking younger than my age glimpsed at a little distance. By this time Zoe Kruller had been dead—murdered—for three years and four months and her murderer had yet to be identified.

Kruller's Auto Repair & Cycle Shop was a garage where every kind of vehicle was brought for repair: autos, pickups and small trucks, tractors, motorcycles. The garage resembled a box laid on its side and spilling contents: vehicles, tools and equipment, loud rock music, mechanics in grease-stiffened overalls. The men's voices were loud. Their laughter was loud, grating. I took care to bicycle on the farther side of the road for I did not want that laughter directed at me, I did not want to attract the notice of anyone at the garage—workers, customers, Aaron Kruller who might be one of the younger mechanics glimpsed in the corner of my eye.

Often there were other bicyclists on Quarry Road but mostly these were teenaged boys. It was not common to see a girl out here, alone. In jeans and a pullover shirt I might have passed for a boy except for my pale-blond hair in a ponytail streaming behind me. If someone at the garage whistled at me, called after me *Hey there girl! Hey baby!* My heart kicked with alarm—unless it was with excitement—but I never glanced around for I knew that it wouldn't have been Aaron Kruller who'd called after me—Aaron Kruller wasn't one to call after girls—and for sure it would not have been his father Delray and whoever it was, one of the mechanics, or a customer, or just some guy hanging out at the garage where lots of guys seemed to hang out, he'd have ceased seeing me in more or less the same instant he'd singled me out for fleeting male attention and he wouldn't have had a good enough look at my face to realize *That girl! Eddy Diehl's daughter.*

22

DIDN'T SEE WHO IT was who'd hurt me. Never knew his name.

This would be my statement. My testimony. There was no way of speaking of what had been done to me that was not a way of acknowledging what I'd wanted done for otherwise why would I have gone with these individuals, why in the battered van that day after school instead of to the yearbook editorial meeting where our advisor Mrs. Finder would be waiting for me, and disappointed in me.

Hoping he'd be there, at the other place. At the depot.

It was where certain individuals hung out after school. Though not all of them went to school any longer. Older guys in their twenties who supplied the dope. Aaron Kruller was known to be among their friends. *Druggies* Ben would say sneering *dopers junkies losers* but there can be happiness in such risks. *Want to party with us Krissie? Want to get high? You look like you need to get high sweetheart, c'mon I know the way.*

And so I went with them. Maybe it was a mistake—maybe all of my life has been a mistake—how'd I have known, unless I took the risk?

Turned out, Aaron Kruller wasn't there.

But then, Aaron Kruller was there.

. . . didn't see who hurt me. Any of them. Didn't see their faces, don't know their names.

Where it started to go wrong, can't remember. Or why. Maybe there's no *why*. When it's your fault. When you invited it. When you know beforehand this is wild, this is risky, this is reckless, these girls are not your friends. Why are you here but there's no *why*.

Wet, and cold. Inside the depot, like a cellar. Coughing, and choking. Gagging. Whatever they'd given me—*Krissie c'mon! You need to get
high sweetheart*—was coming back in hot coins of vomit like acid soiling
the front of my sweater. *Stoned out of her mind who the fuck is she? She's
just a kid Jesus she's freaking out, crashes and O.D.'s who's gonna dump her?
Not me!*

One of the girls caught at my arm digging in her nails. Whose name I
didn't know, or her face except it was a face of fierce concern, impatience.
Maybe I'd been crying, her boyfriend was trying to comfort me. *Hey Baby:
wake up! Open your eyes Baby Girl you're gonna be O.K.*

This girl was tugging at my hair, to wake me. This girl made my head
jerk like a puppet's, the others laughed. We were crowded together. Out
of our closeness a frantic heat was generated. Still, in the stone-walled
depot it was cold, damp as the farther, unfinished section of our cellar
beyond the furnace room. And the other girl—Bernadette. They were
high, and they were laughing. Buzzing voices, how many I could not have
said and afterward could not recall, overcome by fits of nausea, vomiting hot-acid clots of liquid like rancid milk and the girls who'd been my
friends were disgusted and the girls were furious with me *Puking on my
boots God damn Krista you did that on purpose.* The guys were laughing.
Laughter like animals shrieking. Girls fighting girls are so funny. I wasn't
to know that *Baby Girl* was a gift they'd brought, for the guys.

In fact it was *Baby Tits, Baby Cunt* they called me. To my face *Baby
Girl.*

How the fuck old is she, she looks like a kid. This could be bad.

She's our age, for Christ's sake! She's in our class at school.

These girls I'd thought were my friends. Hot-skinned, eyes glittery as
broken glass. One of them tore my sweater. One of them took hold of my
head to turn it, to cause me to vomit—if I was still in danger of vomiting—
into a corner of the room where there was a pile of refuse already reeking
with the stink of urine. Why this was so funny, I didn't know. Laughter
ran like wildfire around the room like blue sparks leaping from one of my
tormenters to the other and there was Duncan who'd just arrived demand-

ing to be introduced to Baby Girl/Baby Tits/Baby Cunt who's some kind of a trade for the dope he's bringing. Puking, and on my knees, and laughing wanting to think *But they like me, too—don't they? Think I am pretty, and want me with them.*

Passing joints, a "joint" burned in my clumsy fingers, one of my friends had to steady my hand. There came hot searing smoke into my mouth, into my lungs, it was a mistake to breathe, I could not help but breathe for otherwise I would have choked, yet now I was choking, there passed before my eyes a quick vision of my mother staring at me appalled and disgusted *You are not my daughter any longer, you are his.* Tears running down my face and I'm gagging but laughing and the girls who'd brought me here—Mira, Bernadette—my friends from school—are shoving me away squealing with laughter *Don't you puke again girl! Jesus* unless this has already happened and is somehow happening again, this sour taste in my mouth, the front of my pretty pale yellow sweater embroidered with rosebuds now splotched with vomit, dark-yellow stains like rancid buttermilk, my clothes are smelly and damp and beneath the sweater is my little white cotton brassiere that's been torn, too.

One of them must've reached up inside the sweater. Hard male fingers you might mistake for tickling, or a caress.

Why's this?—started off they'd been nice to Baby Girl then abruptly there's a change—like a cold wind picking up from the river—brackish-smelling, evil—can feel the meanness like heat coming off their skins—their ice pick eyes. Duncan Metz is an older guy—in his twenties—long out of Sparta High—thick-muscled neck and straggly hair and a spiky goatee gives him the look of a mean goat, a billy goat that's got to be boss. Duncan Metz was a friend of Aaron Kruller's. I had seen the two together on the street. Maybe, Duncan Metz worked at Kruller's Auto Repair and riding past the garage I'd seen him, or he'd seen me, maybe Duncan wasn't one of the mechanics but just a guy who hung out at the garage, took his car there to be serviced or purchased a car from Delray Kruller, he'd have wanted work done on, a Chevy Camaro maybe, or a Pontiac Firebird, Daddy would've known the names of this class of car not special enough for Eddy Diehl. Seeing Duncan, I thought *Now Aaron will be here. Now my life will be changed, all this will become beautiful.*

It isn't true, Krista Diehl is a senior at Sparta High, in the same class with Mira Roche and Bernadette Hedwig. Krista is in tenth grade, a sophomore. Krista is fifteen years old and under-age and Duncan and Jake and R.J., older guys in their twenties, are pondering this fact. Duncan has been admiring Krista's hair, pale-blond hair that isn't bleached, asks is her pussy blond, twists her hair in his fist making her whimper with pain, pulls her head down, toward his groin, Duncan means to be funny (doesn't he?), he's showing off for his friends, Krista is whimpering like a scared little girl which is always funny. Mean billy-goat Duncan Metz yanking Krista's head up, now forcing Krista up on her toes like a dancer, Baby Tits on her toes is even funnier and with part of her mind that isn't doped and dazed she knows that this is a mistake, pleading with one whose pleasure is hurting you displaying you before others is a mistake but Krista can't help herself begging *No don't please don't hurt me please* and one of the other guys tries to intervene, his objection is practical, common-sense *Duncan leave off she's too young, Baby Tits will get you arrested, man* and Duncan says *Baby Tits is stoned out of her mind, she'll be damn lucky her brains ain't fried when she comes to.* Inside the depot the air is fouled by a fire somebody has started, smoldering-garbagey stink of old rotted newspapers, rotted lumber, rotted leaves burning giving off an acrid smoke so the fire has to be stamped out. Still it's cold and damp inside the abandoned old train depot, you can see where the ticket sellers' counter used to be, benches for passengers now overturned, wrecked, a smell of urine/excrement in here, for homeless men sometimes sleep here in cold weather on the wrecked benches, or beneath them wrapped in newspapers on the filthy floor. Passing joints, crouching together around the remains of the fire that gives off no heat only this smoldering-garbagey stink you want to think *This is like family, sharing* except the dope Duncan has brought is hash mixed with speed, so strong it's like fire, the inside of my mouth is throbbing with heat, my head, my skull, my heart begins to race, there comes then a wave of sudden happiness, warmth, a crazy good feeling making me want to laugh as Daddy could make me laugh tickling his little girl out of a sulky mood, that quick, within seconds squealing with laughter or maybe it's the start of being smothered, suffocated—they've brought me here to suffocate me—too much is being crammed into my skull, my brain is swelling inside my skull like a balloon close to exploding. *Girl you must've wanted this, why else are you here. God damn stupid Baby Cunt why else you here.*

Somehow, Zoe Kruller was consoling me. On tiptoes leaning over the counter at Honeystone's asking *What can I do you for Krissie?* Desperately I needed to know if Zoe had been here, too. If this was a place she'd been brought to. And when she'd known, what would be done to her. Where she was going, and would not come back from. When she knew that she would die. When he began to strike her with the hammer, when he cracked her head like a melon, threw her onto the bed, unless already Zoe had been thrown onto the bed, must've been such rage in him, such a need to do harm, a frenzy, a madness as he twisted the towel around her neck and tightened it until her terrible thrashing waned, and ceased—until she'd ceased breathing—ceased struggling. And beyond this, there is no Zoe. And three and a half years later no one knows why. No one knows who. Nothing has changed. Nothing has been resolved. The man's face is a blur, the man's name is not known. Not a day, not an hour I am not aware of whose daughter. To this very day as an adult woman and as powerfully then as a girl of fifteen thinking defiantly *But I love him, I will never not love him. I will never not believe him.*

Early afternoon in fifth period study hall that day where I was staring at my geometry text, chewing at my lower lip, that emptiness inside me like a hole that can never be filled and there was Mira Roche whom I scarcely knew, an older girl, a senior with the face and figure of an adult woman, smiling at me leaning over to whisper to me *Hey Krista: want to party with us? Tonight?* And Bernadette Hedwig who sat behind me leaned close so I could feel her fluttery breath against the back of my neck saying *There's this guy Krissie, this really cool guy wants to meet you.* And Mira says *Yeah he does! He told me.* And in the girls' lavatory afterward where they followed me Mira on one side of me, Bernadette on the other, I was blushing so flattered, so confused, why'd these older girls care about *me?*—and Mira said I was sexy as hell, that blond hair *to die for* and Bernadette was stroking my hair, leaning close as if to kiss me and I felt a sudden happiness, I believed that these girls were a way to Aaron Kruller, it was Aaron Kruller of whom they spoke. The thrill of being chosen like this! The thrill of being liked thinking *These girls want to be my friends. My special friends.* For I no longer had any friends at Sparta High. The girls in my class I had believed I could trust, I could no longer trust. Or I did not wish to trust. It had been a long time since I'd stayed overnight with a girlfriend in Sparta, as I'd once done. Before *the trouble* had come into our lives changing our lives so Ben and I were conscious of people feeling sorry for us, pitying us and we'd come to hate them, it was a mistake to confide in a friend, both Ben and I had learned. If I confessed to a friend that I missed my father, if I told her where Daddy was living now (which was Buffalo), and what kind of work he was doing ("Like his work here"—which wasn't exactly the truth), if I said how the fact was he'd never been arrested, the Sparta police had never arrested him because they had no reason to arrest him, no proof, no "evidence," they'd never had any and yet so many people thought he'd killed Zoe Kruller, more and more recklessly I might be led to confess to my friend, I might begin to cry, my friend might console me, and encourage me to say more, and so I would say more, I would tell her how sad my mother was, how sad my brother Ben was, how angry we were, how unfair it was and how unjust, so much about Edward Diehl on TV, in the papers, and none of it was true, and there was no way to erase it, or make it right. And this girl would pretend to be sympathetic, pretending to be my friend, saying *Oh Krista it must be so hard, it's like somebody dying in the family, my mother feels so sorry for you and for your mother she says she can't imagine how your mother has lived through it having to wonder if he'd hurt that woman maybe he'd hurt* her?

But Mira and Bernadette are not like that, I think.

Her and me goin for a ride. Just us.

Duncan is taking me outside he says. Twisting my hair in his fist. He's the kind of guy, a girl would go easy for, a girl would go with him not fearful and not needing to be forced but Duncan doesn't want that, that is boring to Duncan, in a loud braying voice Duncan declares *Bor-ring!* Which is why Duncan requires a change of scene and a change of people often. He's angry at Baby Tits/Baby Cunt or maybe just pretending—pretending to be angry, and to scold—like a stern daddy—pulling me by the hair so I'm limping after him like a dog on a short leash trying to laugh, I know that Duncan Metz is a joker, Duncan Metz takes pride in making people laugh and so if I'm laughing like the others it isn't cruel—is it? If I'm laughing and not whimpering in fear or pleading for him to stop this isn't going to hurt—is it? Or, if it hurts, if my scalp is screaming with pain, it's an accident and not intentional, Duncan is just joking.

Outside the depot it's been raining. A wet sweetly-rotted smell of earth, spilled fertilizer in the Chautauqua & Buffalo freight car Duncan is trying to lift me into—*C'mon baby, cooperate! One two three*—there's a logic to this, Duncan Metz is going to dump me inside the abandoned freight car and crawl in after me maybe, or Duncan Metz is going to dump me inside the abandoned freight car and force the sliding door shut trapping me inside, there must be a logic to what Duncan is trying to do and to my panicked laughter but my brain seems to have shut down except to register that someone seems to have intervened—a stranger—another guy grabbing at Duncan's arm furious and disgusted *Let the girl alone, Metz get the fuck away from her*—suddenly the two guys are struggling, exchanging curses, quick hard blows—Duncan falters and backs off—lets me go—even shoves me at the other guy with a muttered obscenity *Fuck you Kruller!*—I see that the second boy is Aaron Kruller—Aaron is incensed as if he's been watching Duncan and me from a distance not wanting to get involved but somehow he has become involved, God damn he has no choice.

When Duncan shoved me, I lost my balance and fell to the ground. No strength in my legs. So tired!—so exhausted!—wanting suddenly desperately just to sleep, to escape into sleep on the wet pavement except

Aaron Kruller is crouched over me pulling at me *Get up, c'mon girl get up you can't go to sleep here—*

He manages to get me on my feet. At a little distance, Duncan is jeering at us. Aaron ignores him saying *Okay lean on me don't shut your eyes try to stay awake. Jesus, come on!*

How badly I want to sleep. Lie on the ground curled into the shape of a little white grub, no eyes, no ears, scarcely a heartbeat and my bones are hollow filling with sleep like ether except that Aaron Kruller is shaking me, gripping my shoulders and shaking me, won't let me sleep *Wham! Wham!* the flat of Aaron Kruller's hand against my face waking me so that my eyes fly open.

Later, I will see the logic of this. I will think *This was meant to be, in just this way.*

My mouth is bleeding. My upper lip has been cut. Maybe from Aaron Kruller's slap, or one of Duncan Metz's blows. There's vomit dribbling from my mouth down the front of my clothes. Silky blond hair falling in vomit-clotted tatters in my face. *Stay awake* Aaron says. *Keep your eyes open. Fall asleep you'll O.D.* Roughly walking me as you'd walk a staggering drunk. Half-dragging me to the street his arm tight around my waist supporting my weight while Duncan Metz shouts after us like someone crazed.

Aaron ignores Duncan Metz. Aaron is saying, urging *C'mon girl, you can walk. We're almost there.*

There's a car parked on the street, motor running. Aaron helps me into the passenger's seat. My legs are limp, I seem to have lost one shoe. My head feels loose on my neck as if it might fall off. Still I am so sleepy, so dazed!—stricken by another spasm of nausea—gagging and vomiting though there is virtually nothing to throw up—my guts are sick— poisoned—so ashamed you would think *This can't be happening to me, I am not a girl to whom such an ugly thing can happen* but when the vomiting seems to have run its course Aaron Kruller wipes my mouth matter-of-factly with a wadded tissue out of his jacket pocket. He has to be disgusted with me but half-marveling too *Jesus, girl! Look at you.*

And I know that I am safe with him. Thinking *He knows me. All these years Aaron Kruller has known who I am.*

IT WAS SAID *They grow up fast, the mixed-bloods.*

My mother and her people said this. In Sparta, Caucasians said this. Not in contempt or disdain or anyway not always but in a kind of guilty wonder.

They grow up fast. They don't have much choice.

And so it seemed to me Aaron Kruller was no boy like my brother Ben. Aaron Kruller wasn't a kid. Not yet eighteen—I think this is right— yet Aaron behaved like an adult man tall and decisive and cursing beneath his breath as if knowing that what he was doing was bad luck, damned bad luck but he had no choice.

Getting involved with Krista Diehl. He'd had no choice.

He drove us to a brick row house. Somewhere in Sparta, not far from the train depot. A red-brick row house dripping rain and inside smelling of fried potatoes, grease. Walked me into the house his arm slung hard around my waist and I was slipping-down, near-falling, near-fainting and too dazed even to cry. Briskly Aaron walked me past an astonished-looking woman—a relative of his—middle-aged, a stranger to me—she'd come to open the door when Aaron rapped on the door with his fist and called to be let in—"It's me, Aaron!"—walking me then past this woman and down a narrow corridor tilting like something in a fun house and into a cubbyhole of a bathroom ordering me to wash my face, clean myself up, if he drove me home and my mother saw me looking like this she'd freak and call the cops.

And if the cops saw me, I'd be busted.

At the sink I had difficulty turning on a faucet. My knees were weak, I could not seem to keep my balance. Aaron cursed faintly beneath his breath—what sounded like *fuck fuck fuck this*—but pushed down my head, ran cold water from a faucet and splashed it onto my heated face until I was coughing, sputtering, part-revived.

Aaron asked how old I was. I told him. Aaron shook his head in that way of his half-disgusted half-marveling. *"Fuck."*

Meaning, I was under-age. I was a minor. Being in my company, in my drugged state, and looking the way I did, as if something had been done to me, something crude and nasty and sexual, meant trouble.

"Aaron? Who's this?"

The woman pushed into the bathroom behind us excited and blustery as if her patience were beyond frayed, she was seriously pissed. In the exasperated familiarity with which she spoke Aaron's name you could hear an accent echoing Aaron's, they were of the same family, the same kin. Aaron gave her a highly truncated account of what had happened at the depot. He spoke of *she*, *her* as if I were not present. As if I were a problem that had been presented to him, he had not wished for and could not abandon.

"Oh, Jesus. Did she—is she—*hurt*?"

"I don't think so."

"She's high on—what?"

"Ask her."

The woman pushed Aaron aside. She would fuss over me now as you'd fuss over a sick child. Her breath smelled warmly of beer, her red flannel shirt strained over her wide heavy breasts. Her name was Viola: it seemed to me, I'd seen *VIOLA* on a name tag somewhere, maybe at Kmart.

Viola was an aunt of Aaron Kruller's—a sister of Delray Kruller— with some of the same facial features, the swarthy skin, heavy dark eyebrows.

Aaron's aunt Viola might more plausibly have been Aaron Kruller's mother than Zoe Hawkson had been.

Vaguely I was made aware of a stained porcelain sink with exposed pipes, an antiquated toilet with a pink chenille toilet-seat cover, a large scarred bathtub into which laundry seemed to have been dumped—dirty towels, bedding, women's underwear. I was made to think how revolted my mother would have been by such untidiness. Such slovenliness. Such letting-go. Viola was asking Aaron if anyone had followed us here and Aaron said he didn't think so. She asked if he'd seen police cruisers in the neighborhood and Aaron said he didn't think so. She asked if this had anything to do with—the name sounded like *Dutch-boy*—and Aaron said, "Fuck, no."

Aaron didn't care for this line of questioning. Aaron left me with his aunt whose breath came fiercely as if she'd been running up a steep stairs. Roughly she was swiping and slashing at my hair with a grimy hairbrush and with her fingers—her nails were oddly shaped, square, and had been painted a lurid red-orange, now chipped—she picked out snarls and clots of what she hadn't immediately recognized as vomit. In exasperation she gave a breathy little scream: "Ohhh shit."

"What's the problem?"

Aaron had returned, with a fresh-opened can of beer. Through my stuck-together eyelashes I saw him drink in thirsty swallows as a drowning man might suck at air. I fell in love with him then. I fell more deeply in love.

The Kruller boy, Aaron. The boy I had so long pursued and dreamt-of and seeing now how coarse his face was, a bristly dark beard pushing out on his lower jaws, the heaviness of his jaws, in his forehead and cheeks old acne-scars or lacrosse scars or maybe scars from fights and in his left eyebrow a particularly nasty-looking scar like a fishhook. And seeing him now at such quarters I thought that I might not have recognized him, I was frightened of him and yet hopelessly I loved him, a sick sinking love must have shone in my bloodshot eyes for Aaron stared at me, and looked quickly away.

Muttering again what sounded like *Fuck fuck fuck this* under his breath.

Viola was asking Aaron why he'd brought me here "stoned out of her head"—and "so young"—and Aaron said it wasn't like he'd had any choice. Viola asked if he knew who I was and Aaron didn't answer at first and then he said, with a harsh mirthless laugh, "Guess."

"'Guess'? How the hell am I going to 'guess'?"

"Her last name is 'Diehl.'"

"Last name—what?"

"'Diehl.'"

Viola was standing at the sink beside me and she lifted her head now to stare into the splotched mirror above the sink, at Aaron who stood behind us lounging in the doorway drinking beer.

"'Diehl'—? You mean—him?"

"Fuck who else I mean, Vi. How many 'Diehls' are there."

Aaron shrugged. In the mirror Viola continued to regard me with something like fascinated dismay. More clearly now than before I could see the family likeness between her and her nephew: not just the facial features and the dark-tinted skin but her way of tensing her jaws as if she were trying to bite back terrible words, she dare not reveal.

I wanted to take comfort in this woman's nearness. I wanted to take comfort in her physical warmth, the way the material of her frayed flannel shirt strained at her breasts and the way in which she stared at me as if unable to know what she felt for me. She was my mother's age, perhaps. Fine worry-lines beside her eyes and a tiny pinch of flesh beneath her chin, but still Viola Kruller was a good-looking woman, men would turn to stare after her in the street.

In a kind of delayed rebuke, she gave me a little push.

"Ed Diehl's daughter! Jesus."

I had no response to this. At the sink, my face flushed and my hair in my eyes, I could pretend that I didn't understand. I was high—"stoned." I could pretend to not understand many things.

Viola said, relenting, working her mouth into a kind of forced smile, "Well. I guess it isn't your fault, is it. You're just a girl. His kid. Like it isn't anybody's fault whose kid they turn out to be, murderer or not."

I wanted to protest *But my father is not! Daddy is not* but my throat was shut up.

Suddenly I felt faint. The faintness came and went in waves and this was a bad one. The woman caught me beneath the arms and helped me to sit on the lowered toilet seat. Fuzzy-chenille toilet seat. Viola Kruller and Lucille Bauer had at least one thing in common: toilet-seat covers of fuzzy chenille.

In the downstairs bathroom Mom had a yellow cover. In the upstairs bathroom rosy-pink.

I smiled to think *Mom wouldn't like to see this!*

I was feeling light-headed again. Wanting to slip down, curl onto the stained linoleum floor of the little bathroom and sleep.

A tight-curled little white grub. The kind you might crush underfoot, without noticing.

"No, hon! Not that. You aren't going to nod off, hon. You know that's not a good idea, in the state you're in, hon. Bet-ter not. No-oo—" Briskly the woman shook my shoulders to keep me awake. With weak fingers I fumbled for one of her hands, gripped it with a tenacity that must have surprised her. I could not recall when I had last gripped any adult's hand in such a way. "O.K., hon. I got you. You're all right. You're going to be all right."

Behind us Aaron spoke—startling how close his voice was—I'd forgotten he was there—"If I can get her out of here and get her home, if she'd sober up"—and the woman said, "God damn Aaron, you should've thought of that before you brought her here," and Aaron said, "This was the closest of any place I knew. Vi, you'd have done the same thing," and the woman said, "Why didn't you take her to the hospital, if you thought she was O.D.'ing," and Aaron said, "She was breathing O.K. and she could walk," and the woman said, "So—you could take her now, get her off our hands," and Aaron said, "I'm scared of fucking up my probation," and the woman said, "Your probation? What about mine? God damn you, Aaron. Kids like you don't *think*."

Scolded, Aaron fell silent. You could tell that this was a familiar routine. There was an exasperated fondness in the aunt's voice, something conciliatory and trusting in the nephew. I thought how fascinating it was, these strangers were speaking of me as if I mattered. As if, if I O.D.'d on drugs, that would matter. And how strange, that they spoke of me as if I were a young child, not responsible for my behavior. The woman asked another time if I'd been *hurt*—I knew to translate this as *raped*—and Aaron said he was pretty sure not, there'd be "signs" of that if I had been. "Looks like she wetted herself, poor child," the woman said, dabbing at my clothes with a wet towel, and Aaron said, with that harsh mirthless laugh, "Long as the wet isn't blood, I don't mind wet."

They laughed together. Aunt and nephew laughing together. Krullers laughing together. The woman slapped my face with the wet washcloth sharply scolding—"I told you, hon. Don't fall asleep." To Aaron she said, "If she goes into a coma, if she dies on the floor right here that will fuck up your probation real good, mister smart-ass," and Aaron said, "Fuck, Auntie. She'd be dead by now, she was going to die."

My lips twitched in childish relief. I wasn't going to die!

The woman went away. Seeing that I was steady on the toilet seat and not about to fall off. In another room I heard her on the phone. I didn't think that it was an emergency number she was calling.

Alone together, Aaron Kruller and me. It seemed a different kind of alone than before.

As if we were known to each other now. We'd been identified and declared to each other now.

"You. You're 'Krista'—right? Some days, after school—I'd see you."

Meaning *I'd seen you following me. And I'd known why.*

This was not a question. Aaron knew the answer.

I had only to remain silent, Aaron knew the answer.

"That asshole brother of yours—'Ben.' He knows to stay out of my way."

Such contempt in Aaron's voice. The ugly fishhook scar in his eyebrow glared waxy-white.

It was disconcerting to think how young my brother Ben was—my "white" brother Ben—set beside Aaron Kruller. How Ben hardly needed to shave, his voice was a cracked boy's-voice, and there was stubble on Aaron Kruller's jaws, and his voice was deep and mocking and his big hands more resembled my father's hands than my brother's that were still the hands of a boy and so the hatred between them might be dangerous, for Ben. I wanted to plead for him *But Ben never hurt you!*

In the doorway Aaron Kruller loomed over me. In the close air of the little bathroom I could smell his body, and I could smell the briny beer-odor of his breath. He'd removed his jacket and was wearing a black T-shirt with a faded lilac logo—*Black River Breakdown*. His shoulders were broad and his arms were ropey-muscled and both his forearms were covered in mocking little hieroglyphics of tattoos that gave his dark-tinted skin a purplish-phosphorescent glimmer.

These tattoos were new, I thought. Since Aaron had been expelled permanently from high school.

Delray Kruller, too, was "covered" in tattoos. So it was said. My mother's relatives spoke of the man with disgust, indignation. They believed the husband of Zoe Kruller to be not only a *mixed-blood half-breed* but a *crack-head Hells Angel murderer.*

Openly they said—many in Sparta said—at least, those who were sympathetic with my father—that a man who'd done time in Attica, a known convict and biker, it's no surprise a man like that would kill his wife by beating her with a hammer and strangling her and whatever else he'd done to her, sick and perverted as Delray Kruller was.

As if hearing these thoughts Aaron said suddenly, crudely: "Y'know, Krista—you stink, Krista. You stink of puke. Better rinse your mouth."

Such hatred in Aaron Kruller's voice! His face seemed to shift shape, triangular as a cobra's.

Roughly then Aaron nudged behind me—pressed me against the hard unyielding rim of the sink and ran cold water into a sparkly pink plastic cup he'd taken from a windowsill—that had to be his aunt's cup, that held her toothbrush. The plastic rim was crusty with old lipstick yet when Aaron lifted the cup to my lips I didn't turn aside in revulsion but like an eager child hoping to forestall punishment I rinsed my mouth obediently and spat discolored water into the sink.

My mouth was bleeding, inside. Blood mixed with saliva mixed with tepid tap-water.

Shutting my eyes then and leaning my forehead against the sink wanting to slip into a dream and sleep on the filthy linoleum floor but Aaron shook me again: "God damn! I said *no*."

My lips moved, too faintly for the incensed boy to hear. I was trying to say *But I just want to sleep for a few minutes. Then I can go home.*

"Just keep your damn eyes open, Krista. You can do it."

In your arms, I could sleep. Then I could go home.

Aaron was saying, in a lowered voice so that his aunt couldn't hear, "Your father was screwing around with my mother, wasn't he? 'Eddy Diehl.' I saw them together. Plenty of times. 'Eddy Diehl' is the one, not my dad—whoever killed her, it was *him*."

In his excitement Aaron wasn't speaking very coherently. Yet I understood him perfectly.

"You want to get me in trouble too, don't you? Why you were following me! Looking at me! Like saying, 'Here I am. Come after me. Try it.'"

Aaron was pressing hard against me, hunched over me as in a clumsy wrestler's grip. His heavy upper body, his groin, I could feel tension in him like the crude vibrating of a motor, a sudden hot wave of sexual need. I knew boys' bodies—I knew what boys' bodies were—though the only naked boy I had ever seen was my brother, when he'd been much younger—I knew that it was Aaron Kruller's penis pressing against my buttocks, ropey-hard, urgent, and Aaron's big-knuckled hands were closing around my throat "This how he did it? Like this? *This*?" Faintly I was struggling, too weak to throw him off, the big fingers tightening around my neck, the big boy hunched over me grunting and his weight on my back, his weight jamming my belly, my pelvis, the sharp little wishbone of my pelvis against the porcelain rim of the sink. *Oh! Oh! Oh!*—I tried to hold myself still, knowing that if I continued to struggle Aaron might squeeze my throat harder. This was my instinct, to surrender. To placate the one who hated me, who wished to hurt me. I believed that if I did not resist he would take pity on me. I thought *I must make him love me, so he will not want to hurt me.*

This knowledge came to me from such a distance, through my life I would attribute it to God.

For God speaks to us only at such times, as instinct.

Or maybe I was beginning to die. Maybe these were symptoms of the onset of death. When you can't breathe but the will to breathe is so powerful you begin to hallucinate your breathing and you begin to hallucinate the prospect of being all right in another moment so long as you hold yourself very still and don't resist your assailant. You do not ever want your assailant to know that you are resisting him, he will want to punish you more harshly. And maybe I was beginning to faint for lack of oxygen to the brain, maybe the hands around my throat were tighter than I wished to believe, maybe Aaron Kruller was no brother to me but wished only to hurt me and to take pleasure in hurting me and I could have no way of resisting him for to resist would be to provoke further rage and this was a sexual rage, once begun it must run its course.

What little I knew of sex, I knew that. Once begun sex is a stream into which frantic little tributaries flow, swelling the stream, accelerating the current, rushing downhill, flooding the senses to bursting.

In sex, there is the *little death*, drowning. You fear it and you anticipate it and there is no alternative but to rush to it as one rushes to a precipice, to sink into the flooding abyss, and drown.

"*This* is how he did it—huh? Like *this*—"

It was my father Aaron Kruller meant, I knew. My father, his hands around Zoe Kruller's neck. Strangling, assaulting. That was what Aaron Kruller meant.

In the other room the woman was still speaking on the phone. It was not that she was ignoring what her nephew was doing to the under-aged girl he'd brought home with him, in fact she had no awareness of it. She had utterly no awareness of it. For I did not scream, if I had tried to scream Aaron Kruller would have clamped his hand over my mouth. If I had tried to struggle Aaron Kruller would have hurt me, there was such rage in him.

Very little time had passed. Scarcely two minutes had passed. Through the splotched mirror of the medicine cabinet I might have seen Aunt Viola in the other room, turned away, speaking into a plastic phone receiver and oblivious of us in the bathroom not fifteen feet away.

A strangled little cry issued from Aaron's throat, his panting breath ceased, his thrashing body froze. It was over.

"Jesus . . ."

In a delirium he pushed me from him. He'd finished with me, he had used me up. Pushing me away like a soiled rag.

When he caught his breath he said: "Hey. You're O.K. Nobody hurt you, girl. Look here."

I could not look at him. His fingers clutched at my face now, as you'd lift a mask.

I was dazed, I wasn't thinking clearly. My shoulders where he'd gripped me—my back, my belly—much of my body—throbbed with pain.

I was trying to breathe again, trying to breathe normally, gasping for air. An artery in my throat was pounding.

"God *damn*. I said, nobody hurt you. Breathe."

I did as I was told: I breathed.

I managed to stand, shakily. I did not whimper, and I did not flinch with pain. I was able to show this furious boy with the blood-heavy face and glaring eyes like something chipped with an ice pick that I was breathing, and I was breathing normally.

Nobody had hurt me. This was so.

Not Duncan Metz. Not Aaron Kruller. If my body ached from their rough hands and if my throat was reddened from the grip of steely fingers and by the next morning my skin would be luridly bruised I would disguise myself, I would wear a turtleneck sweater, no one would see, no one would know, if my mother were to discover the more obvious of my bruises, if my mother were to pull away my clothes and scream seeing the marks of my assailants on my arms, my thighs, my ribs I would tell her as Jacky DeLucca had told police *Didn't see who it was, who hurt me. Never knew his name.*

HE DROVE ME HOME. To the house on the Huron Pike Road, Aaron Kruller dared to drive me that night.

We spoke little on the drive. It was late, near midnight. Aaron's aunt Viola had made instant coffee for me to drink, grimly she'd said *Some caffeine will help you. What you're going to tell your mother is anybody's guess but don't involve Aaron and for sure girl, don't involve me.*

I promised, I would not.

I'd gagged at the first taste of the hot strong black coffee but I managed to drink it, all that the woman gave me.

As I'd rinsed my mouth that stank of vomit, using the woman's sparkly plastic cup.

Close to dying, you learn to obey. You learn to take pleasure in obeying, a sweet piercing pleasure you could not imagine otherwise.

Good thing you didn't die, back there. They'd have dumped your body, girl. In a freight car. Down the river embankment. Aaron saved your life so don't get him trouble girl, hear me?

I heard. I thanked her. Seeing in her face—as in his—how they wished to be rid of me as if this night had never happened.

Aaron drove me home without needing to ask where I lived. He might've pretended he didn't know the location of Eddy Diehl's house but sure, where Eddy Diehl had lived all the Krullers would know.

Aaron Kruller would know. As I'd bicycled past his family home and his father's auto shop on Quarry Road, so it might've been, Aaron Kruller had once bicycled past our house on the Huron Pike Road.

Mostly in silence we drove. Now I was sobered up—or almost—my face rubbed hard with a wash rag in Aunt Viola's chiding hand so it felt like my skin had been scraped with sandpaper and the last of the vomit-clots picked out of my hair—every question I had to ask seemed foolish to me as words in a balloon floating over some cartoon-character's head.

I do remember asking Aaron what was it—"What's that m-moving thing?"—in a voice of sudden fright. I'd been trying to focus my aching eyes on the road rushing at us in Aaron's yellow-tinged headlights and in the corner of my vision like a crack at the edge of my brain there'd emerged something liquidy and shivery like molten lead or mercury not fully visible or identifiable in the shadows to the left of the road and Aaron said it was the river.

"R-river?"

"The river. Where you live."

I was staring at this shadowy rippling thing like something molten. It did not seem to me that I'd ever seen this thing before though I'd been living on the Huron Pike Road beside the Black River for all of my life.

Maybe Aaron saw the fear in my face. Maybe Aaron looked away not wanting to see it.

After a moment saying, "You're O.K. Get some sleep, you'll be O.K. How you feel won't be permanent."

I thought *Yes. It will.*

At the end of our driveway Aaron stopped his car. Wary and cautious seeing the length of the driveway Aaron hesitated, scowled—"Think you can make it? I'm not going in there."

Quickly I told him *yes.*

"See, if I drive in there, it'd be a hell of a time turning around. If your mother wants to see who I am."

I told him *yes* I could make it on my own and I told him *yes* I'd explain to my mother some plausible excuse to make sense of why I was so late, why I hadn't called her, *no* I would not tell her where I'd been or with whom.

23

April 17, 1985

Dear Aaron,
    Thank you for saving my life.

Krista Diehl

But this wasn't right. Probably not. This was an exaggeration.

Duncan Metz would not have killed me, I didn't think so. The more thought I gave to it, which was considerable, the more I'd come to see that he'd been teasing me, maybe he'd been intending to hurt me, yes maybe rape me, but I didn't think that he would have killed me, and I didn't think that the dope I'd smoked would have killed me, either.

Say Duncan had dumped me in the freight car. Say I'd been left there. All night. My mother would have called the police when I hadn't returned by midnight at least and in whatever state I was in, comatose, part-conscious, groaning and whimpering and crying for help in the morning a railroad worker would have discovered me.

Or better yet, as I thought about it harder, in subsequent days, one of the girls, Mira, or Bernadette, would have felt sorry for me, and worried about me, and would've called 911, sometime that night. Anonymously she would have reported a girl in the freight yard—*Seems like she'd O.D.'d on some drug—or maybe somebody beat her*—and police and emergency workers would have gone looking for me, and found me before it was too late.

I was sure of this. They'd have found me, I would not have died.

Duncan Metz and his friends wouldn't have wanted me *dead*.

April 17, 1985

Dear Aaron,
Thank you.

Your friend
Krista Diehl

But I couldn't send this, either. So terse, so plain, it sounded stingy, silly. It wasn't anything like what I meant.

Like the silence that surrounds the tolling of a bell allows you to hear the bell. Without the silence there would be only noise. That was how I needed to speak to Aaron Kruller. In short simple words cutting as sharp stones.

But I could not, in writing. I had not the ability. The words I wrote in my schoolgirl hand were not adequate.

These little notes I tore into pieces and threw away. I could imagine Aaron Kruller tearing open an envelope, frowning as he unfolded the sheet of notebook paper. This might have been the first "letter" Aaron Kruller had received in his life and it would have embarrassed him, or made him flush with annoyance.

If his father had brought in the mail that day, Delray would have teased him.

Some girl writing to you? Who the fuck—?

May 23, 1985

Dear Aaron—
I think there was a time when I was a little girl when I loved your mother. Don't hate me for saying "Zoe" was a name I loved. "Zoe" was like music to me. Like the songs "Zoe" sang at the bandstand to make you smile. Sometimes cry but most of the time smile. When your mother worked at Honeystone's & remembered each time that my name was Krissie. A little girl can love someone else's mother as much as her own. A little girl can wish that some-

one else's mother was her own. Even when she doesn't know that person really. As I don't know you really. Yet I love you.

Krista Diehl

So ridiculous! Embarrassing.

If he'd received such a letter Aaron Kruller would have torn it into pieces. Aaron Kruller's coarse-skinned face screwed up as if he were smelling a bad smell.

June 12, 1985

Dear Aaron—

 I need to try again. I can't find the words. I will never forget your kindness to me. You and your aunt who took care of me that night. You were ashamed, I think. What you'd done to me. The sex part of it. Things I do now to myself thinking of you Aaron. Squeezing my hands around my throat till almost I can't breathe. My vision is splotched, I can't see. The sex is so strong. The sex is so sweet. You said This is how he did it, strangled my mother *but that is not right, Aaron. You are thinking that my father was the one who strangled your mother Aaron but that is not right. I know this.*

Krista

This and other letters to Aaron Kruller I would tear into pieces, in disgust. Of course I never sent any letter to Aaron Kruller in even the weakest and most lovelorn of hours but I remember his address to this day: 1138 Quarry Road.

After that time I never bicycled past Kruller Auto Repair. I never bicycled on Quarry Road again.

After that night in April 1985 I didn't speak to Aaron Kruller for seventeen years.

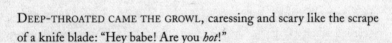

24

DEEP-THROATED CAME THE GROWL, caressing and scary like the scrape of a knife blade: "Hey babe! Are you *hot*!"

Deafening whistles. Teasing catcalls. With a snaky twist of my torso, a quick grab of my hands I'd wrested the basketball from one of the big busty girls from the Seneca reservation, now fierce-eyed Irene Griggs charged into me both elbows cocked knocking me to the floor—*wham!* The referee blew her whistle. Girls on both teams were laughing at me. Must've seemed comical to them—what the hell had gotten into Krista Diehl? Three or four times this game I'd gone for the ball, as if my life depended upon it weaving beneath a guard's arm, rapidly dribbling the ball down the court in the direction of the basket as if I might have a chance to score, the most remote chance to score, before being stopped by a girl like Kiki, or Dolores, or spiky-haired Irene Griggs knocking me down hard on my ass.

The referee was our gym coach, we called Mz. Ritsos. Her first name was Marian which sometimes the older girls called her, who were her special friends.

"Krista! You'll be hurt, you play reckless like that."

Mz. Ritsos was protective of me but disapproving: why didn't I play basketball with girls in my tenth grade class instead of these older girls, juniors and seniors? I was the youngest and smallest player, always being fouled. Knocked down and picked myself up flushed and embarrassed and limping but eager to get back into the game.

Need to be more aggressive he'd said. He'd chided me *Meaner, take more chances.*

If you don't want to be hurt Krissie maybe you shouldn't be playing at all.

I was laughing. Wiped my hot face in my Sparta High T-shirt. I liked it that I had two foul shots coming: I missed the first but scored with the second. My teammates cheered: "Krissie is fuckin' *hot.*"

What impressed them, even as they laughed at me, was I wasn't afraid to be hurt. I wasn't afraid to be reckless.

Playing basketball gave me a rush, a harder rush each time there was risk. Since Daddy had seen me, and chided me. Since Daddy had discerned what was flawed in me, and needed fixing. Now something white-hot stabbed in my belly, the excitement of risk, of being hurt if I wasn't fast enough or skillful enough. In the corner of my eye imagining it was Daddy I saw by the gym doors where some guys were standing, several older guys watching their girlfriends on the court, preferring to lean against the doors and not sit on the brightly-lit bleachers. *He said he'd be in Sparta this week. Staying at the Days Inn.* He'd come into the gym unobtrusively, suddenly he'd just be there. He'd be impressed, seeing how much more aggressively I was playing now. Holding my own, or almost, against these big hulking girls.

One of the guards on my team passed me the ball. Almost I fumbled it but no!—got it!—ducked and turned and dribbled the ball down-court so swiftly the guard looming over me was taken by surprise, lost me as I rushed down-court, leapt and tossed the ball and sank the basket—

Whistles, cheers for Krissie Diehl. Except spiky-haired Irene who was guarding me was seriously pissed, tripped me and elbowed me in the back for good measure, like a love tap. Sent me sprawling for the second time in five minutes and again Mz. Ritsos blew her whistle this time angry and exasperated standing over me, "Krista? You O.K.?" and I told her *yes* rising to my knees though my head was pounding and there was a ringing in both my ears. A circle of girls staring down at me, a long hushed moment when I wasn't sure that in fact I was O.K., the right side of my head had struck the hardwood floor, my right ankle felt as if it had been caught in a vise and my back was throbbing with pain from Irene's sharp elbow and— Jesus!—blood dripping onto the floor, a cut in my right eyebrow.

Mz. Ritsos said, "C'mon Krissie, let's get you to the infirmary"—but I resisted her, wanting to return to the game, two foul shots were owed me and I was determined to score except the gym walls were tilting and the ceiling high above shimmered with a glowering gassy light and it seemed to me that Daddy was here observing me, proud of Krista now, his daughter was not a quitter. Tears spilled from my eyes *Daddy come get me take me away, I am so lonely.*

That was the last time I would play basketball with those girls, in fact with any girls, at Sparta High.

CALLED THE DAYS INN. Asked to speak with "Edward Diehl" and the desk clerk told me that no one with that name was registered there.

I protested no, that couldn't be right. That man was my father and he'd promised he would be there.

The woman checked again, or pretended to. Repeating "No one named 'Edward Diehl' is registered here."

"Maybe another name? He might be registered under another name."

"Well. I can't help you with that, miss."

"I have to speak to him, it's urgent. He's . . ."

My father. He is my father.

Help me to find my father.

I hung up the phone. I was upset! I was hurt for hadn't my father said he would be in Sparta for several days; it was only just Thursday today. The bond between us was so strong, I couldn't believe that Daddy would have left Sparta without saying good-bye to me.

Such desperation I felt for him, I could not have explained. By this time he'd been gone from our lives for years. And yet, I wanted him so badly. *Help me to find my father.*

The right side of my face was bruised from striking the basketball court, there was a thin cut in my eyebrow. It would heal and leave no scar, unlike Aaron Kruller's fishhook-scar. My right ankle ached, I walked with a wincing little limp. On the stairs at school I stumbled. *My father did this* I would claim. *My father is responsible.*

Yet when my mother noticed my injuries and asked me what had happened I told her: basketball.

She said, "Basketball! I didn't think it was such a rough game for girls."

"Anything you play hard at, it's rough."

I spoke with a shrug. It was a remark my father would make.

My mother drew in her breath sharply. She'd heard my father's intonation in my words, she'd felt the rebuke.

Later she said, as if she'd been preparing this announcement with care, and meant to deliver it calmly, "If that man tries to see you again, Krista. If he turns up where he's forbidden to. You will not go with him, Krista. *You will not.*"

I said nothing. I did not meet my mother's eyes.

She told me she'd called the high school. She'd spoken with the principal, and the vice principal, and the guidance counselor who was a former high school friend of hers. She said, "I've alerted them, and warned them. They know about the court order. If my daughter is abducted from school property by her father, in violation of that order, they will be held legally responsible."

I wondered if that could be. I smiled hesitantly, as if I wasn't sure I'd heard correctly.

"Yes! They will be held legally responsible. And he will be arrested. Do you understand?"

Bitterly my heart beat in opposition to this woman. Yet I said nothing.

My mother's skin looked like putty. Vertical striations in the flesh beneath her eyes as if tears had worn rivulets there.

I thought *Yes I know he has wounded you. He has betrayed you. Yes I know you are hurting but I don't care, I am my father's daughter and not yours.*

Was this true? Or did I just want to think it could be true?

"Krista, are you listening?"

"Yes."

When my mother was frightened—threatened—she had a way of speaking in short gusts of words like broken-off breaths. I saw how her hands yearned to snatch at me. Those hands that were more familiar to me than my own. I saw my mother's hands yearning to touch me, to caress me, to poke, pinch, hold me as they'd done when I was a little girl but dared not, now.

I was too young and heedless to understand *Love must be touch, a mother must have that right. Otherwise she is bereft. Otherwise she has no idea who she is.*

" . . . need to know that I can trust you, Krista! After all we've endured in this family because of your father. You must know, your father is . . . is not . . . a stable person. Of course he is 'attractive' . . . in the eyes of some people. But he is destructive, and . . ."

Her mouth moved. Her words stung in the small way of such insects as gnats, midges. I saw her hands seek each other in that gesture I'd come to dread, for I had begun unconsciously to imitate it: a clasping, a wringing of the hands as if a cloth were being rung. To protect myself from feeling sympathy for her I recalled the angry words that had spilled from that mouth the other night *You disgust me Krista! Deceitful going to turn out like your father a betrayer. . . .*

" . . . will you? Promise me . . . ?"

"Yes, Mom. I promise."

"Because it's over, you know. No matter what he tells you, what he begs from you, it's over. There's no more."

I thought *I will warn him.* But there was no way that I could make contact with him, to tell him not to step onto school property. Anxiously waiting through Thursday—and then Friday—and he hadn't returned, and a new anxiety came to me *Maybe he has left Sparta. He has left without saying good-bye.*

The weekend passed in a haze. I knew that my father would never come to the house from which he'd been expelled. He knew that my mother would call the police and have him arrested and to stop her he'd have had to hurt her and he wasn't that desperate, yet.

Ben said, "Did you see him? What the hell does he want?"

I said I hadn't seen him.

"You're a liar. I heard Mom talking to you. What's he want—to come back *here*? Fuck him."

I said nothing. I was thinking that Monday would be the crucial day: he would find me at school. It was the logical place to find me, away from this house.

But Monday!—Monday was a disappointment. No basketball practice and so I had no reason to remain after school lingering at the rear doors as my classmates pushed through into the cold air and buses pulled away from the curb in spewing exhaust. Nothing nastier than freezing air fouled by school bus exhaust. Alone I stood as if waiting—waiting for what?—for whom?—as others pushed past me without taking much notice of me, or glancing at me in annoyance, or bemusement, I understood how I did not belong here, I did not belong with these strangers, even Ben had become a stranger to me, I could not trust him. Sending my thoughts to my father who must have been thinking of me for I was thinking so intensely of him promising *Daddy I will take risks, I am not a quitter!*

The bus that would have taken me home pulled away, with the others. Foolishly I remained behind and waited, waited just inside the rear doors too unsettled and anxious to find an empty classroom where I could work on my homework, stood there at the door pressing my forehead against the pane until after an hour the late-bus appeared at the curb, I would take this bus home with the others.

And the next day: sleepwalking through the crowded halls buzzing like the interior of a hornet's hive trying not to be touched. Trying not to be collided-with, nudged. There were boys who deliberately careened into girls—solitary girls, like Krista Diehl—and I had to avoid these boys while giving no sign that I was aware of them. Even those teachers who'd seemed always to like me and who smiled at me were somber with pity for me *Diehl? Isn't her father the man who killed that woman a few years ago....*

Or *Poor Krista. Her father is in Attica isn't he....*

I wondered how Ben endured this. For certainly Ben knew. And Ben's resentment would be so much stronger than my own.

Like one of the school druggies, I hid away in a girls' lavatory on the first floor. Missed my English class which was my favorite class knowing the teacher would peer at my empty desk, say *Is Krista Diehl absent today? There's no record that Krista is absent.* How many times at Sparta High I could not bear being seen and had to hide in a lavatory in one or another toilet stall with its sides defaced by scrawls and scratches, crudely drawn hearts and initials as in a secret code of desire. At such times as often in my bed at home my hands moved to close about my throat. Gently, tentatively—then a little harder—as Aaron Kruller had closed his hands around my throat. Experimentally I squeezed until I felt the pulses quicken. Squeezing into my vision erupted in pinpricks of light. The fierce life of the blood, the fat artery that thrummed with life. The body has its own life, that the mind can't control. *This is how he did it? Like this? This?* I smelled Aaron Kruller's body, heated with desire. I felt that I would faint with yearning.

I had not seen Aaron since that night. At this time, it had been more than a year ago. A full year! I accepted it as part of my punishment for being Edward Diehl's daughter, whom Aaron Kruller wanted never to see again.

And there was Daddy who loved me, and would come for me. I was confident of this. I could not not believe this. Daddy's love for me was pure and not like Aaron Kruller's for Daddy wanted only to protect me, he would not have left Sparta without me, I was certain.

Tried to remember if he'd actually promised he would see me again on this visit to Sparta. I thought I'd heard him say so but maybe not. I thought *Yes of course! Like this? This?* Fingers on my throat, teasing, tightening. Aaron believed that my father had strangled his mother but Aaron had to be mistaken, I knew.

Like this.

Those zombie-days when I was waiting for my father to return.

To come for *me*. To protect and love *me*.

Later I would learn—it would be revealed publicly—that during this period of time Edward Diehl made more than thirty telephone calls from his room at the Days Inn, some of them repeatedly to the same number: demanding to speak with the Sparta PD detectives Martineau and Brescia and the police chief Schnagel; demanding to speak with the Herkimer County district attorney, a man named Decker; demanding to speak with the editor in chief of the Sparta *Journal*, and several county judges who'd had nothing to do with his "case." . . . My father was demanding the release of all "confidential"—"classified"—documents pertaining to the Sparta PD investigation into Zoe Kruller's murder, among other things; when his phone calls led nowhere, he tried to speak with these individuals in person, at their offices, and was rebuffed; the following day he tried again, and was again rebuffed. In a state of "extreme emotional distress" as eyewitnesses would testify, Edward Diehl turned up on Friday morning at the Sparta *Journal*, demanding to speak with the editor, this was in fact an old demand my father was reviving that the *Journal* publish a front-page retraction of the numerous articles that had appeared in the paper since February 1983 defaming Edward Diehl as a "prime suspect" in Zoe Kruller's murder and now he had a new idea: the *Journal* should publish an interview with him as an "innocent man" who'd been persecuted by Sparta police and had never been arrested and never formally charged with any crime and consequently never cleared of suspicion and his life—his life as a husband, father, citizen—ruined. He had lost his family, and he had lost his job. He had lost his house. He had lost his *life*. Now he wanted justice and this was justice—wasn't it? Why was justice being denied *him*? Did a man have to be a millionaire, to afford high-priced lawyers, just to clear his name? Was there some sort of cover-up here? Were the detectives and the police chief and the district attorney covering for someone? Had they accepted bribes? Was there a network of bribery, police corruption? Was the Herkimer county sheriff involved, too? Was the Sparta *Journal* involved?

When nothing came of these repeated demands, my father drove to the Sparta TV station WWSP-TV demanding "airtime"—and was turned away by a frightened office manager. Driving then to the office of a lawyer in downtown Sparta whose name he'd found in the yellow pages, insisted upon speaking with this lawyer, a man named Schell, hoping to interest him in taking on his case in lawsuits charging "slander"—"libel"—"defamation of character"—"loss of income"—against the Sparta police, the district attorney, and the *Journal* and other newspapers through the state that had defamed him, but his excited and belligerent manner as well as his lack of money didn't encourage Schell to take him on as a client.

Even on a "contingency fee" basis?—Edward Diehl would gladly have signed over 90 percent of the money the lawsuits brought him, which, he believed, would be "millions of dollars"—but no, Schell declined.

Nor would Schell recommend another lawyer.

Saying afterward, "Jesus, the poor bastard! Looking at me like a drowning rat—that's just realized he isn't going to be hauled up and saved from drowning."

And so, my father Edward Diehl came at last to see that these men, seemingly unlinked to one another, were secretly allied. Far from feeling sympathy for him, as some of them pretended, the men were in fact contacting one another and laughing at him, in his misery.

Once, they'd accused him of murder. They'd tried to get him to confess, they'd tried to blame him for a crime he hadn't committed. But now they'd given that up. Not a one of them, he was sure, seriously believed that he'd killed Zoe Kruller. They hadn't been able to prove that Delway Kruller had killed her, either. All that was past, forgotten. They were laughing at Eddy Diehl now as a crank, a "nut-case," a figure of scorn.

It was like pack animals: one of their kind was injured, limping and doomed. The others detached themselves from him. He would die alone, expelled from the pack; unless the pack turned on him in a frenzy of bloodlust, tearing out his throat.

The wild laughter of wild creatures. Of wolves.

Blood on their muzzles. Beautiful cruel creatures cavorting and leaping in the snow, and on the ground the fallen animal, a gutted carcass.

TUESDAY AFTERNOON, dusk when Daddy arrived at last at my school. I had not given up waiting for him and yet it was a shock to me to see my father in the dark-coppery Caddie Seville as I'd last seen him a few days before. *So this is real after all! Daddy is real.*

Much of that day he'd been drinking. Now it was 4:40 P.M., he'd been drinking since late morning both whiskey and ale. He hadn't slept for several days in succession. He'd made his decision.

"Krista sweetheart! Climb in."

Quickly I ran to the new-looking Caddie Seville. Maybe I was being observed by some of my classmates—envied, I would have thought.

She has a father. He came to pick her up. Classy car!

Smelling whiskey on Daddy's breath as he leaned over to hug me hard enough to knock the breath from me. I laughed excitedly, I loved Daddy's whiskey-breath, Daddy's stubbly chin.

"I knew you'd be here, Puss. Sorry I'm late. I had business to attend to. Now I'm clear. I knew you'd be the one not to let me down."

We drove out of the parking lot. I saw that there was a change in my father since the last time I'd seen him: he was still wearing the suede jacket but it looked soiled, even torn. His graying-red hair was disheveled as if he'd been sleeping and had not combed it. His face was ravaged and yet radiant and his eyes were bleary, bloodshot yet alert and alive. Eddy Diehl was a desperate man but he was a righteous man. In history we'd been learning about John Brown the Abolitionist leader, the "bloodthirsty madman" reviled by others who'd sacrificed his life for a principle. He had been hanged, he'd become a martyr for the sake of ending slavery in the United States. In our textbook the photograph of John Brown resembled my father, I thought.

"From now on, it's you and me, Krista. I need my girl with me."

And I said, blinded by happiness *Yes!*

"But if you come with me now, see?—you can't go back to *her*. You can't go back to any of them, you will be with *me*."

And I said, blinded by happiness *Oh yes!*

"Because she would never have you back. Your mother would never want to see you again."

And I said *I know this, oh Daddy this is what I want too.*

At the Days Inn, he showed me the gun.

Calmly removing it from a duffel bag, where it was wrapped inside a white cotton T-shirt. The duffel bag—soiled, adorned with mysterious seals and insignia as if it had originally belonged to someone else—he'd set carefully onto the bed, to unzip. As his boyish grin unzipped in his battered face part-shy part-boastful. And his quickened breath.

A gun! A handgun! Many times I'd seen rifles up close, .22-caliber rifles, and boys' air rifles: Ben had one, my father had bought him when he was twelve. And there was my grandfather's shotgun, he'd used to hunt pheasants when he'd been younger, Ben and I were warned never to touch.

But only in movies and on TV had I seen a handgun, a revolver.

Blunt-nosed, ugly and dark-dully-gleaming, an alarming sight in my father's just-perceptibly unsteady hand.

Both hands, as he gripped it. Sighting along the barrel like a TV cop with a deep-furrowed brow and in that stance regarding himself in the mirror above a bureau of drawers.

"Our secret, sweetheart. Yes?"

I was too surprised to react, at first. Smiling stupidly as often I was left standing on the basketball court in the first dazed moment before my nose began to leak blood from a ball carelessly or cruelly flung at my provoking little-girl Caucasian face.

"Krista? Don't look so scared, sweetie. A gun is our friend, when we are in danger. When we have enemies who are armed. See, honey—"

Daddy was showing me something about the gun, I was too upset, too distracted to understand what he was saying, what he was showing me, later I would think *The safety lock was on, was that it?*—"I would never resort to a 'deadly weapon' except if I was forced. Like for self-protection, or to protect my family. To protect *you*. If for instance they break in here and try to take you away from me."

This too was confusing. This too I could not comprehend.

"'Break in'—? Here?"

"If they locate us. If they know that Edward Diehl is in this room."

My heart was hammering inside my skinny rib cage. My father's words made no sense to me. Lines from the song Zoe Kruller sung in her teasing-sexy throaty voice *Little bird of heaven! Little bird of heaven right here in my hand!* ran through my mind, mocking me for my heart had become the little bird wildly thrashing its wings to escape.

Still gripping the gun, Daddy went to shut, lock, and bolt the door of the motel room. Briskly Daddy yanked the Venetian blind down over the single window, that overlooked a cracked asphalt parking lot nearly deserted at this time of day.

Daddy tried to shut the drapes, too. But the cord broke in his jolting hand.

"Just to take precautions, sweetie. Nobody should know that I'm here—or you, with me—unless they'd been spying on me, or on *you*. Unless your vindictive momma put them on my trail or one of the Krullers, still hoping to cast the blame on me and not on Delray they've all got to know is the one. . . . God damn their sick sorry souls to *hell*."

I was swallowing hard. My mouth had gone dry. Daddy spoke in a reasonable-sounding voice as if knowing that I would agree with him.

Wanting to say *Daddy why do you have a gun? Daddy please put away the gun!* but the words caught in my throat. Daddy paid no heed to me, not the slightest heed, as a father pays no heed to the prattling of a very young child he loves, but has no need to hear.

Light-headed I needed to sit down quick but was fearful of sitting on the bed where Daddy had tossed his things, the unzipped duffel bag weirdly decorated with a stranger's private icons, a brown paper bag out of which long-necked bottles glistened—whiskey?—and a cardboard box containing manila files grimy from usage. Nor would I have been comfortable sitting in the room's single chair near the TV for the chair was covered with Daddy's soiled clothing, sweated-through undershirt and boxer shorts he must have worn to bed, and stretched out to dry that morning.

His smell pervaded the room. It was a smell I would long remember, briny and sweaty and acrid and despairing, the smell of a desperate man.

As if Daddy could read my thoughts he said cheerily, "Krissie honey! Give your old Daddy a smile, eh? Like you were smiling when you got into the car? See, this gun is a damn good high-quality Smith and Wesson thirty-eight caliber. This gun *is not going to hurt Krissie. This gun is for self-defense only.* All you need to know is we're safe here. If they'd been following us they'd have broken in by now."

On the drive to the Days Inn my father had peered into both the rearview mirror above the dashboard and the outside mirror. At the time I'd thought that another vehicle was crowding him from behind. Sharply he'd turned corners, brazenly he'd driven through intersections as the yellow light turned red. Now I knew that he was making sure that no one was following us.

Daddy's enemies. Our enemies. But we were safe in this locked room.

I wondered why we were here. What would be perpetrated, here.

"Want a Coke, Krista? You look thirsty. There's a machine outside —I'll get you a Coke. You stay right here."

Quickly I said Daddy no, no thank you.

If he'd unlocked the door and stepped outside, maybe there would be danger for him. Maybe—these thoughts came fluttering through my brain like dazed moths—I would push past him, run outside and call for help and Daddy would never trust me or love me again.

"You sure? I'm having a drink, myself. Sure you don't want anything?"

Still the revolver was in my father's hand. Not pointed anywhere purposefully, it was not at that moment, strictly speaking, a *gun,* a *weapon;* you might argue that it was simply an object.

We were in a first-floor room at the far end of a two-storey stucco building of just discernible shabbiness and melancholy; something in the very jauntiness of the sign *Days Inn Vacancies* exuded this air of shabbiness and melancholy. In books there is said to be meaning, in our English class our teacher was reading poems by Robert Frost to us and it was astonishing to me, and a little scary, how the words of a poem have such *meaning*, but in actual life, in places like the Days Inn motel there is not much *meaning*, it is just something that *is*. And outside our room was a scrubby evergreen hedge that looked as if it was dying and beyond the hedge a nasty-smelling Dumpster. The room itself was depressing, as you'd expect—the bed so carelessly "made" as to suggest mockery, or anger—someone, seemingly my father, had risen from this bed and only just yanked the chenille spread up to cover the bedclothes at a diagonal, knocking a sweat-stained pillow to the floor. In our house my mother insisted upon making beds daily, even Ben was trained to make up his bed shortly after getting out of it, like brushing our teeth this was, washing our faces and combing our hair, something you *did*. But not Daddy, and not here.

Strewn about the room were Daddy's things: manila folders, legal-looking documents, newspapers, an empty Four Roses bottle on the bedside table, a two-thirds depleted six pack of Pilsner Ale. At home it had been understood that Daddy's territory in the basement, which was most of the basement, was not to be disturbed: Daddy's "workbench" as he called it, a long plank table where he kept his numerous carpenter's tools, his "power" tools, some of them hanging from hooks, always in the same order. You could see that Eddy Diehl was a serious man, for all his joking and kidding-around and liking to drink with his men friends, Eddy was a serious man who took his work and his work-tools seriously; here there was no *fooling around*—still less *fucking around*—at Daddy's workbench, not ever.

But in this room, this terrible room at the Days Inn, Daddy's things looked as if they'd been flung down, as if a windstorm had swept through the room yet leaving the stale-smelling air intact.

Afterward it would be revealed that several nights earlier my father had registered at the motel under the name "John Cass." It wasn't clear—from the motel clerk's vague testimony, you might infer that the clerk hadn't looked carefully at the ID my father had shown him—why he'd chosen the name "John Cass" but immediately I knew *It's for Johnny Cash*.

I would smile to think this. Not a happy smile but one that I could have shared with Daddy. One of his secrets, I would not tell anyone.

Nor would I reveal most of what Daddy confided in me, in the next two hours. At last speaking of having been in the U.S. Army—in boot camp at Fort Pendleton, and in Vietnam for five months; how "weird and scared" he was in Vietnam; how the black soft earth had seemed to erupt from inside, as if the explosion had come from beneath his feet and not through the air; how recalling it he wanted to laugh, it had been so *easy*; falling, losing consciousness, giving up—so *easy*; so he knew that dying could be *easy*, it was coming back to life, it was living your life, waking in a hospital bed delirious with pain and for the rest of your life walking with pain, and certain memories, that was the hard part. And working construction in the Thousand Islands, after he was discharged, sent home, limping and having headaches and a fucking ringing in his ears he'd have to live with, how he'd had a glimpse the summer he was twenty-two of "wealth"—"the real thing"—not just the "cottage" his work crew was building for a millionaire businessman from downstate but most of the properties on the island, which was Harbor Island—summerhouses with as many as fifteen, twenty rooms—and these were not small rooms—the highest-quality woods (redwood, cedar)—the highest quality kitchens, bathrooms, furnaces, every kind of electrical fixture; and the thirty-foot docks, and the yachts, so many yachts, all of them dazzling-white and some so large they required crews to man them; and sailboats of a size and quality Eddy Diehl had never known existed, high-class speedboats, even canoes. Canoes! You could spend hundreds of dollars on a canoe! That summer was what you'd call an "eye-opener" Daddy said, wiping his mouth as he drank. "Made me wonder what the hell life is, that I could get to be the age I was, after I'd been in the God-damned U.S. Army like I was, and thought I knew some things, like seeing people blown apart and feeling your own self drain away like something down a sink, but that was nothing, just movie stuff, comic-book stuff, not like what the world actually *is*. What the world *is*, Krissie, is people owning things, and owning *you*. That's not something you are taught or you can see in the plain daylight. I was twenty-two and didn't know shit. Not a fraction of what's going on. No more than a beetle would know crawling over the hull of one of those forty-foot Chris-Craft yachts. See what I'm saying, Krissie?" He squinted at me. He drank again, roughly wiping his mouth. "You get to realize, it hurts like hell, like a tire iron shoved up your ass, all that you are not going to have. All that you are never going to have no matter how you work your sorry ass off, every drop of your blood squeezed out of you and it wouldn't be enough, see? It's never enough, a guy like me. I knew that, then. It was a harder thing to know, than about dying. Because this, you have to live with; the other, you just give up. Right then, I was just a kid really, I knew how it would play out. My own father, and his father. And guys working construction, making 'good money' in the union. I never had delusions of grandeur like some people. Your mother, she'd have liked me to 'invest' with her brothers—she'd say maybe I could start my own construction business—didn't know the first thing about the business, pissed me off trying to tell me what to *do*. So, Krissie, this wasn't a kind of knowledge that helps you with your life, but at least you see how things are. And there it was."

Daddy paused, smiling. Daddy was wiping the revolver on a corner of the chenille bedspread, tenderly, distracted.

"Every fucking place in the Thousand Islands I helped build, I'd have liked to come back at night and set on fire. I had dreams like that, and woke up laughing. But you never do."

Daddy was sitting heavily on the bed, that creaked beneath his weight. He'd begun to sweat visibly. He'd removed the suede jacket and tossed it aside—I was surprised to see how cheap a jacket it was, lacking a lining, and wondered how I could have mistaken it for something more expensive. Daddy's face was ravaged-radiant, oily with sweat but he seemed hardly conscious of his discomfort, wiping the gun in that tender exacting way as if he could conjure out of its grim and obdurate ugliness something magical. I remembered how at my grandfather's farm we'd been told not ever to touch Grandpa's guns; now he'd become an old man, he no longer hunted; he seemed to have turned against hunting; though he refused to talk about it, there'd been a "gun accident" in the family some years ago involving an older cousin of Ben's and mine whom we'd never known, who had died somewhere on Grandpa's property. My mother warned us not to ask questions about this cousin, or about pheasant hunting; she'd warned us not to go anywhere near Grandpa's old guns he kept in a cabinet in the rear of the farmhouse. And now it seemed to be my mother to whom I was pleading *But Daddy would not hurt me, Daddy loves me.* Seeing my mother's scornful expression I protested *Daddy would not hurt himself, if I am here with him.*

"Krista, hey—y'sure, you don't want a Coke?" Daddy squinted at me with a fussy kind of half-drunk courtesy just this side of coercion. "'Cause we might be here a while, in this room."

Numbly I shook my head *no.* I wasn't hearing this.

"We're going to decide a matter tonight, Krista. Your mother and me. That woman is still my 'wife'—I am her 'husband'—that won't change. It involves you, that's why you are here. And also—hell, y'know—your old man loves you."

Daddy splashed bourbon into his glass, and drank. For a long moment he sat brooding, gazing at me. Weighing the gun in his hand.

I wanted to say *I love you too, Daddy.* My throat was very dry.

Daddy's eyes shone with such emotion, such love—I wanted to think it was love—it was frightening, for it came so strong. He was saying he had evidence to show me—and to show my mother—he'd been assembling—how long?—years?—to take his case to the public—if that was the only alternative. "See, they've made me a desperate man, Krista. But they've made me a better man, I think. Stronger. My soul like—*steel.*"

Spread out on the rumpled bed were sheets of paper covered in handwriting—notebooks—folders crammed with newspaper clippings—

photocopies of letters both handwritten and awkwardly typed, with numerous corrections—which, Daddy said, he'd sent to Sparta police—to local, state, federal police—to local TV stations—to national TV networks—to the Sparta *Journal*, papers in Buffalo, Albany, the *New York Times*, and *Time* magazine.

He'd written to judges, he said. Herkimer County, New York State federal judges. All the names, addresses of judges he could locate. He'd written to the attorney general of the United States and to each of the justices of the Supreme Court of the United States, Washington, D.C.

Seeing my startled and pained expression, Daddy said quickly, "Hey sure, sweetie, I know: most of these sons of bitches won't read mail from ordinary people. From 'citizens.' But they have secretaries, right? Someone opens the mail, someone reads it. Has to be, otherwise—what if a letter contains a 'threat'? They'd have to know. They'd want to know. There's nothing in any of my letters like that, Krista—no. I'm not a fool. I don't even *hint*. I just state the case—the way I was treated by the 'law'—by 'the authorities'—just facts—no 'threats'—my hope was that someone would take note, someone would care—I realize that—that probably—"

His voice began to falter. I was trying to smile, my face ached with smiling and with my attentiveness to what my father was saying which I knew to be crucial, knowledge he was imparting to me for a reason. In my own faltering voice I told my father that it was wonderful he'd done so much work, he'd collected so much evidence, maybe I could help him—somehow, I could help him—

"The God-damned ironical thing is, if they'd arrested me? If they'd 'tried' me? Like it's said—a citizen has the right to a trial?—to 'clear his name'? Because if they'd done that, they would've had to find me 'not guilty.'" The word *ironical* was strange in my ears, in my father's urgent voice; here was a word no one in the Diehl family was likely to utter, except now Eddy Diehl could lay claim to it; as if to punctuate its strangeness, and confirm his claim, Daddy paused to drink, wiping again at his mouth. In these recent years he'd become a transformed man: no longer young. No longer a swaggering good-looking man after whom women gazed with longing in public places. On his jaws coarse dark whiskers had sprouted, unevenly. There was a merriment to these whiskers, Daddy resembled a pirate in a children's adventure film, you expected such a bewhiskered figure to wink, and laugh. Instead Daddy said, "I asked to be given a second lie detector test—'polygraph.' The first one, they said was 'inconclusive.' What the hell's that mean—'inconclusive'?— means it didn't show that I was lying, right? But my God-damned lawyer steps in and says no, not a good idea, don't take a second test. Because I was in a state of nerves, my blood pressure was up, he thought the test might 'incriminate' me if it went the wrong way, and I'd be truly fucked. So I never took it, I listened to him. I was in a fog, I wasn't thinking clearly. And later I realized that was a mistake. Lots of mistakes I made, back then. Now, it's too late. I would have to pay for a private test, and I can't afford it, and anyway the fuckers wouldn't credit it—lie detector results are not 'admissible' in court. They won't even talk to me, now. I mean the Sparta police, the persecutors—*prosecutors*. Like I have ceased to exist. They never found the guilty man because they never looked for him in the right place. Delray—he had his rotten luck with lawyers, too. Bastards suck you dry like leeches. You get the impression they don't know what the hell they're doing, or give a damn, it's just a job to them. Then you run out of money and they drop you, you're on your own. Why'd the cops never arrest Delray? *He* was the one killed her. Who else? Zoe was always saying, 'Anything happens to me, better believe it's Delray. But nothing is going to happen to me.' Then she'd laugh in that way she had, like something was destined to happen, it couldn't be averted. When you're high—Zoe loved to get high—you can't ever comprehend that you will crash. That was Zoe's mistake. One of Zoe's mistakes. She thought she knew what was coming but in her heart she couldn't truly believe it. Like all of us, I guess." Daddy paused, rubbing his jaws. A thought had come to him like something wedged in his brain, suddenly shifting. "You know—Delray was maybe not the one. I'm remembering now, things I've been told, that were a surprise to me, I mean a considerable shock—there were other men who'd been seeing Zoe. Men she'd taken money from. Delray and me, that poor bastard—we needed to talk. Badly we needed to talk and we never did. Just Delray and me, and this gun—Delray might've told me what happened that night, you think?"

Daddy laughed. Daddy was not speaking very coherently, his thoughts swerved and lurched like a drunken skier rapidly descending a treacherous slope. Impatiently he'd begun to shove papers back inside folders, as if they were embarrassing to him, he fumbled and dropped some of the yellowed clippings, without thinking I stooped to gather these neatly up and place in his shaking hand.

Daddy's knuckles were skinned, bruised. As if he'd struck something. Someone.

"Thanks, honey. You're a sweet kid. Christ! I'm so tired."

The shaky hand holding the gun—the heavy dull-gleaming ugly gun—relaxed; the gun slipped from Daddy's fingers and fell softly onto the bed. I thought *I can take that from him now. He wants me to take it from him.* And yet, I could not move. I was standing less than eighteen inches from the gun where it had fallen but I could not move. Always I would recall, I could not move. Not to snatch up the gun. For if I had—what would I have done with the gun? Would I have turned it on my father?— I would not have turned it on my father. I would not have backed away, lifted the gun in both trembling hands, aimed the barrel at my astonished father. Not ever.

He was oblivious of me, swaying on his feet. The animal-smell lifted from him, my nostrils pinched with a kind of thrilled disgust. Long ago when he'd lived with us my father had sometimes smelled like this returning from work, having sweated through his clothes through the long summer day, and my mother visibly recoiled from him—not rudely, not to insult—yet of course she'd insulted him—"Excuse me, Lu*cille*." You wanted not to be near them, not to be a witness. In Daddy's face the instinctive male resentment of the female—the too-fastidious female—he'd have liked to slap with his open hand, in that instant.

He hadn't slapped my mother. Not ever, that I was a witness.

I would swear to this. When I'd been "interviewed"—not "interrogated" but just "interviewed" with my mother and a Family Court officer present—I'd sworn to this.

Again Daddy was saying Christ how tired he was. With an air of surprise and chagrin and I thought *He will lie down now, he will sleep. I can run for help.*

On the bedside table a digital clock made a whirring noise like a defective heart: the time was 6:56 P.M.

At home my mother would be awaiting me. And anxious for me. And angry, and hurt knowing that in my innermost heart I loved my father more than I loved her. Despite everything *It isn't anything I can help. Even now. Forgive me!*

It was help for my father I could run for. Not for me.

Outside the motel there were uplifted voices, a sound of car doors being slammed shut. On the highway the steady hum of traffic. But no one would come to room 23 of the Days Inn. No one would come to this room registered to "John Cass" to give aid to us, who were in such need.

I must have made a sudden involuntary movement—wiping my eyes with the fingertips of both hands—Daddy's head jerked up and his eyes were alert and wary and I saw he'd snatched up the gun.

"What's it—somebody outside? Who's there?"

"Nobody. Just—somebody parking a car."

On lurching feet Daddy went to the window. I saw that he was sodden with drink, narcotized. Yet his eyes shone dangerously. Eagerly he licked his lips like a ravenous dog. He poked fingers into the Venetian blind, to peer through the slats. Whoever was out there must have seemed to him of no consequence, finally. Daddy turned back to me, that tremor of merriment in his whiskers.

"Krista, you know that I love you, honey—you know that."

Yes, I knew. How like doom it felt, to concede this.

"You were always my heart, Krista. My 'little bird of heaven.'"

We were both remembering how Daddy used to swoop me up in his arms when I was a little girl, toss me into the air light as a cushion, catching me almost immediately as I squealed, kicked. Never was I in danger—

Daddy held me safe. If I panicked, began to cry—if I squealed and kicked too hard—Daddy hadn't liked that.

"I think you should call your mother, Krista. It's time now. Tell her that you're with me, and I want her to speak with me, not over the phone but face-to-face. Explain, 'Daddy will not hurt you.'" Daddy paused, smiling. The effort of that smile was of a man stooping to lift a weight that will shatter his spine.

Nervously I said that my mother might hang up, before I could explain.

Nervously I said I wished that he would put away the gun. It was frightening to me, that gun.

Daddy frowned. He was a daddy who did not like to be told what to do, not ever.

Sometimes you forgot that. When he appealed to you, when he seemed to be softening toward you. When you realized that it was a mistake, a mistake you must learn not to make, to confuse Daddy's love for you with Daddy's respect for you. A child is loved but not respected. You forgot that.

"She won't hang up the phone. She will know not to hang up the phone this time."

"Well, but— You know how Mom—"

"Fuck 'Mom'! What's 'Mom' done for you. I'm your Daddy, who loves you, right?"

"Yes but Daddy, the gun makes me—"

Wanting to say *afraid*. But my voice was weak, guilty-sounding.

In reproach Daddy said, "I would not hurt you, Krista. You must know that. It would end in an instant. A heartbeat. It would spare you pain. Honey, life is mostly pain—it's like the Bible says—'All is vanity beneath the sun.' Vanity, and bullshit." He laughed, like one who has said something witty by chance. With the gun he was indicating the phone on the bedside table. "Your mother is waiting for this call, Krista. Your mother is a smart woman, a shrewd woman, she knows that her 'former husband' is in Sparta, and if she knows this she knows why I'm here, and that this is the last time I am going to beg her. This is the last time for all of us. She knows this, I think. I think she knows this. I want my family back that was taken wrongfully from me. I want my life back that was taken wrongfully from me. The decision is your mother's. It's her responsibility. She calls herself a Christian—right? She kneels, and prays, and whoever the fuck she prays to, God the Father, or His son the Savior, they've got to be giving her good advice—right? 'Till death do you part.' 'In sickness and in health.' *Better do as your husband wants, Lucille. He is your husband!* When I signed over the house to her, all of the property, I said, 'I'm putting this in your trust, Lucille. I hope I will be welcomed back one day.' Your mother did not say *no* to this. Between us was the understanding, she would say *yes*. Because I was sure that my name would be cleared. Because I had not hurt that woman, I had not hurt anyone. Not of my volition, and not ever you kids! That was my trust in her, in your mother. It was true, as she knew—I'd been an 'adulterer.' That was true. But not the other." Here Daddy paused, as if acknowledging *the other*—the unspeakable act, the irrevocable act of *murder*—was exhausting to him.

Outside, more car doors were being slammed shut. The Days Inn was moving to evening, night. Families were arriving, couples. A drunk-sounding couple in the adjacent room.

Daddy paid them no heed. Daddy was motioning with the gun, toward the phone, in a way that made me very nervous.

"You will call your mother, Krista and explain the circumstances. How you've chosen to come with me. How you are safe with me. How nothing is going to happen to you, or to any of us, if she accepts her responsibility as she has not done yet. If she comes to see me, tonight. Just get in the car, and come here, and see me. If she loves you the way a mother should. I'll tell you what—you tell her: 'Daddy says I can leave, if you come.' Call her 'Mom'—she's 'Mom' to you. Tell Mom that Daddy will let you leave here if she comes. If 'Mom' takes your place. See, Krissie, the marriage bond is the fundamental thing. The vow—'Till death do us part.' Lucille comes, and Krista can leave. With a promise not to tell anyone about us—right? A promise not to interfere. All I need is some time face-to-face with your mother, I think we can work things out. I know we can work things out. These papers, I want to show her. She's got to realize. You've got to realize, Krissie—your daddy would never truly hurt you. Nor your brother, not ever. That's a promise. That doesn't even need to be a promise, that is understood. That is fact. But Lucille has got to see me, tonight. Tell her."

I stared at him. He spoke so reasonably. His mouth twisted in a rueful smile, as if everything he was saying was so very obvious, he hardly needed to say it.

"But Daddy, if Mom knows that you're here—with me—I'm afraid like I said she'll just hang up the phone. She won't even listen."

Daddy's face flushed with blood. "No. She will not. She wants to speak with me, in her heart."

Was this so? I didn't think it could be so. I wanted to think *yes* but I was trembling with fear, there was Daddy with the gun in his hand, not exactly aiming the barrel at me, but holding the gun in such a way that the slightest movement would turn it toward me, at chest level. Or maybe this was Daddy teasing Krissie. Maybe Daddy wanted me to laugh. Maybe in another moment Daddy would smile, and wink. A daddy can be so funny! I thought *Daddy is joking. Daddy is such a tease.*

"You know the number, Krissie. Dial it."

There was my hand lifting the plastic receiver, sticky from strangers' sweaty hands. Numbly I dialed our home number but all that resulted was a frantic beeping and Daddy said, "Baby, you have to dial 'nine' for an outside line, this is a motel." Daddy laughed, and I tried again, this time I dialed nine and then our home number and I prayed that Mom would answer as the phone rang and on the first ring as if she'd been waiting anxiously by the phone, Mom did.

"Mom? It's—"

As soon as she heard my voice my mother said sharply, "Krista! Is he there with you?" and I said yes and my mother said, "Has he been drinking?" and I said yes and my mother said, "Is he—dangerous?" and I hesitated, I could not say yes, I could not betray Daddy; and my mother said, "Where are you?" and still I hesitated, for Daddy was leaning close, his eyes shone with excitement, a kind of elated dread, I could feel the clammy heat lifting from his skin, the ugly revolver tilted downward toward the floor and in that instant I thought *I can, I must*—I must wrench the gun from his fingers, this might be my last opportunity, I must scream at him, I must surprise and frighten him, I must run with the gun to the door—but the door was not only bolted but chain-locked, the door could not have been opened as quickly as I would need to open it, to save my life. Within seconds this man would be on me, this large heavy sweating desperate man would be on me, furious that I'd disobeyed him, flaunted his authority, dared to take something from him to which I had no right. And so I would be punished. I would be hurt. I knew. I stood paralyzed, helpless as at the other end of the line my mother's voice lifted in anger, agitation, fear asking where? Where had he brought me? and Daddy lost patience and snatched the receiver from me.

"Lucille! We're in Sparta, Lucille. Come to be with us, all this will be cleared up." Daddy was cradling the receiver in his left hand in an awkward gesture that required lifting his elbow, bringing the mouthpiece of the receiver close to his mouth at an angle. He spoke in a voice of subdued eagerness, smiling.

I could hear my mother's uplifted voice but not her words and Daddy said, calmly, "It isn't like that, Lucille. Maybe it pisses you but she's with me because she wants to be here. That's how it is, Lucille. So come be with us, we will clear up these misunderstandings." And again I heard my mother's voice but not her words and Daddy listened patiently for several seconds before interrupting, "D'you know the Days Inn, Lucille? On the highway? Sure you do. It's beyond the Holiday Inn, and Mack's—you know, the traffic circle. The Days Inn. Can't miss it, the sign is all lit up. I think it's a yellow sign. Just past Mill Road. I am in room twenty-three, Lucille. *Two-three.* I will be awaiting you, Lucille. No need to knock— just walk up to the door, Lucille, I will be watching for you. Krista and I are relaxing here—just waiting for you, Lucille. We need to be a family again. We can call Ben a little later. We'll begin with just you and Krissie, Lucille. You know how I've been wanting this, Lucille. You know my heart. Krissie wants to be here, Lucille. She is *not hurt*. And she *will not be hurt*. No one will be, I promise. You won't be hurt, absolutely not. Just come here, Lucille, come alone, right away and we'll straighten this out. Tell you what—if you think that Krista is upset, if you're concerned about Krista I will let her go, as soon as you step into this room. I mean—Krista can step outside. Krista could wait in the car. Maybe later, if things work out, we can call Ben, we can pick him up and all of us have pizza somewhere. How's that sound? The kids love pizza. Lucille, we never really communicated, I think. I'd been led to suppose something from you that maybe was a misunderstanding. It seemed to me you'd turned from me, you'd hardened your heart too soon! But now, we can make amends. It isn't too late. You'll find that I am a changed man, Lucille. Just get in your car, honey, and drive out Garrison, to Mohawk, and Mohawk straight north to route thirty-one, it won't take more than ten-fifteen minutes, Lucille. But you have to leave right now. *Don't make any calls to anyone.* Just get in the car, and get here. You know how I love you, Lucille, you are my wife—'till death do us part'—this is a decision I have not made lightly, you know it's the right decision, and a long time coming. Lucille?"

Daddy listened. Daddy scowled and interrupted: "No, Lucille. Now." And Daddy hung up the phone.

THE END, when it comes, comes swiftly.

You can't foresee. Of course, you have foreseen.

The trouble that came into my life must have an end, simultaneous with that life.

For of course my mother called the police. There was never a glimmer of a possibility that Lucille would comply with my father's demand to present herself to him at the door of room 23 of the Days Inn, still less a glimmer of a possibility that she would wish to present herself in my place, that I might be allowed to leave. Terrified and near-hysterical my mother called 911 and stammered what she knew, all that she knew, of my father who was "holding their daughter captive" at the Days Inn on route 31; of my father Edward Diehl who'd been "involved" in the murder of Zoe Kruller, in 1983, but never arrested; of Edward Diehl who'd been her husband who'd "threatened my life, and my children's lives, many times. . . ." And within six minutes of that call Herkimer County sheriff's officers began to arrive at the Days Inn. And Sparta police vehicles began to arrive. In all, there would be twelve vehicles, in addition to a medical emergency vehicle; there would be, shortly, a van bearing a local TV camera crew; there would be sirens, flashing red lights, the amplified voices of strangers demanding that Edward Diehl open the door—step outside with his hands in the air—drop his weapon if he had a weapon—*and do it now.*

By this time I was cowering in a corner of the musty-smelling motel room like an animal paralyzed with terror. I had wedged myself between the wall and a bureau, sprawled and panting telling myself *If my mother intervenes. If my mother is here. She will speak to him, they will let her speak with him, it will be all right.* Telling myself *They won't hurt him, or me. It will be all right.* Daddy saw me, and Daddy took pity on me; didn't chastise me, didn't scold; moving restlessly about the room gripping the gun and speaking to himself, breathing heavily. His face shone with elation, excitement. Flashing red lights from the parking lot illuminated his battered and bewhiskered pirate's face and his glassy-glaring eyes.

"Loveya, Puss! You better know that."

Now the voice had become a megaphone voice, deafening as if it were in the room with us. A shout, an angry male voice, instructions repeated to *Edward Diehl* to lay down his weapon, unlock and open the door and release his daughter; to step through the doorway slowly and with his hands raised and visible and he would not be hurt repeated *Edward Diehl would not be hurt* and my father might have laughed, I think yes I heard Daddy laugh, or was it a sobbing sound that resembled laughter, Daddy's face dazed and flushed and with that look of piratical merriment about his whiskers and twitching mouth and his racing eyes caught in the glare of a powerful spotlight aimed at the motel door and window penetrating the cracked and grimy Venetian blinds Daddy had yanked down over the window to shield us from the eyes of strangers. In these last staggering minutes of his life my father did not speak, he did not speak to me as if in the urgency of the moment he'd forgotten me, a kind of oblivion had washed over his soul, his *hard-as-steel soul* and he'd forgotten me, he'd forgotten his wife whom he had so desperately summoned to his side. He'd forgotten his family, his life that had gone bad. For it was his secret knowledge that death is *easy*, death is so much *easier* than life. At the door calmly unlocking and unbolting it as he'd been commanded and through my fingers as I lay in a paralysis of terror in a corner of the room rank with odors and dust-balls I saw through the crooked slats of the Venetian blind the brilliant dazzling light that was aimed against us from outside, a harsh blinding light, a white-tinged luminescent white, a white you might mistake for the purest star-light, illuminating and consecrating all that it touched even as it meant oblivion, annihilation, extinction and bathed in this light—for now the door had been kicked open by my father, now the musty-smelling motel room would be exposed to the stares of strangers—I saw Daddy crouching, his shoulders hunched and his head lowered, now his face was turned from me and I could not see if he was smiling, I would never see Daddy's face again and must surrender him now, in his shaky right hand the revolver to be identified in the media as a .38-caliber Smith & Wesson in the *illegal possession* of Edward Diehl, I saw Daddy step confidently into that blinding light and lift this gun as if about to fire it in a seemingly spontaneous mocking gesture that would be the final gesture of his life.

25

Two-inch gloating headlines in the Sparta *Journal*—

FORMER SPARTA RESIDENT DIEHL
SUSPECT IN '83 KRULLER HOMICIDE
KILLED BY POLICE IN MOTEL SHOOT-OUT

In the *Journal* and elsewhere you would learn that my father's full name was Edward James Diehl and that the dates of his life were 1942–1987. You would learn that he had been born in Sparta, New York, and so it seemed appropriate that he would die in Sparta. You would learn that, though never arrested for the crime, he had been a "prime suspect" in a homicide: for always Edward Diehl must be a *suspect*, even in death.

Falsely it was reported in the *Journal* as elsewhere that my father had died in a "shoot-out" with police officers but in fact it had not been a "shoot-out" with connotations of lurid melodramatic TV tabloid crime but a massacre: my father had not fired a single shot. Though his gun was loaded with ammunition the safety lock had not been released, clearly my father hadn't intended to fire a single shot and this fact would not be reported, this was a fact I would not learn until months later.

Daddy had wanted to die. He had not wanted to kill. He'd had no intention of harming me. This I would come to believe. This I know to be true.

It was determined that eight police officers had fired at Edward Diehl within a space of several seconds and not one of these police officers had missed his target. It was Herkimer County policy, police officers must fire no less than two shots at their target. And so eighteen bullets had torn into my father's head and upper body, some of them as he was falling, some after he'd fallen, some as he lay writhing and dying on the carpet inside the room where the power of the bullets had sent him sprawling on his back, out-flung and the Smith & Wesson revolver flying from his hand.

This, I did not see. I have no memory of this. Though I was the daughter of Edward Diehl who'd been "taken hostage" in that room, I was the fifteen-year-old daughter of Edward Diehl whom police had "rescued" from that room, I did not see my father die, I would not remember anything beyond the deafening gunfire.

Part

Two

26

IT'S A SNOW-BLINDING SUNDAY morning slowly he's pushing open the door at 349 West Ferry with the silver-tinselly Christmas wreath on it, sprig of blood-red berries and big red fake-velvet ribbon though Christmas is—Christ!—a long time past and he knows something is probably wrong, his mother's life has gone wrong, he'd like to think it isn't because of him, she'd gotten fed up being his mother like she'd gotten fed up with being Delray Kruller's wife, who could blame her? So he's steeling himself for what he's going to find inside. Shades pulled at every window upstairs and down he'd seen from the street, walked around to the rear of the bruise-colored row house in the snow blinking and staring and it's weird, it is not a good sign Aaron Kruller thinks, the front door is not locked.

No one here? No one downstairs? The living room—if that's what you'd call it—is pretty messed-up. Like they'd been partying but never got around to clean-up. And a single lamp burning, in daylight, with a crooked shade. Aaron is hoping that he won't meet up with Zoe's woman friend close as a sister Zoe claimed though Aaron had neither seen nor heard of this Jacky before, shiny face and dyed-beet hair and pushed-up breasts in some sort of corset-looking nylon thing Aaron was made uncomfortable to see, there was Jacky licking her lips gazing at him like she knows his innermost thoughts and they are not-nice thoughts, frankly filthy-sexy-teenage-boy thoughts, her friend Zoe Kruller doesn't look old enough to have a kid Aaron's size, at least six feet tall with a bumpy shaved head and a stippling of scars on his face and steely eyes like the wrath of God judging her.

Any woman, could be older than his mother, like Jacky DeLucca, one of his teachers at school or the mother of a friend he'd see stopping by the home of one of the guys after lacrosse, and Aaron finds himself staring at the woman like he can't help seeing her inside her clothes, the actual naked body of the woman, the female, fascinating to him, appalling and astonishing and his wonderment is like something squeezed through a narrow pipe coming out a smirk of disdain, can't bring himself to smile at them in dread of them guessing the kind of thoughts he was thinking O Christ couldn't wait to get away from the DeLucca woman to beat himself off going off like a gun making a mess like whipped egg white in his pants.

But Jacky isn't here, seems like. Not even the TV is on.

Last time he'd been here, the front door had been unlocked too but there'd been people inside. He'd heard voices inside. This time it's weird and unsettling, so quiet.

"Hey: Mom? It's me."

Asshole thing to say it's me, it's me Aaron, calling out in his voice Zoe said was loud as a young calf bellowing, she'd laugh pressing her hands over her ears but now Zoe doesn't seem to be here, to complain of him.

Aaron is disgusted, and Aaron is angry. Seems like Aaron is always disgusted and angry and not wanting to think he's anxious what he might find inside this house.

Because she hadn't called him, for a while. First she'd moved out she had called him—Aaron—at certain times she'd promised and he'd been home to answer and he'd been sullen and insulting to her but O.K., that was O.K., she'd called him, and talked to him, and even if he'd said Fuck you Mom and hung up the phone, it was O.K. between them and she knew it. And he knew it. But now, hadn't heard from Zoe in maybe two weeks. And had not glimpsed Zoe in Christ how long—maybe a month. There was Christmas—a shitty time he'd like to forget—and New Year's—worse yet—that passed in a drunk-drugged blur and she'd called to tell him she had his Christmas present for him all wrapped up but never got around to delivering it. Come by the house to pick it up, she'd said.

How the fuck is a fourteen-year-old kid going to do that, on a bike?—Aaron's old junker Schwinn?—sliding and skidding in the snowy-icy streets?—sure as hell Delray isn't going to drive him.

Not there. Not to the house on West Ferry. Delray'd said not ever was he going there, couldn't trust himself what he'd do, if he did.

Your slut-mother. Slut-junkie mother go check the bitch out, see for yourself.

Delray's heavy hand fell on Aaron's shoulder. With a shiver like a horse casting off flies with its rippling skin Aaron cast off Delray's hand like he's holding himself back from slugging the old man in the face.

Don't believe me she's a slut, eh? That just proves you don't know shit who a slut can be.

Loudly he called: "Mom?" The calf bawling for his mother.

A few times he'd actually heard a calf bawling, it was something to hear!

Thinking maybe she'd shout at him down the stairs. Say Oh God Aaron that's you? You're here? Jesus wait I'll be down in a few minutes you're thirsty go get something from the fridge, sweetie, O.K.? Don't come up here it's kind of messy, O.K.?

And he'd think with a shiver of disgust She's got somebody up there— has she?

He'd seen his mother with a man, just once. Maybe more than once. Maybe he hadn't exactly seen them, quickly he'd looked away. Or maybe—they'd been at a distance—it had not been Zoe but another blond woman who'd resembled her. It was mostly what he'd heard—what he'd overheard. Delray on the phone. Delray's relatives complaining of her. Maybe it was all bullshit, how'd Aaron know? Them saying that's how a white bitch behaves, can't trust them, comes down to it they're white and you're shit on their shoes like Delray was a full-blooded Seneca which he was not, still less was Aaron, and Aaron was Zoe's kid not just Delray's and maybe he looked Indian but there was more to him than that. Hell yes.

Aaron poked his head into the kitchen—nobody there. Vinyl chairs looking like they'd been kicked partway across the floor. Bottles, glasses, plates soaking in the sink. Like the party spilled into here like high tide lapsed to low tide and the surf drained away and what remains on the beach is litter you don't want to examine closely. And beneath a stale-garbagey smell, a scent of Zoe's perfume.

It's too quiet here. Zoe isn't easy with quiet. In the house on Quarry Road which was too damn far out of town to suit her, miles into the country Zoe always had the radio on loud or was singing to herself, practicing her Black River Breakdown voice you'd hear through the house and it was a sound that was both comforting and unsettling for it meant Zoe Kruller's other life, the life she lived away from the house and in the eyes of admiring strangers, the life she'd yearned for that Delray and Aaron could not give her, and that they resented. Why aren't we enough for you was a question never asked for neither Delray nor Aaron would have had the vocabulary for such a question. But there were good memories too, overall mostly good memories Aaron thought, when he'd come home from damn fucking school where he was treated like shit or from lacrosse bruised and banged up and bleeding from cuts in his face and there was Zoe singing in the kitchen and she'd sounded happy.

Proud of his lacrosse scars. The older guys respected him. If he had his lacrosse stick he'd bring it into the kitchen with him but Zoe wasn't allowed to touch it know why?—Females are forbidden to touch your lacrosse stick. Even your mom.

What kind of damn old Indian superstition is that, Zoe asked.

He'd shrugged and muttered in reply. Zoe laughed annoyed saying it's an insult like I would contaminate the damn thing and Aaron said smirking That's the way it is, Mom. That's l'cr—.

Zoe made a swipe to touch the stick. Knowing she'd do this Aaron lifted it high over his head. Laughing red-faced, and Zoe said O.K. smart-ass make your own supper, you're so smart.

He hadn't had to, though. By supper, it was O.K. between them.

On the stairs he's calling in the bawling-calf way, "Hey Mom—you up here?"

27

MARCH 1990

THE WOMAN TURNED TO HIM, at his touch she turned to him and seeing his face began to scream. And he didn't like that, God damn he did not like being screamed at. Reaching for her to quiet her with his hands blunt and clumsy as a beast's paws and at his touch she began to scream louder shrill and piercing in his ears in her terror he'd needed to silence her but instead he was waking and there was no woman—the woman had vanished—except the screams were a telephone ringing close beside his dazed head where he seemed to have fallen at a sprawled angle across a soiled bare mattress in just boxer shorts, T-shirt yanked halfway up his back and fumbling for the damn phone he'd knocked it onto the floor, snatched up the receiver and there was an actual woman's voice frantic in his ear *Aaron! God damn answer the phone! It's Delray come get him immediately.*

In his drunk-dazed state Aaron managed to sit up. Where he was exactly he'd postpone for later. Head felt like he'd been struck with a shovel. Mouth sour as puke. His grimy bare monkey-toes dug into the stained carpet like that part of him was instinctively grabbing hold of something solid. The woman he'd been with seemed to have vanished. There had been an actual woman here with Aaron on this mattress naked and grunting and straining but she was gone now. By a luminescent watch seeing it was 4:20 A.M. No moon to reflect snow outside the window thus so dark it was like the bottom of the sea. He'd seen a TV documentary on the depths of the sea where no light ever came, weird fish-shapes there in the perpetual gloom no human eye had ever seen nor could the deep-sea creatures see one another. Why such creatures existed was a mystery no one could solve. What purpose to life on earth, no one could solve. But the situation was, you were here, you'd got born, you had to play the cards dealt to you. Aaron rubbed his eyes seeing through the part-opened doorway—into the bathroom—there was a light, a scent of steam from the shower wafting to his nostrils but the woman was gone.

"Jesus!"—seeing on the doorframe and on the wall beside the bed what appeared to be smears of blood of a kind made by a swiping hand.

Could've been blood from a bloodied nose he seemed to recall a woman's nose he had not meant to injure, or was it his own nose, the woman had smacked with her elbow. Aaron wasn't sure.

Out of the phone came the female voice urgent and bossy more clearly now: "Aaron! Are you there? Are you awake? God damn this is Viola I'm talking to you! I said Delray is hurt bad. Must've passed out hit his head on the pavement. Or somebody hit it for him. If you don't come pick him up he's your God damn father you owe him that, if you don't get your ass over here Aaron I'm going to call 911 to come get him. Take him to the ER. God damn Delray isn't going to die on these premises."

Aaron was stammering telling his aunt not to call 911, don't call for help, Pa wouldn't like that—"Tell me where he is, Viola—I'll come get him."

"'Where he is'—didn't you just hear me, for Christ's sake! Are you drunk? Are you high? He's here! He's at my place! He's got no right here! All of you, you and him, and her, your damn mother—all you are has been trouble to us! To the family! Last time Delray showed up here it was half the night trying to locate you, you took your own sweet time getting over here, and this time I am not hauling your father inside, and up the stairs, and him puking on me—the hell with that. Where he is, Aaron, he's in the driveway here, outside my house in the snow where somebody dumped him. One of his biker buddies. Or a cop friend. You know that crowd he runs with. Has to be somebody knows that I am his sister. I'm in bed I hear a car horn, someone yelling, look out the window and there's somebody laying in my driveway dead or too drunk to stand. Delray must've left his car somewhere, at some tavern and he couldn't drive in that condition so they brought him here and dumped him on me. Oh, God." Viola paused breathing heavily. When she resumed she was sobbing, furious. "What if your father has some brain injury? You know he's half-crazy as it is. What if his liver is poisoned? Try to talk to him he says yes, sure he will cut down on drinking, check into detox, there's half of us in the family offered to drive him there and visit with him while he's in then this happens, scares the hell out of me. I'm Delray's sister not his mother! Not his wife! Or his son! *You're* his son—see? So get over here, Aaron, take him back to your house with you or I'm calling 911 and if it's the police or the ER the hell with you both."

Aaron said he was coming. Be there as soon as he got his clothes on. By this time he was on his feet, and reasonably alert. Stone cold sober in ten seconds. Telling his aunt not to call any God damn cops or ambulance, Delray might get busted—"Like if they 'commit' him and he can't get out like that time at the VA in Watertown, that almost killed him."

His aunt had hung up. Aaron lost the receiver, it clattered onto the floor. It was coming back to him where he was. A familiar place made unfamiliar. In a shaft of light from the bathroom he saw something that made the short hairs at the nape of his neck stir—a snake? A snake in the house? In winter? Had to be more than just a garter snake it was thick-bodied, dark, lustrous as grease. Or maybe Aaron's eyes weren't focusing right, like his brain. If this was a meth high it had taken a malevolent turn. If this was just a drunk maybe he had D.T.'s. Another wrong thing was this wasn't Aaron's bedroom but a back room on the first floor of the house on Quarry Road, dirty old mattress on the floor and a filthy fiber carpet strewn with mysterious articles of clothing, shoes, stained towels, cigarette stubs and husks of dead insects, but—a *snake*? Maybe in summer, the back door has been left carelessly open, chinks and tears in the screens, possibly a snake could get in that way or through the cellar, crawl up the stairs to the first floor but this snake looked lifeless, or in a deep sleep. Cautiously Aaron approached it and dared to prod it with his bare foot: what's it but a hair braid, dark shiny fake-hair, has to be ten inches long.

Fake hair! Showy-looking brunette braid must've been twined in with the woman's own hair, shiny and sexy and the first thing Aaron had noticed about her but it's fake.

Why you can't trust women. Even young girls. Can't know what the fuck they are thinking, can't know what they are feeling, can't know how they will surprise you except you know it won't be a surprise you will like.

Drove to his aunt's house on Dock Street. Viola hadn't fully forgiven him for bringing the Diehl girl there, that night. And now, there was Delray. In a state of dread driving the utterly deserted late-night streets of Sparta suspended as an inheld breath thinking *God don't let my father die. Not like this he deserves better* and as the van skidded on the icy streets thinking *If he's dead when I get there—whose fault is that?* Aaron loved his father but frankly he'd been putting up with the old man's bullshit for too long. Since Zoe was killed, and Delray a "suspect." Since Zoe left the house saying sure she'd be back, give her a few months. A few months just to breathe Zoe had promised but Delray had never believed her.

Third time since New Year's he'd been wakened from sleep to drive out and bring Delray back home. It was shocking, shameful, an ugly sight to see a man like Delray Kruller sick-drunk and helpless as a baby. There were guys his age with fathers like Delray that'd been alcoholics for longer than Delray, you get fed up with them, you've had enough of them, still they don't go away, and they don't die. A long time they hang on. God damn Aaron resented it. Wanted to keep his good memories of Delray— like his good memories of Zoe—what they'd been when Aaron was a little boy. Not like now. This wasn't right.

It was a night of unnatural stillness, very cold. Not even a wind from the mountains, or the river. Smelly clothes he'd thrown on back at the house, bare feet shoved into boots. And there on Dock Street beyond a block of darkened store fronts and a shuttered A & P was the red-brick row house where Viola rented a second-floor apartment. In the driveway was what might've been a bundle of old clothes. A body carelessly tossed into the snow, unmoving. You could see where the body had been dragged in the snow a few yards toward the house as if despite what she'd said on the phone Viola had intended to get him into the house but given up and covered him with a blanket in a gesture of dismay and disgust hiding most of the man's face so your first thought seeing him was this was a corpse.

Loudly Aaron said: "Pa? Wake up."

Cautiously he pulled the blanket away from his father's face. Wanting to think what you always want to think at such times *This isn't him!*

The old man's face was battered, swollen. It looked like a football that has been kicked too much. The graying hair Aaron remembered used to be glossy-black Delray had worn with a headband like a Comanche warrior to strike fear in the hearts of Caucasians was now thinning at the crown and matted and messy and his jaws were covered in whiskers sharp as an animal's quills. Delray was only forty-eight—forty-nine?—Aaron wasn't sure which but looked a decade older, or older than that, bruises under his loose-shut eyes and mouth slack as a dead fish's. There was some mangy old Seneca death-mask Aaron had seen in a museum display, hollow eye-sockets, mouth in an open O and owl's wispy feathers in the headdress and God damn if Delray didn't resemble that death-mask the kids had laughed at, trooping through the dusty museum displays. The Indian kids in a tight little band had laughed hardest, harshest.

Looked like Delray been beaten, kicked. This wasn't just falling-down drunk. Aaron guessed that all over his father's body he'd soaked up considerable hurt.

From a doorway in the row house came a woman's voice. Aaron's aunt hunched inside an overcoat calling to him, "Just get him out of here! I can't take more of this! He's killing himself, God damn he is not going to kill *me*."

But seeing Aaron struggling with Delray, Viola relented and came to help him. The two of them grunting as they tried to lift the heavy man, managing finally to heave him—now he was part-wakened—to his feet.

"Hey Pa, you can't sleep here, see? Freeze your ass? It's me, and Viola. C'mon *wake up.*"

Viola slapped snow onto Delray's bruised face which helped to revive him. Aaron slung an arm around him to hold him up. Jesus, the old man had put on weight! Like a sack of potatoes. No taller than Aaron but outweighed him by thirty pounds at least. Delray was muttering as if incensed, indignant. Shoving at Aaron not seeming to know who Aaron was, and he meant to help. Aaron pleaded, "Jesus, Pa, come *on.* I got to get you home before the cops come by."

This kind of serious drunk, it's like brain damage. Nothing funny or jokey about it. Delray'd been drinking vodka lately to take him to a place where, just maybe, he would not come back from.

Where you could see him, at a distance. A vapor in the shape of a man fading the harder you peered at him.

With Viola's help Aaron managed to walk Delray to the van, lift and shove him inside where he sprawled across the front seat groaning and cursing. Viola was laughing in exasperation, her face wet with tears. She'd had enough, Viola said. Delray was her big brother she'd looked up to all her life and Delray had taken care of her at crucial times in her life—when her first husband had gone kind of crazy and tried to kill her—before he'd been incarcerated at Potsdam, where he died—and some other times—but now, this was a new turn, this was more than Viola could handle.

Among the Krullers it was openly said *Delray is headed for hell, after her.*

Her meaning Zoe. Who was already in hell.

Viola said: "Take him to Watertown tomorrow, the VA hospital. They've got his files. They have to take him. Get him into detox. Another night like this, Delray will be dead."

Aaron said O.K., he would. Aaron said he'd see how things were in the morning.

Viola said sharply: "I said take him. Commit him. Fuck how 'things are in the morning.'"

Aaron said O.K. He was frightened of his aunt's anger, a woman's anger has a way of translating into claw marks on your face if you aren't vigilant. Thinking how seven years after Zoe had been murdered—seven years!—his mother was still to blame. Whatever was happening in their lives now, a consequence of what Zoe had started. *Headed for hell, after her.*

Aaron drove out to Quarry Road slowly. Cautiously. His drunk old man could start flopping like a fish, puking or fighting him—a drunk in such an extreme state is dangerous, like a meth tweeker. Aaron's own adrenaline high had peaked and was now ebbing. His head began to pound with pain as if the veins and arteries inside his skull were rubbery and stretched tight to bursting, and it scared him.

Ahead, a Sparta police cruiser was turning onto Post Road. Aaron slowed the van. Didn't want to attract the attention of law enforcement officers tonight. He was pretty sure he was sober by now but earlier that night he'd been drinking and if cops stopped him and made him take a Breathalyzer test maybe it would show alcohol in his blood and he'd be charged with driving while "impaired"—lose his driver's license and then what? Can't live without a driver's license.

At the Grotto he'd been drinking with his friends after work. Two guys from Delray's garage, older married guys reluctant to go home to their families. And there was this girl—woman—a few years older than Aaron—named Sheryl?—Shirl?—she'd given Aaron some kind of speedball, wanting him to get high with her, no damn good getting high alone she said, and Aaron said O.K. like doing drugs was some special thing for him, at age twenty-one, she'd be the one to turn him on. Now it was coming back to him, a little: Sheryl with the tight-braided hair she'd swung like a horse's tail, and a quick panting breath in his face like hissing steam. In the parking lot behind The Grotto the two of them fumbling and grunting and later he'd taken her home guessing that Delray wouldn't be there—which Delray was not—and whatever happened between them at the house, in that back room, Aaron wasn't sure.

Except she'd left the shiny fake hair-braid behind, like a taunt.

The worst possibility was, he'd hurt her, or insulted her in some way unknown to him, she'd reported him to the cops and they've got a lookout for him right now checking the license plates of vehicles and with sick-drunk Delray sprawled in the seat beside him Aaron will be pulled over, his driver's license examined, van registration, check the computer and for sure *Kruller, Aaron* is in the system, Aaron has a juvenile record for fighting at school, "assault" and misdemeanor offenses, under New York State law this record is sealed but still his name would be in the Sparta PD data base and you had to suppose that *Kruller, Delray* would be in the system too. *Drunk-and-disorderly, impaired driving, resisting arrest* Delray Kruller's driver's license suspended for six months back in 1987.

But it would be the connection with *Kruller, Zoe* that would trigger the cops' interest most.

"Pa, chill it. We're almost home."

Delray had begun thrashing about in the passenger's seat. In the confined space of the van's cab he smelled strongly of alcohol and vomit and his body. Demanding to know where in hell Aaron was taking him, and why he wasn't driving—this was his van, wasn't it? Aaron said, "Pa, I picked you up at Viola's just now. Some friends of yours dumped you in the driveway, you could've froze to death if Viola hadn't been awake."

Adding, "See Pa, I'm taking you home. You need to get to bed."

Need to get to bed. As if that was Delray's greatest need.

Aaron was thinking what a wrong thing it is, taking care of your father like this. Like he's a baby. It was unnatural, supposed to be a father takes care of his children.

You can't help being resentful. Like with Zoe who'd stopped loving him in that special way. Like a mother loves you no matter what and will always forgive you except one day this love can wear out, you're on your own. He'd gotten too big for her, maybe. How was this Aaron's fault! *Love ya sweetie and your father too it's just that I want my own life now some place I can breathe.*

It was a cruel joke, then: strangled like she was. So the breathing ended.

Past 4:30 A.M. when Aaron turned the van into the lane leading to the house he'd lived in for all of his life he could recall. Old farmhouse Zoe had had painted peach-color which was a pretty color but weatherworn now it more resembled dirty concrete, and since she'd left more than seven years ago the shutters were faded, and some of them rotted loose. Flower boxes Aaron had helped Zoe attach below the windows, where she'd planted bright red flowers—geraniums?—until she'd lost interest, and these window boxes too were rotted. Neither Delray nor Aaron saw the house only just lived in it the way shell-creatures live in their shells except sometimes Aaron took notice, what a sad wreck it was getting to be, how sad Zoe would be to see it, a beaten-up ship drifting in some remote sea.

Oh honey! How has this happened! I never meant for anything like this to happen.

Sure she still talked to him. More than he talked to her. Almost he could feel her hand touching his wrist. Almost he had to stop himself from turning to her desperate and yearning *Mom? Where are you?*

" . . . never touched her, Aaron. Your mother."

"O.K., Pa. Right."

"You know that, don't you? Aaron?"

"Sure."

Grunting and cursing he managed to maneuver Delray out of the van and into the house. Not an easy job without Viola to help and the old man too drunk to cooperate and inside the house Aaron led him into the back room—no question Delray could be walked upstairs—where a few hours before Aaron had brought the shiny-fake-braid woman Sheryl, or Shirl. Let Delray sink down onto the dirty bare mattress, tugged off Delray's boots, Delray's filthy wool socks, vomit-splattered sheepskin jacket. Delray tried to assist by lifting his arms, lifting his legs, apologetically now mumbling, ". . . loved her. You don't believe me but I did. A kid like you, you don't understand these things. I loved your mother. . . ."

"Pa, I know. Sure."

Aaron squatted loosening his father's trousers, this was an awkward procedure that made him ashamed, couldn't look the old man in the face. Going then to get a wetted cloth from the bathroom to wash roughly at

Delray's battered face. Maybe Delray looked worse than he was. Boxers who bleed easily always look worse than they are. Or anyway, the serious injuries are not visible. Blood is not a serious injury. Playing lacrosse a guy can be bleeding from a half-dozen cuts but stay in the game. It's a matter of pride staying in the game. Aaron was determined to stay in the game. Some guys, friends of his living out on the Seneca reservation, they were giving up, enlisting in the army. That was the way out—the army. But Aaron Kruller would not. He was going to hang on here in Sparta, help his father at the garage and one day *clear his name*. This was not a mission Aaron ever spoke of to anyone. Certainly not to Delray.

Examining now his father's big-knuckled hands, seeing with a smile sure the old man's knuckles were skinned, must've been he'd been in a fight that night and had hit somebody, hard. Maybe Delray had provoked the fight, he'd brought this onto himself. "Who were you with tonight, Pa? Just, I'd like to know."

Delray didn't seem to have heard. Delray grabbed the wash cloth from Aaron and pressed it against his eyes, moaning softly.

Saying after a moment: ". . . believe me, don't you? About your mother? Yeh?"

"Pa, sure. Never mind that."

"You would not ever in-form on your own father, would you, Aaron? Right?"

Aaron laughed uncomfortably. This was not a new subject between them. "Why'd I 'inform' now, Pa. I never 'informed' then."

Better back off now, Aaron thought. Let his father sleep it off. Maybe that's all Delray needs is to sleep it off, by the time he wakes around noon Delray will have forgotten this episode and Aaron means to forget, too.

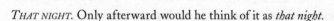

28

THAT NIGHT. Only afterward would he think of it as *that night.*

In fact Aaron had not been home until late *that night* himself.

Meaning the night when Zoe died. The night when Zoe was murdered. *That night everything changed. And I had no knowledge of it until hours too late.*

It was their pattern now. The pattern of their lives. Living together in the house on Quarry Road after Zoe moved out. After school—this was before he'd been expelled as a *chronic troublemaker*—Aaron worked at his father's garage. He pumped gas and was learning auto repair taking instruction from Delray and when Delray wasn't there from Delray's right-hand man Mitch Kremp. In the tow truck he'd ride with Mitch and assist him and after the garage closed at about 6 P.M. most evenings Aaron hung out with his friends for as long as he could before returning home where most nights Delray wasn't likely to be.

Turning up the lane to the house he'd see a single light burning in a downstairs room. Though knowing better—for sure, Aaron knew better—he'd feel his heart leap with the thought this might be Zoe returned. Though probably Aaron had left the light on himself, that morning.

That night which was February 11, 1983. When Aaron's life was struck in two. He'd hung out with some guys he knew at the reservation, out North Post Road. There was a crossroads community there lacking a name, a 7-Eleven store where the older brother of a friend of Aaron's bought the guys six-packs, cigarettes. One of the older guys drove into Sparta where he had a contact at the train depot, to score nickel bags of weed. Aaron was one of the younger guys but reckless, hopeful. Any crazy thing that came up, Aaron volunteered. They'd been looking to break into cars at the mall behind Sears but came away with kids' toys and women's crap like towels, underwear, socks in shopping bags they tossed away in disgust. Anything expensive, people had enough sense to lock in their cars and it was more than they dared risk, to break the window of any car. Must've been noisy entering the mall at the CineMax in the wake of some high school girls eyeing them but the CineMax manager must've alerted security, there came a guard to chase them away. *This is private property boys. This is not a public place.* One of the guys overturned a trash can, shattered glass and the fat-faced guard couldn't chase them more than a short distance into a field where Aaron and his friends were running like dogs in a pack excited and aroused whopping as their feet broke through the ice crust and the guard shouted after them in disgust *Cocksuckers next time you're gonna be arrested. Get the hell back to the fucking rez where you belong.*

Laughing together but the feeling drained away like air hissing from a slashed tire, Aaron wanted to get the hell home.

Past 11 P.M. when he returned to the house. Now that Zoe was gone seemed like nobody gave a damn how late Aaron stayed out or if he cut classes at school or failed to show up at school at all. If he had meals to eat, or ate like an animal foraging what he'd find in the refrigerator—leftovers, take-out Chinese and pizza, hoagies. All Delray kept in stock was beer and ale.

That night. Delray had not been home when Aaron returned nor did Delray return while Aaron was watching TV, drinking beer from a can and finishing off a stale hoagie from the refrigerator sprawled on the sofa but there was no question, Aaron would believe Delray when Delray claimed he'd been with a woman at that time, whose name he could not reveal because she was still married to her husband and desperate not to lose custody of her children. This woman's name would not be revealed to Aaron but it seemed that she lived in Star Lake, not in Sparta, and so Delray was driving forty minutes or more, all this sounded plausible. No question, Aaron believed his father swearing to him he had not been in

Sparta, he had not been anywhere near West Ferry Street, *he had not seen Zoe that night.*

Saw in his father's bloodshot eyes the sincerity of his father's words *Did not commit bodily harm against my wife Zoe I love to this day you believe me Aaron don't you?*

Sure. Aaron believed.

Questioned by police where had Delray been on that Saturday night and in the early hours of Sunday morning Aaron had said, "My dad was home, with me. We were home together."

Sullen-faced kid, evasive eyes. Under duress Aaron looked dark-red-skinned, that singed-looking skin of the Native American though he'd had a blond Caucasian mother.

"All that night? That night and into the early hours of Sunday morning, you were in your father's presence? That's what you're telling us, Aaron?"

Yes. That was what Aaron was telling them.

The older detective—his name was Martineau—suggested in a mock-sympathetic voice maybe Aaron was lying to protect his father? That it?

For a long moment Aaron did not speak. Dark blood beat heavily in his face. But he would not be baited, he would say only no he was not lying. His father had been home with him, the two of them together all that night.

"In the same room? In the same bed? All that night?"

The detective spoke sneeringly. Still Aaron would not be baited but sat stubborn, impassive. He was not lying. He did not think of it as lying. If Delray had sworn to him that he had not hurt Zoe, that he had not been at 349 West Ferry Street that night, Aaron believed him.

You know I would not lie to you son. This is the utter truth I am telling you.

Questioned further, Aaron told the detectives in a slow halting near-inaudible voice yes it was so, that night had not been a typical Saturday night for his father. Or for him. Some nights Delray was gone all night, two or three days Delray might be away somewhere, and Aaron wouldn't know where, but the night of February 10 had been different: Delray had been home. Maybe he'd had some kind of flu, he'd gone to bed early. Aaron had stayed up watching TV. So he'd been home, and his father had been upstairs in bed, Aaron could swear that. He would swear that in court if necessary.

And in the morning his father was still in bed when Aaron left the house, he was sure. He'd decided to drop by the house where his mother was staying with a woman friend, she'd asked him to come and pick up a Christmas present she had for him before she left on some trip—Aaron thought it was "an airplane trip"—"auditioning" at some nightclub. No, Aaron didn't know details. It was like Zoe to speak of her plans yet remain secretive about details.

But she'd wanted to see him, Aaron said, before she left on this trip, it had seemed important to her.

How frequently had Aaron seen his mother, since she'd moved out of the house on Quarry Road, Aaron was asked. Aaron shrugged saying not too often.

"'Not too often'? When had you seen your mother, before that morning, son?"

Son. A sour taste filled Aaron's mouth, he'd have liked to spit out onto the table.

Not too often, he said. But Zoe called him, at the house.

"She said she had a 'Christmas present' for you? Where is this 'Christmas present'?"

Aaron shrugged. He had not given the *Christmas present* any thought until this moment.

"And your mother didn't mention who was taking her on the 'airplane trip'? And where?"

Aaron shook his head, no. She had not.

"Did you have any 'premonition' something might have happened to her? That's why you went to see her?"

Aaron shook his head, no. He had not.

The word *premonition* was new to Aaron. But he knew its meaning.

So he'd gotten a ride into Sparta with some Quarry Road neighbors going to church. This was around 9 A.M. Bright winter mornings he'd wake up early.

"And your father was still there? In bed? Asleep?"

Aaron shrugged. As far as he knew, yes.

The detectives exchanged looks of bemused skepticism. Aaron understood that they thought he was lying but would not be baited into speaking insolently to them.

The younger detective Brescia said: "Now you're sure, Aaron? You're telling the truth and not lying to protect your father—you want us to believe that?"

Believe that bullshit almost the detective had said. Aaron felt the sick sour tarry taste in his mouth, stronger now.

Aaron shrugged. Aaron smiled. Yes. He was sure.

In these first weeks of the investigation, Sparta detectives had to acknowledge that they hadn't been able to find any *physical evidence* linking Delray Kruller to his wife's murder. Of the fingerprints of numerous individuals discovered at the crime scene like flyspecks scattered throughout the shabby row house the fact was that not a single print identified as a print of Delray Kruller's would ever be discovered.

No witnesses in the neighborhood would claim to have seen Delray anywhere near 349 West Ferry that night, as they would report having seen one or two men including Eddy Diehl in his shiny black Olds.

Which didn't surprise Aaron. He'd known that Delray had not lied to him. Just Delray swearing to him, Aaron would have staked his own life.

Eddy Diehl was the name most often heard, in connection with the Zoe Kruller murder.

Eddy Diehl had been Zoe's lover, who'd been seen at the West Ferry Street address.

Eddy Diehl, a married man with children. Known for his quick temper, his heavy drinking.

* * *

PUSHING OPEN THE DOOR, that was slightly ajar. In that instant seeing what lay in the bed. Part-naked female body falling out of the wrecked bed and one bloodied arm sprawled on the floor as if beckoning.

A cry erupted from him, his throat. The cry of a wounded animal, that scraped his throat.

He would not cry *Zoe* but *Mom*.

Many times he would cry *Mom Mom Mom* both at this time and at subsequent times through his life.

Recalling how in this first terrible moment something seemed to rush at him, at his face, shaped dark as a bat, as if to smother him. He'd begun to black out—his knees lost all strength—he was on the floor on hands and knees gagging.

Hot-acid vomit. Spilling and leaping out of his mouth.

What *dead* means. If you are meat you are going to rot. That is what *dead* means.

He'd smelled her, he thought. He was sure.

Despite the freezing-cold air. He was sure.

It would not be publicly revealed in the media, what Aaron did in the next several minutes.

He had not run from the room, as another person would have done. He had not run downstairs screaming for help. For not a moment did he give a thought for the danger he might be in, if the murderer or murderers of his mother had still been in the house.

He had done none of these things. He had managed to get to his feet and went to his mother where she lay battered and bloodied in the wrecked bed, and he'd grunted with the effort of pulling her back onto the bed, and lifting her stiffened arm from the floor. He had tried to straighten her awkwardly bent arms, he'd tried to cover her nakedness. The bed-clothes were soaked and stiffened with blood. For the bedroom was very cold, near-freezing—a window had been forced open. Yet there was the unmistakable smell of urine, feces. In even his state of shock Aaron was mortified and ashamed. For Zoe's sake he was mortified and ashamed. His mother, his mother's naked body. There was such shame in a naked body.

And in the urine and feces smearing the thighs. Zoe Kruller had been a beautiful woman in her glittery costume highlighted on the bandstand stage but her mangled and mutilated body was not a beautiful body. And the smell was not a beautiful smell.

Someone had opened the window partway. Snow had blown inside. Aaron stumbled to the window and forced the window open as high as it would go.

Why? Why take time to do such a thing?

Were you crazy Aaron? What was going through your mind?

Like Zoe's bed, the room had been wrecked. You might be led to believe that it had been systematically, deliberately wrecked. A frenzied struggle had taken place here. Everywhere on the floor were fallen things. Aaron stumbled over a woman's high-heeled shoe. A torn lamp shade, a cracked ceramic lamp. A woman's underwear, stockings. A soiled sweater, inside-out. A torn brassiere flesh-colored and gauzy as cobweb. Outside the window the February sun was blinding-bright reflecting new-fallen snow. The grimy wallpaper splotched with blood was starkly exposed. It looked as if a deranged child had flung red paint against the walls. There was a blood-soaked towel, tightly looped about Zoe's neck, knotted at the nape of her neck. For her scalp had been bleeding, her skull had been cracked. Items had been swept off a bureau top. A woman's blue-sequined handbag with a fake-gold chain. A woman's toiletries. A container of white talcum powder spilling onto the floor. The talcum powder smelled of lily of the valley and quickly Aaron squatted sprinkling the talcum powder in handfuls over his mother's body, and over the bed. Talcum powder onto the floor and onto the walls sticky with coagulated blood. And Aaron pulled more bedclothes over the body, a heap of bedclothes to hide the battered body, whatever he could find, anything his groping hands could find, what remained of the talcum powder he emptied onto it.

"That's better. That will be O.K."

Exhausted then he left the bedroom. Staggered from the wrecked bedroom now smelling of lily of the valley. Everywhere he'd left his fingerprints not giving a thought to it nor to who might still be in the house, hiding in one of the rooms. Jacky DeLucca who'd licked her pushed-together smiling lips at him, who might've been murdered too, elsewhere in the house, he did not give a thought to, he'd forgotten Jacky DeLucca entirely. He would not pause to glance into another room. He would not glance into the bathroom close by. In a daze of unnatural calm descending the stairs like one who has been shaken out of a dream yet not fully wakened. Yet there was a smell, a smell of blood and death and now a smell of lily of the valley, sickly-sweet, on his hands. And blood, on Aaron's hands. And a mixture of talcum powder and blood, on Aaron's face where he'd touched his jaws. Close to fainting on the stairs but he managed to stagger outside into the fresh freezing air and sat down heavily on the stoop. The strength had drained out of his legs, he had no more strength in his body. Still he felt that strange calm, a sense of satisfaction, completion. What he had been able to do for Zoe, he had done. Too weak now to walk away. Too weak to call for help. On the dirty cement stoop and the door ajar behind him, the tinselly Christmas wreath knocked askew. Maybe Aaron had knocked it askew himself. Open-eyed and calm-seeming in his trance of sorrow where they would find him.

A few blocks away at Dock Street church bells were ringing: St. Patrick's. For it was 11 A.M. of that Sunday morning in February 1983 when Aaron Kruller's life was torn in two.

How long had Aaron sat there on the front stoop instead of going for help?—he would be asked afterward. And he'd had no idea. Ten minutes? Fifteen? A half-hour? In his trance of oblivion he might have been waiting for Delray to come fetch him. He might—almost—have been waiting for Zoe to come fetch him. He was not even registering the cold, which was below ten degrees Fahrenheit. Though shivering convulsively, his parka and trousers blood-smeared, smears of white talcum powder weirdly mixed with the blood. Until a neighbor noticed him, lonely-looking kid just sitting there on the front stoop like an abandoned dog, bareheaded, gloveless, hugging his knees to his chest. The dazzling-white snow caused Aaron's thoughts to move with unnatural slowness. He could remember Zoe upstairs in the bed but had no clear memory of having opened the window beside the bed or of sprinkling the powder onto her. *Why did you do such things Aaron* the police officers would ask him and Aaron said simply *Mom liked things to smell nice. Mom would've felt bad how she was left.*

This was so. Everyone said this of Zoe Kruller. How Zoe had never left the house looking less than good. It was Zoe's intention to look *terrific, a knock-out.* Zoe would've been deeply shamed to know she would be discovered by strangers naked and in a bed filthy with her own urine, feces, blood. The shame of it would follow her after her death. *If I could help a little* Aaron said *maybe that was it.*

29

ON THE DAZZLING-LIT STAGE at the park there was Zoe in her sparkly red dress and high-heeled shoes looking so beautiful you just stared and stared, seeing yes it was Zoe, it was Mommy yet at the same time a stranger with a special connection to the crowd that adored her singing her best-known song "Little Bird of Heaven" at a fast bright pace so different from the way she'd sung this song to Aaron, as a lullaby when he'd been a small child thinking it was a special song just for him, that Mommy had made up. *Who's my little bird of heaven?* Zoe had asked leaning over the bed to nuzzle her face against Aaron's face, kissing Aaron's nose, tucking him into bed *Who's my little bird of heaven—you are! You are my little bird of heaven.* And now to Aaron at the age of eight it was unsettling and disturbing, it was a betrayal to hear Zoe sing the song he'd believed was special to him in this new, altered way and to see Mommy smiling and winking at the audience of strangers and in this sparkly dress he'd never seen before that dipped in front to show the tops of her breasts, and the tight fabric that clung to her narrow ribcage, waist, hips like something liquid.

> *I looked up and I looked back*
> *Walked a hundred miles on the railroad track*
> *Alls I can tell from where I stand*
> *There's a little bird of heaven right here in my hand.*

Of course Aaron understood: Zoe was a singer with a band, and this was what you did, if you were a singer—you dressed in special costume-clothes, you stood up on the stage at a microphone, you smiled and sang like someone on TV and the audience cheered and applauded. Aaron understood and yet—Aaron was hurt. Seeing the glamorous blond woman who wasn't Mommy in the spotlight singing with the band that called itself Black River Breakdown that Daddy resented, those guys Daddy disliked and complained of to Mommy—the white-haired fiddler, the Elvis-looking guitarist, and the heavyset man strumming what looked like a large violin resting on the floor that had a deep bass sound like frogs croaking out back of the house on Quarry Road.

Though Daddy said yes, he was proud of Mommy, too. He was.

Aaron and his father were sitting in the first row close by the band-stand. Had to crane their heads back, to see. And the loud music-sound swept over them, like waves. These first-row seats had been *reserved* for special family members and friends of the band, it was a privileged place to sit close by the bandstand. There were other songs of Zoe's the audi-ence liked, too—"Big Rock Candy Mountain," "You Are My Sunshine," "Footsteps in the Snow." You could see how excited and anxious Zoe was for the audience to love her, to cheer and applaud. With narrowed eyes Aaron looked over his shoulder at the rows of seats, so many people, faces unknown to him, all of them staring at Zoe on stage, Aaron counted thirty-two rows of seats, and in each row there were twenty-five seats, and so there were—was it 800 people at the bandstand? But others were standing, and in the grass there were people sitting on blankets and close by in the park people at picnic tables and outdoor grills. Maybe 700 people. Black River Breakdown was the third or fourth band to be playing in the Labor Day concert and had the largest audience. Aaron knew, he should be proud of his mother. He wanted to be proud of his mother. He did not want to think how Mommy had betrayed him, that was a wrong thing to think Aaron knew, a baby-way of thinking, and he was older now, and happy for his mother except it made him feel strange, it made him feel dizzy like seeing somebody wearing a mask, or a department store mannequin he'd mistaken for a real person, there was something wrong about this, hearing *little bird of heaven* in this place and in an altered voice of Mommy's that was not the voice of the lullaby, the voice that was special for *him*.

And beside Aaron in the folding chair seated with his legs sprawled, an opened can of beer on his knee there was Daddy listening with his face shut up tight staring at Mommy on stage and lifting his hands to clap only at the end of a song, not in spontaneous applause like others in the audience. Deliberately and loudly and lifting his hands so Zoe could see—if she wished to see—how he was clapping, and proud of her, and happy for her.

He *was*.

Not just clapping but other noises were disturbing to Aaron, and to Delray. Cheers, whistles, shouts—these were from men, boys—and the looks in their faces—you could tell. Aaron was only eight, but Aaron could tell.

Showing off your body like that. Don't tell me you aren't. The way you move your mouth, too. Think I can't see?

That was Daddy, telling Mommy what she had not wanted to hear.

What Aaron was not meant to hear.

After the concert there was a reception. Aaron believed that they were going to the reception but before even the applause subsided Delray lurched to his feet and walked away leaving Aaron to follow in his wake. Maybe Delray had murmured *C'mon!* or maybe he'd said nothing at all and so Aaron had no choice but to make his way through the crowd jostled by strangers and feeling anxious, excited. Feeling the sting of Zoe's betrayal like sunburn on his face.

Nearing the parking lot Aaron said, dangerously, "You let Mommy do it—you didn't stop her."

Delray was walking ahead, unhearing.

"Why'd you let her, Daddy? Why didn't you stop her?"

Now Delray heard. Delray was unlocking the car. Delray said, as if this were a subject he'd given thought to, and not a subject that made his mouth sneer, "'Stop her'—what? It's something for your mother to do that makes her happy. She's got a good voice. She always wanted to sing with some band. She won't always have this chance." Delray laughed, and now you could detect the sneer. In the car leaving the park—Delray was one of the first to leave—it seemed he'd forgotten to switch on his headlights until other motorists signaled him. Aaron said, "Why didn't we stay with Mommy? How will Mommy get home?" and Delray said, laughing, "Don't worry. Mommy will always get a ride anywhere she wants to go."

In his bed without Mommy to tuck him in he'd been miserable not able to sleep feeling restless, itchy—he'd been bitten by mosquitoes at the damn park. He was excited, yet—shut his eyes and saw Zoe on stage—heard Zoe singing—and the deep-bass bullfrog-sound from the man with the oversized violin. You had to resent how Zoe drew the light and warmth from him in his bed—from any room she left—you could feel the temperature dropping, the chill of her absence. The emptiness.

30

MAY 1978

"MOM? HEY MOM—"

Wandering through the house calling for her. Knowing she wasn't there. Everything so quiet: no radio, no humming/singing in the kitchen. Early mornings Zoe would rap on the door to Aaron's room, come inside to poke, prod, tickle and urge him out of bed if he wasn't up yet. Calling him *sleepyhead, lazybones.* Yanking the covers off him as he woke with effort his skin clammy and heartbeat slowed like the heartbeat of a creature drowsing in the mud of the deepest sea.

But not this morning. This morning was quiet. Nobody gave a damn if Aaron woke in time for the school bus. If he got out of bed at all.

In a quiet choked voice Delray said *There's no way to stop her what she wants to do. What she thinks she wants to do, that we can't give her.*

He was nine years old. He was a big-boned child with somber staring eyes and lusterless dark hair standing up in tufts around his carved-looking face. Rubbing his fists into his eyes in hurt and in fury at his departed mother. He knew that Zoe had done a very wrong thing and that Pa was disgusted with her and Aaron must side with Pa so that Pa wouldn't be disgusted with Aaron.

He'd seen Pa take after Zoe, a few times. No one had known he'd seen. Pa would not like it if he'd known. How Pa slammed out of a room in pursuit of Zoe grabbing her shoulders and shake-shake-shaking her and his yellow teeth bared in a wide mean Hallowe'en pumpkin grin but he'd never hit Mommy he would claim, he would claim to Aaron *never with closed fists.*

And Mommy would dare to slap at him, her hair in her flushed face. And Mommy would dare to claw at him, breaking her fingernails. *Bastard you son of a bitch hitting a woman. Weigh twice as much as me you big brave man you sorry son of a bitch.*

If Aaron rushed out of his hiding place, Pa would turn on him cuffing him, balling up both fists to punch him in the head, in the gut, in the buttocks if Aaron dared to get in Pa's way.

Mommy was gone but Aunt Viola came by to cook for them. Viola was Delray's younger sister who'd defend Zoe to him saying Delray had got to learn to ease up some, you know how much it means to Zoe this singing career of hers, what a sweet voice Zoe has, everybody says so. And Delray said meanly what my wife has is a nice sweet ass. Nobody's listening to her damn voice.

Viola said laughing, Well. Delray would know.

One night when Delray was out and it was just Aunt Viola and Aaron in the house eating macaroni-and-cheese out of Aunt Viola's casserole dish and watching TV she told him a secret: that Zoe and her music-friends Black River Breakdown had driven to New York City for an "audition" with a recording company and if this "audition" went well Aaron would be seeing Zoe on TV one day before long and hearing her on the radio. Maybe they'd be invited to Nashville and appear on Grand Ole Opry. Maybe they'd be friends with Dolly Parton, Johnny Cash, June Carter. People would buy their records and they'd all be rich and could move out of Sparta to some city like Nashville or New York or to a better part of Sparta like Ridge View where people had their docks and boats on the river.

Aaron was astonished to hear this. Delray had never told him any of this. Viola drank Delray's ale from the can eating and talking and her eyes dreamy saying how she'd gone to see Zoe off and wished her good luck. No she didn't approve of all that Zoe did but she understood why Zoe needed to do it. Traveling with her musician-friends in a cream-colored

Chevy van with *Black River Breakdown* in purple letters on its sides and in this van they carried their instruments (guitars, drums) and sound equipment to what they called "gigs"—weddings, family gatherings, summer concerts, bandstands. Black River Breakdown was three musicians and a female singer and they all had full-time jobs and families and no one knew of them yet beyond Herkimer County though they'd been doing these "gigs" for almost five years now and as Zoe said *Not getting any younger!*

In the house on Quarry Road there was an antiquated upright piano Zoe had bought as a girl for forty dollars from an elderly neighbor. Zoe kept wanting to take piano lessons but in the meantime had learned to pick out melodies on the keyboard with two fingers replicating songs she heard on the radio or in records. In this way Zoe learned many songs, she was very patient, and very hopeful. Hearing Zoe pick out tunes on the piano Aaron listened closely as if the notes of the piano—sometimes halting, sometimes fluid—were a special code, for him to decipher.

When Aaron struck the keyboard with his clumsy fingers, or with his fists, the strings inside vibrated with alarm, pain. In frustration Aaron set his thumb against the keyboard as far to the right as he could get and run his thumb hard and fast down to the left making a terrible noise and skinning his thumb so it bled.

Zoe had another hope: to write songs!

Wanting to write "love ballads" most of all for Black River Breakdown to record but each time she wrote a song, no matter the song sounded original at first, soon it shifted into something by the Supremes.

"Like their music has burrowed into my brain. Damn!"

Each day Zoe was away in New York City she called home at 6 P.M. speaking first with Delray and then with Aaron. Delray was brusque and sullen with Zoe saying little before handing the phone over to Aaron, who felt strange hearing his mother's voice on the phone, a novelty for him, and yet so warm and intimate as if she was leaning over him in bed, blowing in his ear and tickling him awake.

The first three calls, Zoe chattered excitedly telling Aaron what a wonderful time they were having—what a "fantastic" city New York was—next time she came, she would bring her family with her. But the fourth, final evening Zoe burst into tears saying she couldn't wait to get back home, she was missing them so.

Hearing his mother cry over the phone, Aaron was astonished. Almost Aaron began to cry too, except his father took back the receiver from him.

"Zoe? Get the hell home. Or I'm coming down there after you."

After Zoe returned home crestfallen and discouraged it would be revealed, maybe Black River Breakdown had made a mistake hurrying off to New York City as they had. Arranging for "audition recordings" to be made at Empire Music Productions, Inc., for a fee of $1,650.

"This terrible 'studio'! On the twelfth floor of the rattiest old building on Forty-third Street just a few blocks from Times Square, you would think it was *legitimate* at such an address, wouldn't you?—we sure did. After we paid our fee it turned out there were all sorts of 'surplus fees'—'hidden expenses'—and this contract we had to sign so confusing to read, we just gave up and signed it. Should've known it was a bad sign this building where junkies and vagrants—'homeless people' they are called in New York City—were camped out on the sidewalk out front, you practically had to step over them to get inside. And this 'Mr. Goetsche' who introduced himself as 'CEO of the company' takes our money, a cashier's check, and there's a 'sound engineer' and this room supposed to be a 'recording studio' and we spent at least six hours making these short records you can actually play, I mean they are real records, but small, and they give them to you and I'm feeling shy asking, Is this it? So much money and all we are getting in return is these little plastic records of Black River Breakdown singing, that we already have tapes and cassettes of, at home? Mr. Goetsche says we will be hearing from him in another day or two about our 'audition'—whether we will be moving to the 'next stage'—and in the meantime we're staying in a Howard Johnson Motel on Forty-seventh Street, and there's roaches in the bathrooms, terrible noise all night long—sirens, ambulances, fire trucks—firecrackers?—maybe gunshots?—like the worst stories you'd hear of New York City, you'd have thought were exaggerated. Oh God, I had to check my bed for *bedbugs*. Seems like I could feel those nasty things crawling over my skin! Days we went sightseeing for instance to the Empire State Building and Rockefeller Center which we did not think was so very impressive, nights we saw shows like the Rockettes, so that was all right but very expensive, worse even than what people here might think and all the money I'd been saving from my work at Honeystone's is mostly gone, I am so sad about that. I am just sick about that. . . . So a day goes by, and another day, and a morning, and we don't hear from Mr. Goetsche who said he was going to send our 'audition records' out to agents, music companies, radio DJs and some TV people for feedback but he doesn't call us and when we try to call him, some switchboard operator puts us on hold. So I think—I'm feeling desperate like there is nothing to lose at this point—so by myself I go back to see Mr. Goetsche, and sure enough in the 'recording studio' there is another group being auditioned, looks like high-school-age kids trying to imitate Mick Jagger, and Mr. Goetsche stares at me like he's pretending not to recognize me, says he doesn't have time for me right now, but I tell him he had better make time for me, or I am going to the police. Mr. Goetsche all but laughs in my face, I must appear so foolish to him.

"He's older than he'd seemed the first day. Kind of oily-skinned and puffy-faced and the whiskey fumes coming off him and it isn't even noon. He takes me into his office—takes my hand, and squeezes it—like there is some special feeling between us—his office is so cramped and depressing and looking out onto a blank wall and I'm saying, Mr. Goetsche I know that there are all kinds of amateurs in music hoping to be discovered, just tell me is there any chance for Black River Breakdown, or for me?—and Mr. Goetsche starts in saying, Yes of course there is, dear Zoe, this is America there is always a chance for success, but then he stops as if he has run out of steam, he gives me this sad crooked smile and paws around in a drawer, pulls out this large glossy road map of the United States, opens it on his desk top like a school teacher might do, he's put on his glasses, bifocals, he's breathing heavy through his nostrils that are thick with hairs, with a pencil he's tapping this road map north and south, east and west, saying in this somber voice, Zoe you look like a sweet decent young woman and I know you have tremendous 'heart' and could be a legendary performer but I am going to level with you, dear, like you deserve: see all these towns? cities? everywhere, in every state?—in each of these there is at least one very pretty girl with a good voice, a 'promising' voice, hoping to make a career for herself in 'entertainment,' hoping to be famous and rich and make her family proud of her and her high school classmates green with envy, and it's her hope that one day strangers will come up to her on the street and ask for her autograph and to have their pictures taken with her. All the far-flung states of the United States, all the cities, towns, desolate little crossroads settlements shortly to become ghost towns, covered in dust in the next few decades, and no one remaining to remember, or give a damn—just dots on the map, see? And the tragedy is, Zoe, there are just too many of you. Too many 'Zoe Krullers'—and not enough places for you. Like sea creatures in the ocean, all so hungry, and never enough food. And so the sea creatures themselves must become food. If there were not all the other 'Zoes'—plus 'stars' desperate to hang onto what they have with their fingertips, whose names would be known to you—you might have a chance. But there isn't, see, Zoe?—and so you don't."

Telling this story Zoe lowered her voice to imitate Goetsche's deep-bass voice. You could see that Zoe meant to entertain her listeners yet tears came into Zoe's eyes always by the end of the story, she wiped at lightly with her fingertips.

Aaron wondered was he meant to laugh? Did Mommy want him to laugh? Each time Mommy told this story, to different people, it was becoming a funnier story, the voices more exaggerated, and Mommy's expression more comical, yet there were those tears, Aaron saw.

How he hated the man in New York City who'd told Zoe such things!

Hated to think of anyone making his beautiful mother cry and hated to think of people like starving-hungry fish, and so many of them. And so many to be eaten.

"Oh hell—I have to concede he was right. He is right. There in Times

Square, in the vortex—is that what I mean?—'center'—of all that hunger, and all that hope. And he knows. Maybe his name was even 'Goetsche'— we were thinking later, driving back to Sparta in the van, maybe the name meant 'Got-cha'—like 'I gotcha, sucker!'—maybe it was a joke-name. But maybe it wasn't. Maybe he wasn't joking then. With just me, I mean. Other people, that was different. With me, he spoke sincerely. I'm sure he spoke sincerely. He'd been drinking some but he wasn't drunk. He called me Zoe in such a tender way, he asked would I like a drink, just the two of us could toast Break River Blackout—that was what he called it, but he wasn't joking—and I said no thanks and he said O.K. Zoe, he kissed me on the cheek. O.K. and *bonheur toujours*. And I took the elevator back down out of that place, and walked out onto Forty-third Street, and was crying, and laughing too, and I thought *Too many Zoe Krullers, and all so hungry.*"

Aaron said protectively: "Mom, I like how you sing!"

"Well! That's all that matters, then."

Zoe smiled and leaned over to kiss Aaron, lost her balance and her pursed lips missed his nose, and there was a sweet-sour smell to Mommy's breath too, Aaron wondered if she had brought back from New York City.

31

HE WAS ELEVEN. He'd been kept back in fifth grade. Among his ten-year-old classmates at Harpwell Elementary he was everything wrong, he could see in their eyes. He could see in his teacher's eyes. Wrong-sized thoughts began to push into his head.

Krull began to push into his head.

At the landfill on Garrison Road he'd seen them. Straddling his bike he'd seen them. This wet-smelling April day he was alone. Spending much of his time alone. He knew, that kick in the heart, the woman in the pickup was his mother. Even if his eyes misted over and his vision was blotched and his heart kick-kick-kicked like a frantic animal yet he knew, the woman was Zoe. Had to be Zoe with her bushy blond-streaked hair tied back in a red silk scarf. He knew that scarf. He knew that laughter like a bird's sharp beak pecking. The man's voice was lower, murmurous.

This was a man Aaron had seen at Honeystone's more than once. Aaron didn't know his name but he'd seen him with his kids, a boy who was Aaron's age, a girl who was younger. He'd seen the man wait until Zoe was free to take their orders, he'd seen the way the man tried to be unobtrusive holding back, watching Zoe out of the corner of his eye. And how Zoe laughed in delight seeing this. Like a big cat shivering with pleasure in her skin, licking her lips as she leaned over the high counter on her elbows murmuring *Hey there what can I do you for today?*

Aaron shut his eyes remembering *Eddy.*

What can I do you for today, Ed–dy?

Zoe's special voice. Soft throaty teasing voice. The way Zoe leaned over Aaron's bed when he was sleeping and slow to wake up blowing in his ear.

This man, Eddy. Sure he was a Caucasian. Not a drop of any kind of dark blood, Aaron could see.

Good-looking guy in T-shirt, khakis. Baseball cap with the rim pulled low over his forehead. Muscled arms covered in fair hairs and an air of expectation about him, he wasn't one to wait patiently in line for anything yet would wait for Zoe Kruller.

Ed–dy thought it was you out there you are looking good

Zoe and so are you

The landfill was a place Aaron came to. Usually by himself but sometimes with friends. At the garbage dump there were large ungainly birds that kept up a raucus din, you could hear out on the road. Like something being killed. Crows, gulls, turkey vultures. Turkey vultures were something to behold! *Scavengers* these were called. Older boys bicycled to the landfill to pop these birds with air rifles and twenty-twos. *Pop* was a way of speaking Aaron admired. *Pop* meant that the terror, the hurt, the terrible thrashing death inflicted upon a living creature was only just a popping noise like something in a cartoon. *Pop* was what Krull might do, some day he had a gun.

Delray had a gun. Delray had what he called a *deer rifle*. Delray hadn't kept the rifle clean and oiled and last time he'd taken it out, to examine, there'd been rust on the barrel. *Damn thing might blow up in my hands* Delray had said in disgust.

Aaron was crouched behind a packing case. Aaron was trying not to breathe too deeply, the smell of rotting garbage was strong. He had not noticed the dark-green pickup as he'd approached the landfill on his bike but then he'd noticed it, parked just outside the fence, in an area overgrown with trees and tall thistles and rushes, where there was a service road through the underbrush. He'd heard voices but could not decipher words. Through a stand of scrub trees he could see the occupants of the pickup—a man wearing a baseball cap, a woman with hair tied back in a red scarf. He wasn't sure if he liked the way his heart was pounding. Maybe he liked it. He heard laughter. The woman's high-pitched laughter, that was familiar to him, he thought. He thought it was familiar. A sensation like stinging red ants ran over his skin.

It was a lonely afternoon, he'd biked out to Garrison Road. That morning he'd hung around the garage hoping his father would find use for him but Delray had not and then Delray went out with the tow truck and took a young mechanic with him, and Aaron wasn't wanted.

Zoe had gone out shopping. Or wherever Zoe went, Saturday afternoons. Used to be Mommy took Aaron with her in the car maybe just for a ride but no more.

You're a big boy sweetie, where are your friends can't you go play?

It's too boring with Mommy today. You'd cause me trouble. Yes you would!

Aaron dared to approach the pickup. Squatting and moving on his haunches like some ugly stunted creature. In gym class the other boys stared at him warily. The size of Aaron Kruller, his dark eyes and smudged skin. At Harpwell Elementary there were no other boys like Aaron, as there would be in middle school and in high school, to which children from the Seneca reservation were bused. *What did you say to those boys did you threaten to hurt those boys* Aaron's teacher asked him in a hissing voice and Aaron was utterly astonished not knowing how to defend himself.

Sit here. Here in this desk. Don't squirm! Don't turn your head.

Just leave the other children alone. You are older, you are bigger than they are.

Rage smoldered in him, seeing the blond hair pressed against the pickup window on the passenger's side. Where the man had pushed her, and she'd given in. Big lazy kitty giving in, stretching her arms. And now the man was leaning over her. Eddy, in the baseball cap. The woman's arms came around the man's neck gripping him tight.

Krull knew what they were doing. Krull knew what *fucking* was, what it meant: the nastiest thing you could do. Older boys had told him. At the garage the mechanics said *fuck, fucking* often. Delray said *fuck* in an explosive way when he was angry but you didn't need to be angry to say *fuck* it was just a way of talking, even women said it sometimes, even Zoe said *fuck*. But if Aaron did, Zoe would scold him.

Watch that mouth! There are ladies present.

A joke of Zoe's, who was not a lady. Why was that funny?

Krull at age eleven knew what *fuck, fucking* was and was disgusted by it. Krull could not have imagined why any woman would consent to be *fucked* by any man.

Whoever Eddy was, he drove a dark green Chevy pickup. New model in good condition and Aaron wondered if he'd seen it at his father's garage. Maybe at the gas pumps. Maybe he'd pumped gas for Eddy himself.

Delray would not like it. Zoe with this man.

Krull didn't like it. Stinging red ants in his armpits where coarse hairs were sprouting, and in his crotch he scratched with punishing vehemence.

Krull knew all about Aaron, but Aaron knew little about Krull. *Krull* was a special name the older boys had for him, to signal they liked him, maybe. *Aaron* was Zoe's special name for him she'd selected, she had told him, before he was born, out of the Bible.

Never was an *Aaron* she'd known in all of Sparta, Zoe said. Why he was special and must live up to his name.

Why am I special he'd asked her.

Because you are mine! Mommy said.

Mommy laughed and kissed his nose. Like it was a joke? Or was not a joke? Mommy was so wonderful Mommy could make you believe anything if it was something you wanted to believe.

Because you are mine and also Daddy's. That's why you are a special boy.

Krull knew better. Krull bitterly resented being kept back in fifth grade lacking in *reading skills* and *social deportment*. Shamed and angry he would not trust any God-damned teacher not ever again.

Words were scrambled in his eyes, when he tried to read. And numbers were scrambled. He hated just the look of a page of print and writing on the blackboard he shut his eyes against, he hated so.

And if Aaron was called to the blackboard to take the chalk from the teacher and if Aaron could not comprehend which numbers to write on the blackboard it was Krull who consoled him *Fuck them just walk out. Walk out of the fucking room just do it, man.*

Staring at the Chevy pickup on the far side of the fence. No one was visible inside the cab now, even the flash of red scarf had disappeared. And the laughter had ceased. You would think if you'd just bicycled to the landfill now, that the pickup was empty, abandoned.

You'd think that whoever had driven it might be at the landfill somewhere or in the woods nearby, with a gun. A rifle. Hunting.

Pop! Pop pop pop! Krull could hear the guys sniggering, one of them handed him the rifle.

32

THOSE YEARS. *Krull* grew.

Blunt-sounding as a fist: *Krull*.

Heavy density as a block of concrete: *Krull*.

At home his father called him *kid*. Sometimes *Aar-on* if he meant to criticize. There were many ways to displease Delray and not so many ways to please Delray but overall, Aaron and his father got along. At the garage where Aaron worked part-time—for no pay—*room-and-board is what I'm paying you, kid*—Delray sometimes took Aaron aside to speak to him in what you'd call a special way, a personal way, almost tenderly, often teasingly, rubbing his big grease-stained fingers over Aaron's head saying *O.K. kid, you didn't fuck up this time. In fact you did pretty damn good.*

Like at lacrosse. One of the older guys staring at Aaron, nodding his approval of Aaron. Though Aaron lived in Sparta and not where they did. Though Aaron had a white mother, their mothers despised. (How did Aaron know this? Aaron knew.) Lacrosse was the *medicine game*. Lacrosse was the *war-game*. Not just anyone could play lacrosse: girls were forbidden. Even the heavy hard-muscled Indian girls who more resembled boys were forbidden. Players wore their *war marks* with pride, bruises, scars, knees and ankles and shoulders that throbbed with pain, it was an insult for *females* to take up a lacrosse stick still less run out on the field wild to play. Aaron had long been hearing tales of lacrosse players from the Herkimer reservation who'd been picked out by scouts for Canadian pro teams, brought to Canada all expenses paid to play lacrosse for a living.

Renounce their U.S. citizenship and take on Canadian citizenship which they readily did.

Mostly now, now he was older, in high school Aaron was expected to work at Kruller's Auto Repair longer hours. There wasn't time for lacrosse. There wasn't time for schoolwork. Homework assignments Aaron left behind at school in his locker or homeroom desk. Zoe objected saying their son was too damn young to be working like a damn grease monkey in that garage, he was just a kid, what about him learning something at school and getting a diploma and going to the community college? Delray said he'd never gotten any high school diploma still less gone to the community college and Zoe said *Yes that's exactly right, that's why our son should not model himself after you.*

Delray laughed *What's this "model"—you're thinking, that should be you?*

Zoe worried that Aaron might be injured in the garage. If a jacked-up car or motorcycle slipped, and broke his leg? Crushed him? Kruller's garage was not the best-equipped garage in the Sparta area. Kruller's garage did in fact have accidents, mechanics were occasionally injured. Delray himself had a crushed and nerveless finger on his left hand as well as a crushed left toe with a dead toenail thick and discolored as a hoof, he laughed at such injuries saying at least he hadn't had to have anything amputed like his buddies who'd been in 'Nam. Nothing irked Zoe more than her young teenaged son returning to the house slump-shouldered as a middle-aged man, in grease-stiffened overalls and stinking of oil, gasoline, sweat, she insisted that Aaron wash his hands and forearms with Twelve-Mule Team Borax and before she'd let him sit down at the supper table she insisted upon digging the black grease out from beneath his ragged fingernails herself with her metal nail file, clipping his nails with her tiny nail scissors and even filing them where they'd been broken or torn. Grease on his face like Indian war paint, in his very eyelashes and in his hair. So Delray took Aaron out to have his hair cut short like a Marine recruit. Delray laughed at Zoe's concern: *Bullshit. Aaron's O.K. with me.*

This was so. Aaron was O.K. with Delray. Most of the time.

It felt good to have a father like Delray who knew cars, motorcycles.

A father who owned a Harley-Davidson he still took out sometimes, with his biker-friends.

Rumor was, Delray Kruller had once belonged to the Adirondack Hells Angels. If anyone asked Zoe she would shrug evasively and say *Ask Del. He's got the tats.*

Tats: tattoos.

Must've been, something had happened with some biker-band, years before. Something had gone wrong. Maybe that was the time his father had gotten *incarcerated* up at Potsdam. Aaron knew better than to ask. Even when he'd been a younger kid he'd known. You kept your mouth shut, if your father wanted to tell you something he'd tell you. Nothing made Delray angrier than to overhear someone ask something of Zoe that had to do with *him*.

Younger, Aaron had been invited occasionally to come ride with Delray on the Harley-Davidson. In a trance of happiness Aaron would climb into the wide fleecy seat behind Delray, arms around Delray's midriff in a way that would have been unthinkable except on the 'cycle at such a time. So physically close to his dad! And how muscular his dad was, though the flesh of Delray's lower back and waist was going flaccid, fatty. There was no call for Aaron and Delray to touch each other any longer, still less to touch in such an intimate way. Aaron's trance of happiness was a kind of oblivion which, in times of deep unhappiness, at school for instance, or lying twitchy and sweaty in his bed unable to sleep, he could play and replay in his memory like rerun TV footage.

Zoe protested *Del make him wear a crash helmet at least! Both of you.* Delray teased saying *Chill out sweetheart, the kid is safe with me. We ain't gonna crash.*

In fact both father and son wore crash helmets on the Harley-Davidson, when Delray believed that crash helmets were required. Not for brief teeth-jolting rides along dirt lanes between cornfields where seven-foot cornstalks whipped in the wind and blew and slapped like forlorn living creatures as the cyclists rushed past. If the ride was longer and on an actual paved road—along Quarry to Post, and to the River Road for instance—with a stop at the Post Tavern—Delray strapped helmets on both his and Aaron's heads and without protest Aaron bowed his head like a young fighter pilot, or an astronaut, being geared-up by his superior, on a mission that might end in a fiery death.

Hang on, kid. Might be a little bumpy at first.

With Aaron behind him hugging him tight Delray rarely took the thunderous-roaring Harley-Davidson past seventy miles an hour. And this on clear stretches of country road. Beyond seventy, seventy-five, the vehicle began to vibrate and shudder ominously, Delray wouldn't risk a crash. Not with his son on board. Much of his life he'd been a reckless son of a bitch—no one was quicker to acknowledge this, than Delray—but now in his forties he was learning caution. Even half-drunk Delray took pride in his instinct as a cyclist knowing to brake in quick little jerks going into curves—never to slide into loose gravel at even a moderate speed—hadn't he witnessed such accidents in full daylight, one of them damn messy, and fatal.

Gripping Delray tight around the midriff as they sped on the Harley-Davidson Aaron was dry-mouthed with wonder seeing the familiar countryside begin to blur like something in water, ripples in water—oncoming vehicles on the road sped at them at astonishing speeds and were jerked past like toy objects on a string—overhead the sky dissolved pale as vapor penetrated by winking patches of sunlight through clouds like fire and it came to Aaron *This is the happiest you can be, you will never be happy like this again.*

Later in their lives Delray rarely took the Harley-Davidson out. In fact he was trying to sell the damn thing. He had back trouble—"cervical spine strain"—getting older, you acknowledged certain risks.

Still Delray was a tall stocky-bodied man with sharp-chiseled Indian features and dark shaggy hair like the hide of a bison as Zoe said half in disgust and half in admiration—her crazy biker-husband she'd married young—"too damn young to know what the hell I was doing"—who in the heat of summer wore a headband like a hippie of another era, drank beer and sometimes even smoked pot at Kruller's Auto Repair which by the early 1980s had become a just-barely-solvent business Zoe had come to realize could only lose business as newer and better equipped auto repairs were established in the Sparta area. First thing you noticed about Delray was his tats: muscled shoulders and arms covered in black hairs and glistening with fantastical colors, a U.S. flag twined with a cobra etched into Delray's right forearm, a U.S. eagle with glaring bronze eyes etched into Delray's left forearm and on his back, which was broad and pale-fleshed and covered in dark wiry hairs like a pelt, a lurid-grinning black skull with flames shooting from its eye sockets and beneath this skull the mysterious letters **aha61**.

Adirondack Hells Angels 1961?

What Aaron figured. Not that Delray would reveal any secret of his.

On his craggy right knuckles, a crimson heart with *Zoe* in black script.

Man-to-man Delray confided frankly in Aaron he had second thoughts about his tats, especially the U.S. flag and U.S. eagle.

"See, it's like your skin is given out to something not-you, you can't get back. Like some asshole billboard or something. You'd have to skin yourself alive to get it back, see kid?—ain't fucking worth it."

Because you are special. You are mine!

Bullshit he was. Never was. Shrinking from his mother as she tousled his hair, poked and tickled him in that way of hers. Zoe was one who liked to touch, as she talked. Or touched without needing to talk.

Now he was *Krull*, he ceased believing her.

Came to the realization that so much she told him was bullshit because she was his mother, and she loved him.

Krull understood, such a love was weakness. It bore into you, weakened you. Like some kind of bone-marrow-cancer. Aaron had been shy and self-conscious in school, had difficulty reading and hated to be called on by teachers, feared stammering, giving a wrong answer and the other students would laugh at him and so he'd acquired a reputation for being sulky, "uncooperative." His teachers had been uneasy with him mistaking him for a boy he wasn't—yet—and then there came *Krull* when Aaron was thirteen and beginning to get his height, weight, muscled body and there was no mistaking *Krull*.

Beginning to like, in eighth grade, the way his classmates drew back when he approached. Some of them looking quickly away as if they hadn't seen him. (But their eyes drifted back, covertly. Especially girls' eyes.) It made Krull laugh, that glimmer of fear in their faces. Krull had no need even to push at them, collide with them, shove them against a stairway railing or a row of lockers to provoke that fear.

First fear. Then respect. Krull grew.

Krull had the respect of older guys. Some were from the reservation and others lived in the outlying northern district of Sparta near Quarry Road, a few were his neighbors. They were guys like himself. Their fathers were men like Delray Kruller: quarry workers, construction workers, truckers, welders, factory workers, mechanics. The guys shared cigarettes, joints, beers and even whiskey with Krull. You had to have an older brother or cousin to acquire such things for you at the 7-Eleven or Circle Beer & Wine or to steal them from home. In boys' lavatories at school and sometimes—brazenly—in school corridors between classes they drank hastily and carelessly from cans of lukewarm beer and ale and the liquid stung their nasal cavities as they snorted with laughter, wild-dog-yipping laughter that attracted attention. For it was to attract attention, to alarm, intimidate and display themselves that they behaved in such ways with a hope too of being expelled from school, sent home permanently and totally *fucked-up*. Sure they smoked on school property—they'd been smoking since grade school. Some of them—though never Krull, who had too much sense—sniffed from plastic bottles of glue inside paper bags held to their faces. It was a sick giddy dazed "high"—a killer "high" said to fry the brain. Like crystal meth, they couldn't afford. They got into scuffles with other boys—"good" boys—who reported them to authorities. They defaced park benches with spray paint, broke windows, slashed tires. Krull was rarely a part of such roving gangs of boys, Krull had to be working at his father's garage. In seemingly aimless surges like packs of dogs they moved bristling with energy. Their language was close-cropped and explosive, repetitive and incantatory—*fuck, fuckhead, fuckface, motherfucker, cocksucker, shithead, cunt* and *cuntface*. This language was sacred to them, words with the power to intimidate others and even to inflict a kind of hurt upon them—girls, women, weaker boys. If you were a boy you wielded that language, or you did not. Krull wielded the language as if he'd been born to it. Thrilling, to utter such words. To inflict such hurt. Like shooting at the landfill. Popping scavenger birds. Popping squirrels, ground hogs, raccoons, stray dogs and cats. *Gonna pop that fucker* one of the guys would say. *Pop out his fuckin eye, you watch.* One of Krull's friends was Richie Shinegal who lived a mile away on Quarry Road. Richie was fifteen and in high school in some indeterminate grade awaiting his sixteenth birthday when he could quit. He was taller than Krull, and heavier. He was meaner than Krull. He had a Remington air pistol that shot BB pellets with the power to kill small creatures and to maim or blind others. If Richie aimed his BB-pistol at you, he'd aim for the eyes. He'd aim to make you wince, and to make you hide behind your hands, but he wouldn't pull the trigger if you were his friend. One day the guys had biked to the landfill and Richie was showing off target-shooting—crows, ravens, rats scurrying in the garbage—and Richie handed the pistol to Krull telling him how to use it, how to cock it, and pull the trigger lifting the gun, sighting along the barrel and holding his breath but when Krull pulled the trigger as he'd been instructed aiming at a crow some thirty feet away something went wrong, some mysterious action in the pistol sprang shut and slammed over the knuckles of Krull's right hand and Richie howled with laughter at Krull whimpering with pain like a shot cat, white in the face the sudden pain was so intense. Krull's hand was inflamed then turned blue-black and swelled to twice its size, he could hardly grip the bicycle handle to ride back home.

That night at supper Zoe saw the swollen hand and asked what the hell had happened to him but quickly Krull pulled away his hurt-boy-face set in opposition to her like a clenched fist, didn't want his mother to touch him, not ever again.

33

AUGUST 1981

SIX YEARS AT MINIMUM WAGE, treated like shit by prune-faced old Adele Honeystone who rarely had a smile for her just plain jealous of Zoe's popularity with customers especially men, abruptly Zoe quit. Busiest time of a Sunday afternoon in summer, Zoe quit. Adele was saying in this simpering voice like there's a poker up her bony rear *Zoe please could you sponge the counter here it's so sticky!—use the clean sponge please not the old dirty one THANK YOU* and Zoe stood very still not daring to speak nor even to move and then slowly detached the God-damned fucking hairnet from her hair wadded it into a ball and tossed it into the trash.

"No, ma'am. I don't think so."

"What?"

"I said no, ma'am. I don't think so. I quit."

Oh this was a long time coming! Months and even years of hiding her resentment behind sweet-Zoe smiles, needing the extra cash, Delray refused to help finance anything to do with what he called her *music career* like it was a joke and not Zoe's oldest dream from when she'd been a girl. *Music career* was something Zoe would have to find money for herself and so God damn she'd swallowed her pride and her fury having to endure being criticized by snotty Mrs. Honeystone for scooping too much ice cream for customers, heaping too many nuts and too much Reddi-wip onto sundaes, most of all what Mrs. Honeystone called *carrying-on—*

laughing like a banshee—meaning flirting with the (male, admiring) customers and generally having a good time.

So, every nerve twitching in her body, Zoe quit.

"Zoe, *what*? *What* did you say?"—the astonished old woman was staring at Zoe through thick-lensed bifocals like some docile pet had kicked up at her, or nipped her—following Zoe around the counter and in the direction of the door as customers looked on alert and smiling, bemused—"Zoe, you can't *just quit*! Not *like this*! Don't be silly, Zoe, put your hairnet *back on*, you can't *just quit* in the middle of—"

"Ma'am, I said I quit. Get someone else to put up with your old-biddy shit, ma'am. Zoe has had it."

Ma'am. Old-biddy shit. Zoe has had it. These words uttered in Zoe Kruller's sweetest girl-singer voice would pass into local Sparta legend, by sundown of that very Sunday.

In the wake of Zoe Kruller walking out of the dairy like a stage actress tossing down her hairnet, untying her apron and laying it on a counter there teemed rumors like rushing water in a gutter: Zoe had in fact been *behaving strangely* for months not just at Honeystone's but elsewhere. Wouldn't be surprised if Zoe had been *embezzling* from Honeystone's or at any rate pocketing money instead of ringing it up in the cash register or possibly stealing outright though no one could claim to have seen her. Anyway it was known—in some circles it seemed to be known—that Zoe was *slipping around* with some man not her husband except which man?—the guitarist for that hillbilly band was too young for her but knowing Zoe it might've been him, or the old-guy fiddler you could see gazing at her with such love right on the bandstand, had to be embarrassing for the old guy's family. And there were men, a half-dozen, a dozen, who patronized Honeystone's frequently but only on weekends when Zoe Kruller worked, and making sure, when they did, that Zoe and not another clerk waited on them. Zoe's quick sharp laugh sounded like *uppers, speed*—amphetamines—a kind of epidemic in Sparta of women and girls addicted to diet pills—cheerleaders at the high school, nurses at Sparta General, housewives, even grandmas. *Speed* was most popular with working women in their thirties hoping to maintain some edge of glamour and vivacity.

It made a woman sexy, too. Sexed-up: *hot.*

Nastiest rumors had to do with Delray: he was the one who'd forced Zoe to quit her job out of jealousy, resenting the men Zoe was meeting at Honeystone's. Yet more, Delray resented Zoe singing with that country-music band. Delray was an ex-con, ex-biker, wife-beater. It was known he was one-quarter or maybe one-half Indian. You could see the Seneca features clearly in his face and in that hair. Why he went crazy if he had a few drinks. Why he had such a fiery temper. He'd blackened his wife's eyes, why she wore dark glasses sometimes. Bruised her wrists, why she wore so many tinkling little bracelets. Half-strangled her, why her voice was so throaty-sounding. Widely it was known that Delray was a heavy drinker, drug-user, *man-handler* of his wife to keep her in line.

Why did I quit 'cause I am ready for a change that's why.

Fuck you all of you looking at me like that, I deserve some happiness or at least the chance of it. That's why.

"Pursuit of happiness"—that's in the U.S. Constitution!

"All men are created equal"—that means women, too!

Not getting any younger, that's a fact. None of us are.

If I'm going to be on my feet smiling at customers might's well be a cocktail waitress. There's tips!

I'll get my chance one day. I know this.

I am not a superstitious person. Or a religious person. But I believe.

You must have faith in your destiny. You must not doubt.

At Checkers there's a different clientele. More money, and classier, than the rest of the Strip. The owner has promised me, some Friday nights I can sing. A lot can happen.

How's my husband feel about his wife working out at the Strip?—ask him.

And ask him why. Why's she there. Ask him. See what Delray says.

* * *

HE WAS TWELVE. Grown to a height of five feet six and a half inches and weighing 117 pounds sinewy-muscled and edgy-quick and looking older than twelve. And feeling older.

Wouldn't talk about his mother. What was happening between her and his dad. Stayed away from the house, when they quarreled. Slept outside in the old barn, in all his clothes and in his shoes.

Sure he'd seen this coming. When Zoe ran out to climb into the cream-colored van with *BLACK RIVER BREAKDOWN* on its sides. Carrying her suitcase, and Delray hadn't been home.

Since the landfill, he knew the name of the man who drove the Chevy pickup: Ed Diehl.

Maybe he'd seen Zoe with Ed Diehl another time, too. He wasn't sure. He wasn't sure. But he was sure he'd seen Diehl at his father's garage getting gas.

One day on his rat-colored bike he showed up at Honeystone's. No reason. Much of what he did had no evident reason. Once he'd picked up a skinned-looking little bird that had fallen out of a nest, and the parent-birds—robins—squawking and fluttering overhead—and he'd had a choice of crushing the little bird between his fingers or climbing up on a pile of lumber to put the bird back in the nest and for no clear reason he returned the bird to the nest as the parent-birds swooped and squawked dangerously close to his head but another time, no more reason, he'd kicked a turtle off a roadway, down an embankment and maybe its shell cracked on a rock, he hadn't gone to investigate.

He'd have liked to have Richie Shinegal's air-pistol. Better yet, a twenty-two rifle. Not sure why. Not yet.

At Honeystone's he leaned the rat-colored bike against an outside wall and pushed the screen door in inhaling the milky smells, chocolate, sugary baked goods like an old lost dream of child-comfort. Though Zoe had worked at the dairy for several years Aaron had not been there in a while, he'd grown self-conscious seeing his attractive young mother in the white uniform behind the counter, how pretty she was, how fluttery and girlish and glamorous, how people looked at her, how men looked at her. When she'd seen Aaron come in immediately she would wink and smile at him calling out *Hey there sweetie! C'mere.* Now Zoe was gone from Honeystone's. Now there was not any reason for Aaron Kruller to push his way inside out of the shimmering heat of late summer. Behind the counter a cat-faced girl stared at him in surprise. Others looked at him, too. Halfway across the floor to the counter where Zoe used to work when an old-woman nasal voice sounded sharply: "Aaron Kruller! You are not wanted here. Please leave."

Behind one of the refrigerated display cases Mrs. Honeystone stood purse-lipped and tremulous. Krull's mouth twitched. Not a boy's uneasy smile—not Aaron Kruller's uneasy smile—but a rude grimace baring teeth. Adele Honeystone had known Aaron since he'd been a young child—she had known Zoe Kruller for fifteen years, or more—but this did not seem to be Aaron Kruller. This was not a young boy but an adolescent male of an age no one might guess, taller than she and wearing a soiled black T-shirt and grease-stained work pants and in imitation of an adult biker he wore a black leather band on his left wrist. You would think that this was a wrist watch but it was just a black leather band. His eyes were deep-set beneath heavy eyebrows and glimmered with a kind of boy-mockery that unnerved the old woman. Hysterical Mrs. Honeystone would afterward claim to have glimpsed the handle of a knife—or some other weapon, like a hammer—protruding from one of the Kruller boy's trouser pockets for clearly he'd come to commit a robbery and to terrorize and so the white-haired old woman began to scream, "Stop him! He's a thief! Call the police!" Krull was taken by surprise. Even Krull, who had not expected this. Like an asshole he'd entered into the presence of his mother's enemy naively with no plan. Fear and loathing for him glinted in the old woman's glasses as daringly she advanced upon him, seeing that he was backing away, wildly she swung something at his head, might've been a baking tray she'd snatched up behind the counter, shedding brownie-fragments of which some would be caught in Krull's clothes—"Help! Thief! Vandal! He's Zoe Kruller's son! She's sent him here! *Call the police!*"

There were few customers in Honeystone's at this time. Several stood in line waiting to be served, other were seated at the wrought-iron tables. These were mothers with young children. None would see the weapon in the boy's pocket still less in his hand as Mrs. Honeystone would one day claim but they were quick to take up the alarm, frightened and clutching at their children as white-haired Mrs. Honeystone swung the baking pan at the boy's head as if to drive him to the door and in a sudden fury the boy punched blindly at the old woman, struck her on the hip causing her to lose her balance and totter as with a face contorted as a snarling animal's he crouched low to deliver a second punch, would've been a wicked sucker-punch except suddenly a warning thought came to him he'd better not, better get the hell out of this place, running outside to the rat-colored bike awaiting him as inside Honeystone's female screams lifted shrill as the shrieks of terrorized birds.

Never did! Never said that I would kill her.

Didn't mean to hit her, the old bitch hit me first.

Never had a knife. Nobody saw a knife!

. . . telling lies about my mother. Guess that was why.

They came for him at the address on the arrest warrant: 1138 Quarry Road. In two police cruisers racing up the bumpy dirt drive to the peach-colored house amid cornfields. Advanced upon him with drawn pistols as if he were an adult known to be armed and dangerous. Spoke harshly to him and when naively he resisted—lifting his arms against them, turning as if to run away—he was thrown by three arresting officers to the floor (the linoleum floor of the kitchen, which Zoe did not keep quite so clean as sparkling-shiny linoleum floors in TV ads)—his pockets were turned inside-out, searched for weapons—wrists cuffed behind his back in an expert way to make him whimper in pain. Hauled then to his feet—two young flush-faced cops gripped his upper arms, tight—forcibly walked outside to the first cruiser nearly fainting with pain. Delray wasn't home nor was Delray at Kruller's Auto Repair out at the road and where Zoe was, Aaron stammered he did not know.

What he'd vowed was *not to cry*. God damn he *would not cry*.

At Sparta police headquarters he was booked on charges of *criminal physical assault, attempted robbery, threatening human life and property*. The complainant was *Mrs. Adele Honeystone*. The name on the arrest warrant was *Aron Kruller*.

At the time of the arrest, Aaron was twelve years, eleven months and six days old. Having been *kept back* he was in sixth grade at Harpwell Elementary.

It was hours later Zoe answered the phone at home, was summoned to police headquarters and arrived shaken and frightened and furious and her son was released in her custody after several further hours' consultation involving the arresting police officers and a representative from Herkimer County Juvenile Court. Stammering and red-faced as if guilty—for sure, he was looking guilty—he repeated he'd gone to the dairy for no reason he'd just bicycled out to the dairy, gone inside for just the hell of it not intending to rob anyone, not intending to "vandalize" or "threaten" anyone, the old woman had begun screaming at him immediately like a crazy person, *he had not done a thing to provoke her*.

Maybe he'd hit her, yes maybe with his fist he'd hit her to make her back off while she was hitting him with something like a platter, on his head and shoulders. To *defend himself* he'd hit the old woman but just once, he swore. And not hard.

Driving home in the late afternoon Zoe stopped at a liquor store for a six-pack of beer and in the parking lot began to drink to soothe her shattered nerves. Telling Aaron who was rubbing his wrists and arms already darkening with bruises, "Oh, take one—take a beer. I know you kids drink. God damn you." He'd been trying to explain to her why he'd gone to the dairy in the first place—this was the crucial question, Zoe kept asking—where he should've known, for Christ's sake he wasn't an idiot, or an asshole, should've known the Honeystones wouldn't want him, and no explanation he could give made any sense even to Aaron himself until at last he gave up and Zoe said: "Why you did it, Aaron, was for me. For your mother. But it was a wrong thing to do, see? It was a reckless and mistaken thing to do. Even if you'd come after the dairy was closed, like to 'vandalize'—'set fire'—it was a wrong thing to do. Not because the Honeystones don't deserve it but because you'd get caught. For sure, you're get caught. So fuck them, we'll get you off these charges. These are chicken-shit charges, that old bitch can't prove any of it. Let her try! Let all of them try slandering me, telling their nasty lies about me, I don't give a damn for them anymore. This is just my old life here in Sparta, see?—I'll be laughing at this, some day. And you too, sweetie. You just wait."

What these exuberant words meant, Aaron didn't know. Zoe drained her first can of beer and opened another and drank thirstily and avidly as he'd never seen any woman drink, still less his mother. He too was drinking, but cautiously. He felt queasy, nauseated. One of the young cops had struck him with his knee, in Aaron's abdomen. In the struggle he'd been kicked, punched, slapped many times. His mistake was that initial attempt to get away from them—like a panicked animal—which was a desperate asshole thing to do for within a second they had him on the floor, on his face, arms twisted up behind his back, one of the cops kneeling on his lower back, the weight of a full-grown man on his lower spine—at least three law enforcement officers of the size, heft, and belligerence of Delray Kruller shouting *Lay still! Lay still punk! Fuckin' little punk! Threaten some old lady, punk, there ain't no old ladies here* and he could not draw breath, he could not explain, all his effort had gone into staying alive, his wrists, his arms, his ribs, his back, his thighs, his belly and the right side of his face were bruised and scraped as if he'd been dragged along the ground which maybe he had been, out there in the driveway. Maybe he'd stumbled, or they'd knocked him down again, and dragged him half-conscious whimpering and trying God damn so hard not to cry knowing Delray would be disgusted with him, if he cried. And Zoe would not be so proud of him, if he cried. If for instance he pissed himself *which he had not.* Staring out the kitchen window at the police cruisers racing up the drive like TV cops he'd thought this had to be some sort of joke—was it?

His friends would talk of nothing else for days. For weeks marveling *You heard? Krull was arrested!* Faintly smiling trying to feel good about something, at least.

Zoe cuffed him on the less-bruised side of his head. "What? You're smiling? This is *funny*?"

No, no! Quickly Aaron protested. Nothing was funny.

"Like your father. Del had a juvenile record, too."

There came Zoe's fingers icy from the beer can brushing Aaron's sweaty matted hair off his forehead. With a detached sort of tenderness as you'd gaze at a wounded animal at the roadside, as you're driving by, Zoe said: "You are like your father, I can see that. There's good in Delray, a lot of good in Delray along with the other, that's how he is. A certain kind of man, that's how he is. You're growing up faster than I'd expected, I guess. A hell of a lot faster than I can monitor. The cops didn't hardly believe you're the age you are, frankly I might not if I wasn't your mother. But I don't need you to intervene on my behalf, see? Honey? That can bring only harm. That can hurt you, too. In my life I'm moving in some other direction now. You'll have to have faith in me, that I love you deep in my heart and forever even if things change, for a while. You'll have to let me go, see? You, and him."

Him. By which Zoe meant Delray.

Let me go. Aaron didn't want to think what this might mean.

Framing his face in her hands, to kiss him. Wet beer-smelling kiss on his nose. Aaron laughed uneasily, wanting to slip free. They were laughing together, a little wildly. What was so funny? Why'd anybody laugh, in the situation they were in? He'd been arrested on the complaint of a hysterical vicious old woman and charged with serious adult crimes and he'd have to be taken back to the courthouse and if he was lucky the family court judge would give him probation not a few months at the county juvenile facility. And that evening his father would break his ass when he returned home, when Delray heard the news which Zoe could not keep from him. Even Krull was made anxious by the possibility of being sent away to juvie like certain of Krull's friends nor did Krull relish the prospect of having his ass broke by the old man, in the beat-up state he was already in.

"Wish I'd seen that old biddy's face, when you came at her. This will give old Adele something to think about, at least." Zoe wiped her eyes that were damp from so much laughter.

"I didn't 'come at her,' Mom. It wasn't like that."

"Well—did you have a knife? Like they said?"

"Mom, no. It wasn't like that really."

"Long as they didn't find any knife."

Zoe turned the key in the ignition with her bronze-crimson two-inch cocktail-waitress nails to drive them home.

34

MOVING IN SOME OTHER DIRECTION. Have to let me go.

You, and him.

After she was murdered they continued to live together in the house on Quarry Road except that they lived together now not as a father and a son awaiting the wife and mother who linked them but simply as a man designated as a "father" and a boy designated as a "son." Though neither Delray nor Aaron could have explained it, the distinction was crucial. And sometimes it was not much evident that the man was a "father" and the boy a "son" for often they went for a full day, a day and a night and yet another day without seeing each other and without speaking like sleep-walkers or ghosts inhabiting an identical accursed space. Since Zoe had moved out in the early winter of 1982 approximately two months before her death the house had begun its slide into chaos, dissolution. As Delray would say with a sigh of peeved satisfaction *Gone to hell.*

It had been Zoe's wish that the farmhouse be painted peach-color and now Zoe had vanished from the house the peach-color began at once to fade like a light going slowly off. The dark-green shutters began to rot and the roof developed leaks. Long before Zoe's actual death miles away in another house muddy footprints were tracked onto carpets, bare floors. Dishes collected in the sink, dirty cutlery and glasses which Aaron would "wash" by dumping boiling water over them once a week or so. Debris collected everywhere including the stairs. There were dust-balls the size of mice, grimy handprints on the walls. Windows left unwisely open, rain lashing through the screens, puddles and stains on furniture, walls, floors. Large shelled insects died and turned to husks underfoot. When drains became clogged or the God damn toilet backed up—this happened often—Delray dumped in Drano and stood back out of the fumes. Aaron learned to dump cleanser on the floors, run hot water on an already filthy sponge mop and in a frenzy of concentration mop everywhere until abruptly he lost interest and the floor was clean, or wasn't.

She'd said *Sure I will be coming back sweetie. Maybe just to get you. But I will be back. Sometime.*

After she died it took time for the fact to sink in: Zoe wasn't coming back. These months they'd shared the vague idea unexamined as the cause of spreading stains in the ceilings that yes, she'd be back, for sure Zoe would be coming back and they'd hear her singing/humming in the kitchen as always and her cheery voice lifting to them except now the new fact was she was not returning to Quarry Road not ever.

Delray's younger sister Viola began to drop by the house every week or ten days. Viola and Zoe had gotten along well enough but Viola hadn't approved of Zoe's hopes for a singing career still less had she approved of Zoe moving out of the house as she had. *Sure he's hell to live with but Delray was her husband. And what about Aaron?—he's just a kid.*

There came Aunt Viola noisily running Zoe's Electrolux vacuum cleaner through the rooms of the house whistling in a way to remind Aaron of Zoe, that grated against his nerves. Halfway down the stairs staring at his husky-bodied aunt in overalls and a man's flannel shirt and when Viola frowned at him saying why didn't he give a hand, God damn there was a lot of housecleaning here, Aaron said: "Nobody asked you. You don't need to do this."

"Well—somebody 'needs to.' What kind of pigsty would this be, things just were let go?"

Aaron brushed past his aunt, head bowed. Except he didn't mumble the words audibly Viola was sure he'd said *Fuck you Viola.*

She laughed, shocked. Or maybe not shocked. Aaron was that kind of kid.

Still, Viola wouldn't report this to Delray. Viola wasn't one to provoke trouble within the Kruller family, when there was trouble enough in the family. Especially she wouldn't provoke trouble between Delray and his son, in a state of what they didn't know or could acknowledge was grief.

And he'd lied for his father. This was generally believed within the Kruller family. No way Delray had been home on the night—a Saturday night!—that Zoe was killed, yet Aaron had given a statement to the police, and would swear by it.

"There's a special bond between you and me, Aaron"—so Viola told Aaron who had no idea what she meant.

No idea what most women meant. Most adults. The words they uttered might've been in some foreign language, for all you could trust them.

This *special bond* meant that the Kruller family would hold together, the family would not split apart because of what had happened to Zoe. *Even if Delray had killed her. That was Delray's business.* Aaron supposed this must be the meaning. Other Kruller relatives had hinted as much to him eyeing him anxiously, with a kind of alarmed respect.

Lying to protect Delray. Shows the kid must love him.

Aaron felt no emotion for any of it—Aaron felt, if he could have defined the sensation, like a pig that has been hacked open and gutted but was still alive somehow. That was the weird, wild thing: how he was still alive. After he'd walked in on his mother's corpse that morning. After he'd seen her, and her half-closed eyes like burst grapes had seen *him*.

At school in science class they'd studied evolution: "The Theory of Evolution." Aaron had not done well on tests and quizzes but took away from the unit the thought that *Things are always changing. Nothing stays what it is.*

Without Zoe between them it was hard for Aaron and his father to connect. If Aaron was in the kitchen preparing a quick breakfast for himself, wheat flakes dumped in a bowl, near-rancid milk dumped on the cereal, he'd eat standing at the sink staring out the rain-splotched window at a cornfield fifty feet away, Delray might pass by the kitchen door as if unseeing, or with a muttered greeting but Delray preferred to have breakfast most mornings at the Star Grill Diner on Garrison where the waitresses knew and liked him and the sentiment was he'd been a husband treated badly by his wife who'd left him and was promiscuous with other men and a heroin-user and whoever killed her, it had not been Delray Kruller who left the waitresses sizable tips, smiled and joked with them so you could see the hurt in the poor man's heart, he was trying so damn hard to heal.

And if Delray stood in the twilit living room watching TV, remote control in hand and flicking through the channels too restless to sit down or to watch anything for more than a few minutes Aaron might pass silently behind him, up the stairs and into his room and the door shut behind him.

Hey you know I'd never hurt her, right? I loved her.

You know that Aaron don't you. Aaron?

C'mon watch TV with me. Just a little. Hey Aaron?

The one reliable place father and son saw each other was the auto repair. Here, Delray exuded authority, gave the other mechanics instructions. Delray ordered supplies over the phone, spoke with customers and dealt with complaints, gave estimates and rang up final charges, ran credit cards, vetted checks, counted cash. Delray was the one to pay bills and to hand out salary checks. There was satisfaction in this, Aaron thought. The other mechanics liked his father and respected him—Delray was an expert mechanic, when he took the time. Aaron's happiest memories of Kruller's Auto Repair were how Delray would take him into his private office which was partitioned off from the noise and bustle of the garage, and in this office there was an old rolltop desk with a swivel chair Zoe had bought for Delray at a "bankrupt auction" when she'd loved him and there were shelves of mechanics' manuals and automotive catalogues and on the walls advertisements, posters, a calendar of Vargas females in various stages of seductive undress, at which Aaron scarcely dared to look, such sexual excitement rushed to his groin in an instant. And at the rolltop desk Delray might take time, if he was in the mood, if the damn phone wasn't ringing or somebody out front with a complaint, to draw diagrams showing Aaron what needed to be done on a vehicle—"See? Like this."

Fascinating to Aaron, to be shown the logic of engines; how gearshifts, piston rods, cylinders, fuel lines and ignitions worked together; this was the only time Delray spoke to him in such a way, describing what needed to be done as if what needed to be done was the crucial thing, and a thing to be taken seriously and respected, and not who did it.

"See, kid, a good mechanic is half-instinct, you get born with it. But the other half, you have to learn. I can teach you."

35

MUST'VE BEEN THE WEEK following Easter there came an unfamiliar car up the driveway to the house on Quarry Road and out of the car which was a not-new Ford Escort—cheap compact, cheesy-green exterior—there climbed, like a soft-oozing mollusk squeezing out of its shell, the DeLucca woman.

Krull stared in disbelief. Her!

(More now since Zoe died, he was Krull. Especially alone with his thoughts which were hurtful raging thoughts like a blizzard of driving nails he summoned Krull to him.)

Uninvited and without warning the DeLucca woman—"Jacqueline"—"Jacky"—was coming to knock on their door. This woman with whom Zoe had been living at the time of her death, in the row house on West Ferry. This woman whom Aaron had only glimpsed, once. Who in the local media was quoted as saying in a wavering little-girl voice *So many men in poor Zoe's life it would be hard to find just the one, who hurt her.*

And *There's some of them, I never knew their names. I don't think Zoe did, either!*

This terrible woman Delray denounced to anyone who'd listen as a *whore, hooker, junkie* to blame for Zoe being murdered. This woman who took Zoe in to live with her, helped her get a job on the Strip, introduced her to the men who'd provided her with hard drugs like heroin—Delray was sure, previously Zoe had only smoked dope now and then and dropped diet pills—never anything you'd inject in a vein. But what made Delray murderous toward Jacky DeLucca was allegedly she'd told Sparta police that if something happened to her, Delray was responsible.

See Zoe was scared of her husband he'd beat her she said but worse he said what he would do, she ever left him. Not just her but their son he said.

No I never saw him actually there. At the house. I never did. But I was gone a lot. That night, I was gone.

In the Sparta *Journal*, on local TV the DeLucca woman said such things. Not once but numerous times. Such accusations can be made by "witnesses" and quoted widely—newspapers and TV stations are only reporting "news."

In the days and weeks following, business at Kruller's Auto Repair fell off abruptly. And since then, a slow-skidding decline. Especially women ceased to patronize the garage. Even at the gas pumps sales were off. Delray blamed the Sparta PD and the media—"Making people think I am a murderer, for Christ sake *of my own wife*."

Krull backed away from the kitchen door not wanting the DeLucca woman to see him.

She must have gone to the auto repair first, looking for Delray. But Delray wasn't there. For weeks she'd been hoping to see him. Trying to speak with him on the phone but Delray eluded her. At Kruller's Auto Repair Delray's assistants took messages for him on smudged scraps of paper *Plese Call Jaky DeLuca URGENT!* and in disgust Delray ripped these to shreds. Once, Aaron picked up a ringing phone in the house and at the other end was a breathy female voice *Ohhh h'lo!—DelRoy? Is this Del-roy Krul-ler? Hel-lo?* He'd hung up quickly seeming to know who it was.

Now, she'd dared to come to the house. Making her way in itty-bitty open-toed shoes up the hill to the front door carrying in her arms what appeared to be two large shopping bags. DeLucca was a fleshy woman moving at a quickened if erratic pace as if she were bearing something precious she was fearful of dropping. From behind a filmy curtain Aaron observed her. In fact, Krull observed her. It was Krull who was required.

Seeing how the woman paused squinting toward him in the chill April sunshine, her face shiny as if polished with a rag. Her voice was girlish, high-pitched.

"Hello? Hel-*lo*? Is anybody home? Is it—*Aar-on*?"

She'd seen him, inside the door. He had not ducked away in time.

Not Krull but DeLucca opened the door. Stumbled at him with a look like she wanted to hug him, hard. Her mascara-smudged eyes were bright with tears. As if no time had passed since Zoe's death and now the two of them could grieve together.

"Why, Aar-on! Oh honey—I tried to c-call you—and your dad—so many times I tried to call you and Del-roy and n-never—"

Shorter than Krull by an inch or more yet DeLucca outweighed him by possibly twenty pounds and most of this weight packed into her upper torso and into her hips. Giving off a perfumy-talcumy scent she passed uncomfortably close to him and entered the living room as if she'd been invited. (That talcum scent. Krull's knees went weak.) It wasn't a warm day but DeLucca wore no coat or jacket just salmon-colored polyester stretch slacks and a black V-neck pullover in a fabric shiny as shellac that made her breasts appear enormous as twin dirigibles seen at close range. Her plastic-looking shoes were open-toed, to display her pudgy small waxy-pale feet and painted toenails. Between the heavy breasts, in the cleavage of the black V-neck, there glittered a small gold cross on a gold chain. Despite folds of excess flesh Jacky DeLucca was coarsely glamorous and radiated a powerful sexual aura. Her dark-maroon hair glinted like wires lifting from her scalp in giddy filaments and her eyebrows were pert little triangles, strokes of red-brown pencil. Her mouth was crimson and moist as an open wound. The pupils of her eyes were blackly dilated as if she were on some drug: Quaaludes? Krull knew plenty of people taking this powerful tranquilizer and some who dealt it at Sparta High School.

"—a sorrowful mission, Aar-on! I've been procrastinating— 'castrinating—for too long! Wanting to bring Zoe's things over here— Zoe's pretty things—I knew Zoe would want her family to have if f'instance there's some young cousins or a niece or someone who could fit into 'petite' sizes—*I* surely can't!—but Delroy seems never to be home nor to answer his phone, I am hoping *not because of me*. I mean—*not because he has taken a dislike to me.*"

DeLucca spoke wistfully and with an air of flirtatious reproach as if guessing that Delray might be somewhere near, listening.

Krull mumbled she could leave the bags with him but DeLucca seemed not to hear. She'd edged closer to the boy staring hungrily at him.

"Y'know, Aar-on—you look *changed*. You look *older*. I was reading about you in the paper, Aar-on. Ohhhh your eyes are not a child's eyes! What those eyes have seen. . . ."

Krull was taken aback and could not speak.

"—see I had to leave that place, Aar-on. That accursed place. It could never be cleaned, Aar-on. 'Exercised.' I live somewhere else now—I am looking to change my life. Those sonsabitches—'Sparta PD'—the Herkimer County sheriff men, too—interrogating me like they did!—threatening to 'incracerate' me—'abfucscation of justice'—*I never knew a thing, and had nothing to do with anything!* I—I am waiting for forgiveness."

Forgiveness! Krull backed off uncertain what this was about. Krull had not quite recovered from the whiff of female-talcumy-sweat.

Wishing now that his father was home. Delray would take hold of this pushy female and fast-walk her to the front door and if she didn't leave as he wished, he'd give her a nudge with his knee in the small of her back.

"If only I'd been there that night, Aar-on! With Zoe. I would risk having been k-killed too—if I might have saved her. That night when I went away knowing it might be a mistake. And with a man—a man I kn-knew was a mistake! I am awaiting my redeemer now. Aar-on!"

Awkwardly Krull was backing away from Jacky DeLucca even as Jacky DeLucca lurched forward. Her eyes brimming with tears of sympathy were fixed on him like a hypnotist's. In his confusion Krull had no idea whether this fleshy woman his mother's age—or older—was tormenting him deliberately, as certain Sparta girls were known to do, in the safety of public places and in the company of their friends, or if she spoke naively and sincerely and was appealing to Krull to be her ally "Your father Del-roy has said such hurtful things about me, Aar-on! Of course I understand—I am trying to understand the hardness of the human heart—I am trying to forgive. Since this tragic thing that happened to my closest dearest friend Zoe and spared me—only God knows why I was spared, I have tried every day to pray, and comprehend. Zoe speaks to me sometimes, Aaron! Not in actual words but in a whispering in my soul. She is so changed, now. She 'sees both sides now.' She wants me to tell you, she loves you. Her changed state does not mean that she doesn't love you, Aaron, or continue to think of you—she does."

To this, Krull had no reply. His clumsy boy-fingers were clenching and unclenching into sweaty fists.

"This one time Zoe was drinking and she said suddenly, 'Jacky, I feel so bad—I'm not a good mother.' Zoe laughed and said, 'I love babies, I loved my son as a baby, but babies grow up.' Another time, it wasn't long before the terrible thing happened, Zoe was a little high and in one of her flighty moods she said, 'I don't give a damn what happens to me, Jacky, as long as *something happens*.' Zoe said this! And I said, 'Zoe, you don't mean that,' and Zoe said, 'Don't I?' and just laughed. Any wild thing that came into her head in such a state, she'd say. Just getting on an airplane like she was planning to fly out to Vegas she'd say, 'It's a crap game. You shake your life like dice.'"

Krull was cornered, somewhere. Krull's head was throbbing. Trying to tell this woman he *did not want to talk about Zoe with her.*

"—so good to cry, honey! You're just a child. Boys like you grow up too fast, it's Del-roy's blood in you, that Seneca blood—I know, all too well—I was engaged to one of you, once—you don't know how to cry, and that's bad. Like a man—a boy—needs loving, too. Not just women. If it's denied you, some kind of poison festers." It seemed that for an eerie unsettling moment Jacky DeLucca glanced down at Krull's lower body—his legs, his groin—where a single great pulse was beating quick and hard. "You and I, Aaron, we're the right ages, I think. I could be your mother—Zoe would bless me, where she dwells now. Never had a baby of my own yet and this would be a clear sign, Zoe forgives me."

In a croaking voice Krull repeated he did not want to talk about his mother. If she'd like to leave the things she'd brought. . . .

"Zoe's piano! Is that it?"

In a corner of the living room was Zoe's old upright piano. She'd bought at some auction or garage sale. The keys were yellowed and thick with dust since certainly neither Delray nor Aaron had tended to it since her departure; Aaron avoided even looking at it. Now Jacky DeLucca hurried to the piano to strike several keys dramatically. The sharp sounds grated against Krull's nerves. Badly he was wanting to cry, gnawing at his lower lip so hard he'd nearly split the skin. "Zoe just loved piano! She'd get people to give her little lessons, like. Like at Chet's. Mr. Csaba who was our boss there said he'd pay for lessons for Zoe but she never took him up on it. At the Club if it was a slow night Zoe would pick out some tunes on the piano and get all dreamy. And sing, in her wonderful voice. Oh, Zoe could sing! This person who hurt her, whoever he was, he took a terrible advantage of Zoe, her yearning to sing. This is what I think."

Krull was trying to think *So she doesn't think Delray is the one.*

Trying to make sense of this *She knows who it is, then. That's what she is revealing.*

Seeing the expression in Krull's face that was both pained and abstract, Jacky DeLucca said, "I'd better take these things upstairs, hon. And hang them. Zoe would want that. The wrinkles might shake out some and you can ask some girl cousins over. Or, maybe, if you have a girlfriend, some sexy size two, you can ask her over to pick what she wants."

Krull winced. Who in the family would have wanted anything of Zoe's! And a girlfriend of *his*—the thought was repugnant to him.

Boldly DeLucca brushed past Krull to the stairs. As if she'd been in this house before and knew the way.

There was no choice but for Krull to follow this pushy woman upstairs. Hoping to hell he wouldn't have to explain anything to Delray *She didn't listen to me, Pa! Just barged past, I couldn't stop her.*

After the incident at Honeystone's, where Krull lost control and had punched the old woman in the hip, he knew better than to touch any female again. Not for a long time.

He'd been charged with *second-degree assault*. Through the pleading of a young-woman Family Court officer the other charges—*attempted armed robbery, attempted destruction of private property, threatening great bodily harm*—had been dropped. The case had been heard in a Family Court judge's private chambers and the judge—also female, middle-aged and frowning—spoke harshly to the young defendant and to his sober-faced parents sentencing him to six months at the Youth Facility at Algonquin and after a pause adding *suspended sentence* which caused Zoe to burst into tears of gratitude. *Thank you Your Honor! Thank you, from the bottom of all our hearts.*

At the hearing, both Zoe and Delray were dressed as if for church—Delray in a corduroy coat and tie and his wild hair tamped down for the occasion and Zoe in a dark blue dress primly buttoned up the front and her hair too tamped down and drawn back neatly into a chignon. The judge told them that during Aaron's six-month probation one or another of his parents was obliged to bring him to weekly meetings with a Herkimer County youth probation officer and if he missed a meeting without a legitimate excuse his probation would be revoked and he would be remanded to Algonquin to serve out the remainder of his sentence. Aaron had not missed any meetings but by the time the six months had passed, Zoe had moved away and Delray was the one, exasperated and embittered, to bring him to the probation office.

God damn good thing you didn't kill that old woman. You'd be up at Potsdam and that's too fucking far to drive.

On the stairs Krull stared helplessly at the woman's hips above him in the tight-fitting salmon-colored slacks. Seeing the suggestion of a crack between her buttocks Krull felt a sickish stir in his groin of the kind he felt sometimes—Christ, this was sick—seeing a mangled dead thing, raccoon, young deer, broken and motionless at the roadside.

DeLucca said, breathless from the stairs like a zestful girl athlete,

"There's some surprises here, I think! Some of Zoe's dresses are really glamorous. Classy! This weekend she was in New York—with a friend— around Christmastime—he bought her some really nice things—except back here where'd you wear them?—out on the Strip?—'cast your pearls before swine'—Zoe said you grew up having to do that, being female."

Though she'd never been in the house before—Krull was sure— yet DeLucca made her unerring way to the bedroom at the end of the hall where she shook items out of the shopping bags onto a bed: a black silk dress with thin straps, that resembled a slip or was in fact a slip; a cranberry-colored velvet sheath with a deep V-neck studded with tiny pearls; a shimmering gold dress that looked as if it would fit a woman's body tight as a glove; a bronze-colored dress of some crinkly fabric with stains beneath the arms. And high-heeled shoes, and jewelry. Purple silk brassiere, matching cobweb panties. Krull stared feeling hot blood beating in his face.

DeLucca lifted the black silk garment to her face, to smell. Wordless then she held it out to Krull who shuddered at the talcumy scent and pushed her hand away.

"What's wrong, Aaron? This is a mission of sorrow, have you no respect for the dead?"

Primly now DeLucca meant to take her time smoothing wrinkled garments with the edge of her hand, against the bed. There was a sly druggy glisten in her damp eyes, Krull saw. The bed, that had once belonged to Krull's parents, was now unused by Delray, who slept elsewhere in the house; it had been carelessly covered in a faded gold brocade spread waterstained from drips in the overhead ceiling. Beneath this spread, the mattress was bare. Viola had stripped it months ago. Delray slept on a sofa downstairs when he slept at home; after Zoe's death, he'd been avoiding this room. He'd instructed Viola to pack up Zoe's things in boxes and take them to Goodwill but Viola had not done this. Each time Krull entered the room he had no idea why except something drew him, a sensation of anxiety and fatigue and wanting to cry for sometimes crying felt good and you had to be alone. He'd gone through Zoe's bureau drawers numerous times as if looking for something she'd left behind but had not found anything except a stray button, a near-empty tube of lipstick. Once in a box in another part of the house he'd discovered a cache of old snapshots, he hadn't wanted to see, yes but he'd looked, there was Delray Kruller seated on his Harley-Davidson looking young as Krull had never seen him, long straggly dark hair and dark-tinted glasses and a cigarette in his mouth and in the crook of his arm a blond girl, had to be Zoe looking young as a high school girl which was possibly what she'd been in that long-ago time before Krull was born. And how beautiful Zoe was, smiling her dazzling smile. In a little halter top and short-shorts, bare legs and bare feet.

Damn he didn't want to *care*. Too fucking late for him to *care*.

"C'n you give me a hand, hon?"

DeLucca was chiding him as you'd chide someone you knew well, with both exasperation and affection. Hanging Zoe's dresses in the closet with an air of fussy ceremony. "Zoe would like this, I think. Her spirit can settle here and not be so drifting and lonely. Oh she was flighty! Last thing she told me, 'If I don't make it back, Jacky, you can come visit me in Vegas, and bring Aaron. Maybe I'll have a suite at Caesar's Palace.'

"She was thinking of you, see? What I trust now is the inner spirit. Zoe speaks to me in a whisper. I wish you weren't so angry, Aaron, and would trust me. 'We are here on earth to love one another, that is all.'"

Krull wondered if that was the Bible? It didn't sound like the Bible.

Badly Krull wanted to run from the room but couldn't seem to make his legs move. Knew he should get out of there but could not. Could not look away from the moist crimson wound in the woman's face.

Now in a lowered voice DeLucca said, "I guess it was you, Aaron?—the talcum powder."

At first Krull didn't know what DeLucca meant. Talcum powder?

Then it came to him. The shock of it.

"It was a loving gesture, Aaron. To 'purify.'"

Krull had been told by the detectives months ago that this information—how, panicked, he'd reacted to having discovered his mother's body—would be kept confidential and not be released to the public. Yet somehow, Jacky DeLucca knew.

He'd been Aaron, then. Not Krull. Climbing the stairs to the second floor of that row house smelling of death. And what awaited him, in that room he'd never seen before. . . .

"Poor Aar-on! You loved her."

Jacky DeLucca spoke warmly and would have embraced him except quickly he stepped away lifting his elbows. It was panic he felt now: Don't touch! Get away from me! He could not bear it, if this woman touched him.

He was fifteen: his birthday had been the previous week, unheralded. Delray had no awareness of birthdays and no interest in birthdays nor could he have said his son's exact age, as Delray in his indifference might not have recalled the name of the president of the United States, nor of the governor of New York State. It was enough that some people knew these things, why the hell would *he*? Zoe had never forgotten Aaron's birthday but Zoe was gone now.

"Why do you look so angry? Or—are you *afraid*?"

DeLucca laughed softly. She was teasing him: she'd backed him against the bed. He had a choice of sitting down heavily on the bed or pushing past her, escaping. But he had a dread of touching her. Seeing that the dark red polish on her fingernails was chipped and her nails were uneven and it came to him in a sudden flash of memory that when he'd discovered Zoe in that bloodied bed smelling of her body Zoe's fingernails in which she'd taken such pride had been chipped too and broken as if she'd fought desperately with her assailant to save her life.

"To 'purify' what was fouled. To ease that poor woman's shame. I understand, Aaron."

Krull wanted to ask *But how do you know? Who told you?*

"It's a secret, Aaron. I know. Shouldn't have said anything to you but wanted you to know—'Jacky DeLucca is your friend.' In Zoe's place, I can watch out for you. So many nasty secrets, Aaron, and this is a beautiful secret we will keep between us. Yes?"

DeLucca was fumbling in a pocket of the salmon-colored slacks. On the palm of her hand she held three pills—darkly shiny as the shells of beetles—she seemed to be offering to Krull? He shook his head, *no*. Whatever these were—speed? Quaaludes?—wasn't for him. Not at this time of day, and not with this woman. "No? You sure? Well—I don't want to crash, Aar-on. Nooo not yet."

She released him. She'd been standing very close to him, breathing into his face. As if accidentally she drew the back of her hand across his belly and groin where he'd become hard and all his senses clamored like a struck bell.

"Excuse me, please. I will be right back."

DeLucca went to use the bathroom just outside the bedroom door. Again as if she'd been in this house on some previous occasion and was an invited guest now. Krull flushed with indignation. He wasn't a child, to be manipulated. He was incensed, DeLucca was using the bathroom without troubling to shut the door all the way—he could hear her inside, on the toilet—pressed his hands against his ears and ran from the room and down the stairs thinking he would run out of the house and hide in the barn or better yet in the woods at the rear of the property where frequently he'd hidden as a child for no reason, for the hell of it. Yet on the first floor he paused. Hearing the sound of faucets and plumbing in the old house, the woman's footsteps overhead, a female's footsteps that were not his mother's. Almost calmly he thought *She is waiting for me. She is naked up there.*

His heart beat with excitement. His cock had stiffened with blood so that he felt impaled upon it like a creature that has been stabbed and gutted with a sharp blade. Hesitantly he ascended the stairs he had just descended in a panic and there was Jacky DeLucca emerging from the bathroom smiling at him—"Oh! Aar-on there you *are*." Her voice was teasing and sing-song, her manner was meant to be girlish and shy. She was not fully naked but part-naked: she'd removed the dark V-neck top, and must have removed her brassiere, for her breasts were bare enormous and drooping with prominent nipples like berries or eyes. He could not look at those breasts and yet he could not look away. Gently DeLucca cupped her breasts in her hands, lifting them. Krull wondered if her breasts were filled with milk—warm sweet milk, to bursting. DeLucca smiled at Krull liking the way he stared at her and in a whispery voice she said, "He isn't at the garage. He isn't anywhere. I tried to call him. I looked for him first. He wants to know, you can tell him." Krull made no sense of this. He had not approached the woman, she had approached him; he saw that her feet were bare. She'd kicked off the open-toed shoes. Still she wore the salmon-colored slacks, that fitted her hips and belly so tightly. She pulled Krull's head down to her, he was so much taller than she was. She kissed his mouth, the damp crimson mouth enveloping his mouth. There came her tongue into his mouth sudden and darting.

She was pressing against him—her bare, spilling breasts, against Krull. She laughed at him, and led him back into the bedroom. Led him as you'd lead a drunken man, or a blind man. The gold-brocade cover that had been one of Zoe's purchases was already rumpled and stained as if strenuous couplings had been enacted upon it numerous times. The last thing Krull saw clearly was the gold-glinting cross between the pendulous breasts swinging above him.

Zoe would bless me, where she dwells now.

In her place, I love you!

36

WAKING HE HAD NOT KNOWN what day this was.

Downstairs there was the Sparta *Journal* on the kitchen table left for him, opened and askew—he'd heard Delray slam out of the house a few minutes before—also he'd heard Delray on the phone, his voice raised—seeing now what had upset his father for there on the front page of the paper was the prominent headline—

SPARTA PD: NO NEW "LEADS" IN KRULLER HOMICIDE

—and there was *Zoe Kruller, Victim of Unsolved '83 Slaying* beneath the photograph the *Journal* had printed how many times Krull could not bear seeing it again!—yet stood hunched over the table, staring.

It was terrible to think—a full year had passed. A full year Zoe had been dead. And the smiling blond woman in the photo continued to smile as if in defiance of her fate, though surely her fate was a mockery of that smile.

Beautiful thick-lashed eyes widened in an expression of naive surrender to whatever was being promised, by way of the camera eye—

Yes! Here I am. Love me.

Further down were photos, seemingly matching, as of brothers, of *Delray Kruller, Edward Diehl*. These photos too had been printed numerous times in this paper and had appeared elsewhere, for Sparta police had interviewed these men as *persons of interest* in the case.

Not *suspects* exactly for neither man had ever been arrested.

Must've been in disgust that Delray had left this for him. Just as easily, Delray might have torn the God-damned paper into shreds and tossed it away but maybe he'd thought that his son should see. The son of the *murder victim*, and the son of a *person of interest.*

Frowning Krull scanned the article, that covered three lengthy columns on the front page and spilled over into page eight. The point of the article seemed to be that on the "first anniversary" of the "unsolved local murder" Sparta police investigators, though working now with state investigators, apparently had "no new evidence, no new information, no new leads, and no new 'persons of interest' or 'suspects' in the case."

Krull tore the paper. Krull in a sudden rage.

Wishing he could tear at whoever had written this, printed it. Using his mother's face to sell papers. A dead woman's smiling face.

"Fuckers."

THAT EVENING his aunt Viola called.

"Just checking in, Aaron. Seeing how you are."

Viola spoke in a hesitant voice. Krull mumbled a vague reply.

"Is my brother home?"

No. Delray was not home.

"You know when he's coming back?"

No. Krull did not know when Delray was coming back.

"I suppose you saw . . ."

Yes. He'd seen.

" . . . damn them why don't they leave us alone! Why don't they leave your father alone, he has endured enough."

Viola was breathing harshly. Possibly, she was sobbing. That kind of quick-breathing sobbing indiscernible from anger.

"Those pictures in the paper! Always the same pictures! Poor Zoe, and poor Delray! You never think what these things must be like for people until they happen to you. . . . Jesus."

Delray's family was a large one and there were relatives scattered across three counties in the southern Adirondacks and along the Black River and the Mohawk River and Krull supposed that they'd all been on the phone that day upset and indignant and resentful at the unexpected news story. And perhaps there were similar stories on local TV, Krull didn't know and would not investigate. *One-year anniversary of the unsolved murder of Sparta resident thirty-four-year-old Zoe Kruller.*

Viola spoke at length, bitterly. Viola said why didn't the God-damned journalists do a "human interest" story about an innocent man who'd been hounded by police and reporters and his auto repair business near-bankruptcy as a result. Why didn't they do a story on the family of the *murder victim* whose wounds could never heal, being clawed open by such stories.

Viola asked Krull what he was doing. Krull mumbled what sounded like *Nothing*.

In fact Krull had been scrubbing the kitchen floor. At last disgusted at the sticky linoleum underfoot. Using Dutch Cleanser and hot water and a wooden-handled toilet brush to push into those narrow cracks between the counters and the refrigerator and stove where months of filth had accumulated.

"So—what are you having for dinner tonight, Aaron?"

Trying to sound cheery, chatty. Like she really cared for him, her brother's son.

Krull mumbled he was O.K. He had some things here, Delray had left for him.

"Yes? Like what?"

Krull mumbled inaudibly. Wished to hell his aunt would hang up the phone, this conversation was making him nervous.

"Delray needs to watch over you more, Aaron. He's going to pieces which isn't fair for you. He knows this, I've talked to him. But where the hell is he. At the garage they're always saying 'Del stepped out for a few minutes.'"

Krull said well, he couldn't help that. His dad did what his dad wanted to do, he guessed.

"Yes. Right. Your dad always has. That's the trouble."

Krull could think of nothing to say. In the background at Viola's there came a sudden swelling of sound, like a radio. Or a man's voice, and someone responding. Laughing.

"Aaron, hon—I have to hang up now. I hate to just leave you. It sounds to me like—well, it doesn't sound good. On this day of all days. 'One-year anniversary.' Del should be with you, damn him. You're not a little kid but still he should take more care with you." Viola paused. Krull was waiting for her to hang up. He was feeling anxious, resentful. Why'd his aunt call him, if she was just going to hang up? If she wasn't going to ask if he was hungry, if he was alone and might want to have supper with her that night? In the background a clatter as of bowling pins—was that what that noise meant? Might mean the Ten Pin out on the highway next to B & B Barbeque. . . . As if she'd just now thought of it Viola said, "Aaron? If you're alone there and hungry, I could swing around and pick you up. I'm with some people after work, it wouldn't be any trouble. We could have pizza, or barbecue, O.K.?"

Krull dropped the receiver onto the phone and broke the connection.

Viola didn't call back.

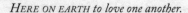

37

HERE ON EARTH to love one another.

A beautiful secret we will keep between ourselves.

Could be your mother, Zoe would bless us!

Afterward in a frenzy of repugnance he'd closed off the room.

His parents' old bedroom with Zoe's flowery, faded wallpaper.

The bed they'd lain on. Torn like the mud of a pigsty.

And Zoe's sad-glamour clothes hanging in the closet—these he could not bear to glance at, let alone give away as the DeLucca woman had suggested.

He'd never told his father about Jacky DeLucca who'd come looking for him but had settled on Krull, instead.

Never wished to think of her—the DeLucca woman—but always he was thinking of her. The things she'd done to him—her mouth, her hands, her pearly-fat thighs, the way she'd drawn him into her so deep—deeper—until his senses exploded in crazed white heat, blindness.

Could be your mother Aar-on. We are the right ages.

In dread that she might show up again at the house, or at the auto repair—looking for Delray Kruller. But then, she'd see *him*.

She'd been high. Some kind of speed. Her skin scalded. Her kisses were frantic bites. Her eyes rolled back in her head. The beet-dyed hair exuded a sweaty-chemical smell. Panting and grasping and groaning like some convulsing sea-creature *Oh oh ohhhh help me Jesus love love you.*

What sprang out of Krull, out of his cock, something like hot mucus. He guessed was his soul.

Weeks later his hands, his hair still smelled of the beet-dyed hair.

His back was riddled with nail-marks. Some of these had become infected and itched badly. His mouth still felt raw, bitten.

Nights when he couldn't sleep, roughly stroking his chafed cock. And when he did sleep, dreaming of the woman, wakened from sleep by an explosion in his groin that made him gasp aloud, stricken with both intense pleasure and intense shame.

Ohhh Aar-on! Love you.

The mattress beneath the tangled sheets of Krull's bed was stained with the leakage of his sperm. That unmistakable reek. In desperation he opened the windows of his room wide, let the wind, rain inside. Still the smell prevailed. The smells.

"Pig."

Not sure if he meant DeLucca, or himself.

His old morbid thoughts of Zoe were being crowded out by DeLucca. God damn he resented her! In his bed trying to sleep he'd be thinking of what they'd done together—what the woman had made him do—his cock perpetually aroused and increasingly chafed and he could feel the sex-desire like a fat lazy snake curled up inside him in the pit of his belly where unbidden and unwished-for it uncoiled, violent as a trap you'd set for rabbits, you had better take care you did not trip yourself.

Ohhh Aar-on! You are fantastic, I adore you.

Business was down at Kruller's Auto Repair, only one or two guys came to work most days. Krull worked the pumps, the least of the jobs. Whenever a compact turned off Quarry Road in the direction of the gas pumps wondering if it might be the cheesy-green Ford Escort and inside Jacky DeLucca. How she'd roll down her window and stare at him with a pretense of surprise, how she'd smile licking her fleshy lipstick-lips *Ohhh Aar-on! been missing you* while Krull remained stony-faced, unsmiling.

As if not recognizing her. *That* would freak the woman.

But Jacky DeLucca never returned to Quarry Road so far as Krull knew. As if she'd given up looking for Delray Kruller or had found him some other way and Krull would be the last to know about it.

Maybe it was a relief, Zoe wasn't living with them any longer. Zoe would strip Krull's bed to launder his sheets seeing splotches of stiffened mucus everywhere and the mattress shamefully stained. Zoe would make some joke to embarrass him—*Used to be, you'd pee your bed, kid! That was bad enough.*

Babies grow up, she'd said.

She hadn't loved him. That was the secret between them.

"Glad she's gone. Bitch!"

Now they didn't have to worry about losing her.

38

DELRAY WAS SAYING he'd made some mistakes in his life.

Hoped to God that these mistakes would not follow *into the next generation* like the Bible warns us.

Making such pronouncements though he wasn't drunk. His heavy hand falling on his son's shoulder and the son shuddered but did not shrink away. Thinking *Pa isn't drunk. Not any ordinary kind of drunk.*

In such a somber and penitential mood Delray might speak of his father and his father's father and the *Indian-blood* connection. The *Seneca Nation* connection that had gone wrong somehow in Delray.

"What they want from you—it's like sucking at your blood. They can't even say what they want. What it is, it's the 'white' in you—like bone-marrow. They'd like to suck it out. When I married Zoe, that fixed it for me, with my relatives out on the rez. Fucked it. I had a close cousin, he never spoke to me again. And he's dead now, and that can't be remedied."

The son listened to the father uneasy at what was being disclosed.

The son loved the father for all that the father was a man capable of inflicting sudden hurt.

"—so I'm saying, don't think you can go back there. You can't. You play lacrosse with some guys, don't mistake that for anything more. Don't think like you're gonna be a 'blood brother' or any shit like that with them, you're not."

Delray's father had been a half-blood Seneca and his father's father a full-blood Seneca and both men were unknown to Delray's son who had never met them nor even glimpsed them.

Zoe had said: "If your father wants you to know about this, he will tell you. There's plenty of things he hasn't told me and you know what?"

What, he'd asked.

"It's for a purpose, that's what. What we are told and what we are not told. So don't ask."

News came of the DeLucca woman, on the following morning.

A *savage assault* the Sparta *Journal* reported.

> Thirty-nine-year-old East Sparta resident Jacqueline De-Lucca, cocktail waitress at Chet's Keyboard Lounge, left unconscious and bleeding in a parking lot behind Big Boy Discount Appliances. Discovered early Monday morning by a security guard.
>
> Assailant or assailants unknown. In stable condition, Sparta General Hospital. Sparta police investigating.

The news item was brief, on an inside page of the paper. There was no accompanying photograph. Krull would have missed it except at the auto repair there was a copy of the *Journal*, loose pages a customer had left in the waiting area.

Numbly his lips moved: "'Jacqueline DeLucca.'"

Not wanting to think—he had no reason to think—that Delray might have had anything to do with this assault. He had no reason to think that Delray had anything to do with DeLucca at all. Nor had Krull anything to do with DeLucca since more than two years ago when she'd come to the house bringing Zoe's things.

Could be your mother, Zoe would bless us.

Krull had not seen the woman since that day. Except in his most lurid sex-dreams. But in person, no he had not. The actual woman who'd been, as the article in the *Journal* noted, *a close friend of the 1983 homicide victim Zoe Kruller*, he had not glimpsed and had done his best to forget.

* * *

THAT NIGHT WITH HIS FRIENDS, at the train depot. Nights he didn't have to work late or help with the tow truck which was a twenty-four-hour service Kruller's Auto Repair provided he'd begun hanging out with these new friends who were older than Krull and admirable in Krull's eyes. For Krull was under-age and they were not. What a swift transition it was— one year you dropped out of high school, a few years later you were in your mid-twenties, or older. Like Delray these guys would try anything. And the occasional girls, too. Krull had a weakness for beer but also he'd come to like the sensation of dreamy not-caring he got from smoking dope. Like Novocain this was. The buzzing turned numb and you experienced a kind of wavy tunnel vision, faces in a slow spin and melt, to be laughed at.

Zoe had been a *junkie, a heroin user.* So it was said of the dead woman, after her death.

What Krull liked about smoking dope was the way the faces lost substance, the more you stared at them. Anything you might see in such a state, pushing a door open, seeing what lay tangled in bloodied bedclothes on that bed, how could you take it seriously?

Mellow out Krull's friend Duncan Metz advised him. *Any fucking thing that happened it's over with, you're not going back to change it.* Metz was older than Krull by as many as ten years but had taken a liking to him, it was said that there'd been a murder, maybe more than one murder, in Metz's family, also you could see that Metz had mixed-blood, an olive-swarthy skin darker than Krull's and the same deep-set dark eyes and naturally those kinds of guys were drawn together like cousins, or brothers.

Another kind of weed Metz gave Krull to smoke he called *Jamaican*, that was more expensive and harder to acquire that gave a nasty kick of a high, made your heart thump like a crazed thing which was why not everybody wanted to smoke it especially girls were wary of smoking it and of being in the close company of guys who smoked it for this weed when you smoked it and sucked in the smoke really deep into your lungs made you want to fuck, or fuck somebody up bad, and Krull came to like *Jamaican* best of all.

39

DIEHL, B. ONE OF a dozen names of Sparta High juniors posted outside the chemistry lab on the second floor of the building.

Krull would not be taking a course in chemistry. Krull would not be taking courses in biology, physics, advanced math or in any language. Krull was not a college-entrance major but a vocational arts major—a "shop" major—and all that such majors were required to take, to receive a Sparta High diploma, were courses in English, social studies, health, physical education and driver's education as well as courses in shop.

Driver's education! As if Krull hadn't been driving cars, even trucks, since he'd been eleven.

It pissed Krull to see *Diehl, B.* on that list, and beside the name a grade of A–. Eddy Diehl was a construction worker, a "manual laborer"— wasn't he?

So far as Krull knew, Ben Diehl's father Eddy no longer lived in Sparta. He'd been allowed by the Sparta PD to move away and Krull had not heard that he'd moved back.

In the pickup he'd seen. At the landfill. Before she'd left home. Before she'd been killed. When it was Eddy Diehl she'd been with and Delray had not known.

It seemed to be happening to spite Krull, how frequently he saw Ben Diehl at school this year. Must've been that their schedules were bringing them into proximity. That proximity felt like taunting. In the school cafeteria, on the stairs, in the halls Krull moved tall and lanky and quick as a cobra sighting the smaller boy with red-coppery hair and a pinched face walking stiff-legged away from Krull without seeming to have seen him, like there's a broomstick up his ass. For sure Ben was aware of Krull as the cobra's prey is aware of the cobra but too terrified to acknowledge this awareness.

There was a girl, too. Ben Diehl had a sister. She was younger.

When it happened that first time, it was purely by chance.

Krull had not been stalking Ben Diehl. Krull had been thinking of other things. Seeing then Ben Diehl entering the guys' locker room, a few steps ahead of Krull. The boy was alone as frequently he seemed to be alone whenever Krull noticed him. The boy moved jerkily as if parts of him wished to go in separate directions but were held together by a brittle and inelastic skeleton. Here was a boy not a natural athlete—you could tell. Somber-faced, ashy-faced, downlooking. His forehead was creased. His mouth worked silently as if he was arguing with a voice inside his head. He was perhaps five feet six inches tall. He weighed perhaps 120 pounds. He wore the clothes—shirt, jeans, running shoes—favored by most of his classmates but on Ben Diehl these clothes were unconvincing. *Diehl! Some kind of freak.* Krull took note of this for it was surprising, how Ben Diehl scarcely resembled his father Eddy who was a good-looking man, or had been. Even as Ben Diehl seemed to be bearing something of the shame and notoriety of his father which meant that he was guilt-stricken and would understand why he had to be punished.

Fifth hour, this wasn't Krull's gym class. Krull was a sophomore and not a junior, for Krull had been *kept back*. Yet by instinct following the Diehl boy into the locker room bypassing other boys without seeming to see them until he sighted Diehl just setting his backpack on a bench in a far corner of the locker room. Those who observed Krull swiftly approaching Diehl with the obvious intent of inflicting hurt upon him fell immediately silent and backed away and those whose lockers were close by Diehl's quickly departed so that, as Krull advanced upon Diehl, taller than Diehl by several inches and heavier by at least twenty pounds, there were no witnesses remaining to see how the smaller, seemingly younger boy glanced up in surprise at Krull, yet a kind of guilty surprise, as if he'd been expecting this; how Diehl had time to stammer only, "What—what do you—" before Krull seized Diehl's narrow shoulders and in virtually the same movement slammed him against the lockers with such force that the entire row of lockers rattled and shook. The attack was silent, unerring. The attack seemed scarcely to have required much effort on the larger boy's part.

Diehl hadn't had time to protect himself or had not the strength to protect himself having fallen onto the cold tile floor cringing beneath the long narrow bench as Krull kicked the bench aside to get at him, looming over him hot-faced and trembling.

"Get up. God damn cuntface *get up*."

Now witnesses would report hearing Ben Diehl beg, "Don't h-hit me! What did I do to you! L-Leave me alone I didn't do anything to you"— a look of such fright in his face, such abject pleading, Krull gave him a punch, another punch and a kick and turned away in contempt.

Without seeming to hurry Krull left the locker room. Krull no more than glanced at Ben Diehl's classmates observing him, seven or eight boys keeping their distance from him in such respectful silence, Krull saw no need to threaten them. They understood.

Now you know, what I can do to you. Any time.

What you deserve, your father killed my mother.

For a time then ignoring him. The Diehl kid. He'd have liked to murder with his bare hands. Stomping, with his booted feet. Sensing that the time of their proximity was rapidly diminishing as Aaron Kruller's days in the Sparta public school system were rapidly diminishing for soon it would be his sixteenth birthday and so badly he wanted to quit, he could taste it.

You stay with it God damn it you know your mother wanted that.

And he'd protested *Pa you didn't graduate from high school—why should I?*

Because you can't turn out like me. The time for people like me is past.

These words out of Delray's mouth were chilling to his son. It was not possible that Delray Kruller could think such thoughts still less give voice to them.

In the aftermath of death, strangeness was released in their lives like a toxic gas.

Delray saying *Your mother never liked you working with me, so young. She said, Aaron can try different things. Not be a slave to fixing engines.*

Fuck her.

Delray looked at him, as if he hadn't heard.

Fuck her. Mom. Fuck what she wants for me, she left us didn't she?

Snake-quick came Delray's backhand slap, striking his sulky-faced son on the side of his head and nearly knocking him over.

You don't talk of your mother like that, you little pisspot. You show respect or I will break your ass.

IF THERE'D BEEN DOUBTS before, now there were none. Ever after the son's allegiance to the father was unquestioned.

OUT OF NOWHERE it must have seemed. By accident it must have seemed. The tall hulking Indian-looking boy known as Krull—the boy whose mother had been murdered—appeared at the edge of a dirt path descending to the river just as Ben Diehl was climbing the path to the footbridge above the river.

You could see the look of fright in Ben Diehl's face: *should he run?* Or—was it better *not to run?*

Since the attack in the locker room that had been unpremeditated and seemingly spontaneous it might have been that Ben Diehl was hoping that there would not be another for guiltily he had acquiesced to Krull's anger and hadn't reported him to the boys' gym instructor or to school authorities nor even to his own mother explaining with convincing self-irony how he'd tripped over the bench in the locker room and fell against a locker.

No other boy confirmed this. No other boy seemed to be involved.

Now it was weeks later, in a damp-wintry season. Ben Diehl was wearing a brown corduroy jacket with a hood he'd drawn over his head, Krull was wearing a jacket that looked as if it were made of silver vinyl, with no hood. Ben Diehl was carrying a backpack that looked to be crammed with books. Walking, he tended to look down. A kind of gravity drew his gaze down. Krull's gaze was a predator's gaze uplifted, alert. He'd had no conscious plan to follow—to "stalk"—Ben Diehl that day except somehow it had happened.

I don't like it but I guess things happen that way.

Was that Zoe's voice? Zoe singing one of her bluegrass songs?

Almost, Krull could hear. It was a famous song—maybe by Johnny Cash—but Krull heard it in Zoe's voice, intimate in his ear.

No plan for any second attack. Except it wouldn't be in the presence of potential witnesses this time.

Thinking *This is it! This makes up for the other.*

Meaning his sudden happiness. Like a lightning-stroke. About twenty feet behind his frightened classmate Krull broke into a run, his legs were suffused with strength, hard-muscled and there was a sinewy joy in all his limbs and fleetingly he saw the warning PEDESTRIAN BRIDGE CLOSED FOR REPAIR DO NOT USE but Ben Diehl couldn't turn back, Krull was driving him forward and onto the bridge and within seconds he'd overtaken Ben Diehl and grabbed his arm and shook him as you'd shake a rag doll—"You running from me? Turn your back on me, I'll break your ass."

Ben tried to push away. There was a frantic strength in his arms, his teeth were bared in a grimace of terror and fury and Krull was surprised, like a frenzied little rat the Diehl boy was, fighting him. Krull shook him harder, slammed him against the bridge railing so he heard the other's breath knocked from him. His own breath was coming in short steaming pants. Below, the Black River rushed darkly swollen from a recent rain. Krull thought *I can kill him here, no one would know. The body would be lost for weeks.*

What he said to Ben Diehl was: "Your father—where is he?"

Ben Diehl stammered he didn't know.

"You know! He murdered my mother."

Ben Diehl stammered no.

"He did! And he got away with it! And he's living somewhere else now, he was never punished!"

Clumsily the boys struggled, for Ben Diehl was trying to loosen Krull's grip on his shoulder and neck. Krull had caught him in something like a wrestling hold. There was a wish to hurt here but there was an awkward intimacy as well. Krull said, as if pleading, "Why'd he do it! Why'd he kill her!" and Ben protested, "He didn't. He *did not*." Somehow then out of a jacket pocket Ben Diehl drew a knife, a jackknife, managed to get the four-inch blade open and to stab wildly at Krull before Krull comprehended what was happening, the blade glanced against Krull's jacket sleeve and recklessly Krull grabbed at it, closed his fingers around the blade cutting his fingers in that instant though scarcely aware that he was cutting himself, pain came so sharp yet fleeting, in the exigency of the struggle so fleeting that Krull could not register it. Ben Diehl was sobbing trying to wrest the knife free so that he could stab Krull with it, a frenzy overcame him. Krull cursed him struggling for the knife, both Krull's hands were bleeding now but he managed to strike Ben Diehl with his fist, a tight bare-knuckle punch, felt like he'd cracked the bone beneath Ben Diehl's right eye socket. The knife was loosened from Ben Diehl's fingers and fell, and Ben Diehl fell to his knees stunned from Krull's punch, a rain of punches directed at his face, head, shoulders. Ben Diehl's face was a sickly white now smeared with blood, Krull's face felt hot, flushed. He was saying, "Could kill you, God damn you! Could push you over, you'd drown. Nobody to see." The jackknife glistening with blood Krull had to suppose was his blood had been kicked a few feet away, Krull snatched it up and threw it over the railing into the river. So he could not use the knife. In his murderous mood he understood that this was a wise thing to have done. Pushing Ben Diehl into the river was different, there would be no stab wounds. There would be nothing to incriminate another person. He was kicking at Ben Diehl who had curled up on the plank bridge as a worm might curl to protect itself. Kicking at Ben Diehl's legs, thigh, buttocks not in the ribs, he'd break the kid's ribs if he did, and taking care not to kick him in the face, he'd already bloodied the poor kid's face. Short of breath half-sobbing, "Could kill you—see? Tell your son of a bitch father! Tell him 'Aaron Kruller could've killed you, and he didn't.' You tell him."

He'd left Ben Diehl there, on the bridge. Turned his back and walked away and at the dirt path he began to run and he did not look back. His face was damp as if he'd been crying. His hands were bleeding, he'd been wiping them on his clothing. The sight of his own blood was strange to Krull, he was beginning to feel pain now, a sharp throbbing pain in his hands and he thought *This is a good thing. Something is decided.* And that night drunk and stoned at the depot he hooked up with a girl named Mira, there was Mira high and giggling and straddling Krull at the groin and Mira was kissing his mouth and moaning and Krull wiped his hands where the clumsy bandages had come loose, his greasy-bleeding hands on the girl's tangled hair.

40

AND THE GIRL. Ben Diehl's younger sister.

Krull had to think it was a coincidence. At first.

Essentially she was too young to register on Krull's sexual radar. A slight-bodied blond girl with somber eyes and a way of shrinking back when Krull happened to glance at her—in the 7-Eleven store near the high school for instance.

And too quickly the girl turned away, retreating into the back of the store. Krull stared after her thinking *Jesus! She isn't following me is she?* He was bemused, appalled. He was fifteen years old, this girl looked to be several years younger.

Recalling then that he'd seen her somewhere else. And would see her, as if by chance, on subsequent days—on the street as he bicycled past, in the alley that ran behind Post Street which was a biking shortcut for Krull, behind the high school where students left their bikes and Krull left his, a stripped-down old Schwinn with a hard-rubber seat and handle bars adjusted low, the chassis stippled with rust like acne. Belatedly Krull would wonder why a girl not at Sparta High would be in such a place, gazing at him. At a little distance.

Realizing then *It must be her. Diehl's daughter. What's she want with me!*

Krull felt a touch of alarm, fear. A touch of panic.

What he hadn't done to the brother. What he'd stopped himself from doing. And now the sister—following *him*.

There was danger here. Krull knew the danger. Better to ignore the girl. Not make eye contact with her. As she watched him with those wistful inscrutable eyes as he turned away, began pedaling his stripped-down old Schwinn without a backward glance.

Since the footbridge, Krull stayed away from Ben Diehl.

As if there were an understanding between them. A kind of truce. For it was enough for Krull to know, and for Ben Diehl to know, that he'd spared Ben Diehl his life. Might've shoved him off the bridge to drown in the river, might've stabbed him to death with his own knife. (Pulling a knife on Krull, of all people! You had to hand it to Ben Diehl, he'd had guts.) Krull's restraint had been an act of mercy that had not needed to happen. And it was enough, Krull had cut his fingers and the palms of his hands on Ben Diehl's knife and the cuts were God-damned slow to heal.

41

All things that hapen to any one, they are things to hapen to the soociety. But not at the one time. If there is a dead Person that does not mean you cant speak to them and sometimes they will speak to you. Except in a dream the dead Person does not speak usually. The dead Person might look at you in a sertain way to say *I am here.* You would want to beleive theres a god to believe theres Justiss. But that does not mean there is either one of these.

MRS. HARE his remedial English teacher encouraged him. Returning Aaron Kruller's painstakingly handwritten compositions with comments in purple ink like lacework. No matter the assignment Aaron could not seem to write more than two or three paragraphs terse as a stream of muttered words and there was often a riddle-like nature to these words, its meaning not immediately evident to Mrs. Hare. Even in the remedial class half the students handed in typed work of varying degrees of neatness and clarity but Aaron wrote in a large childlike hand like one who wielded a pen with difficulty; his notebook pages were creased from the strain of his effort, bearing faint smudges of grease.

Grades in remedial English at Sparta High were not numerical as in other classes but only just *P* or *F*: "pass" or "fail." (In remedial English, most grades were *P*.) If Aaron didn't receive *P* for one of his assignments he was likely to receive an ambiguous *???* with a note from Mrs. Hare to come see her during his study period.

Purple ink was Marsha Hare's signature—unlike red ink, which the other teachers used. For Mrs. Hare believed that purple ink was "not cruel" like red ink. Red was the color of stop signs, danger signs, exits and fires—red ink, on a student's paper, suggested blood eking from miniature wounds. By contrast, purple was a "kind" color—a "soothing" color. Mrs. Hare had been a longtime substitute teacher in the Sparta public school system hastily hired in the fall of Aaron Kruller's junior year to replace a teacher who'd had to resign for reasons of health. Mrs. Hare was known for wishing not to offend or hurt or discourage her students for these were adolescents afflicted as with severe acne by "reading disabilities"—"limited aptitude"—"personality problems"; and a number of these adolescents, like Aaron Kruller, exuded an air of sullen unease verging upon threat.

"'Aaron Kruller'! Hel-*lo*."

Brightly greeting the boy when she saw him in the school corridor, or slinking into her classroom just as the final bell rang. He was taller than Marsha Hare by several inches and an oily odor wafted from his close-cropped Indian-black hair, his eyes were heavy-lidded, evasive and narrowed and yet—Aaron seemed to Mrs. Hare the *most promising* of the thirty-seven students entrusted to her.

Given his family background, the *most dangerous*.

Mrs. Hare was in her late forties, an attractive woman in whom small whirlwinds of maternal warmth seemed continually to be stirring, leaving her breathless, eager and yearning. Her eyes were thinly-lashed, a watery hazel that glistened with emotion; her face was a girl's face faded and smudged, like a watercolor. Almost alone among the Sparta High faculty Mrs. Hare made an effort to dress "stylishly"—she wore designer blouses with lavish bows, tailored pants suits in hues of cranberry, fuchsia, flamey-orange-red. Her dun-colored hair was elaborately arranged, held in place by tortoiseshell combs; her makeup was putty-colored, and her lipstick red-orange. As Mrs. Hare spoke to her students her voice ascended in arias of enthusiasm and encouragement—her speech was riddled with such words as *promise, keep trying! yes you can! Never say never.* It was said that Mrs. Hare had had female surgery of a sinister sort: a breast mutilated, a uterus removed. It was said that Mrs. Hare had an elderly husband in a wheelchair—unless the elderly husband was Mrs. Hare's father or, more sinister still, Mrs. Hare's terribly afflicted son. Boys joked about "Mrs. Hair-y" behind her back—if Mrs. Hare wore short sleeves, you could glimpse wiry patches of hair in her armpits; the more sensitive girls shuddered and exchanged pained glances. Once, cruel boys placed what appeared to be a used sanitary napkin in the wastebasket beside Mrs. Hare's desk, only part-covering it with crumpled paper; but before class began, red-faced Aaron Kruller carried the basket out, to dump into an incinerator. Mrs. Hare never caught on what the joke could be, that aroused such hilarity and embarrassment in the classroom, and so the joke came to nothing.

Mrs. Hare reminded Krull uncomfortably of the DeLucca woman. The moist eyes fixed upon his face, the girl-body grown fleshy, middle-aged. Some indefinable air of hunger, female yearning. "Aaron? If ever you want to speak about anything with me—just let me know. Anytime."

And: "If ever there is anything to share, Aaron."

Not meeting the woman's eager gaze Aaron muttered what sounded like *Yes ma'am*.

Between the two—the middle-aged remedial English teacher, the near-sixteen-year-old boy—there was a curious, clumsy connection. As between relatives—an aunt, a sulky nephew.

One afternoon, Aaron reluctantly came in for an appointment with Mrs. Hare, at her request. The teacher was sitting at her desk with one of Krull's compositions before her, covered in a filigree of purple ink.

Krull sat in a vinyl chair that felt flimsy beneath his weight as Mrs. Hare clasped her long narrow hands against her chest. She drew a deep breath and began, like one running to dive from a high board before she has lost her courage: "Aaron. I've debated telling you this. There was a crime in my family, also. My mother's family in Troy. A terrible thing that happened—a girl who was my cousin—my older cousin—abducted, stabbed to death—her body thrown into the canal—missing for weeks before she was discovered. This terrible murder—of a beautiful nineteen-year-old girl engaged to be married—was never 'solved'—through the years, it has been decades now, this crime cast its shadow upon our lives. I was a girl of twelve then—I am a middle-aged woman now. So I understand, Aaron." Mrs. Hare's voice quavered with daring, and with hope. "I hope I understand."

These words were like a jolt of electricity, Krull hadn't been prepared. He'd needed to steel himself and he had not.

" . . . if you should, you know, wish to speak of it. Or write of it. More directly, Aaron. I sense that you are always writing about this certain subject—I won't say what it is—but you are never *confronting* this subject. It has swallowed you up, nearly. You must *break free*."

Squeezed into one of the classroom chairs—cheap vinyl, aluminum legs—Krull held himself stiff, unyielding. He appeared confused, his mouth worked silently. Nervously Mrs. Hare continued:

"Well! My point is, Aaron, you have a choice nonetheless. I mean— beyond the classroom. Beyond this school. You can be a citizen, or you can be a 'rogue.' Like—a 'rogue' elephant. You can live outside society for the reason that you have been wounded and are angry—clearly, very angry—I know how the other students fear you, and that you've been involved in fights and 'disruptions'—I am grateful that you've done good work for me—very good work—promising work—but let me say, so long as you're young this is a way you can live, and for a while into your thirties, perhaps. But then—it's over. If you've made yourself into a citizen, the crime will heal over and you can have a life—a useful, adult life. But if you are a rogue and an outcast, in thrall to your hurt, you will not have a life." Mrs. Hare paused. Her voice was tremulous, uncertain. As if she'd climbed to a dangerous height and was now peering down at Aaron from this height. "You will not live long—that's what I fear for you."

The pretext for their conference that afternoon was an assignment Krull had handed in the previous day, on the theme "The Individual in Society." Krull had managed to write only a single paragraph of two sentences. Twenty-one words choked and clotted on which he'd toiled at the auto repair shop, seated at Delray's desk. He'd had to break the composition off when a sudden call came in—he and another mechanic were wanted out at the Interstate, there'd been a car wreck and a tow truck was needed. Afterward reading what he'd written *All things that hapen to any one, they are things to hapen to . . .* he felt a wave of shame, fury. God damn he knew what he wanted to say yet could not say it, the words were stopped up inside him.

Peering now at the paper Mrs. Hare had handed back. Seeing he'd spelled *society* wrong. He'd spelled *happen* wrong. Wanting to crumple the fucking paper in his hand.

"Aaron? You are listening, aren't you?"

How close Mrs. Hare had come to *You are listening, dear, aren't you?*

Krull muttered something vague. Krull felt blood rushing into his face. Krull shifted in his seat preparatory to leaving.

"You seem so—sad, Aaron. Your expression is—"

Krull stood, clutching the paper. God-damned paper he'd crumple in his fist as soon as he left the classroom.

"Well. In any case I hope—I hope you will revise the composition. I mean, I hope that you will develop it. You always seem to have so much more to say, that you haven't quite said. The minimum word count was five hundred words, Aaron. No need to count, but—"

Krull was miserable to leave. Krull was hoping this would not have a bad ending. A flash came to him of Zoe's battered face, the bruised and broken eye sockets. Krull muttered *Yes ma'am!*

Mrs. Hare walked with Krull to the classroom doorway. Like a TV lady of the house showing someone to the door. The room was Marsha Hare's homeroom—she'd decorated with glossy photos of animals, landscapes, river views. She'd decorated it with what Zoe would recognize as *nice female touches*—artificial sunflowers in vases, ferns and African violets in clay pots, curiously little wood carvings. Seated, Mrs. Hare had seemed nearly Krull's height but once they were standing, you could see how short Mrs. Hare was, beside Krull; how her authority rapidly diminished. *Sure O.K. thanks Mrs. Hare* he'd rewrite the assignment *Yes ma'am* except next day in gym Krull got into a scuffle with two boys—"white" boys—pissing him off looking at him like he had a bad smell and other boys joined in, some on Krull's side, mostly not on Krull's side, there was a free-for-all that lasted for several clamorous minutes, and this time there were witnesses to Krull's behavior including the gym instructor Mr. Casey whose nose was bloodied and so within the space of a few flurried hours Krull was arrested by Sparta police officers and taken to police headquarters and booked on charges of *assault*, *disorderly conduct*, *resisting arrest*. Never would Aaron Kruller return to Sparta High, he'd been permanently expelled. He would not graduate with his class. He would not see Marsha Hare again.

42

THE GIRL. Eddy Diehl's daughter.

Now he knew her name—Krista. Knew exactly who she was. But not why she was trailing him. A girl with pale blond ghost-hair, too young to merit a second glance from Krull.

Still she was watching him, from a distance. Drawing back when he saw her. But not drawing back too quick.

There was something pleading in the girl's face. In her somber eyes. *Hurt me! You can try.*

Krull had hurt her brother Ben, maybe she knew that. Maybe Ben had told her. (Though Krull had to doubt that Ben had told anyone about being so humiliated.) But Krull would never hurt a girl. Not even Eddy Diehl's daughter.

Nor would he come near the girl. Not ever.

NOW THAT KRULL WAS AWARE of the girl—Krista Diehl—who was Eddy's daughter—he realized he'd been hearing about her, from Mira Roche. How young she was, and how trusting. Kind of sweet, naive. Poor kid you felt sorry for her almost, what with her father . . .

Krull didn't ask about the father.

. . . her father who'd been in trouble with the police, people said he'd moved away from Sparta.

And there was Duncan Metz and his friends, Krista hadn't a clue what plans they had for her.

Mira laughed, uneasily. Seeing that Krull had lapsed into one of his moods.

(For sure, Krull wasn't going to get involved. Trying to put distance between himself and that crowd. You couldn't call them friends—Krull wouldn't have known what to call them. The girls were crazy for him—for Krull—but it wasn't flattering, these were garbage-heads who'd do anything a guy asked, for drugs; once they were stoned, they'd do even more, until they passed out. And such good-looking girls, like Mira Roche . . . There was Duncan Metz who claimed to be Krull's good friend, Krull never fully trusted. It was said of Metz admiringly that he'd been busted numerous times since he'd been sixteen but had never spent a day in any facility not even juvie. And now Metz would never be busted, he was too smart. He made too much money. He had some mysterious connection with the Herkimer County sheriff's department, one of his cousins was a deputy, or Metz was a trusted snitch, trading information to law enforcement for special favors. Last time they'd been together Metz took his Firebird convertible to ninety miles an hour on the Interstate—ninety-five—one hundred—and beyond one hundred—and Krull in the passenger's seat saying *Slow down! Jesus* but Metz high on crystal meth just laughed. *Chill it Krull, I don't make mistakes.*)

Since he'd been expelled from school Krull worked longer hours at the garage. Now it was winter, Kruller's Auto Repair hired out for snow-removal services, and the lagging business improved substantially. Still, Delray had only two full-time mechanics now and two or three younger men who worked part-time. As Delray's son Krull was paid haphazardly and some weeks not at all. When Delray wasn't on the premises it was Krull who took over answering the phone, talking to customers. He was learning the skill of estimating repairs. No one hearing him on the phone *Yes sir, yes ma'am* would have guessed he was only seventeen. Ever more Delray entrusted him with the tow truck, late-night snow removal. The kind of work you end up doing through the night after a heavy snowfall, having put in a full day's work beforehand in the garage. *Shit-work* Delray called it *but it pays.*

In fact Krull liked snow-removal, especially at night. Something crazy and thrilling about it like lacrosse: you worked with other guys, you were a team, it could be dangerous work but as long as you kept going and never shut your eyes for a moment's respite you were O.K.

The trick was to take as much work as you could get. Just say yes, and do it. And do it well. And charge a few dollars less than your competition. That made a difference.

There was the feeling, too, of being *of use*. People grateful for you turning up. Especially women, or elderly people. Damn grateful for you since without snow removed from their driveways they were trapped.

Of use—it was a way of feeling Krull grew to like. He was thinking of Mrs. Hare, who'd been so hopeful for him. Weird how this teacher had seemed to like "Aaron Kruller" and how after he'd been expelled—months after—Krull would think of her suddenly, and miss her; Krull, who'd hated school, and had dreams about returning, knocking down walls and dealing devastation. What she'd told him—you can be a "rogue"—or you can be a "citizen." It was a sensible distinction. Not that Krull believed in a "useful" life—useful for who?—still less did he want to be a "citizen" but he needed to help out Delray. And he didn't want to die young.

EACH TUESDAY MORNING AT 9 A.M. Aaron Kruller reported to the county courthouse on Union Street, Sparta. Waiting his turn at the Probation and Parole Office of the New York State Department of Corrections. After the arrest at school he'd been sentenced to three years' probation. Delray had been so disgusted with him and beyond disgusted he'd looked sober, scared. Krull was resolved not to fuck up anymore if just for the sake of his father.

So, the girl. Eddy Diehl's daughter.

An under-age girl. You could see at a glance. Real sweet, Mira Roche said. Real trusting.

Kind of pathetic, so trusting.

Krull had no intention of going anywhere near Krista Diehl. Whatever Mira said of her, Krull wasn't going to give a damn. She wasn't his problem. There was no connection between them. Still, that night after the garage closed Krull drove into the city, to the depot where the guys hung out. Where the girls were, and the little blond ghost-haired Krista. There he encountered Metz, with the girl. No choice but to intervene. Metz must've been high, a serious crystal high, weird flamey look to his eyes and scarcely registering who Krull was, his friend. And Krull told Metz to let the girl go—Krull said he'd drive her home. There was an exchange of words, there was a struggle. Krull would not recall clearly what happened, afterward. Except he'd been surprised, Duncan Metz had backed off from him. *Fuck you take her. Fuck you both. Who gives a fuck.*

These were Metz's exact words. Krull would've laughed except this was actual life, and not funny.

So, the girl: Krista Diehl. Here was Krull with the responsibility of driving her home.

Eddy Diehl's daughter. The girl who'd been trailing him, at a little distance. Regarding him with somber eyes. And Krull thinking *This is a test. Like from God, a test to see where I will take her. What I will do.*

Krull wasn't a believer in God. Krull wasn't a believer in much of anything. Still, there was something to this. Something like in the Bible.

Put to the test to see what you will do. Being judged.

Zoe hadn't believed in God, most of the time. But Zoe was shrewd to perceive that, if you didn't believe in God at the right time, when it really mattered, you were fucked.

Other times, when it didn't matter, you were O.K. But you had to be cautious not to grow careless and confuse one time with the other.

"Stay awake. Keep your eyes open. Fall asleep now you won't wake up."

Jesus! Krull saw with disgust the girl's shimmering blond hair in clumps caked with puke.

Her puke, it had to be. Dribbled down the front of her clothes, even on her shoes. A thrill of disgust coursed through him.

The way Krista Diehl was breathing, quick and shallow, and her face deathly white, Krull thought she might be O.D.'ing. Krull had seen a girl start to O.D. on speedballs the previous summer, back of the depot in somebody's van, eyeballs rolling up inside her head and her young face slack and mouth opened like a sick baby. The guy who'd been with this girl had shaken her to keep her awake, slapped her face, and so Krull shook Krista Diehl as you'd shake a rag doll, her head flopping on her shoulders. Weakly she whimpered for him to stop.

At least, she was conscious. With Krull's help she could stand. Suddenly gagging again, and vomiting the shit she'd been given, puking up her guts. Krull cursed not getting out of the way in time, his boots were splattered.

"Jesus! Look at you."

He was disgusted, indignant. Yet had to laugh at her, this wanly pretty little blond girl, looking like a wetted bird, feathers stuck to its skull.

It was thrilling to Krull to think, here was Ben Diehl's sister. Here was Eddy Diehl's daughter. Looking to *him*, for help.

Krull bundled her into his car, vomit-splattered clothes and all. Krull in thrilled disgust drove along Ferry Street to Union and to Post not knowing where the hell he was going thinking *Dump her at the ER! Let them empty out her guts.*

Sometimes it happened, a user O.D.'ing on drugs was dumped behind the Sparta hospital. At the curb, and the driver pulled away, fast.

Instead, Krull took the girl to his aunt Viola's. Shocked the hell out of his aunt seeing the limp part-conscious blond girl, so young, before even she knew the girl's identity Viola was shocked, and disapproving, thinking this under-age girl—fifteen? fourteen?—was a girlfriend of her nephew Aaron who'd had sex with her, given her drugs and had sex with her which was equivalent to rape, a girl so young, and now it looked as if she was O.D.'ing, in a few minutes she'd be dead. Why the hell did you bring her here? Krull's aunt asked him, and Krull said he hadn't known what else to do. Couldn't take her home in this condition and didn't want to risk dumping her at the ER, if someone saw his license plate, or his face. Nor had he wanted to dump her on a street corner or in a field or in a freight car at the railroad yard which was where it looked that bastard

Duncan Metz had intended to dump her. Viola asked if the girl was his girl and vehemently Krull said No she was not. He didn't have sex with girls that young and he'd never have sex with this girl, for Christ's sake. And Viola said, flush-faced:

"It's rape, Aaron. They call it 'statue-tary' rape. When the girl is under age and you're not."

"I said, *I did not have sex with her.*"

"Is there somebody else, who did?"

Krull didn't know. Didn't want to think what Metz had been doing with Krista Diehl, in the depot.

He was staring at the girl as she swayed on her feet. His aunt was holding her now, wiping at her face with a tissue. The Diehl girl who appeared to be only minimally conscious of her surroundings. Krista Diehl, here! Krull was made to think of what linked them, him and her; what the connection was between them, powerful as a blood-bond, of which neither could have spoken.

Hurt me! You can try.

What happened between them, then.

No way of speaking of this either.

After he'd told his aunt who the girl was. After she'd stared at him in disbelief. After she'd gone to make a phone call and Krull was alone with the girl, in his aunt's bathroom. Krull turned on both faucets and the girl was trying to wash her face, swaying against the sink, light-headed, clumsy.

He had not wanted to touch her further. He'd given her a washcloth, she fumbled in her fingers. And suddenly his hands were closing around her neck. He was standing close behind her, at the sink. Couldn't seem to control his hands, closing around the girl's slender neck. And feeling her immediate fear, her panic, in that instant, he was hard. Blood in his penis, hard as a hammer. His brain was close to extinction, annihilation.

Taunting her: "This how he did it? Your father . . ."

How Eddy Diehl had strangled Zoe, in her bed. Except Krull seemed to recall there'd been a towel twisted around his mother's neck. But maybe Eddy Diehl had strangled her before using the towel. Maybe there had been the marks of a man's fingers, shadow-fingers on the discolored skin.

Krull hadn't seen his mother's throat but he'd seen her face. Always at all times shutting his eyes Krull sees his dead mother's face. A swollen face like a bruised and broken melon, sallow skin, bloodied skin, broken cheekbones and broken eye sockets and the opened eyes, like grapes. And in the eyes the burst capillaries, the pressure of strangulation.

Krull had seen his mother dead, and he'd smelled her. Krull's beautiful mother except not beautiful now. This was Zoe's reward. This was Zoe's punishment. *Got what she deserved for Christ's sake. That poor woman* it was said. Krull had heard such utterances, or had almost heard them. A terrible choking rage rose in Krull, to punish.

" . . . this? Like this? *This* . . ."

He was pressing against her, his weight against her back. He was squeezing her throat. Weakly the girl picked at his fingers but lacked the strength to free herself. Not daring to claw frantically at him as another girl might out of a fear of provoking him to greater anger. For maybe—the terrified girl might be reasoning—Krull was just teasing, wasn't really serious as—maybe—Duncan Metz had not been serious and had not intended to rape her and let her die of a drug overdose in a freight car; maybe in another moment Krull would loosen his grip on her throat, and laugh at her. Laugh at her terror. Reveal this as a joke.

Guys did such things. Took you to the edge. Showed you what was beyond the edge. And if you believed, a guy would laugh at you, scorn you. He'd tell his friends and they would laugh at you, too.

But you couldn't know. Sometimes you couldn't know until it was too late.

Mira Roche had told Krista this. And Bernadette. Krista's friends!

The fact was, Krull had not been alone with Krista. Close by in the apartment his aunt Viola had been on the telephone. If he'd been alone with Krista, if he'd brought her out to the farmhouse on Quarry Road, something different might have happened. But Krull's aunt was in the apartment, and Krull only just rubbed hard against the girl, through her clothes. And through his clothes, he had not unzipped his trousers. He had not taken out his cock, to force against her. Hadn't pulled down her jeans, to force his cock into her. The crack of her tender little ass. He'd have torn her badly, he'd have caused her to bleed but this had not happened, for Krull's aunt was close by. Within several swift seconds he came, and came hard. He came nearly fainting. He would think *She doesn't know. Neither of them will know.*

Abruptly then it was over. His fingers released her, he lifted his weight from her. Half-fainting and his knees near-buckling yet telling himself *Nothing happened. Didn't touch her.*

In a choked voice he spoke: "Hey. Nobody hurt you. C'mon, breathe."

He laughed. He prodded her. He would behave as if nothing had happened between them. The girl half-lay slumped over the stained sink, gasping for breath. Krull hoped to hell he hadn't wetted her clothes—but there was water in the sink, water issuing from the faucets, she'd been trying to wash her face. Must've weighed no more than eighty-five pounds in his hands. A cold sweat came over Krull, he could've broken her spine forcing himself against her, could've broken her neck losing control as he had, the sex-hunger was so strong, unstoppable.

By the time Viola returned it was over. Krull wanted to think it was over, he'd stepped back from the girl, adjusted his sweaty clothing. And there came Viola agitated and fussy like one who has made a difficult decision: "Let me. I'll wash her face. For Christ's sake! Here's puke in her *hair.*"

It was Viola's idea to have Krista telephone her mother, when she was recovered enough to speak coherently. Explain that she was at a friend's house in Sparta. She'd stayed late at school, there had been a—what?— a meeting of the yearbook, or some sport practice—basketball? Krista would explain how she'd tried to call home earlier but could not get through. Or could not find a phone. Maybe the phone service had been out. Explain she'd had supper with her friend. And her friend's mother was going to drive her home now.

Viola had wanted to drive Krista Diehl home, in fact. But Krull insisted. Krull had begun this, and Krull would end this. Took a beer from Viola's refrigerator to drink while driving the girl out to the river road where he knew the Diehls lived. Scarcely a word passed between them. By now Krull was forgetting how he'd near-strangled the girl, how he'd rammed himself against her oblivious of how he might be hurting her, he would forget how he'd come, and how hard he'd come, weak-kneed, whimpering, he would come to think that probably this had not happened. None of this had happened. Or it had happened in some different, alternative way. Possibly he'd wanted it to happen, but his aunt had appeared. His aunt had appeared in the doorway of the bathroom and so he'd stopped. Whatever the hell Krull was doing, crude-pig-Krull humping the girl he'd brought home to save from O.D.'ing, that had not happened. His aunt would be a witness, it hadn't happened. No sex-assault. No statue-tary Rape. Not Krull. Not Krull who was too shrewd, and too cautious.

Left the girl in her driveway. Drove home to the darkened farmhouse on Quarry Road to which Zoe had abandoned him, God damn her. He would not forgive her. He would not forgive any of them God damn them. Took another beer from the refrigerator out of a six-pack of Delray's he had to drink fast to keep from gagging, wipe out any thoughts he might've had to disgust him like cockroaches slithering out of the tears in the wallpaper as he stumbled to his room, fell onto his bed and into a stuporous sleep of no dreams.

43

NOVEMBER 17, 1987

DRIVING TO BOONEVILLE to haul a wrecked Dodge Colt out of a drainage ditch where the drunk-driver kid had died behind the wheel in fact mashed into the wheel as the cheap four-cylinder engine beneath the hood was mashed like the snout of a hog and a stink of gasoline and oil made his head ache Krull was distracted hearing the tow-truck radio turned up high *breaking news! news bulletin!* thinking he'd heard the name *Diehl* but uncertain until on the 11 P.M. local TV news he caught at a tavern on Garrison Road he saw blurred film footage of Sparta PD vehicles in a motel parking lot, there came a female broadcaster's excited voice and photo-inserts of a man identified as *Edward Diehl, suspect in unsolved 1983 murder.* And in the morning the Sparta *Journal* was ablaze with news of how *Edward Diehl, 45, longtime "suspect" in the Zoe Kruller murder case* had been *shot and killed* by Sparta police and county sheriff's deputies in a *shoot-out* at a Days Inn on route 31.

First reports suggested that before his death Diehl had "confessed to" the murder of Zoe Kruller in February 1983. The "longtime suspect" had taken his fifteen-year-old daughter "hostage" with him in the motel room and had demanded that his former wife come to the motel to speak with him but the former wife identified as *Mrs. Lucille Diehl, of Huron Pike Road,* had called 911 instead.

Krull was stunned thinking *It's over then? This is it?*

In subsequent news bulletins it would be revealed that Edward

Diehl had not fired "a single shot" at police officers outside his motel room though allegedly he'd been holding a gun identified as a .38 Smith & Wesson revolver, allegedly he'd aimed this gun at police officers and threatened to fire it.

Later, it would be revealed that Edward Diehl had not admitted killing Zoe Kruller, either.

On the front page of the Sparta *Journal* was a prominent photograph of Eddy Diehl with a pinched half-smile, the narrowed eyes of a boy who seems to have wakened in the body of a middle-aged man, bemused, distrustful, yet hopeful: Krull had seen this photo of Diehl many times before, in the *Journal*, in other local papers and on TV, he'd come to know Eddy Diehl like a relative. (The man he'd seen with his mother, at the landfill! Where, it seemed to Krull, all this unhappiness had begun.) And for sure there was, in the adjoining newspaper column, the same photograph of Krull's mother the God-damned paper had printed a thousand times above the gloating caption *Zoe Kruller, victim in brutal 1983 slaying.*

Krull looked for a photograph of Diehl's daughter the *fifteen-year-old hostage Krista Diehl* but there was none.

Anyway, he knew her face.

"Krista."

For hours, days afterward Krull could think of nothing else. No one else.

Badly he wanted to see her. The girl.

Not knowing what the hell he would say to Krista Diehl if he saw her but maybe—if he saw her—some words would come.

Too shy to call. Though Krull could deal with auto repair business over the phone in the way that Delray called *expediting* yet Krull hated speaking on the phone in any personal way.

He was nineteen. He had a woman he saw frequently, a divorcee in her mid-twenties with two young children. He saw other women. He did not much see "girls." He had sex with these women, sometimes. He did not stay overnight with them, usually. He wasn't comfortable in close quarters. He wasn't comfortable with speech. Wasn't comfortable with emotions that felt to him crude and outsized as the gigantic blades of windmills turning in sporadic gusts of wind. *Keep away from her. Keep your pig-hands off her. Might've torn her insides, raped her and be sent to Attica for twenty years. You have been warned.*

44

MID-AFTERNOON OF THE DAY following the night he'd been summoned by his aunt Viola to her house, to haul his sick-drunk father home, dump him on the mattress on the floor of the spare room in the house they shared on Quarry Road, Krull said to his wrecked father he'd take him to detox at Watertown, meaning the veterans' administration hospital there where Delray had been a patient once, a few years before, briefly; and Delray shuddered, and rubbed his bloodshot eyes with his skinned-knuckle fists, and said, in a voice of chagrin Krull could not determine might be sincere, or mocking: "Right. I better."

Krull persisted, as if the old man hadn't given in like a rotted door pushed open: "Or you're a dead man, see Pa? Your liver's shot."

"Yah right. Din't I just say. I better."

Delray was seated in the kitchen slump-shouldered in a chair where he'd staggered, to sit hard, heavy as a bag of gravel. Squinting his broke-egg eyes on his son as if hoping to bring him into sharper focus.

Delray was bare-chested, in work trousers worn without a belt. His torso was a mass of bristly gray hairs, fatty flesh, stippled discolorations that were moles, pimples. Vague as part-recalled dreams were tattoos in bright but fading colors—eagle, skull, scripted words on flowing banners. In the ironic light of afternoon Delray's old glamour-tattoos had a comic-strip look.

Krull lit a cigarette, exhaled smoke like disbelieving laughter.

"You're going? You will go? You *will*?"

"God damn I said yes din't I. You and Viola, you talked me into it."

There remained just the decision: whether Delray would commit himself to the VA hospital alone or whether Krull had better come with him, and maybe his sister. Delray insisted hell he could drive to Watertown by himself, he was cold stone sober now and would remain sober and he'd done this before, with good results.

Krull asked, "What kind of results?"

"Good results. Two weeks in, and they discharged me."

Krull wasn't sure that this had been so. Krull thought he remembered some scene with Zoe screaming at Delray, crying and breaking things in the kitchen. But maybe this was some other time. Some other hospital visit. Maybe it hadn't been Delray who'd been in, but some other relative. Krull was eager to believe this good news, that Delray was agreeable to Watertown.

On the phone when Krull called her with the good news Viola broke down. Saying God had intervened, must've been God had listened to her prayers all that day she'd been pleading with Him saying if Delray didn't get professional help for his drinking she was finished with him, her big brother she'd always loved she would not speak with ever again, her soul would be damned. Which God could prevent, if God only would.

Now it seemed to Viola, God had intervened.

"And I pray for you, too, Aaron. Let God into your heart, some."

Arrangements were made at Watertown. Phone calls were made. There was a bed for Delray in the detox ward. Krull thought *He must be scared as hell. Zoe would never believe this.*

By 4 P.M. of that very day Delray left for Watertown which was a three-hour drive to the northwest, on the St. Lawrence River. By this time Krull had helped Delray take a long steamy shower to cleanse himself of the accumulated filth and shame of days and with one of Zoe's small scissors Krull had trimmed Delray's coarse matted hair growing down his neck and the wild-man whiskers threaded with gray so that his father no longer looked drunk or crazed or the most pathetic thing there is, an aging biker. Viola arrived excited and hopeful and helped Delray pack a single suitcase and a duffel bag into which, she'd confided in Krull, she had placed a Bible; and both Viola and Krull offered to drive Delray to the hospital and help him get settled but Delray insisted he wasn't a God-damned invalid, he'd made up his mind to quit drinking by his own choice and by his own choice he would check himself in.

And when he was dried out, Delray said, he'd check himself out.

"Zoe said the most shameful thing about a drunk is, he gets his family tangled in his misery. This time, I will spare you."

So it was Zoe, of whom Delray had been thinking. All this day they'd been preparing for Watertown. All this day Delray had been brooding, somber. Stone-cold sober Delray called this condition.

"Like raking your insides with a hand rake. Hurts so much, it almost feels good."

OUTSIDE THE FAMILY there isn't much. It was a consoling thought, or a terrible thought. Krull didn't know which.

THAT EVENING a call came from the hospital at Watertown, a supervisor at the detox clinic. Informing Aaron Kruller that his father Delray had checked himself into the alcohol rehab program and wanted his family to be informed. Delray's name and records were already in the hospital computer and his veteran's status had been confirmed. Krull asked how long would his father be hospitalized and was told six to eight weeks minimum.

Six to eight weeks! That long, Krull would have to run his father's business.

He was twenty-one at this time. He'd been an adult for as long as he could remember, before even Zoe had died. Only vaguely could Krull recall a boy—a little boy named "Aaron"—on the far side of Zoe's death as in a shadowy corner of the house on Quarry Road.

Krull asked when his father could have visitors at the hospital and was told that visitors were not encouraged until the patient was progressing "significantly." For a patient in Delray's condition this could be four or five weeks.

Krull said they'd be there. Soon as his father could see them, him and his aunt would drive up.

At the auto repair Krull told the mechanics that Delray would be "out of town" for a while. This meant that Joe Susa, the most experienced mechanic, would oversee the work of the garage while Krull answered the phone and took care of invoices, bills, orders, customers as well as filled in where he was needed. The startled and somber way Delray's employees took the news, not meeting Krull's eye, he guessed they knew: Delray had to be back in detox, or worse.

45

"KRULL? OPEN UP."

Krull. This was a name none of the mechanics called him, or anyone who knew him as Delray Kruller's son. So Krull knew this had to be trouble.

Past 10 P.M. at the rear of Kruller's Auto Repair & Cycle Shop which closed at 8 P.M. Since that time Krull had been hunched over his father's battered old rolltop desk trying to make sense of his father's bookkeeping. There were bills, invoices, supply orders, illegible handwritten notations, loose checks of which some had been cashed, and others had not. There were drawers stuffed with old receipts, state and federal income tax documents, bank statements. It wasn't clear to Krull whether Kruller's Auto Repair & Cycle Shop was making money—a "profit"—each month, or whether Delray's erratic bookkeeping didn't reflect the economic reality. Delray had a way of paying out checks without subtracting sums from the business's checking account; he had a way of stuffing bills into drawers without paying them. And there were old, scrawled checks from customers dated so long ago, the checks had become worthless.

Owning your own business sounded good. *Running your own business* was the problem.

It was less than three days since Delray had checked himself into the VA hospital at Watertown. In that time Krull had been putting in fifteen-hour days minimum at the garage. *Your own business* meant you never had a free thought for anything else.

Why a man had to get drunk, Delray would claim. Why a man had to get high.

Most of that damned day Krull had been lying flat on his back beneath a jacked-up Jeep having a fucking hard time repairing the engine, Jeep repair wasn't Krull's specialty, God damn he missed Delray. Stained with grease and his eyes ringed with grime looking like a raccoon's startled eyes and his hair around the edges of his baseball cap stiff with dirt. The snaky-purple tattoos he'd acquired in a Niagara Falls tattoo parlor with some friends not long before were blurred like a bad drunk dream. But Krull didn't want to go back to the house and get cleaned up until he'd located some crucial records in Delray's desk which it looked like, at this point, he wasn't going to locate.

Owning your own business meant some kind of pride. That was the idea. *Going bankrupt* was not the idea.

Now came—was it Dutch Boy Greuner?—banging his fist against the rear door of Kruller's Auto Repair in a way to suggest that he'd done this before. The garage was shut, darkened; just a light at the back, in Delray's office; through the window Krull saw the scrawny-tall Dutch Boy like an apparition. And when Krull opened the door Dutch Boy said, blinking his pale-lashed eyes, "W-Where's your old man, Krull? I need to speak with Del-roy. Where the fuck is Del-roy?" Dutch Boy spoke rapidly to overcome a stutter that seemed to begin in his solar plexis and move up into his throat in peristaltic jerks. His enunciation of *Del-roy* was mean, mocking. Dutch Boy had a reputation for being unpredictable, dangerous. Like Duncan Metz you could not anticipate how he would greet you—friendly, not-so-friendly. When he'd been in high school and for a while afterward Krull had had dealings with Dutch Boy who'd worked for Duncan Metz and whose family had kicked him out of their house at the age of fifteen. Dutch Boy was three or four years older than Krull, taller than Krull by an inch or two, bony-shouldered like a vulture with papery folds of skin over his eyes, stained teeth amid bright gold fillings. Dutch Boy had been incarcerated at Potsdam on drugs and weapons charges and had maxed out on a three-year sentence which meant he wasn't on parole and Sparta police had no legal right to keep a watch on him or run him in for "suspicious" behavior. It was rumored that Dutch Boy had participated in the execution of another prisoner at Potsdam, at Duncan Metz's bequest. Dutch Boy wore black leather and biker boots except the black leather was cheap black vinyl and smelled wrong; the boots weren't leather but vulcanized rubber. Dutch Boy's pale-lashed eyes shone with a flamey-meth heat and his dyed-brass hair stuck up in spikes. In an excited quavering voice Dutch Boy said, "Del-roy owes me, Krull. Where the fuck is Del-roy. Next time Del-roy's head is going to be broke not just his sorry old ass."

Krull understood, then: his father had been deliberately beaten.

His father had been beaten in some way connected with Dutch Boy Greuner which meant drugs. It could be high school weed and speedballs but also harder stuff like crystal meth, cocaine, heroin. Selling out of the rear of Kruller's Auto Repair, not Delray personally but one of the young mechanics, and Krull had a good idea which one. God damn, this was too much.

"You looking like—what? You don't believe me? Huh? Go ask your old man, Krull. Ask him why his ass got broke the other night, he'd tell you."

Krull said his father was *out of town.*

"Yah? 'Out of town' what the fuck's that mean? Like—'out of town' he's on the run?"

"How much does he owe you?"

"'How much does he owe us'—like it's that simple, Krull! See, it ain't that simple."

Needing money. That was it. Desperate to repay loans, the Goddamned interest on the loans which was killing him. Delray had taken out a second mortgage on the house. After Zoe died when everything went to hell. The business wasn't generating enough profit, Delray's reputation was *wife-beater, wife-killer.* You would have thought that people would ease up after Eddy Diehl was shot down by police, but that hadn't happened, or anyway not enough. It was like Sparta residents had made up their minds what they wanted to think about both Delray Kruller and Eddy Diehl, and couldn't be troubled to change their minds.

Plus there were new gas stations and auto repairs out on the Strip. A new Harley-Davidson franchise. Delray was of a Vietnam-vet generation beginning to fade. Like being eaten while you are still alive, Delray called it. And not yet fifty years old.

Dutch Boy had invited himself inside Delray's office. This was a small cluttered space partitioned off from the garage by a plasterboard wall adorned with calendars, posters, advertisements. Krull had not so much as glimpsed Dutch Boy in maybe a year. Of Krull's circle of loser-druggie-friends most had had dealings with Dutch Boy that hadn't turned out so well like Mira Roche who'd O.D.'d on a combination of meth and crack cocaine, dead at eighteen and her picture in the papers and on TV for a day or two then dropped.

POLICE CHIEF CLAIMS "DRUG EPIDEMIC" AMONG SPARTA TEENS

SPARTA POLICE, COUNTY SHERIFF'S DEPT. JOIN IN WAR AGAINST DRUGS

FOURTH DRUG-RELATED DEATH IN HERKIMER COUNTY THIS YEAR

Since Delray needed him, Krull had tried to put distance between himself and the drug scene. Krull who had a weakness for anything speedy that could fire him up, make him think *O.K.! This is it!* but the downside of it was seeing his hands shake, dazed and dizzy after he'd slept for twenty hours sodden like a waterlogged tree trunk. One day putting on clothes he discovered that the waist of his trousers was loose like he'd begun to shrink, must've lost ten pounds within a few days—scared as hell of losing muscle-tissue like the meth-heads he knew, teeth rotting in his head.

Now Dutch Boy was crowding Krull. His stammer was ringed with spittle. Saying there were people he owed—him, Dutch Boy—Krull had to figure it's like a ladder, someone owes you, someone on the rung below you, asshole doesn't pay what he owes so you can't pay who you owe on the rung above you, there's a *breaking point*. There's a *point of no return*.

"Like, the ladder can break, see Krull?"

Krull shrugged. How was this his problem, Krull suggested.

"See, you better call him, Krull. Your old man. You know where he is, you can call him. Get your old man on the phone, K-Krull. Don't fuck with me."

Calmly Krull thought *I could kill him here. Who'd know?*

"Krull, you hear me? Call him. Here."

There was a phone on Delray's desk and this phone Dutch Boy pushed in Krull's direction, but Krull lifted his hands away. With a shake of his head Krull indicated he didn't know where his father was, didn't know how to call him, Krull was on his feet now disliking the way Dutch Boy was crowding against him, taking up too much space where he wasn't welcome. Seeing behind Dutch Boy's dyed-brass head a heavy wrench on a shelf, if Krull could maneuver in the right space he could (maybe) lay open Dutch Boy's skull in a single blow and the problem would be solved for Delray if not for Krull.

Pumped with adrenaline Krull was thinking he didn't care if he killed Dutch Boy but he'd care like hell if he got caught. Piss away his young life at Potsdam or Attica and maybe he'd die there. *That* would break Delray's heart, losing his only son. Could not risk that.

Dutch Boy's name was Dennis. In school he'd been Dennie Greuner afflicted with a stammer like a seizure, provoking laughter in other children.

He'd been skinny, sickly-looking yet somehow he'd prevailed and in high school he'd suddenly grown taller, acquiring a malevolent sort of strength like a toxic gas set to explode with the slightest spark.

Quietly Krull said his father was a sick man.

Quietly Krull asked how much did his father owe.

Dutch Boy named a sum. Krull whistled thinly. Hoping that, whatever Delray had done with the money it had been worth it.

NEXT MORNING there came a call for Aaron Kruller from the Watertown Veterans Administration Hospital Alcohol and Drug Rehabilitation

Clinic informing Aaron that his father Delray had departed from the facility sometime the previous night. He'd told no one where he was going. He'd told no one that he was leaving.

Krull hung up the phone. Felt like he'd been kicked in the belly.

"Fuck you, then. That's it."

The previous time, Delray had done more or less the same thing. At the same detox clinic. He'd lasted a little longer, but he'd left before he was released. Same God-damned thing he'd walked out. And Zoe had taken the call, and Krull had heard her scream.

This was it. This was the end. Let him drink himself to death. Krull wasn't going to care.

He'd made arrangements to pay Dutch Boy in installments. Five hundred dollars each. He'd made the first payment. There were six more installments to come. He hadn't told his aunt Viola or any of the Krullers about the money. Couldn't bring himself to tell Viola the bad news. *Headed to hell, after her.* Drinking beer till his head buzzed and his gut was bloated like something dead and swollen in the water thinking how it was so, Zoe had plunged into hell and was pulling them after her like dirty water swirling down a drain. The kind of family situation, you could call it an inheritance, you'd naturally need to get high and stay high as long as you could.

46

THESE WEEKS LATER, Delray was still missing.

In the wind you could say of the old man. Krull believed that Delray was still alive, though. Somehow, he knew.

On broken wings Krull was descending. Not in graceful arcs like the wide-winged hawks circling their small-mammal prey preparing to dive and clutch and tear but a drunk-jolting slip-sliding-down through rough currents of air. He'd had a hit of crystal meth in some very early hour of the morning but it was long past morning now.

"Krull? You O.K.? Look here."

Too much effort to turn his head. And when he turned his head it was some later time. Still, there was a sun. Bleeding into the darkness below like a burst egg yolk so he didn't need headlights yet. Not wanting to switch on his lights until absolutely lights were needed, it was a principle Delray upheld as well.

Moving target. Couldn't remember if this was a good thing or not-so-good.

It was a warm-balmy May day. Should've been an ordinary day except Krull had wakened to a premonition. Zoe had had these also: *premonitions*. Like *superstitions*. Like axle grease lodged beneath your fingernails, so deep you can't ever pick or pry it out.

"Krull, shit. Open your eyes, you're gonna crash us."

Krull wasn't what you'd call a meth-head. Krull was not. Not a serious user of any drug. So not susceptible to *premonitions* and *superstitions* but still he had a feeling, when Dutch Boy called him.

Driving out the Sparta-Boonville Road. Glacier hills like the shrugging backs of ancient beasts, drumlins and deep ravines. In the city which was steep hills lifting from the river you could go for days without seeing the sky. Had to crane your damn neck, make an effort to look up. In the country navigating these long slow hills you could see more. There's the illusion, you could see into the future.

"Pull over, Krull. Christ! I'll drive."

Krull shoved whoever it was away. Krull muttered laughing what sounded like *Fuck you fucker!* But it was in good spirits.

The way Dutch Boy spat the name *Krull—K-Krull—*over the phone, almost you could see the outraged spittle.

"He's a shithead. He's fucked. Fuck him."

Krull was driving a 1988 Dodge minivan, he liked. Handled easy for a vehicle of its size. Registered in the name of *Aaron Kruller.* Four thousand down payment supplied by Dutch Boy. In cash.

Except Krull was in that paranoid state, wasn't sure if he'd already accomplished his mission and was to be rewarded or if he hadn't accomplished his mission and was to be reprimanded. As in a dream he wasn't sure what the mission was, or had been. Something important, urgent. Dutch Boy said *This one you don't want to fuck up.*

Like skidding on black ice. Getting turned around. Your vehicle in motion so you'd have a hell of a time saying which direction you'd been traveling in, and why.

"Ma'am sorry. It's a *cash transaction.*"

At the doctor's house on Fairway Lane he'd said this. The doctor's wife Lorene had invited Krull inside though Krull had clearly been in a hurry and his work-boots heavy as horse's hooves were muddy tracking up the prissy oatmeal-colored carpet. Just inside the rear door of the doctor's house on Fairway Lane you could see some kind of luxury-hotel look through paneled glass, an indoor swimming pool?—glimmering aqua.

This wasn't the first time Krull had delivered to the split-level glass-

and-brick house overlooking fucking Sparta Hills Golf Course but the first time the doctor's wife Lorene came on to Krull swaying and leaning against him so crudely, such a yearning to be loved or anyway stroked, touched, fucked she'd actually leaned her face to his, touched his lips with her lips, would've kissed Krull with her tongue except he'd been as shocked as if a snake had poked its forked tongue out of the female's mouth or if a snake had slid up his leg and into his crotch. "Jesus! Ma'am get *back*." His age and size and Indian-looking as he was Krull was easily freaked-out by females careening near him, drunk or high, you heard such tales of rape accusations, sex-assault and death threat accusations, anything a female declared a male had done to her would be believed, today. And this was a fully white woman, and Krull's skin was heavy-dark with blood and his shadowy beard he'd have had to shave twice a day, fuck that Krull had better things to do. So shoving the doctor's wife Lorene—now astonished, hurt like he'd slapped her face—as if Krull was supposed to walk away with no payment for the delivery except a wet tongue-kiss and the promise of sex! And Dr. Jacobi's wife pushing forty at least. To Dutch Boy he'd repeat his terse response like a TV ad lib, "Ma'am sorry. We just do cash transactions" to make Dutch Boy laugh.

Provoking laughter in Dutch Boy was like provoking laughter in some damn beef cattle still with its horns. Slow and stupid but dangerous just to approach. A wrong move, you can wind up on the horns.

Krull was known as Dutch Boy's lieutenant. Dutch Boy's right-hand man. Only man Dutch Boy could trust. He said.

And a guy to make Dutch Boy laugh.

Only when he was high, Krull was funny. If you could call it funny. Weird like something on late-night TV. Switch on the set, there's Krull.

"Krull, c'mon. Pull over here. I'll—"

Krull wanted to laugh but his teeth were chattering. Yet so warm he'd yanked up his T-shirt to his armpits. The skin taut against his ribs was slick with sweat. Shit he'd been losing weight, it was fucking hard to sit still long enough to eat. If you had the appetite to eat. Meth-smoke dulled his taste and his tongue felt numb like some dead thing crawled in his mouth though he had an urge to talk, an itch to talk, only just not any words to say. When the frantic woman pressed against him before even she'd tried to slide her snake-tongue into his surprised mouth she had reached around him adroit as a mother reaching around an intransigent child to clasp him tight against her, mother-hands flat together at the small of his back as she gripped him tight saying she was so lonely, Christ she was so lonely, she could love him, please let her, she'd been crazy for him since the first time she'd seen him, Krull had had to push the woman away, shocked. The hungry female mouth so yearning to swallow his own.

Years ago, Zoe's friend Jacky DeLucca. Krull still dreamt of that female he had not seen since.

He'd never found out if Delray had been the one who'd beaten DeLucca. It wasn't something you could ask of your old man.

Never found out if, before Eddy Diehl had been shot down, he actually had confessed to killing Zoe. If that was maybe why he'd been shot down. But the story had been altered afterward. Out of spite, to ruin Delray Kruller. Out of spite, Delray's enemies in the sheriff's department. Some boyfriend of Zoe's cousin, that was the connection. All of Sparta was a spiderweb of such connections.

In the center of the web was the spider Death.

After Diehl died his family had moved away from Sparta. The exwife, the son Ben and the daughter Krista.

The girl, Krull had almost strangled. Almost fucked. No but he had not, it was only just his hands.

He had not. She would confirm this.

These weeks he'd given in, said *yes* to Dutch Boy. What had happened to Dutch Boy's previous lieutenant wasn't commonly known.

If Krull had been to the doctor's wife this afternoon and he had the cash on his person, then he'd made the transaction. If Krull still had the dope, he hadn't made the transaction. If Krull didn't have either the cash or the Baggie with the rock crystal he was in serious trouble.

Whoever was pulling at his hands, Krull shoved aside. Trying to talk reason to Krull and Krull lost patience suddenly cursed him laughing angrily and reached over to open the door, God damn door handle Krull grabbed and tried to lift the wrong way, then managed to get it, the door swung open, shithead shoved out screaming, Krull jammed the accelerator to the floor.

He'd been there, at the doctor's wife's house. He remembered now. It had been real enough. She'd half-fallen, her hair in her face. Her eyes leeching onto his like she's drowning and Krull was the one to haul her up but had not. *You sorry bastard. You redneck shithead* out of the doctor's wife's peach-colored face.

There was the wish that Delray might return. Krull would appeal to Delray frankly what to do about Dutch Boy. Except if Delray hadn't disappeared, there wouldn't be Dutch Boy in Krull's life.

Duncan Metz was gone, out of Sparta. There was a rumor he'd been told to leave, or he'd be hurt. Maybe he was in Buffalo. Maybe in Erie, Pennsylvania. Dutch Boy had Metz's arsenal, he called it. Military rifles, shotguns and semi-automatic pistols. A single-shot Remington pistol with bolt action. And more.

You plotted killing your enemy before he realized he had a good reason to kill you. Except the risk is, your enemy has already realized. Your enemy is waiting for headlights to approach his house in the countryside darkening like something congealing while the sky is still light and clouds marbled and massive like sculpted rock.

In the wind. But where, no one knew.

You'd have thought that Delray would contact some of his relatives in Sparta. But no word came of him. Then, mid-April Krull heard that Delray had "passed through" Long Lake seeing a cousin and his family there but by the time Krull drove up to Long Lake, in the Adirondacks, Delray had "moved on."

What condition was his father in, Krull asked.

Knowing from the look in his relatives' eyes, this was a painful question to answer.

Another time in April Krull learned of Delray turning up unexpectedly at another relative's home in Plattsburgh, near the Canadian border; this Kruller cousin had enlisted in the army and was shipped to Vietnam at about the time Delray had enlisted. His wife called Krull to say that Delray had "come and gone" and he'd shown signs of "heavy drinking" and "talked kind of confused, sometimes." Krull asked if Delray had said anything about rehab, returning to rehab and Watertown, and if Delray had said anything about returning to Sparta, anything about him, and the woman said, "Him and Luke, they didn't waste a lot of breath talking but mostly just drank. Luke has this bad habit of talking past you—y'know what I mean?—he'd say something about Vietnam, that damn war they were in, and Delray would only just grunt and laugh like it was so long ago, what the hell's it matter any longer. I tried to feed Del some, he wasn't eating a whole lot, I asked how was his family back in Sparta, how was his son—that's to say *you*—and Delray said this thing to chill your heart— 'That's a long time ago, too.' I thought maybe it was an error of mine to call Delray's attention to, y'know, your mother and all, but he didn't take offense against me. Later in the night I woke up hearing him and Luke still downstairs laughing—or maybe not laughing but something else. Next morning Delray was gone."

"Gone where?"

"Aaron, how'd I know? Del din't even make clear where he'd come from."

First of May Krull heard from a customer at the auto repair who'd known Delray since high school, that Del had moved in with some woman at Saranac Lake and was working as a mechanic there. "Why the fuck would Pa do that," Krull said, "—he owns his own place here." By the time Krull could get away to Saranac Lake driving all the hell out route 28 and north into the mountains on treacherous looping roads it was days later and in Saranac he dropped by every garage and body shop and diner, bar and tavern in the vicinity showing photos of Delray at a younger and healthier age so he had to explain how Delray was likely to be looking now. No one in any of the garages remembered having seen Delray which was a bad sign but in a lakeside tavern a young female bartender claimed yes, could be she'd seen this man, he'd been in the tavern several times by himself and not with any woman, she remembered his face "kind of beat-up, wounded-looking"—but he'd left her dollar tips, he was a generous man.

Krull had to smile. Generous! The less cash Delray had, the more he tossed around. There was a reckless giddy air to Delray at such times, like a man on his way to the gallows.

The woman said she'd asked Krull's father his name and he'd just laughed and mumbled what sounded like "That's a long time ago."

Krull spent a day and a half at Saranac. Not wanting to spend money on a motel he slept in his car. Needing a shave and smelling of his clothes, desperation and beer he'd had to drink, in pursuit of the old man, God damn he was determined to find Delray except the search was just one tavern, bar, diner or restaurant after another along the main-traveled highway, a futile quest Krull came to see for this wasn't TV where after a few inquiries a son would find someone—like the female bartender—to help him locate his father and bring him back home and check him back into rehab to save his life. Instead what Krull encountered was strangers of whom some had time for him and others did not; strangers who were mostly sympathetic and wishing to be helpful and pitying, especially women staring at the wrinkled old snapshots Krull spread out before them saying *Oh is this your father? Looking for your father is he sick?* Saying *There is a strong family likeness here, you and him. You can see it in the eyes.*

Looking at Krull as if he, Krull, was the sick one, not Delray. Or maybe Krull had caught the sickness from Delray and already it showed in his young face.

The kind of family situation where your remedy is to get high. Stay high for as fucking long as it's feasible.

KRULL RETURNED HOME to a surprise and not a good surprise.

". . . hate to let Del and you down Aaron but hell: how'd I know when Del is coming back? Or if Del's coming back? I got my family to look out for, see? This body shop in town, I can start next Monday. You tell Del, next time you talk to him, that. . . ."

Joe Susa! Krull was stunned. Krull had not expected this. Joe Susa was the most skilled of Delray's mechanics.

Twelve years of working with Delray, maybe that was enough. Krull saw in the man's eyes how deeply distressed he was, how guilty he felt and what damned relief, at the prospect of quitting Kruller's Auto Repair.

. . . kind of beat-up, wounded-looking . . .

Like tracking a wounded animal. An old buck. The gut-shot old buck leaving a blood trail through the woods, in the snow stubbled with broken limbs, swatches of leaves. Krull had never gotten into hunting but knew it was a code of hunting, especially the Seneca Indians believed that the hunter is morally bound to locate the animal he has wounded and put the animal out of its suffering.

Except you have to find the wounded buck, first.

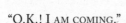

47

"O.K.! I AM COMING."

Krull was in the habit now of speaking aloud. No one else to speak to, he could trust.

At Booneville Junction twelve miles west of Sparta there appeared to be no inhabitants only a rotting granary of about the height of a three-storey house beside the Chautauqua & Buffalo railroad track. On all sides were overgrown fields. The Booneville road was cracked and crumbling. Here you turned left onto Seven Mile Road which was narrow and unpaved leading back, after a mile, to what must have been once a farming-family enclave. Of six houses two had collapsed into their stone foundations and one had burnt down to its foundation and another had begun to burn from the roof down, gutting out the attic, exposing rooms so that you could see fire-scorched wallpaper, splintered glass in what remained of windows, blackened curtains delicate as lace stirring in the wind. In his jittery mood Krull stared at a window of this devastated old farmhouse thinking that a woman was watching him from there, drawing back the black-lace curtain, beckoning.

"Yah? What?"

Krull's voice was raw, weird. Krull heard his voice like something through a funnel aimed back at him.

"You don't know me! I'm not the one."

Krull laughed to show he wasn't serious. For sure there was no woman in that house. No one watching Krull, for sure.

Weird thing was this wasn't Krull's first time, seeing the female face, shadowy figure in the window. That he knew was not there. That he knew was not Zoe for Christ's sake he knew *Zoe was dead*. Hadn't he seen the body, smelled it. Hadn't he sprinkled talcum powder on that body like you'd sprinkle lime on a some dead animal you wanted to burn away quick without that terrible smell.

Krull had been out to Dutch Boy's twice before. First time, when Duncan Metz had owned the premises. Or rented the premises. A rumor was, Krull had heard only the previous week, Metz was buried on those premises.

Dutch Boy's country place, Dutch Boy called it. The important thing, it was beyond the jurisdiction of the Sparta police and just over the county line in Kattawago County. Dutch Boy boasted he had a friend in the Kattawago sheriff's department and possibly this was so.

Krull climbed out of his car: a Ford Charger. Four-door, eight-cylinder, dark bronze, last year's model. The kind of car Delray would've been impressed to see his kid drive except how the hell did his kid get the money for it?—that would've been Del's first question.

"Trade-in. Fucking good deal."

Somehow Krull was outside, kicking at leaves. There were tall grasses here—rushes?—and the wind was rippling these grasses, churning these grasses so Krull's scalp prickled, almost you could see something—some giant thing—animal, or a human figure—not quite visible but you could see it like a moving shadow making its way through the grasses, flattening the grasses, letting them spring up again, and the challenge was not to panic, for *there was no one there*.

A body is a dead thing. You buried a body, or burnt it. Like garbage it was buried, or burnt. It was an asshole kind of sentiment, to imagine that some kind of *spirit* survived after the *body* was shot all to hell. Krull told himself this *Your mother is dead and she is not coming back*.

Krull explored the fire-site. Part-burnt lumber, shingles, scattered and crumbling bricks and parts of dead trees like fallen things from which life had leaked out. Sweet damp grass had begun to grow out of the debris, there was wild lilac grown tall and leggy like the bushes behind the peach-colored farmhouse. *Fallen hearts and fallen leaves, starlings light on the broken trees* she was singing. He'd broken off a sprig of lilac to bring to her, torn the tree limb like an arm wrenched out of a socket but Zoe didn't scold him, hadn't seemed to notice. Wasn't that kind of Mommy to take much special notice except she'd thanked him, kissed him. *All we need is a place to land, my little bird of Heaven right here in my hand.* Now the scent of lilac flooded Krull's senses so he felt drunk, buzzing-high, it was a sweet high though mixed with smells of rot and wood-scorch. Of the six houses one remained habitable: Jimmy Weggens's grandparents' house Jimmy had inherited, in disrepair and oddly aslant as if the very earth had shifted and tilted beneath it, and in this house Dutch Boy and some others were living.

From a distance the house was an old gaunt-looking farmhouse with steep roofs and a sagging front veranda and lightning rods like ice picks on the highest peaks of the roofs. The chimney was brick and partly collapsed, the veranda roof glared with a rich rotted sheen. Translucent rags of plastic flapped at the windows like soiled bandages. There remained some measure of dignity to the veranda which was wide and had a look of soaring, with ornamental-carved posts like something in a picture book. The front yard was grassless and rutted from the tires of numerous vehicles and this evening—somehow, it was evening—Krull was sure he'd left Sparta in the early afternoon—several vehicles were parked there of which the showiest was Dutch Boy's 1984 dark-purple T-top Barracuda with its left side scraped as if with a giant fork and a front bumper fastened to the chassis with wire.

Krull had climbed back into his car and continued up the lane. Parked in the yard in front of Dutch Boy's place. Krull had no weapon except a tire iron shoved partway beneath the passenger's seat. Dutch Boy had several times tried to give him one of the semi-automatic pistols, twenty-two caliber six-shot, small enough to fit in Krull's jacket pocket, but Krull had not wanted to carry any firearm reasoning that if he had a gun the urge would be to use it, to find a use for it. When Krull was high on ice—"black ice" was the worst—his nerves were wound so tight, the least noise and sudden movement like a butterfly beating its wings, hum-mingbird or just some thistle silk blowing in the wind, his heart began to pound with adrenaline which even in his nerved-up state Krull was able to understand was not a good thing.

The wild-flamey-meth high had gradually leaked out of Krull, from eighteen hours before, or whenever. Now his heart was pounding with only just apprehension, fear. He had not switched on his headlights. There was that, he'd done right. The sun had not yet disappeared. Much of the sky remained light in the west, above Lake Ontario, and was ablaze with red.

A waning red sun. Delray had talked of taking him there some time, a friend had a boat, they could go fishing. A part of Krull's mind, this was still a prospect. This might still happen. The old man comes back, he's "retired" from the auto repair and cycle shop. Sure they could do it, some weekend.

Dutch Boy wasn't so crazy in daylight as he got to be sometimes, in dark. Krull was thinking this time of year, it stays light later.

Krull was thinking this melancholy thought: how Jimmy Weggens's old grandparents had lived out here in Booneville off that unpaved road all of their lives and farmed—wheat, soybeans, corn, dairy cows—and had children to whom they'd left the farmhouse and property of some fifty acres but the children had all grown up and moved to Sparta or some other city with not the slightest interest in farming, gradually they'd sold off the property, or maybe it was leased to neighboring farmers, but the old house had gone uninhabited until at last in the mid–1980s it had fallen to Jimmy Weggens who was a meth-head junkie of thirty-five with teeth rotted in his jaws and a grin like a Hallowe'en pumpkin.

Jimmy had been an old-time partner of Duncan Metz and was now a partner of Dutch Boy Greuner in the manufacture of crystal meth. In the basement of the old house was a "cooking lab" and out back a putrid waste-chemical dump. For a mile you could smell this dump but no county law enforcement officers had ever investigated the premises nor were likely to, Dutch Boy boasted.

Dutch Boy was also a source of more mainstream drugs: pot, coke, prescription painkillers and anti-depressants, diet pills and heroin. No weapon except the tire iron which obviously Krull could not carry into the house.

Krull cupped his hands to his mouth. It was always a chancy thing, showing up here even when expected. "Hey. It's me—Krull." He'd seen a face at one of the first-floor windows.

Just inside the door, Dutch Boy's young girlfriend Sarabeth was hugging her bony arms, shivering. There was a shiny metal clip in her left eyebrow. Nervous and embarrassed-seeming Sarabeth told Krull, "He's kind of pissed right now. Don't know why." Sarabeth had once been a girl of Krull's. Not Krull's only girl at the time and not for a very long time but there was a sentimental attachment between them, an air of regret, apology. Sarabeth was eighteen, or twenty. Some tales Sarabeth told, you could figure her for twenty-five, or older. Her tales of herself were seductive and fanciful. She was a rich man's daughter on the run from Averill Park, a classy suburb of Albany. Sarabeth herself had been a classy model, unless it was a classy call girl, in Syracuse. Her small myopic watery tea-colored eyes were dilated and might have registered fear in normal circumstances. Dry-mouthed from whatever drugs she'd taken Sarabeth licked her lips and lay a quivery hand on Krull's arm to warn him in a breathy whisper, "He's kind of excited." In an interior room, that had once been a kitchen, Dutch Boy was speaking on the phone. His voice was unmistakable: a sequence of furious stammering surges. He was speaking with his Syracuse supplier, Krull surmised. Krull had remembered that he'd made five deliveries in Sparta that day and each had gone without any difficulty and so he had money to hand over to Dutch Boy, a wad of crumpled smelly bills. Even new-minted bills handed to Krull from the shaky hands of upscale customers like the doctor's wife had a way of taking on the smells of Krull's body. Time would be required for Dutch Boy to count these bills for Dutch Boy did not trust what he called "intermediators." Now Dutch Boy hung up the phone and fixed his eyes on Krull at first not seeming to recognize him. Then he said, "You. God damn where the fuck've you been." It did not seem to Krull to be a question requiring an answer.

Krull tossed the bills onto the table which was an ancient kitchen table with an enamel top, badly scratched now, and stained. It was an enamel table of the kind Krull recalled from his grandparents' kitchen, Zoe's parents' kitchen in some long-ago time when they'd gone to visit almost every Sunday.

Now Krull wasn't sure if the old people were still alive. If they'd have wanted to see him, his face that would remind them of Delray's face.

The floor was linoleum splotched like bubbles. There were several windows layered in grime but emitting the waning sun, like Technicolor. A chemical stink pervaded the air, a sharp smell of fertilizer. Nitrogen? Krull had nothing to do with the cooking of the drug, he was wary of its dangers and had no intention of becoming involved in its preparation if he'd been asked, which he had not. No one in the house seemed to notice this strong chemical stink except Krull and then only when he first arrived. Dutch Boy was in a mood, excitable as Sarabeth had warned, and anxious. Possibly something had gone wrong. Dutch Boy wore his black-vinyl leather vest, his bare chest beneath clam-colored and concave, hairless. Dutch Boy's nipples were pinched little berries. His shoulders and upper arms were scrawny, he appeared to have no muscle-tissue at all. His dyed-brass hair was brown now at the roots. Except for his stubbled jaws and flamey eyes and creases in his face he might've been a kid dressed for Hallowe'en, a figure to smile at. As he spoke to Krull trying to address something urgent in a strangulated stream of words, his stained teeth shone. His eyes appeared mismatched, unfocused and yet he seemed to be making a genuine effort to speak reasonably to Krull, to convince Krull of something, perhaps to warn Krull, to threaten Krull but somehow his words came out garbled as in a language foreign to both Krull and himself. Krull murmured *Yeh, right. O.K.* in a placating voice. He'd been looking and had not seen any gun visible. Sometimes Dutch Boy kept a pistol in plain sight, sometimes one of his Enfield Military rifles, and there was the twelve-gauge Rottweil shotgun somewhere at close hand. So far as

Krull knew, Dutch Boy had never fired any of these weapons except at targets, fence posts and scavenger birds. Scattered on the enamel-topped table were Dutch Boy's notebooks, pages filled with the elaborate cross-hatchings of a certain kind of comic strip drawing, and Dutch Boy's own comic-strip figures, as well as intricate designs of whirling suns or atoms, grinning skulls, evil-clown faces. It was Dutch Boy's fantasy he'd be an acclaimed cartoonist someday, in the style of R. Crumb.

Krull went on to use the toilet, in a back hall. Dutch Boy continued to speak at Krull's retreating back.

What happened next, Krull would have no recollection. Emerging from the toilet at the rear of the house and there's a flash of headlights turning into the driveway, had to be unexpected since Dutch Boy became so upset. Krull heard Dutch Boy curse as a child might curse in a whimper and there went Dutch Boy limping out onto the veranda and there came three gunshots in rapid succession, loud as if they'd exploded an inch from Krull's head. A moment of silence then like the silence following a thunderclap and then Sarabeth's voice—"Oh no, no. Oh God *no*." Krull saw from a window that a bearded man—was this Metz?—looking enough like Duncan Metz to be his brother—was sinking to his knees at the side of the house where he'd fled stumbling, and there came Dutch Boy shrieking, "Fuck! You f-fuck!" after him as he tried to crawl away into tall grasses moaning and whimpering, and bright blood glistened across his back. If this was Metz, Dutch Boy had not the slightest fear of him for Krull saw Dutch Boy rush at him and fire point-blank into the back of his head and he fell forward with no resistance. Dutch Boy kicked at the writhing body, furious. Another shot, and a great well of blood escaped now from the fallen man's head.

All this happened more rapidly than Krull could comprehend. Almost, than Krull could see.

Like in lacrosse, you can't always see. The plays are so swift, when the players are good, your eyes trail after.

Krull wondering *Is that Metz? Coming from—where?*

Thinking *If I can get through this, I will never deal again.*

Krull backed away from the window. Behind him Sarabeth was moaning, keening. Dutch Boy limped back into the house excitedly muttering to himself and waving the gun in his right hand. It was a pistol with a long barrel, heavy, mean-looking, could be a forty-five caliber, Krull was sure he'd never seen before. Dutch Boy's crazed meth eyes fastened on him. Dutch Boy gestured with the gun at him. "Y-you. K-K-Krull what're you l-l-looking at." Krull felt the dangerous impulse to laugh but managed not to laugh, in fact it was a calm sort of panic *Either he will kill me now, or he will not*. Beside the sink was a drawer yanked partway open, Krull tried to peer inside to see if there might be something in the drawer, a knife for instance, a long-handled knife, he might use to defend himself, but there came Dutch Boy panting like a winded dog, "K-K-Krull? You never saw that, K-Krull—right?" and quickly Krull said that was right, he had not seen anything, and Dutch Boy said, "God damn I thought I could trust that sonbitch, see what he made me do," and Krull said, "That wasn't Duncan, was it?" and Dutch Boy said, "Who? Wasn't—who?" and Krull said, "Just so you know, Dutch, you can trust *me*." Inside the drawer was what appeared to be a hunting knife but Krull knew he couldn't remove the knife from the drawer, couldn't hope to use the knife even if he could get his fingers around it in a clutter of other utensils, there wouldn't have been time.

"K-Krull? You listening to me?"

A spasm of itching overcame Dutch Boy. With the barrel of the pistol he scratched at his left armpit and at his chest shiny with sweat beneath the vinyl vest. In this instant Krull turned blindly and pushed his way out of the back door of the house. In this instant outdoors in the fresher air running panicked and stumbling through sweet-smelling tall grasses and wild rose briars that clawed at him. Dutch Boy was calling, "K-Krull! K-K-Krull!" in a rising voice like a hurt and aggrieved child. Dutch Boy fired a shot, Krull heard the bullet whistle past and disappear into the grasses. Krull ran not glancing back wanting to think that Dutch Boy had only just fired into the air, a warning shot, Dutch Boy would not want to shoot *him*. Wasn't Krull Dutch Boy's lieutenant? Dutch Boy's right-hand man?

Maybe this was a way of indicating that Krull was fired and would be replaced and so Krull ran between a part-collapsed barn and the remains of a barbed-wire fence. Behind him Dutch Boy was shouting and another time fired the gun. Krull heard Sarabeth's thin uplifted voice, and another voice, male, that might've belonged to Jimmy Weggens.

Head-on Krull ran. Ducking and weaving like an animal that has already been wounded, desperate to save its life.

. . . stumbling through marshy fields. Could not risk returning to his car. The sun had vanished now as if it had never been. Sweet damp grasses as tall as his head, and rich soft black earth, a din of peepers, tiny tree frogs. Krull's feet were wet. Krull's head pounded with pain. It was the post-meth headache, the brain's arteries were swollen. Wiping at his face, nape of his neck felt like it was bleeding. (Maybe one of Dutch Boy's bullets had grazed him. Maybe Dutch Boy assumed he was wounded and would crawl away to die like a gut-shot deer.) How many miles he'd half-run stumbling and panting through fields, formerly cultivated fields now given over to weeds, spare stands of trees, thunder rumbling in the eastern part of the sky, in the foothills of the Adirondacks. Hiked along a two-lane blacktop road with no name, hoped he might catch a ride except when headlights swung up out of the dark he ducked away to hide in the underbrush. He had to figure that Dutch Boy and Jimmy Weggens would be pursuing him. By chance then coming upon the railroad track he'd seen at Booneville Junction here elevated to a height of about five feet and Krull hiked along the track in what he surmised to be the direction of Sparta however many miles away, Christ he had no idea. Instinctively you know to head downhill, toward a river. The river was the Black River and in that direction was home. Finally exhausted somewhere in the night Krull stumbled upon what seemed to have been a weighing shed beside the track and inside the earthen-floored shed partly covered by strips of tar paper he lay down cautiously, exhausted and curling upon himself like a kicked dog. Freezing-cold for May, and damp seeping into his bones. Zoe was saying *Just keep warm you can do it hon. Just keep breathing. Love ya!* Felt like his heart was mangled he missed Zoe so. Christ he missed

Delray. He'd come to terms with losing Zoe he'd thought but Delray there was a chance he'd see again. Hadn't tried hard enough to find his father and now it was almost too late. Already he was forgetting what had happened at Dutch Boy's. Had to be some logic to it. Always a logic if you know the circumstances. *Follow the money trail* Delray advised. Sank into an exhausted sleep. Woke and slept again and woke hearing at a distance the furious spittle-edged voice trying to explain something to him except the language was unintelligible. Then Delray crouched beside him explaining which tool to use. Now the language was clear, Krull's heart was flooded with warmth. *The wrench is used like this, and like this. This screwdriver is what's called a Phillips. See?—the little cross at the tip. I can teach you.* Above them was the chassis of a vehicle like a gigantic insect showing its skeleton beneath. Crankshaft, transmission. Fuel line. His child-fingers fumbled the tool and Pa closed his fingers around his and lifted the wrench. *See Aaron, I can teach you. Take your time.* He had not remembered where the hell he was, it came as a shock to wake in the shed on the freezing earthen floor on strips of tar paper and his backbone stiff and joints aching with cold as he'd imagine an old man's joints. From rough reckless lacrosse you acquired aches, sprains, hairline breaks in your bones that would show up years later, older guys claimed. Play your heart out when you're a kid it's the only time you will have, what the hell what comes later. An old man at forty-five. Limping at fifty. Arthritis, slipped discs. He was staring at something moving on the ruined wall. Shadows or a ripple of something outside, and alive. *Hey kid. It's me, kid.* Krull pulled himself up, crawled to the shed entrance and looked outside. It was still night. It was not a true dawn. Gusts of wind stirred broken things on all sides. Flurry of wind in the trees. Hairs at the nape of his neck stirred. Jesus it was a terrible thing to see Pa out there so strangely calm, not twelve feet away. Delray was standing as if bracing himself against the trunk of a large deciduous tree. Pa's dark-stained face was striated, as if creased at an angle. It was a disfigured face, a freak's face, Krull stared astonished. *Kid it's a long time now. Let me go O.K. kid? I'm tired.* And then waking at dawn to discover that the figure he'd believed

to be his father standing with unnatural rigidity against a tree was in fact
a dense striated covering of fungus on a dead tree trunk; ridges of pale
parasitic growth that looked like miniature shingle boards set at uniform
angles. Krull had never seen anything like this fungus-growth that must
have been fifteen feet high, clamped to the tree and eclipsing the very
base of the tree. The fungus-growth had sucked the life from the great
tree, only swaths of dead leaves remained on the broken and tattered
limbs. There was a kind of face in the fungus, a human face if you stared
hard enough but you would not want to approach the fungus to see the
face, and the suffering in the face, at close range.

"Hey there. You needin' a ride?"

A farmer's flat-bed truck approached. Headlights in mist. Krull had
washed his stubbly lacerated face and wetted his quill-hair with ditch
water, adjusted his filthy and torn clothing and walked into the road with
some measure of dignity like middle-aged Delray easing off the Harley-
Davidson, not letting on how his back throbbed with pain. Jesus! You
could pretend to be almost anything you weren't, there were so few things
you could actually *be*.

"Yes I am. Needin a ride. Thanks!"

Conscious of this good luck he had not deserved Krull was driven
eleven miles across the Black River and into Sparta as the city on its steep
glacial hills passed from mist-shrouded dawn to day, to a haze of pale
sunshine; yet some lights continued to burn, streetlights, billboard lights,
porch lights on houses; something about these lights left on struck Krull
as poignant, or sad; or maybe hopeful. And the farmer—whose name
was Floyd Donahower—whose hand Krull shook—who by purest chance
was delivering his malfunctioning John Deere tractor to Kruller's Auto
Repair where he'd known the owner Delray for a long time—brought
Krull to Quarry Road and to his home, he had not thought he would
ever see again; and late that afternoon at the garage the phone rang in
Delray's office and Krull answered it and it was a girl's breathy voice in
his ear, Sarabeth informing Krull that Dutch Boy wanted him to know
there were no "hard feelings" or a "wish for retribution" on his side and

that the problem had been "dealt with"—buried in a rotted old mound of hay and manure behind the barn.

To this, Krull could think of no reply. He'd been working on the tractor fuel line, he'd about repaired the damage. His hands were greasy and just slightly shaky but he was managing.

"Krull? Are you there?"

Krull murmured a sound to indicate *yes*.

"I was so scared last night! Not sure all that happened—I mean, I didn't see any of it—I wasn't exactly *there*. But it's over now, I guess. Things will work out, Dutch Boy says. He just wants you to know—what I told you."

Krull said, "That sounds good. Tell Dennis, good."

He would clean up his life. He was not yet twenty-two. *There's some things I can teach you* Delray had promised. Krull would look to see what these might be.

Part

Three

1

ON THIS DAY I saw him: Aaron.

He'd seen me. He'd been waiting for me. Before he could speak I said his name: "Aaron."

It had been years. Yet Aaron Kruller inhabited my dreams. My most intimate dreams, I would never have shared with anyone else including Aaron Kruller.

"Krista."

He spoke my name flatly. There was no music in his voice, no sign of yearning. And his eyes were narrowed, wary. The eyes of a man of thirty-four years who has lived each of those years and yet calmly I thought *He has come to take me back to Sparta.*

I thought *No love like your first.*

THE HOPE IN THEIR EYES! So blinding sometimes, I have to look away.

Or maybe it's fury. Smoldering-hot acid-fury jammed up inside their ulcerated bowels.

Claude Loomis, for instance. With his pretense of not-remembering me though it has been less than two months since I've seen him in this room, at this very table.

And the way he jerks forward in what appear to be erratic and involuntary muscular twitches against the edge of the metal-topped table that separates us. His voice is a low barely audible mutter *Ma'am? Din't hear you.* His shoulders are bony and misshapen in a way to make you wonder if, beneath the khaki-colored prison uniform, you'd see evidence of amputation, wings sheared bluntly off at the shoulders. *Ma'am din't hear you ma'am.* Mock-courteous, screwing up one side of his purplish-black pitted and whorled face and cupping a hand to his ear, that's pulpy and mutilated.

The ear, that is. Pulpy, mutilated, but "healed."

Between us on the grimy rectangular table is a Plexiglas partition approximately eight inches high. A barrier between civilian-visitor and client-prisoner that must be purely symbolic, suggestive. For either of us could reach over it before a guard could intervene. Lunge, and grab over it.

. . . ma'am? Say that again ma'am?

Claude Loomis has been incarcerated in the New York State Correctional Facility for Men at Newburgh since 1991 on charges of second-degree homicide, assault with a deadly weapon, possession of an unlicensed firearm, and resisting arrest. He is in the eleventh year of a twenty-five-year-to-life sentence and his face has come to resemble one of those primitive-mask faces in certain paintings of Picasso's, the residue of a face that has melted and congealed numerous times. There is a savage white sickle-scar on his upper lip that looks like a living thing and his eyes are shiny-dark and protuberant as if a tremendous pressure were being exerted upon them from inside his skull.

Ma'am din't I tell you! Tryin' damn hard to remember. . . .

Ma'am is what they call me, mostly. Mumbled and near-inaudible like a sound of phlegm at the back of the mouth. *Ma'am* because they don't recall my name from one visit to the next or my name seems problematic because unless you see *Diehl* spelled out it sounds like *Deal* and *Deal* sounds wrong, for the name of an individual whose work is to represent indigent prisoners whose sentences are being investigated or are under appeal.

(Is "Claude Loomis" an invented name? Yes. I am professionally and ethically bound to respect the privacy and confidentiality of all the clients in my caseload.)

(As "Krista Diehl"—the name I have given myself in this document—is an invented name, by just a few letters.)

As I speak to Claude Loomis, as I explain why I am here, what I am hoping to do for him, he stares at me with his yellow-tinged protuberant eyes narrowed in distrust. Here is a man who has been disappointed in the past—not by me, but by someone very like me. Once, he'd been younger and more hopeful and thus disappointed, wounded in his hope. To hope is to risk too much, like baring your throat to a stranger.

It doesn't seem to matter how many times I have come to meet with Claude Loomis. I am a nervously smiling white woman and I am seated on the civilian-visitor side of the table with my back to the door and just outside the door is a guard. I am the stranger.

Ma'am what is your business Claude Loomis asked me, at our first meeting several months ago and I said *My business is helping.*

And Claude Loomis laughed baring big stained teeth *Ma'am that so? Ain't much money in that business is there?*

The guard outside the door is a burly white man from Catskill named Emmet: he has told me, I've asked him, unlike my more aggressive professional colleagues I am always friendly with the staff of any prison or facility to which I am sent. Emmet must weigh 250 pounds, his hair is a crewcut of metal shavings, his face a ganglia of muscles. His stone-colored eyes shift on me when I approach, his mouth twitches into a smile that might be friendly, or just subtly derisive; my profession isn't respected by the prison staff community, in fact we are generally resented, disliked. For we are seeking to *overturn, vacate, release* where they are concerned with *incarceration, maintaining security.* But I'm a young blond woman—younger-looking than my age—and so I have made a friend in Emmet—haven't I? Wanting to think that this burly uniformed man isn't my enemy. Wanting to think that he will protect me if I need him. And not resent me because I've been allowed into the prison as a privileged visitor assigned an "interview" room and not made to meet with my client in the large open clamorous visitors' room where a half-dozen guards are visibly stationed.

Wanting to think, yes Emmet is my friend. An outcry from me, a sound of plastic chairs overturned, Emmet is prepared to open the door and rush inside.

Prepared to save me from Claude Loomis, if I require saving.

Mr. Loomis knows this, all prisoners know this which is why he regards me, his paralegal visitor, with ironic eyes. The lurid scar on his upper lip attracts my attention, he can see. And the purplish-dark skin, the mangled ear. Yet calmly I am explaining: ". . . these documents, Mr. Loomis?—if you could confirm . . . Sorry for the smudged photocopies—this is how they came to me! And your file is still missing a notarized birth certificate, I've tried several times to contact the Haggen County courthouse. . . ."

Haggen County, Alabama. But it's possible that no birth certificate was ever issued for Claude Loomis.

One of those American citizens not born in a hospital—as he has claimed—and no one cared to register his birth which, by my estimate, must have occurred in the mid–1950s.

No birth certificate, no Social Security number. In this stack of much-handled documents pertaining to LOOMIS, CLAUDE T. the information regarding "education history"—"employment record"—"armed services status"—"residence"—"family"—looking as if it has been filled out by someone not Mr. Loomis, is incomplete, inconsistent and unreliable.

(Is Loomis's first name Claude, in fact? On one of the older documents, the initial arrest sheet from the Newburgh Police Department, the typed name is *Cylde. Clyde?*)

In this windowless fluorescent-lit interview room, poorly ventilated, and measuring perhaps ten feet by twelve, crucial information is being sought from Claude Loomis, without conspicuous success. This interview might be taking place in a lifeboat, in a quaking sea! The light is both harshly glaring and dim. My mood is both upbeat-professional and growing-anxious. Claude Loomis is hunched over the documents I have passed to him blinking and squinting as if trying to get them into focus. *Ma'am shi–it.* The disgruntled client knows to keep his voice lowered so the guard outside the door can't hear.

Client is the correct term, not *prisoner*. The organization for which I work deals in *clients* and not *prisoners, inmates, convicts, convicted felons*. For it is our contention that the individual Claude Loomis whose case we have taken up has been wrongfully incarcerated in this maximum-security prison as the final consequence of a sequence of wrongful actions by the state: unjustified arrest—"racial profiling"—by law enforcement officers as a "suspect" in a crime or crimes; a twelve-hour "interview" that was in fact an interrogation; a "confession" by the arrested man, to be subsequently recanted; an indictment by a grand jury, despite insufficient evidence and a (recanted) confession; a trial, with an overworked and ill-prepared defense attorney; a conviction, and a prison sentence that might keep him behind bars for the remainder of his life.

For this visit I have dressed in my usual paralegal clothes: dark blue wool pants suit, white silk blouse and trim little black shoe-boots. For this visit I am determined will be a success and not a failure, I have plaited and wrapped my long silky pale-blond hair around my head, fastened with a tortoiseshell comb at the nape of my neck. I wear schoolteacher pearl earrings, an oversized (man's) watch on my left wrist. Patiently I am saying in my voice of forced calm, ". . . Mr. Loomis *please!* If you can't make out the fine print let me read it for you. What the form requires is . . ."

What the hell is Loomis doing? Hunched so far over the table, as if his spine is broken? In his skimpy record there is no indication of physical ailments other than diabetes and high blood pressure but now he seems to be jamming himself forward in a sequence of shuddery little twitches as if—I don't want to think this, *I am not thinking this*—there is something crudely sexual in his movements, and I am the object.

"Mr. Loomis! Let me read these lines. . . ."

Loomis pauses. Rubs his hands over his head, digging in his thumbs, hard. His glistening eyes remain fixed on the documents spread out before him. As I read to him I am thinking that nowhere in these documents is set down the most obvious and dispiriting fact of this man's life as a *convicted felon: convicted, though very likely innocent*: by chance Claude Loomis had been in the wrong place at the wrong time, late one Saturday night picked up by cruising Newburgh police, arrested and "identified" and charged with a robbery-homicide in the Newburgh jurisdiction that seemed to have been, judging from evidence more recently assembled, committed by another black man of Loomis's approximate age, size, and appearance/skin tone. After hours of interrogation there came to be a "confession" subsequently entered into evidence at Loomis's trial hand-written not by the defendant—who could not write but barely hand-print, in the simple way of a young child—but by a Newburgh police detective, a single sheet of paper at the bottom of which, in a space designated for a signature, Loomis's name appears as CLAUD LOMISS. There was a two-day trial, jurors conferring for forty minutes, sentencing. More than ten years so far served in the Newburgh maximum-security prison.

He'd signed a blank sheet of paper, Loomis had claimed. Not a one of the words of his "confession" was his own.

". . . your original attorney, back in 1991, it's been noted that he failed to cross-examine any of the prosecution witnesses. He failed to . . ."

Failed. Failed to! So many years.

Much of my conversation with Claude Loomis is a repeat of previous conversations. For our cases—of which the Claude Loomis case is representative—move with torturous slowness, like black muck flowing uphill. I can't determine if my client is having difficulty *seeing*—he might be myopic, or have cataracts—or if he simply can't read very well; there is the possibility that he's drugged, also; or slow-witted, or ill. I have no more real knowledge of Claude Loomis than Claude Loomis has of Krista Diehl. If Loomis is, like so many prisoners, illiterate, he wouldn't want me to know; the illiterate have their pride, as we would in their places. Or maybe he's hunched over the table squinting at the documents as a way of not looking at me; maybe he feels, not a sexual attraction, but a sexual revulsion for me. How much more comfortable Claude Loomis would be with a male paralegal, a black or Hispanic paralegal! I know this but there is nothing I can do about it.

In Sparta I learned as a girl: you play the cards you've been dealt. In this case, Krista Diehl is the cards I've been dealt, and the cards I will have to play.

With a smile saying, ever-upbeat, cheerful and encouraging: ". . . my office is optimistic about the appellate court. One of their recent decisions, Claude, overturning a conviction in a case similar to yours, 'corroboration of identification by police-informant witness' . . . the witness your attorney failed to cross-examine and to challenge . . ."

How like a lawyer I sound, though I am only a paralegal. The distinction has been explained to the client but very likely he has forgotten.

"Excuse me, Claude, could you hand the file back to me, and I will . . ."

Calling him *Claude*. Not once but twice *Claude*. Trying so hard to win his confidence.

Not wanting to think *Give up! He doesn't trust you, white girl.*

Why should this man trust you, white girl.

I take back the files from my client. Out of my paralegal's document bag have emerged these soiled manila folders, dog-eared copies of court transcripts, yellowed and brittle legal papers, stapled documents issued by the Newburgh County district attorney's office, and these have been placed on the table between us. Hundreds of pages, thousands of words. No one could hope to read and retain so many words even if his fate is contained within them. How exhausting this is, in this airless room! Like sucking oxygen through a pinched straw, desperate to breathe.

The first time I met with a client alone, unsupervised, was several years ago, not here at Newburgh but at Ossining. After a quarter of an hour I began to feel disoriented and after an hour I believed that I could hear a heavy machine in the distance throbbing, thudding, pounding but this turned out to be just blood-pulses in my head. And I've come close to fainting, and throwing up. And in fact I have fainted and I have thrown up but luckily not with anyone to witness. As Lucille said *You want to prove something with your life, like it's your life-blood you want to spill—but what? All that is over. He'll never know.*

All he'd said to me was if I didn't want to be hurt maybe I shouldn't be playing the game. But I am playing the game, and I think that I am doing all right.

At least, I haven't failed yet.

I am still young. I have plenty of time.

". . . update these forms? 'Next of kin' . . ."

Has Claude Loomis suffered a stroke in prison?—or has someone beaten him, caused a hemorrhage in his brain? That would explain the paralyzed look of half his face. If he'd been beaten, he would not have reported the assault. " . . . let me read this for you, Claude. See if we can make sense of . . ." A stale smell wafts to my nostrils, a smell of despair from Claude Loomis, or from the pile of documents. Badly I want to lay my head down on my arms, cradle my pounding head and shield my face from the fluorescent glare, shut my eyes and sink into sleep.

Is this what Claude Loomis is doing? His protruding eyes are half-shut, his eyelids are folds of reptilian flesh. When I ask if he's all right he mutters what sounds like *Ma'am!* or maybe it's *I am* or *Uhhh.*

In this maximum-security prison Claude Loomis is an old man. He's fifty at least and most prisoners are young men—white, black, Hispanic—in their twenties or early thirties. A few are older, in their forties. And Claude Loomis is physically disadvantaged. Sad to think that there's a chance he will die in this terrible place, if his case is rejected by the appeals court. Sadder to think that the man's spirit has been sucked from him, the marrow of his bones sucked dry. Even if Claude Loomis is finally granted a new trial, even if he's acquitted and released after eleven years of incarceration . . .

This trouble that came into my life.

This trouble that's the end of my life.

When surreptitiously I check my watch—this watch which had been my father's watch, with its white-gold stretch-band—to my horror I see that less than thirty minutes have passed since I entered this interview room. Thirty minutes!

To enter these places of twelve-foot stone walls topped with swirls of razor-wire, these mazelike corridors with no exit signs and heavy metallic doors that open only when a code is punched in, is to enter a primitive time. A warp in time. Though you are a "visitor"—you are "free" to enter and to depart. And when you depart you stagger out exhausted, unable to believe how relatively little time has passed since you'd entered. A single hour is many hours. A single day is many days. A month, a year. Prisoners speak of *doing time*. In such places time is effort, like physical labor.

My father was spared this, at least. He'd arranged for himself a swift execution by firing squad.

Often I dream of him—Edward Diehl. Maybe always, every night. As you dream of something knotted and gnarled in the region of your heart. As you dream of a musical chord repeated to the point of madness. As you dream of the unknowable and unsayable fact of your own death. As the city of Sparta had become, in my memory, a mute, physical sensation that made my heart contract with emotion. *Back there.*

Where I had lost them. My father, my family.

Aaron Kruller, I had loved.

For these reasons—of which I have told no one in my life at the present time—it is a profound occasion for me, to drive to the prison at Newburgh. It is a profound occasion for me to drive here alone and to enter the facility alone through its several checkpoints. The State Correctional Facility for Men at Newburgh is an antiquated stone fortress overlooking the Hudson River wind-whipped and of the hue of molten lead on this overcast November afternoon fourteen years, eleven months and five days after Edward Diehl's death.

Badly I wish that I could confide in Claude Loomis, about my father. Badly I wish that I dared touch the man's arm, his wrist—it would not be difficult for me to reach over the Plexiglas partition and touch him: lightly. My heart is beating quickly—I am so dangerously close to doing this.

Loomis peers at me, alert and wary. As if he senses something dangerous in the air between us.

Don't touch ma'am!

Of course—I would not reach over and touch Claude Loomis! Such intimate gestures are forbidden here. As *contraband* is forbidden. Any kind of personal touch, communication. Each time you enter the prison, you are so warned.

(The interview room, however, isn't under surveillance. Unless the prison authorities are secretly violating federal and state law guaranteeing the privacy/confidentiality of attorneys and clients. There is no camera here, no one is watching or listening.)

Patiently I am trying to explain to Claude Loomis the need to listen carefully to me, and to answer the questions I'm asking him—these are crucial questions. Trying not to sound exasperated with him asking how can he expect to be granted a new trial, how can he expect to be released from prison, unless he cooperates. . . .

Still Loomis stares at me, unsmiling. There is no use my trying to pretend to myself that this man trusts me, has confidence in me. Still less, that he "likes" me. His mouth twitches, his words are unintelligible, what sounds like *even if, see ma'am, they be dead, no family there'd be just me ma'am* frowning and grimacing as if he's arguing with someone. Has Claude Loomis been arguing with me all along? And I haven't understood his hostility? In one of his spasmodic twitches he knocks a manila folder off the table, my ballpoint pen flies off clattering to the floor, suddenly there's noise, excitement in the airless little box of a room. Suddenly Claude Loomis is on his feet and suddenly Claude Loomis is very angry—but why?

So quickly this has happened, afterward I won't recall the sequence of events.

Though I think that I tried to speak quietly to the agitated man, calmly and as if nothing was wrong, just yet. Urging him to please sit down, please don't speak so loudly, the guard will come into the room and our interview will end. But Claude Loomis isn't to be calmed, not by me. Not by this pissy little white-girl paralegal whose eyes are widened in fear. Loomis looks as me as if I am the enemy—he doesn't know me, doesn't remember me, a look of disgust, a look of fury, shiny dark eyes showing a rim of white above the iris like the eyes of a panicked animal. Not knowing what I am doing—maybe this was a gesture I'd made to my father, in the motel room—I reach out toward him and he curses me and throws off my hand as you'd throw off a snake.

Claude Loomis has knocked over his chair, his legs are tangled in his chair legs, violently he kicks the chair against the wall. Reaches over the Plexiglas partition to grab hold of my shoulder, tears the lapel of my navy blue wool suit, shoves me back against the wall. By this time the burly white guard has entered the room cursing Loomis—it's C.O. technique to yell at such times—to yell profanities—grabs Loomis and throws Loomis struggling to the floor. The little room rings with shouts. The men's voices are deafening. All this has happened within seconds, like a car crash. More swiftly than I can comprehend. More swiftly than I can recount. I am clutching at something, to keep upright. I am trying very hard not to faint. Not to lose control of my bladder. My head is ringing with pain—somehow, I'd been thrown against the wall. Precious papers are scattered everywhere. The case file of LOOMIS, CLAUDE T. is scattered everywhere. Documents, folders, transcripts. My leather shoulder bag, my document-bag. By this time Emmet has his prisoner belly-down, facedown on the floor. Expertly Emmet is kneeing the fallen man in the lower back, and cuffing his wrists. Loomis's wrists are thick, the metal cuffs sink into his purplish-dark flesh. Emmet jerks Loomis's wrists and arms up behind his back, to maximize the pain. This is standard procedure, like shouting profanities, obscenities. This is the great thrill of the C.O., the moment of triumph for which the C.O. waits patiently through hours of tedium, boredom. The adrenaline rush to the heart, potent as any drug. Better than sex.

Still I am trying to intervene—though the issue is now exclusively between the guard and the prisoner—between the men—I am trying to explain that what happened may have been my fault—I'd said something inappropriate—thoughtless—I'd made Loomis think of his family—the client over-reacted, he may be off his meds—it wasn't his fault—but another guard, so closely resembling Emmet he might have been a brother or a cousin, has arrived on the run, is leading me out of the interview room, when I try to resist the guard walks me forcibly—here is a man who outweighs me by at least one hundred pounds calling me *Ma'am* saying loudly *Interview's over ma'am this way out*—as I stammer trying to explain that I need to collect my legal papers, can't leave the facility without the papers, to which the guard says, scarcely troubling to disguise his contempt *Ma'am that's for the warden to say.*

DRIVING BACK TO PEEKSKILL, without the papers!

Driving back to Peekskill, chastened, trembling!

Thinking it was my mistake. A blunder of mine. Maybe, I had actually touched Claude Loomis. Mistaking him as a wounded man merely, not a man filled with rage.

Don't touch white girl. Don't come near.

When I'd first begun working as a paralegal for the non-profit organization Prosecution Watch, Inc., I'd hoped to "share"—"forge a bond with"—clients. The indigent, the mentally unstable, a disproportionate number of whom were black, Hispanic, Native American. I'd been eager and naive speaking to both women and men of my father's experience with the law in Sparta, New York. I would say *I am the daughter of a man who was murdered by law enforcement officers. A man who died not because he had committed a crime but because he was suspected of having committed a crime.*

I would say *My father died of being a suspect.*

I would not say that I'd seen my father die. That I'd been a witness to my father writhing in agony in a hail of bullets he'd summoned to him yet in terror tried to ward off with uplifted outspread hands. I would not say *My father took me hostage.*

No need to say *My father took me hostage out of despair, because he loved me. He would never have hurt me.*

No need to say *Daddy loved me, why would Daddy have hurt me!*

Seeing Daddy's hands sometimes, in the hands of strangers. In Claude Loomis's more mangled hands in fact. Daddy's strong capable hands, the fingers broad and stubbed, a workingman's hands.

Sometimes my words were effective, to a degree. That was what I thought.

At other times, no. The client would stare at me indifferently, or with a sneer. Or maybe he hadn't been listening. My little moment of drama fell flat. In my vanity hoping to communicate *Look, I understand! I am one of you, because of my father. Don't push me from you, I am here to share and to help* but they'd seen through me, they had not been seduced.

And so, I rarely speak of my father any longer. Never do I utter the name "Edward Diehl." With colleagues and friends and when it's awkward to avoid acknowledging that my father is "no longer living" and that he'd died "years ago, when I was a girl" in Sparta, New York, in that hilly region at the western edge of the Adirondacks.

And now, I have no "hometown"—only just temporary places in which I live. Since we all left Sparta—my parents, my brother Ben, and me.

"AARON."

Before he could speak, I said his name. I'd recognized him immediately.

He was waiting for me in the corridor outside my office. The office I shared with several other paralegals. Though we had not seen each other in many years he spoke my name flatly, bluntly: "Krista."

Not smiling and not reaching out his hand to shake mine as people do, in my profession—instead I reached out my hand, and gripped his.

"Aaron! It's wonderful to see you . . ."

So soon after the incident at Newburgh, I was feeling light-headed, unreal. A faint roaring in my ears which often I heard when I was overworked and fatigued and now the thought came to me *He has come to take me back to Sparta.*

And *No love like your first!*

(Maybe this was Lucille's voice, mocking. The less I saw of my mother in recent years, the more deeply imprinted her voice in my head.)

Such ease in speech, such warmth in my greeting and a smile that suggested confidence, assurance were not qualities in Aaron Kruller's life,

I could see. He seemed embarrassed, awkward. He'd located me here in Peekskill through relatives of mine in Sparta, he said. He was wearing a sheepskin jacket, work-boots. His dark hair grew thick and wiry and had begun to recede from his forehead. His angular face had filled out, thickened. Still his skin was pitted and faintly scarred and his eyes were steely and unsettling as I remembered. Those eyes I'd seen in the water-splotched mirror above the sink in Aaron's aunt's apartment, that night.

Despite my poise I was shocked to see him. This would be one of the shocks of my adult life.

Why hadn't he called me first, I didn't want to ask. It would have seemed impolite to ask. Why, instead of driving three hundred miles on the chance that he would see me?—there was something dogged and fatalistic in this, the sort of thing my father might have done, driving halfway across the state with the hope of seeing or at least speaking with my mother—or Ben, or me. Not daring to call first, in fear of being rebuffed.

Or maybe, being the person he was, Aaron Kruller hadn't wanted any confrontation that wasn't face-to-face. Maybe telephone conversations put him at a disadvantage. It was a perverse sort of male shyness, in the most aggressive and masculine of men.

When I'd returned to the office from the debacle at the Newburgh prison, I was relieved to see that my supervisor wasn't in. Instead one of the staff lawyers told me that someone was waiting for me upstairs. Is he a client, I said, I don't think that I can face a client right now. The lawyer said he didn't think so. Then: "Or maybe he was, and he isn't now."

Aaron had come to tell me surprising news: there was someone in Sparta with new information about what had happened to Zoe, and she wanted to tell Aaron and me, at the same time.

"'New information'—? What is it?"

"She won't say—she wants us to visit her, together."

It had to be Jacky DeLucca, I thought. That woman who'd befriended me in the brownstone on West Ferry Street, who'd kissed the top of my head with a strange heated ardor, and sent me away. Aaron had no way of knowing that I knew Zoe's roommate. He said that the woman who wanted to see us had been "a close friend, like a sister" to Zoe at the time of her death, who was dying now of cancer and wanted to reveal something to us before it was too late.

"That's what she calls it—'reveal.' To the two of us, together."

In his flat blunt voice Aaron managed to disguise any excitement he might have been feeling.

We were in my office now—the office space divided into cubicles for paralegals like me. Aaron had seemed reluctant to follow me into the room. Maybe he thought that Prosecution Watch, Inc. was a government agency, aligned with the local county prosecutor's office. Maybe he thought I was a lawyer, I had left Sparta to join forces with the world of law courts, law enforcement officers, statutes and penalties. Without exactly looking at me he spoke slowly and with an air of strain like one exerting force against a barely yielding object. I thought—he was still working at Kruller's Auto Repair! He was still living the old Sparta life, that had exuded a kind of romance at one time, a romance exclusively masculine, physical. Ordinary speech was an effort to him, near-painful, as this subject was painful to him.

I remembered how he'd taken me from Duncan Metz's hard hands— literally. I remembered when we were together in his aunt's bathroom, and later in his car, he'd spoken very little to me, yet communicated so much. I thought *He is ashamed, even now. He remembers what he did.*

I thought *He has no idea how I wanted it. Whatever he could do to me, I'd wanted.*

In his manner Aaron reminded me of my brother Ben whom I saw now only once or twice a year, at our mother's home in Port Oriskany in the western part of the state.

Lucille had remarried. Her husband was fifteen years older than she was, a semi-retired manufacturer's representative with a Port Oriskany ball bearings company, a self-defined Christian. Lucille's life was not the old Sparta life, she'd cast from her with the desperation with which one might cast off a water-logged coat, to save oneself from drowning.

"'Jacky DeLucca.' I haven't seen her in twenty years."

If Aaron was surprised to know that I knew Jacky DeLucca's name, he gave no sign. When I pressed him more about what Jacky DeLucca might have to tell us he shrugged saying he didn't know, and he didn't want to speculate. Speaking of his mother hadn't been easy for him, even now. His flat upstate voice had quavered, just perceptibly: *Zoe.*

The reckless impulse came to me, to mime Zoe Kruller in her white Honeystone's uniform. *Well say! Thought it was you.*

In that throaty intimate voice *What can I do you for today?*

And that sly hungry smile. Those hungry eyes.

Aaron was looking at me more openly now. I saw the hunger in those eyes, too: the sexually aggressive male, not entirely certain of his power over me, over the person I'd become. I wondered if he was remembering: the old connection between us.

In his aunt Viola's bathroom. In those minutes his aunt had been elsewhere. Aaron Kruller forcing his weight on me, on my back; Aaron Kruller's hands tightening around my neck.

A flush rose into his face. He remembered. He said:

". . . should leave tonight. Now. I'll drive you there, Krista."

"Tonight! I can't leave tonight. . . ."

This was totally a surprise. My pretense of calm seeing Aaron Kruller here in my office after seventeen years had begun to waver.

But Aaron insisted: "We can get to Sparta by at least eleven o'clock tonight, if we leave now. Then in the morning we can go see DeLucca. On the phone she told me, 'Mornings are my best time.'"

I began to stammer. I was feeling light-headed now, disoriented. It was shameful and astonishing to me, I'd begun to feel a low throbbing sexual yearning, in the man's presence. Though saying, "Aaron, you can't be serious! I can't leave for Sparta tonight. I don't have the kind of job I can just walk away from. I will need . . ." Rapidly my mind worked, thoughts spinning like wheels in mud. I was indignant, insulted. I wanted Aaron Kruller to know that my life was an important life, my responsibilities were considerable despite the small shared office, the utilitarian desk and somber surroundings decorated by unframed wall posters of paintings by Georgia O'Keeffe, Edward Hopper. "I will need to make arrangements about my work, I have appointments all day tomorrow, I'm due to visit Ossining. I'd need to reserve a motel room in Sparta. . . ."

"You can stay with relatives, can't you? Or with my aunt Viola, she knows you're coming."

Knows you're coming. Here was a man used to making decisions forcibly and without opposition; a man accustomed to giving orders.

I told him no, I didn't want to stay with relatives. I didn't want to stay with his aunt. He said he could call a motel for me, from his car. When we approached Sparta—"If you're anxious about this."

He'd been fingering his car keys. He was impatient to be moving on. In his face there was a glimmer of male superiority, subtly sexual, coercive. It was unconscious in him, I felt a stab of dislike. Badly I wanted to protest: Why hadn't he called me, before coming all the way to Peekskill? Why, in seventeen years, hadn't he made any attempt to contact me?

What had hurt was, when my father died, Aaron had not called me. Had not tried to see me. There was the deep, intimate connection between us, deeper than the connection between Ben and me, that could not be undone.

For Aaron Kruller had felt the blood beating in my throat. He'd felt my life coursing through me. And I'd felt the heat and urgency of his male-adolescent body, through his hands and through his groin he'd ground against me, in a trance of desire. There had been nothing like this in my life, there would be nothing like this in my adult life, what had passed between us could never be undone.

It was only by chance that I'd returned to the brownstone offices of Prosecution Watch, Inc. on Seventh Street, Peekskill, instead of returning home. Though it was past 4:00 P.M. and a number of my colleagues, as well as my supervisor, had departed. What had happened in the prison had badly shaken me, the back of my head throbbed with pain and humiliation, my navy blue wool jacket had been torn, my plaited hair was partly undone. I could not bear the emptiness of the apartment that awaited me.

"I can leave in an hour or so, I suppose. But I have to go home first. And I'll drive my own car to Sparta."

"No. I'm driving."

"And then—what? You'd drive me back to Peekskill, tomorrow?"

"Sure. I can do that."

"Six hours? That's ridiculous, Aaron."

Casually I spoke his name: "Aaron." I wanted this name to sound flat, ordinary. I wanted it to sound like a name that meant nothing to me. The man had called me "Krista" in this way—I had to wonder if it had been deliberate.

Were we quarreling? There was the sense that Aaron Kruller didn't like to be contradicted in even small matters. He'd planned on driving me to Sparta with him, and now I was objecting, quite sensibly I was objecting, as Aaron might have anticipated that I would object; it was only common sense for me to take my own car. Maybe he didn't trust me to drive capably enough to get there, and it was crucial that I come with him so that Jacky DeLucca could speak to us both, together.

Or maybe he wanted us to be together, in his car. On the drive back to Sparta in the night, north along the Thruway bounded by stretches of desolate landscape. Arriving late at a Sparta motel.

No love like your first.

I felt a constriction in my chest, a need to resist the man's will, to oppose him. I was not a Sparta girl now, I was a young woman employed by Prosecution Watch, Inc.; I had university degrees, I supported myself and lived alone. I was not married or engaged: my left hand was ringless. There were men in my life but not crucial to my life. I wanted Aaron Kruller to sense this.

I told him that I would drive myself. I told him that I was a capable driver. I said he could keep my car in view as we drove, ahead of him on the Thruway.

He objected that in one car, it would be easier. If it began snowing, as it was predicted upstate.

Predicted upstate? I had not known this.

"Probably you aren't used to driving at night, Krista. I am."

"How do you know—'probably'?"

"Are you? For six hours?"

Six hours. I felt a touch of panic. In my exhausted state, this was folly. This was not a good idea. Yet I would not retract my words, I would drive by myself, and I would leave within an hour. I said:

"I want my own car, Aaron. Without my own car, I'm not going at all."

Rebuffed, Aaron finally gave in. He laughed, to show he was a good sport. "O.K., Krista. Have it your way."

EXCEPT IF YOU HAVE A GHOST LEG THAT HURTS LIKE HELL

YOU CAN'T GET AN ARTIFICIAL LEG TO WORK

On the windowsill facing my desk this remark made by a client of mine is affixed, in hand-printed letters on stiff paper.

I would have liked Aaron Kruller to have noticed it, and commented on it. But that wasn't Aaron Kruller's way.

My client was a heavyset diabetic woman sentenced to an indeterminate "life" sentence on a charge of second-degree murder, for having stabbed her chronically abusive husband to death in 1974. By the time her case had been brought to the attention of Prosecution Watch, Inc., Jasmine had been incarcerated in Lyndhurst for twenty-seven years. She'd had inadequate medical treatment for her diabetes, her right foot had become gangrenous and had had to be amputated; eventually, her entire right leg had had to be amputated. She continued to feel sensation in these missing parts, sometimes severe pain.

Yet, Jasmine believed that the "ghost pain"—the phantom pain—was necessary so that, in her mind, she could locate the missing foot and leg. Without the pain, she couldn't have used the artificial leg she'd been fitted with.

The non-profit organization for which I worked succeeded in getting

Jasmine's second-degree murder charge reduced to voluntary manslaughter and so Jasmine was released from prison for "time served"—after nearly twenty-nine years.

Which was three times the amount of time she'd have probably served under the lesser charge.

By then, Jasmine was sixty-one. You could say that most of her life had been taken from her and was lost to her but Jasmine had not been bitter, she'd been grateful. No client of Prosecution Watch, Inc. had ever been more grateful.

Thank you THANK YOU! You have given me back my life and my hope Krista.

Taking my hands in hers. My smooth unmangled white-girl hands in her sixty-one-year-old dark-skinned hands that trembled with emotion. And when taking my hands wasn't enough Jasmine hugged me, hard.

Know what Krista, I'm praying for you. You are the one I am praying for not me, my prayers are answered.

I wanted to think it was true, I had helped to give this woman back her life and her hope.

I wanted to think it was true, though I had virtually no power to modify my own past, and what remained of my future, yet I could help others like Jasmine. I could do this!

Through the power of Prosecution Watch, Inc., I could try to do this.

In my office that afternoon, I'd hoped that Aaron Kruller would notice the statement on my windowsill. I'd hoped that he would pause, and peer at it, curiously; read it aloud, as other visitors had done, and ask me about it; and so I would tell him its genesis, and what it meant.

Aaron would say *That's wonderful Krista.*

Or, Aaron would say *Krista that is profound. That is something to think about Krista.*

Or *What wonderful work you've done, to bring justice to people who've been cheated of it. Like your father, and mine.*

Of course, Aaron Kruller said none of these things. Aaron Kruller may have glanced at the printed statement on the windowsill, but he had not come nearer, to read it; still less, to read it aloud in a wondering voice. Instead he said he'd wait for me downstairs at the front entrance, badly he needed a cigarette and there was no smoking in this building.

On the Thruway Aaron followed me in his car which was a new-model Buick. My car was a 1999 Saab bought from a colleague at a great bargain. In my rearview mirror his headlights held steady. In these driving conditions—icy rain, wind—I could not drive beyond sixty miles an hour. I mean, I did not want to drive beyond sixty miles an hour. Behind me Aaron Kruller was patient, overseeing. After seventeen years he was protective of me again. I wanted to think so.

My thoughts were in a turmoil: Aaron Kruller had re-entered my life.

Though in ways that would have been astonishing to him, he had never left my life.

And Jacky DeLucca. Of whom women like my mother had said contemptuously *Has she no shame?*

Or maybe it was Zoe Kruller of whom my mother had spoken. The two women, living together on West Ferry Street. "Cocktail waitresses" out on the Strip. A way of saying "hookers"—who deserved whatever happened to them at the hands of men.

Lucille Bauer had not lacked for shame. Not her! My mother's soul saturated in shame as in grease.

Driving north along the Thruway, I recalled Jacky DeLucca: the pale, heavy, vividly made-up face, the widened beseeching eyes and a craving for love so powerful it smelled of her fleshy body. *Zoe was my heart* she'd said wistfully stroking my arm, making me shiver for it was a strange intimate thing for an adult woman to say unlike anything my mother was likely to say in even a weak emotional moment.

Come back to see me Krissie promise?

I'd promised. But I'd never gone back.

No one called me *Krissie* now. No one in my family, even. Not since Sparta.

Only Daddy had loved me in that way, I thought. That way that was unconditional, unquestioning. Which did not mean that Daddy might not be cruel to me—but Daddy had loved me, so Daddy's cruelty had been just a part of Daddy's love. *You know your Daddy loves you Puss don't you* and I had known, yes.

Trying to recall, how Zoe Kruller had come into our lives. One afternoon when I'd returned unexpectedly from school, and there Zoe was—in our kitchen! She had entered my mother's kitchen once my mother was away, like a princess in a fairy tale entering a beggar's hut and always with surprising consequences. I seemed to have known, even as a girl, that Zoe Kruller had entered other rooms in my mother's house, like my mother's bedroom, she had shared with my father.

My mother's bed, beneath the beautiful oyster-white crocheted quilt that was an "heirloom"—Zoe had entered that bed, too.

There was no mistaking this: Zoe had looked at me with loving eyes, Zoe had looked at me and called me *Krissie!*

Zoe had given me an ice-cream cone infested with weevils! I'd had a hard time forgiving Zoe for that, and for my father's anger at me afterward. But I'd forgiven her of course.

Though thinking how unfair it had been, Daddy had seemed to blame me for the weevils. And if the person who'd sold us the cone had not been Zoe Kruller, Daddy would have been happy to bring me back inside Honeystone's for a new cone, for no charge.

Back there, and *back then*. It's better not to think of it, that numbing wound in the region of the heart.

At the Amsterdam exit beyond Albany, we left the Thruway for a late meal. This, too, Aaron had planned. It was nearly 8:30 P.M., we had not made good time on the Thruway which was still thunderous and perilous at this hour with enormous trucks. In the dimly lighted and inexplicably named Lighthouse Café attached to the cinder block Wile-A-Way Motor Court we sat stiffly self-conscious across from each other in a booth. *An ill-matched couple. Something wrong between them. Not looking at each other—why?* Aaron was leaning on his elbows, on the tabletop, rubbing his fists in his eyes, yawning. He'd driven approximately six hours to

Peekskill, to get to me; now he was driving back to Sparta with virtually no rest in between.

An obsessive and willful personality. A dangerous personality perhaps.

We tried to assess our clients before we took them on. If their personalities were likely to bear up under the strain of a re-opening of their cases, a re-investigation, possibly a retrial; for some of them were long-incarcerated, and had given up hope. Some of them, in prison, had become mentally deranged. The ideal goal was a commutation of sentence, a governor's unqualified pardon, a prosecutor dropping all charges and a judge ruling a sentence void. But a *retrial* was a double-edged goal.

Returning to Sparta was something of a *retrial*. I would wonder how good an idea this sudden decision had been.

A waitress came to take our orders. Clearly she was attracted to Aaron, they laughed together like old friends, Aaron's eyes moved over her with easy familiarity but with me, he was quiet. He seemed not to know what to make of me. There was an obduracy in him, an air of self-possession that excluded me. I was hurt, and I was angry. I was chagrined.

There was something sexual here, I could not interpret. As in my office Aaron had disdained to take much notice of the surroundings, the colorful posters on my wall or the card on the windowsill.

Finally, drinking ale, Aaron asked me how I was doing?—but he meant the Thruway drive, not my current life.

I told him that I was fine.

I told him that I was accustomed to driving alone and often in bad weather, I liked driving alone. I told him that I listened to music.

I told Aaron that I'd been listening to Bach harpsichord preludes and fugues, clavier concertos. I told him there's no one like Bach to calm the mind—"To give hope."

Aaron said he'd been listening to Axe, Mr. Big, Metallica. He had satellite radio, he said. In the trucks he drove, tow, flat-bed—he'd had satellite radio installed, too.

He spoke in a flat slightly sneering tone. There came that sharp little barking laughter, that grated against my nerves.

Did I know what satellite radio was? I wasn't sure. I had never heard of Axe, Mr. Big, Metallica. But I could imagine what this music was.

Aaron had removed his sheepskin jacket and jammed it in a corner of the booth. The cuffs of his flannel shirt were unbuttoned, rolled up. I stared at his muscular forearms, what I could glimpse of purplish-spiderweb tattoos. I stared at his hands with their large knuckles, covered in scars. And the thick man's-nails, edged with grease. A workingman's hands. Like my father's. I thought *He knows that I loved him, then.*

He could not know how I felt about him now. I wanted to think that I had no discernible feelings for him, now.

Aaron ate quickly, distractedly. He ate like one accustomed to eating alone, paying little mind to food. He drank, ale from the bottle. He would have lighted a cigarette midway in the meal, but smoking was forbidden in the Lighthouse Café.

I had to know: was Jacky DeLucca going to tell us who had killed Zoe? Was this the secret Jacky DeLucca would "reveal," after nearly twenty years? Yet I could not ask.

For how to utter such words to Aaron Kruller: *kill*, *Zoe*. It was not possible.

In the Lighthouse Café in our dimly-lit booth, in the background a throb of music, the murmurous voices of other customers, I was made to think of the County Line Tavern to which my father had taken me that evening. I felt now a sensation of vertigo, helplessness. To think that my father had been alive then, and was not alive now; as Aaron Kruller was alive now, seated across from me.

How distracting Aaron's presence was! His hands that reminded me of my father's hands, badly I wanted to take hold of those hands. As if a fissure had opened in the earth before me, one of those nightmare incidents that occur from time to time, you read of in the newspaper, in fact such an incident had occurred at the Sparta Gypsum quarry when I'd been a girl: a worker driving a bulldozer had fallen into an abyss in the ground that had not been there a second before.

Buried in tons of gravel. Body not yet located.

Suffocated. Declared dead. Body not yet located.

Aaron reached over, nudged my arm. I had not expected this. His touch was abrupt and unnerving. "Hey. You O.K.?"

Quickly I told him yes. I was fine.

Maybe a little dazed—dazzled—by the drive. The Thruway. Pavement, headlights. Those damned trailer trucks.

". . . thinking about the gypsum mine. Out Quarry Road. In your neighborhood. I was wondering if Sparta Gypsum was still operating."

"Sure. There's friends of mine work there."

"And your father's garage—is that still there? On Quarry Road?"

How naive I sounded! As if Aaron Kruller would need to be told the location of his father's auto repair.

"No. It isn't."

To this, I didn't know how to reply. Aaron was drinking ale, eating. His jaws were dark-stubbled and his gaze was down-looking, sullen. Or seemed to me sullen. The waitress returned to our booth brightly asking in a fluttery-breathy voice, "What c'n I do for you?"—Aaron lifted the ale bottle to her, to signal he wanted another, but didn't trouble to speak, nor even to glance at her. The gesture was condescending and dismissive and I felt a thrill of satisfaction, small and mean, petty.

"Do you still have that old bicycle? The one that looked like pipes fitted together."

"Jesus, no."

We laughed together. Suddenly, we were laughing. My question had been an utterly foolish question like my question about Quarry Road but it had the effect of making us laugh. My heart was beating rapidly as if, turning, I saw the earth fallen away at my feet, I could not move away, paralyzed in wonderment.

"What'd you think? I'm still a half-ass kid? Riding that damn broken-down bike?"

Now Aaron was looking at me more openly, I wondered what he saw. If I had surprised him, in Peekskill. I was thirty-two years old which seemed to me an appropriate age for me, who had ceased being a girl at fifteen. I liked my name too, that had a sharp crystalline ring: Krista Diehl. And my public manner which was a matter of poise: holding myself very still as in armor, or a straitjacket, even as others—like Claude Loomis— break down. My hair was so pale it seemed to lack color, a shimmery-silver hair, and I wore it plaited and clamped about my head. A man who'd hoped to be my lover had said that I was a blond Modigliani. I said, But Modigliani's women have only empty sockets for eyes.

Unlike Aaron, I was determined to be sociable. I asked him about his family: his father, his aunt Viola, his Kruller relatives. My voice was lowered as if we might be in danger of being overheard.

Aaron said in his flat, blunt voice that suggested no emotion other than disdain, his father had died a few years ago.

I told him that I was sorry to hear this.

Aaron shrugged. Aaron drank ale from the bottle.

I asked him about his aunt Viola and Aaron said Viola was O.K.

"Got married, finally. I mean, she'd been married before. This time looks better."

I told him that I was happy to hear this—"Your aunt was so kind to me, that night."

Stoned out of my mind that night, stricken with nausea—I could remember little of what happened. Except I knew that Aaron's aunt had called my mother and managed to convince her that I'd been at a friend's house and some sort of domestic crisis there had prevented me from calling her. Apparently Lucille had believed this.

My anxious suspicious mother!—placated by the possibility of a crisis in another Sparta household.

Aaron laughed suddenly, as if he'd been reading my mind. With one of his thick begrimed nails he was peeling at a label on his bottle of ale. "Yeah, Viola's O.K. Maybe you'll see her."

Why would I see Aaron's aunt? I could not imagine.

"Your brother—how's he? Ben."

I would not have thought that Aaron Kruller would remember my brother, let alone his name. Or wish to ask after him.

"Ben is a chemical engineer with Pierpont Labs, in Schenectady. He's married, he has a son." I didn't tell Aaron that there was a strangeness between Ben and me of which we could not speak. That this strangeness had begun in that hour when one of us had come to believe that our father was a criminal, a killer; and the other had continued to love him.

"I didn't think you would know Ben. You weren't in the same class, were you?"

"Sure. We knew each other." Aaron paused, drinking. He'd finished his dinner and had pushed the plate just slightly away. A subtle look came into his face, guarded, half-sneering. "Ben knew me."

Now I remembered the rumors, that Aaron had roughed up my brother.

And that Aaron had lied to protect his father Delray. Lying, Aaron had made the case against my father more plausible.

Not provable, but plausible.

Now, Delray Kruller was dead. Like Eddy Diehl.

There was a brotherhood in death, I thought.

I wanted to ask Aaron about Mira and Bernadette, my friends from high school. My cruel false friends, who'd exuded an air of cheap reckless glamour. I'd heard that Mira Roche had died of a drug overdose but I had heard nothing of Bernadette in years. And there was Duncan Metz.

I asked what had happened to Metz. Aaron said, in his slight-sneering tone, that Metz had "disappeared."

"'Disappeared'—how?"

"Executed in some drug deal, probably. His body was never found."

Executed! The word conveyed an air of finality, vindication.

Thank you for saving my life dear Aaron.

I had never sent any of those letters. I'd torn them into pieces to make sure that my mother never saw them. Yet now I felt a tinge of fear, that somehow Aaron had seen them.

Aaron asked how long I'd been living in Peekskill and I told him: two years. I waited for him to ask if I was married but of course, he did not ask. I told him that my work was fascinating to me, if exhausting and sometimes disappointing, discouraging. Prosecution Watch, Inc. was a non-profit organization originally founded in 1972 to investigate cases of police and prosecutorial misconduct.

"When people are wrongly arrested. Wrongly interrogated, tried, convicted and sent to prison. Sometimes executed."

I told Aaron that I'd gone to college at SUNY Binghamton. And graduate school at Cornell where I'd earned an M.A. in criminology. I was a paralegal, a lawyer's assistant. Most of the lawyers at Prosecution Watch did *pro bono* work, volunteer work, but the paralegals received salaries. I was trying to save money, I told Aaron. I was accumulating experience, I hoped to go to law school in a year or two.

To this, Aaron had no reply. As my brother Ben had no reply.

Aaron hadn't finished high school, I supposed. I remembered that he'd been expelled in his junior year.

These facts about myself I wanted Aaron to know. For they were facts of my exterior life, like armor.

I told Aaron that when I'd first begun to work as a paralegal, I'd tried to contact the Sparta detectives—Martineau, Brescia—their names I would never forget—who'd investigated his mother's death. But Martineau had retired, and Brescia never answered my calls. I'd tried to speak to the police chief, who'd taken over after Schnagel retired, but the police chief too never had time for me. Whoever I spoke with, I was put on hold. The last time I called, I'd threatened to get a subpoena, to be allowed to see what the Sparta PD had in their files, and a voice had said *Ma'am I'm going to have to put you on hold.*

I laughed. I seemed to have meant for Aaron Kruller to laugh with me. Instead, he looked away. His face stiffened, his eyes became remote.

It was the way of such men, when you seemed to have overstepped, into their territory.

He'd been glancing behind me, at a stream of headlights turning into the restaurant parking lot.

Hypnotic, the stream of lights outside the sleet-lashed window. I saw the reflections in Aaron's face like a play of water-lights over rock. I felt a small stab of satisfaction, he'd come to *me*.

I asked him if Sparta had changed much since I'd moved away in 1988 and he said he guessed so, sure. "When you live in a place, you don't see it. And I'm always there."

I asked him if he'd sold Kruller's Auto Repair and he said yes, if you could call it "selling": he'd sold off the property to pay Delray's God-damned mortgages and loans. But now he was co-owner of a body shop out Garrison Road and business there was O.K.

"I'm like a 'citizen' now. Own a business, pay guys to work for me. But I work, too."

"And you enjoy that work, Aaron? Don't you? What your father did . . ."

"Sure." Aaron laughed, as if my question was so utterly stupid, there was no point in taking it seriously.

Badly I wanted to ask if Aaron was married. I knew he would never volunteer such personal information. Instead I asked about the body shop, where it was located on Garrison Road. I asked who his co-owner was and what sort of work a "body shop" did.

When the waitress brought our check, Aaron insisted upon paying for both our meals. He opened his wallet, and showed me a snapshot of a dimpled, smiling toddler. In an enigmatic voice he said: "Davy. When he was two. He's older now."

"Your—son?"

I stared at the snapshot. My blood beat hard, in sudden envy.

"He's beautiful, Aaron."

"Not looking much like me, that helps. He's O.K."

The child had his father's somber eyes, and something that suggested Aaron in the set of his jaws. But his hair was fair and slightly wavy, his skin much lighter than Aaron's. Very little of the *Indian-look*. I wondered who his mother was. Where his mother was. Why Aaron said nothing about her and why he had no snapshot of her to show me.

Oddly alone the little boy was, in a patch of sunlit grass. With a sweetly trusting smile he gaped open-mouthed at the camera held above him, aimed downward. An adult shadow, his father's, fell slantwise over him.

Aaron took back the wallet, shut it up and put it away. He'd maybe showed me more than he was comfortable with, his gaze was again evasive. Thinking of his son's mother, I supposed. He finished the last of the ale, he'd drunk several bottles. Among my acquaintances no one would drink so much who was driving but Aaron Kruller was not among my acquaintances, nor could I speak to him the mildest words of reasonable caution as I would have spoken to an acquaintance. Aaron said: "Ever think, life's a crapshoot? Toss of the dice. How a kid gets born. All the odds against it. Jesus!" He laughed, it was a joke to him.

I said: "No. I think it has a purpose, there is a meaning."

"'A meaning'—just one? Like—to life?" Aaron was amused, disdainful.

"That we're here together, right now—you and I driving to Sparta together. After so many years. There is meaning in this."

My voice quavered with unexpected emotion. I was feeling anxious, unsettled. Aaron looked away as if embarrassed.

The waitress reappeared with a hopeful smile cast at Aaron. Aaron left a tip of several dollars for her, grabbed his sheepskin jacket and slid out of the booth.

As if we'd been lovers long ago. Before we'd grown into the adults we are now. Impossible to shake that conviction, almost it was a kind of music, sexual music you had only to shut your eyes, sink into sleep, this music would sweep over you in a wave of heart-stopping desire.

Sparta, a city built on glacial hills. Through a misty scrim of icy rain the lights of the city were scarcely visible as we approached in our separate vehicles crossing the Black River which was nearly obscured in darkness beneath us and continuing on to route 31 east and north of the city where I would be staying at a newly built Sheraton Hotel. Aaron had called on his cell phone to make a reservation for me. It was nearly 11 P.M. when we arrived, I was staggering with exhaustion. Aaron walked with me from the parking lot and insisted upon coming with me to my room on the fifth floor. In the corridor as I unlocked the door Aaron hesitated as if waiting for me to invite him inside. Waiting for me to turn to him, to appeal to him. *Aaron I am so lonely, I'm afraid Aaron don't leave me just yet.*

When I told him good night and held out my hand with a smile he turned away saying he'd pick me up at nine the next morning.

2

". . . WANT TO MAKE a blessing. Before I die. I want to bless you—Krista—and you—Aaron. Now that Jesus dwells in my heart I know that I can bless. But I must make amends, for I have wronged you. I have wronged others in my lifetime but you are the living—young—faces of those I have wronged terribly. Please forgive me!"

Jacky DeLucca spoke passionately, in a hoarse husk of a voice.

Jacky DeLucca: so changed, after almost twenty years, I would not have recognized her.

The female body that had been so opulent and brazen seemed to have collapsed in upon itself but not evenly, like sunken earth. There were hollows and bulges and fissures inside her clothing, which was a kind of flannel sweat suit, incongruously flamingo-colored; her formerly sensuous moon-face that had glared with makeup like neon was now shrunken and subdued and sallow; in her flattened cheeks there were fine vertical creases like erosion in sand. Her formerly glittery eyes were lashless and ringed in sunken flesh, her eyebrows that had been penciled in so dramatically seemed to have vanished. Jacky could not have been sixty years old yet looked as if she were in her late seventies. The poor woman! On her head was a pert helmet-wig that shone as if it were made of silver wires. With a wry smile Jacky touched the wig, adjusted it fussily. "My 'hair'! Not going to fool anyone is it! But my poor baldie-head, no one wants to see. *I* don't want to see."

With a muffled little cry Jacky leaned forward to seize my hand, kneading the fingers anxiously. She would have seized Aaron's hand also but Aaron remained out of reach, standing somewhere behind me as I seated myself in a sunken easy chair close by the ratty sofa on which Jacky lay, her wasted legs covered by a frayed quilt. "Reverend Diggs made the purchase for me, out of his own pocket. Reverend Diggs is a saint! I said, 'Just some old head-scarf is good enough for me, I'm past female vanity now,' and Reverend Diggs smiled and said, 'A little vanity is necessary for the soul, Jacky. Female or male.'" I had to force myself to realize, Jacky was talking about the cheap silver-wire wig.

I was badly shaken by the sight of poor Jacky DeLucca and distracted by odors in the room and a mysterious commotion as of voices, shouts and laughter and—was it furniture being moved?—elsewhere in the building. We were in Jacky DeLucca's sparsely furnished room in a residence of some kind, halfway house or homeless shelter and soup kitchen attached to the Central Sparta Evangelical Unity Church. This was a nineteenth-century red-brick church on Hamilton Avenue in a neighborhood of old, large churches and municipal buildings; once, the First Episcopal Church of Sparta had occupied this site. Hamilton Avenue was parallel with Huron Boulevard which had been, in some long-ago time before my birth, Sparta's most prestigious residence neighborhood: sandstone, limestone, brick and granite mansions had been built here, enormous private homes with pillars and porticos and twelve-foot privet hedges. Now the private homes had been converted into small businesses, offices and apartments. The privet hedges had been torn down.

"Sit, please! Aar-on! Just pull that chair closer. . . ."

Reluctant as a sulky teenager Aaron hauled a rattan chair over to sit facing Jacky DeLucca at a slant. His eyes evaded mine, I could see the misery in his face.

" . . . so much to reveal. Before time runs out . . ."

Aaron had parked his car outside in a vast, open wasteland of a lot where a block of buildings had been razed in an effort at urban renewal that seemed to have ceased abruptly. Much of Sparta's aged and decaying downtown was unrecognizable to me, after so many years: a maze of one-way streets, a showy but near-deserted pedestrian mall on South

Main, a half-mile of waterfront parkland bounded by gigantic oil drums on one side and Sparta Quality Ball Bearings on the other, heralded by wind-whipped banners BLACK RIVER ESPLANADE: A COMMUNITY OUTREACH PROJECT. Here on the Esplanade in the chill wan light of a November morning, several heavily bundled vagrant-looking individuals were adrift like flotsam or inert on benches in the way of those bandaged George Segal figures. Except for riverboat sounds there was mostly silence but it was an anxious and not a meditative silence. It had come to me in a wave of something like despair that the Sparta that my father had known so intimately, the city in which he'd grown up, where he'd worked as a carpenter and as a construction foreman and lived a life that had mattered to him, had vanished. And he'd died because that life had mattered to him.

" . . . your father Eddy Diehl, such a handsome man, Krista, I remember the first time I saw Eddy Diehl, this was a long time ago at the old Tip Top Club. . . ." Jacky DeLucca spoke in an eager, hoarse, rambling voice, gripping my hand in her thin chill fingers, regarding me with searching eyes as if hoping to recognize me. Elsewhere in the residence was a grating clatter of voices, scraping chair legs, radio pop-rock. A smell of breakfast: bacon grease, pancakes, scorched eggs. Cloying-sweet baked goods. Making my nostrils pinch, a smell of Jacky DeLucca's decaying body. " . . . never knew your poor mother, dear Krista. I hope she's all right, Krista, is she? I hope that she was a 'survivor' . . . of such a sad, hard time." Jacky sighed, looking confused. I held her hand, hoping to warm it. The flamingo-colored sweat suit appeared to be a kind of sleepware. The silver-wire wig was slightly askew on Jacky's head, I felt an urge to adjust it. That Aaron Kruller was restless in his chair a few inches from mine, that he stared blankly at Jacky DeLucca without seeming to see her, was making me nervous. " . . . my happiest times, working here. In the kitchen. Love to cook! Pancakes, waffles my specialty. Of course there's more to them than just sugary dough, I mix in berries, apples, almonds. Before coming here I was what you'd call a 'cleaning woman'—but got sick—oh I was so sick: hepatitis B. Why my liver was weak. Why I was 'susceptible.' There had come Jesus into my heart, by that time. If there hadn't been Jesus, I could not have made it through that terrible time, and Reverend Diggs to show me the way, and the wonderful people here at Haven House, they have made a home for me, Reverend Diggs has said he will arrange for a hospice for me—'When it is time, and not a day before.' This liver cancer!—they tried all kinds of chemotherapy which is so awful, dear, I hope you will never know, one day they told me the cancer had 'metized' to my bones and there would be no more chemo. The doctor said, 'There is nothing more we can do for you, Jacky. You must put your soul at rest.' Dr. Waldrop is a Christian man, and a good man. And Reverend Diggs . . ." Jacky paused, wiping at her eyes. She squeezed my hand a final time and released it. Aaron lurched from the rattan chair to struggle at opening the single window in the airless room, the window seemed to have been painted shut but by sheer force of desperation Aaron managed to shove it open a meager inch causing Jacky to protest: ". . . not a draft, dear! I can't bear a draft, I will start coughing, dear. Why I have to bundle up indoors and keep a quilt over my legs, my feet are always cold, the circulation in my poor feet is not good. Dr. Waldrop said . . ." Aaron now had to shut the window, yanking downward. I risked a glance at his face that was stiff and guarded and without expression though his gaze drifted onto mine, a look of raw mute misery and rage.

Get her to talk. Hurry her up. Jesus!

As a paralegal I'd had plenty of experience with clients who had crucial stories to tell yet could not seem to find a way to tell them, who struggled almost physically to say what was painfully evident, thus unsayable; I had learned patience, and a measure of sympathy; I had learned the humility of frequent failure. Gently I asked Jacky DeLucca if she'd invited us to visit her this morning because she had "something special" to tell us? Zoe Kruller's son Aaron and me? Did she—remember us?

In a gesture of mock-hurt Jacky slapped at my arm. "Why, 'course I remember you! You are Eddy Diehl's daughter Kristine—Krista?—all grown up and moved away from Sparta and back just to see *me*. And you are"— Jacky's voice lifted in a feeble sort of flirtatious reproach, —"Zoe's grown boy Aaron. Did I thank you for these . . ." It had been my idea, to bring the sick woman flowers: a heavy pot of flaming-pink hydrangea. In the florist's shop the hydrangea had looked less showy but in this bleak room with its shabby sofa-bed, battered Goodwill furniture, and stained remnant-carpet, the gorgeous cluster-flowers exuded an air of subtle mockery. ". . . beautiful flowers that look like . . . some kind of carnation paper . . . crepe paper. . . . *Did* I just thank you, dear? Sometimes I forget what I'm saying, it's this medicine! So many damn pills! Zoe loved flowers she said but never had time to tend them. Fresh-cut flowers some man would give her, a dozen roses that are so expensive these days it's like a joke, or like poin-settas, at Christmastime, Zoe would hand to me—'Jacky, take care of these, will you?'—like she couldn't be bothered. Zoe was always in such a hurry. I was not so different myself, when I was younger. I don't mean to cast judgment on my friend. I was blind to myself, there was a veil over my eyes, I was not one to judge others and I am not, now. Jesus has said, 'Love thy neighbor as thyself.' Jesus has said, 'Judge not, that ye not be judged.'

"In those years before Jesus entered my heart I was not one to judge others, I was not cruel or vindictive. After Zoe died—that way she did—I entered the 'Valley of the Shadow of Death' and lived through a dark time, I was a heroin addict, my addiction was two hundred dollars a day, and more—yes I turned tricks and did not give a damn for my health. So stained with guilt as I was, that Zoe had died in that terrible way!" Jacky paused, breathing forcibly. I did not dare to look at Aaron Kruller who'd remained on his feet, near the window he'd had to shut. "I don't mean that I brought Zoe to her killer, I don't mean that. This man, that owned Chet's, his name was Anton Csaba, he'd have met Zoe some other way if it had not been through me, I know that. Yet I was Anton's friend first, as Anton was friends with many women. When Zoe moved in with me, we both started work at Chet's. Anton had Zoe sing sometimes at the club, and we'd do a few lines of coke together, if guys provided it which they did. It was what everybody did. Damn hypocrite cops, those 'detectives' came to question me acting like nobody'd ever

done coke or smoked dope, you see the bastards off-duty out on the Strip
pretending like they're undercover—bull*shit*. I'm ashamed to say, I liked
it that Zoe was my girlfriend 'cause she was damn glamorous, and singing in that band of hers, Zoe was *real sexy*. And Zoe was a good friend,
like just doing drugs with, she'd look out for me, it can be dangerous,
you need a trusted friend if something goes wrong. A man, you can't
trust. . . . There are people who say if you maintain your health, if you
take vitamins, you can use heroin for the rest of your life if you don't
increase the dosage and your veins don't collapse! Even now, I am
ashamed to say that there is this craving in me. Zoe said, 'Sex is for
people who can't score heroin.'" Jacky laughed at this witty remark with
no heed for how Aaron was staring at her. In another part of the residence there came a muffled thunderous noise as of footsteps on stairs in
a cascading downward stream. Hastily Jacky added, "Of course—Zoe
was not an 'addict'—a 'junkie'—not ever. And I was not, really. There's
men who provide women with drugs to take control of their souls but
Zoe was too independent, she wanted her 'career' and she was fearful it
would never come to her, at her age. Around this time, I'm embarrassed
to say, I was jealous of Zoe sometimes because if there was a man Zoe
wanted it would not matter who Zoe cast aside to get him. And Zoe got
away with so much more than others of us could. If Zoe borrowed
money for instance. A man would 'forgive' the loan, who would not ever
forgive it for *me*. Anton Csaba was one of these. Zoe's mistake was, she
took Anton for granted. You would be inclined to do that if you met him,
Anton was soft-spoken and never raised his voice. Because he was in love
with Zoe, she thought he was in love with her, she made some mistakes
with Anton. He'd promised Zoe certain things. Yet Zoe had this new
man, this 'music broker' he called himself, some kind of 'enter-prenner'
whose business was booking bands. How Zoe met him I don't know for
sure. I guess he'd heard her sing at Chet's one night. Now, I knew that
Anton could be dangerous, he had hurt women before, who'd betrayed
him. It was Anton's way of speech—he would use the word 'betray.' I
should explain, Anton was a gentleman to look at. Anton had the ways

of a gentleman. He'd been born in Budapest, he said. Which is in Hungry—in the real old part of Europe. Anton was a sharp dresser, he wore a sealskin coat and a fedora hat, and gloves made of skins of 'unborn lambs.' (Did you ever hear of—*unborn lamb skins*?) He drove just Caddies and Lincolns and never kept them more than a calendar year, they were always luxury cars with every extra. He had a way of 'owning' women, too. When he was tired of you, he would not care to see you again, and he'd give you a 'gift in parting'—but if he wasn't tired of you yet, you could not just walk away. Anton liked me—'My gal Jacky' he would call me—when I'd fill in at the club for him, he knew he could depend on me, and this was lucky for me, that he only 'liked' me but nothing more. Zoe was the one 'got under his skin.' Anton spoke of Zoe in this way like Zoe was some kind of infectious thing like lice, he couldn't shake off. He wore expensive suits that never fitted him right, made him look like a corpse some undertaker had dressed. Zoe laughed at him behind his back. 'That little mannequin-man' she'd call him. 'My Boris Karloff.' And we would laugh. And maybe it got back to Anton. I forgot to say, Anton could be very generous. Nobody in Sparta was like Anton Csaba that way. If you worked for him and did a good job he would give you presents, if he liked you. Of course if you bitched or made trouble, you were out. Some of those nice clothes I brought to your house, Aaron, that time, Anton had given to Zoe, and she'd always thank him real gratefully but after a few days, you know Zoe, she'd forget. . . . And there's cops who hung out at Chet's. This 'police chief' at the time, he was a friend of Anton's. You'd see them smoke cigars together. It was known that Anton paid off the Sparta police, so they wouldn't interfere in his business which had many facets. When Zoe was killed, 'Anton Csaba' was a name some people told the detectives, but it never went much farther than that. The detectives knew it couldn't be Eddy Diehl who'd killed her because Eddy's prints were all over Zoe's room except not bloody prints. I heard this. This was known. It had to be, whoever killed Zoe was wearing gloves. They knew that Eddy hadn't been there, at that time. The time Zoe was killed. They brought

Eddy in and questioned him and made it hell for him but not because they thought he was the one who'd killed Zoe, it was just some personal dislike of him. You fuck with the cops, they take their revenge on you how they can. They'd have tried to arrest Delray but there was a general feeling in Sparta, that Delray had been badly enough treated by Zoe behaving like she did, and Delray's boy—that is, Aaron—I came to know Aaron—gave his sworn statement, he and his dad had been home together that night, all night. So if it came to a jury trial they figured that Delray would be found 'not guilty'—so the detectives never arrested anyone. Every God-damned question this Martineau asked me, there was a trick to it. Trying to get me to name 'Eddy Diehl.' Which I would not. And I would not say 'Anton Csaba'—I would not have lived beyond a week. Not in Sparta. And where else could I go? Where, that Anton couldn't follow? This son-bitch Martineau would call me, he'd drop by where I was living, had to move out of the house where poor Zoe died, I was living on Towaga and he'd drop by there on his way home he said, off-duty he said, the son-bitch prevert, 'Hey there Jacqueline,' he'd say in this fake-honey voice, 'you named for Jacqueline Kennedy? *You*— named for *her*?" Things that bastard did to me I had to be high, or blind drunk, to endure, and d'you think the bastard ever showed any gratitude? 'Lucky you're not in the female house of detention, fat-twat Jacky, for obstruction of justice, aiding and abetting a homicide, drugs on the premises.' He'd leave me like some broken thing on the bed, or the floor. He never gave me a God-damned penny. A man like that, and the 'police chief' too—Schnabel—Schnagel—things were said of, he'd never sign off on Anton Csaba being investigated let alone arrested. Oh no." Jacky paused, shivering. The room seemed to me overheated yet almost I, too, could feel a draft from the window, I shivered locating a blanket to wrap around Jacky's shoulders. Still Aaron kept his distance from us, like a kid getting more and more dangerous as he's more and more restless and near to explode. The last speech she'd made Jacky seemed to have forgotten that there was a third party in the room, blinking at me with watery eyes of such yearning, I had to look away. The smell of the woman's body seemed less strong to me, as the minutes passed. I thought *When this is over, I can bathe her.*

". . . three years later, when it happened. Nobody knew what, exactly. Anton was in Buffalo meeting with some 'investors' and he 'disappeared'—like that. It was a time he and some partner were buying up property on the Strip and he'd expanded the club and people were saying he'd made some enemies, and they had him killed. You hear these things. There was never any obituary of Anton Csaba in the local papers because there was never any body located but there were stories in the papers, on the front page of the *Journal*—'Prominent Sparta Developer Missing Twelve Days'—that's the one I cut out, and kept. Nobody could believe, in the paper it said that Anton was forty-nine, and he looked ten years older at least. It was a fact he'd been born in Budapest but he was 'survived by' a son living in New York, nobody had any idea that Anton had any family like a normal person. So Anton was gone, this was some-time in 1986. And he had to be dead, buried in concrete somewhere, or dumped in the Niagara River, was what you'd hear. Chet's got sold, and turned into some ordinary strip joint, nothing classy about it now. So there was some kind of justice for poor Zoe—'poetic justice'—and for her family though they could not appreciate it. For nobody knew about Anton Csaba and the ones who did, they kept quiet. Sometimes I'd see Delray out on the Strip, or Eddy Diehl, when he was back visiting Sparta, I'd have liked to explain to them, those poor bastards so harassed, but hell, how could I, there is nothing to be proved, in a case like this there is just nothing because it has been destroyed. If you don't have the police taking in evidence, there can be nothing proved. Even after Anton was gone, years later there are friends of his in Sparta who'd hear if I said anything, this is a damn small town in certain circles!—like that cruel hypocrite and utter bastard Martineau, and his boss Schnagel. So I never said a word. Of this I am ashamed but I had not the strength, then. What I took solace in, Zoe forgave me. I knew this. Zoe was repentant of her life, at the end. She'd seen 'both sides now.' In time, I think it had to be Zoe who intervened with Jesus to flood my heart with rapture, when I had no wish to continue living. I was in the Towaga place, couldn't get out of bed for days, Zoe would come to me—'Jacky? Thought it was you!'—she'd kind of tease, but gentle, the way Zoe teased you if she liked you, or loved you. Only if I was alone, and receptive to her, could I feel her presence like something shimmering in the air, and hear her voice that seemed to come out of the air, that sweet-sexy voice when Zoe sang her special songs. But I could not see Zoe! Except if my eyes were shut, sometimes. There's a special kind of cocaine-high you can get, that isn't so crazy, it's like there is a 'piercing' of the sky, that's inside your head, and sometimes then I could 'see' Zoe—like an angel, all light. And I would say to her, Oh Zoe why did you take so much money from that man? And those clothes? Didn't you know who that man was, did you think he was someone just from Sparta, didn't you know that he is the Devil, he is the Devil come to us on earth, if you take gifts from the Devil you are beholden to the Devil, if you laugh at the Devil the Devil will laugh at you, and pull you down to hell with him. It was the drugs Zoe took—or were given to Zoe, to take—when you are high you lose judgment, Zoe lost 'proportion' it was said. Zoe thought she could cast off Anton Csaba like some man she'd cast off in Sparta, like her husband, or a lover, and there would be no consequences. Zoe was going to Vegas with this 'enter-prenner' and Anton found out, asked me what did I know about him, when was Zoe planning on leaving, and I said, 'Zoe wouldn't stay away from Sparta for long, Zoe would miss her son too much,' and Anton didn't say a word just slapped me, hard across the mouth Anton slapped me and I cried saying, 'Oh! Why did you do that—' and Anton said because I was lying to him, and so I saw there was no hope, the Devil can see into our hearts if Jesus doesn't dwell in them to protect us, so I said, 'Yes Zoe is leaving tomorrow morning, with—' His name was Scroon, I think. Some name like 'Walter Scroon.' This was what Zoe called him though afterward it would be like with 'George Hardy'—there was no man with that name, the police could not locate any man with that name. So I told Anton all that I knew, because I was frightened he would hurt me worse than he had, I said that Zoe was leaving with 'Walter Scroon' who was a 'music producer' and he was coming to pick her up in the morning, maybe around ten, they were driving to Albany to the airport. 'But if you see Zoe, don't tell her I told you'—those were my words to Anton Csaba. And Anton just laughed. And it was then Anton introduced me to 'George Hardy' to take me out—that weekend—to pay me one thousand dollars—we stayed at the 'historic' Inn at Chautauqua Falls—which is so special, and so expensive—and when I returned to Sparta and to West Ferry Street it was like something in a movie, all these vehicles in the street in front of our house, and the street blocked off, and the front door was wide open and cops inside and they told me my 'roommate' was dead—'beaten and strangled in her bed'—and the looks in their faces, like this was some punishment Zoe deserved, that should have been mine, too. There was not a single woman there on the premises—just men—uniform-cops and detectives and emergency medical people—all men—looking at me like I was shit. I fainted, I guess—it was my time to enter 'The Valley of the Shadow of Death'—where I would dwell for years, until . . ."

In short breathless gasps like stifled laughter Jacky had begun to cry. Her face crinkled like the face of an aged baby. The silver-wire wig was askew on her head at a rakish angle. Carefully I straightened it, and adjusted the blanket around her shoulders.

Aaron was somewhere behind me. He had ceased pacing and stood very still. Jacky's eyes widened on him as if, for a moment, she'd forgotten who he was. In a pleading voice she said, to Aaron and to me:

". . . please believe me, Kristine—Krista?—and Aaron—please believe me, Zoe was my closest friend. Zoe was my heart. Never would I have willingly injured her. Never would I have betrayed her. Only, those years before Jesus, I was so weak. The Devil could entice me to any thing with a look, a caress, a promise. Jealousy consumed my heart, too. And envy, and spite. And pride. I did not possess the courage to save my sister in Christ, that is the terrible fact I must live with. For a lie to Anton Csaba that would convince him—if there could be such a lie, from me—might have saved Zoe, but then the lie would have hurt me. If I had said, Zoe was not going away so soon the next morning—Zoe was not going to

Vegas for a few days. Then, Zoe would be gone from Sparta, and Anton Csaba would have to follow her to Vegas to hurt her, which he would not have done, I think. It was how angry Anton was, at that time. But then, the lie would have hurt me. This was my choice, and I was too weak to choose Zoe but only wished to save myself. For this sin I would descend into the dregs and ashes of humankind and I would be broken underfoot as the lowest scum and scorned by the righteous until at my darkest hour after being released penniless and sick from the detention house—this was the Women's House of Detention—down behind the courthouse—it was the 'psych ward' they put me in, I cried so much—I tore my hair, and my face—why they'd arrested me, I never knew—maybe it was 'possession of a control-substance'—maybe Martineau planted it in my room—when I was released I found my way to the Evangelical Unity Church and Reverend Myron Diggs and these wonderful Christians who did not judge their fallen sister Jacky but prayed for me and with me and at last, at prayer service one evening, when Reverend Diggs called for us to come forward, to welcome Jesus into our hearts, I felt such strength suddenly, like a current of electricity bearing me forward to the rail, and Jesus flooded my heart with His warmth and love and has not departed from that hour forward. For so it was, 'Jacky DeLucca' had truly repented of her sins and the terrible sin of 'des-pair'—which Reverend Diggs says is not-caring if you live or die—my most joyful hour was when Jesus allowed me to know *You are forgiven, Jacky*. And that has been six years now. Six years! So I have been granted strength to endure my sickness, that is a test to my faith, washing over me in waves, now that the chemotherapy is finished, and 'there is no more to be done.' And Jesus gives me strength, and will be awaiting me. And so—I am opening my heart to you, that you will forgive me? And—you will bless me?"

I told Jacky yes of course. Yes we would "bless" her. I could not bring myself to look at Aaron Kruller behind me.

I held Jacky DeLucca sobbing in my arms. I held the hot quivering emaciated body. A numbness came over me, I think I was smiling. I was seeing us, Jacky DeLucca in the silver wire-wig, Krista Diehl with her pale plaited hair, our faces shining with tears, a *pietà*, a cartoon sort of *pietà*, though who was the mother wasn't certain, or in whom did God's greatest grace abide. There was a roaring in my ears, I was close to fainting. My lips were dry as sandpaper. I thought *But I don't have to kiss her do I? I am spared kissing her.*

Just the two of us in the room—Jacky DeLucca, Krista Diehl. For the other, the man, Aaron Kruller, had walked out at some point. He'd left us, in disgust or in rage, or in a terrible sympathy for us, I would not know. In the confusion of our embrace the pot of gorgeous hydrangea had been knocked onto its side, now I righted it. Some of the blossoms had broken off. On the table beside Jacky's shabby sofa-bed were several small bottles of pills, a scummy water glass. I saw now that the plaster-board walls of Jacky's room were festooned with religious pictures that resembled enlarged Bible cards. The most striking of Jacky's artifacts was a three-foot-high likeness of Jesus on a swath of black velvet stiffly holding out his pierced and bleeding hands, open-palmed: strikingly pale, with large dark eyes and a crimson mouth like a girl's and on his forehead a crown of bloody thorns crudely painted in bright colors. Conspicuous in the lower left corner were the initials *J.D.*

Jacky saw me staring at the painting. With a girlish shiver she said she'd painted it herself after a vision of Jesus, did I like it?

I said, "It's beautiful, Jacky. Just the way He would look, if He were with us."

"FRESH AIR! JESUS."

Aaron was waiting for me outside the room. Grabbed at my arm and pulled me impatiently out the rear door of the residence cursing *Fuck fuck fuck* under his breath.

Together we stumbled down steps. Crumbling concrete steps. The air was wetly cold. Tears sprang from my eyes and ran down my heated cheeks. I had not realized how, in Jacky DeLucca's sickroom, the cloying-sweet smell of decay had been so pervasive, by instinct I'd been breathing shallowly, taking in little oxygen. I was dazed, light-headed. The impact of the fresh chill air was profound as a slap to the face.

Aaron was disconcerted, furious. And frightened, like a man fleeing a collapsing building. I said:

"Aaron, you have to go back. To say good-bye to her. You can't just run away, she's a dying woman."

"Fuck her. Fuck them all. They can die."

I detached Aaron's hand from my arm. He'd closed his fingers around my arm as if we were intimates—an older brother, an annoying sister— without seeming to know what he did, in his paroxysm of fury. He had the look of a man about to strike out with his fists, at any close target.

"Aaron, we can't just leave like this. I won't go with you."

"Fuck you *will*. Come on!"

We were shoving at each other. Badly I wanted to strike at this stubborn man with my fists, that expression in his face, that expression of obstinacy, willful stupidity, he'd begun unexpectedly to laugh, sharp barking laughter, cruel and without mirth. Somehow I was following after Aaron who ignored my pleas, waved away my good-girl pleas with a wave of his hand, my sensitivity to the dying woman was utter bullshit to this man, unworthy of discussion.

Together we stumbled past an overflowing Dumpster. What a reek of raw garbage! I thought *The poor woman has already died. This is hell she is in, where we had to come for her.*

For this near-deserted area of downtown Sparta there was an unusual amount of activity in the vicinity of the Central Sparta Evangelical Unity Church. The noise we'd been hearing in Jacky DeLucca's room was a U-Haul rental truck being unloaded of shabby donated furniture, by volunteer workers. Close by, unrelated to the U-Haul effort, was a lengthy, straggling line of mostly men—with pulpy veined faces, rheumy eyes and body parts that looked mismatched—as many as forty men— among them a few women scarcely distinguishable from the men—eerily patient, resigned, like penitents, or perhaps they were beyond penitents, these were the damned, like Jacky DeLucca these were residents of Hell, yet unprotesting of their damnation, stoic and contented, for it was a communal damnation, and you could be fed: they were shuffling through an entrance into what appeared to be a soup kitchen. Hot delicious smells wafted to our nostrils, at odds with the stink of the Dumpster. No one took the slightest notice of Aaron Kruller and me.

I thought *Someday I will return here. I will be a volunteer. When I am strong enough.*

In a vast open windy lot partially heaped with rubble from demolished buildings we were walking to Aaron's car. If I'd been brought to this place blindfolded and asked where I was, I could not have said. The ruins of an American city devastated by war, a post-industrial American city in upstate New York—but what exactly had happened here? There was a strange glaring broken beauty to the rubble-strewn lot as of the ruins of antiquity but these were not ruins to be named, let alone celebrated. These were ruins lacking all memory, identity.

What relief, to get to Aaron's car! New-model, American-made, with sleek lines, four-wheel drive for our harsh upstate winters, satellite radio. Suddenly our hands fell on each other. I had hold of the man I'd been wanting to pummel just now, I was clutching and desperate. Aaron's sheepskin jacket was open, I could smell his body. He'd reached inside my coat, opening my coat, dragging me against him. A wet wind rushed at us, smelling of the river. Jocular, teasing. Roughly Aaron shoved me against the side of the car, he'd taken hold of my head in both his hands and he kissed me open-mouthed. We were gnawing at each other's mouth, a sexual frenzy seemed to sweep over us. You would think we'd narrowly escaped some terrible danger. You would think we were both drunk. Seeing us from the rear of the church residence, you'd have thought we were stumbling drunk, shameless-drunk, on a weekday in late morning.

On our way to the Sheraton motel at the northern rim of Sparta, on route 31, Aaron stopped at a liquor store to buy a bottle of Scotch and two six-packs of beer. As he drove he held the steering wheel with one hand and with the other gripped and kneaded my thigh as I pressed close beside him. We were dazed, giddy with desire. So long I'd lived my numb sexless life inhabiting my body as one might inhabit a cocoon, it was astonishing to me how powerfully I felt this sex-need for the man, how my body was reacting, with what directness. Or was this another kind of numbness, a numbness of anonymity, sheer physical yearning. I was very happy suddenly, something had been decided. *It's over, they are all dead. Only we are here.*

The final time: crossing the wide rapidly-rushing froth-tormented Black River that wound through Sparta, over the stately old suspension bridge. Never again to cross this bridge. Not again in my lifetime—I seemed to know this, with an ecstatic fatalism—seeing at the crest of the bridge the sinuous-snaky curve of the river and, in the distance, the hazy peaks of the southern Adirondacks. As a girl I'd memorized those peaks:

Star Lake Mountain, Little Moose Mountain, Bullhead Mountain, White Ridge Mountain, Mount Hammer just barely visible at the horizon.

Never again, these waterfront docks, aging wharfs, warehouses and mills; eighteen-wheel rigs being loaded, unloaded, in the cobblestone streets. Oil drums, oily pools. Refineries, tall smokestacks rimmed with flame like teasing little lips. But where, along the waterfront, was Link Ladies Hosiery?—I could not find it.

This November day was wet, windy, splotched with sudden sunshine, and overhead a vivid blue sky in which enormous clouds like rubble were being blown, broken, scattered.

Aaron said, "It's what I thought. What she said. I knew Delray hadn't ever been the one."

Close beside the excited man, I could not speak. I could not say *I knew my father had not ever been the one.* I could not say *I want you inside me. As deep inside me as another can be.*

At the Sheraton, Aaron entered with me. In one arm carrying the Scotch and the six-packs in a paper bag and with the other arm slung about me as if he feared I might escape. His face was flushed and aroused and not so angry now and I told the desk clerk—whose initial glance at

Aaron and me had turned into a frank stare—that I would be staying another night.

In my room on the fifth floor Aaron shut the door and double-locked it and I pulled the drapes across the windows carelessly and then we were pulling at each other, at each other's clothing, we were laughing, we were short of breath as if we'd run up five floors to this room, and we were on the bed, Aaron heavy and grunting and kissing me the way he'd kissed me in the parking lot, open-mouthed, his teeth striking mine. We were half-dressed, he was lying between my legs, I was clutching at him, our faces were contorted as the faces of swimmers who have slipped beneath the surface of the water, in a sudden panic of drowning. I thought *But is this Krista? Is this—what I want?* Still we laughed together, as we kissed. Our laughter was harsh, stunned. My arms around the man's neck were tight, there was no time for tenderness. My elbows locking together as if, if I wished, I might break the man's neck.

It was like falling together. Falling from a great height. The impact of the earth against flesh. The breath was knocked from me. My brain was extinguished, dark. There were no words, only just sounds. Which of us uttered such sounds, I would not know.

A time for Krista to confess *Always I loved you. Always I dreamt of this.*

Except: there was something impersonal, anonymous in Aaron's love-making. You could feel that you were being swallowed up in a ravenous sexual need like the ravenous appetite of a predator.

Later, Aaron opened the bottle of Scotch. We drank—giddily I drank, from a plastic cup, the liquor burning my mouth—and we made love again, and after a while we drank, Aaron was drinking both Scotch and beer, and we made love again. Our kisses reeked of alcohol. Our bodies reeked of sweat. We had been so gnawing each other's mouths, the pillowcase beneath our heads was soaked with our saliva. Tangled in smelly bedclothes we slept. In each other's arms we slept. Waking I could not comprehend where I was, with whom I was lying as in the grip of a python, one of my bare legs slung over the man's haunch, the small of his back. We woke, we took turns using the bathroom: Krista first, then Aaron. Nakedness seemed to make us unusually clumsy. I stumbled, blinking in the over-bright light of the bathroom. Our laughter was abrupt and unpredictable. We may have been embarrassed. We may have been very happy. We may have been drunk. We were naked and sweaty and careless of the time. We had ceased hearing vacuum cleaners in adjacent rooms and in the corridor outside our room. It was late morning, it was early afternoon and in time late afternoon and we'd begun to hear the voices of a new shift of motel guests arriving. It may have been early evening. Beyond the carelessly pulled drapes, the November day had flared up in a kind of luminous flame and now it had abated, now dusk came swiftly. This was a melancholy time of day, or would have been, in Peekskill. Here in Sparta I fumbled for my plastic cup, that seemed always in need of refilling. Aaron was drinking his way into the second six-pack of beer. He'd ordered room-service meals for us, cheeseburger, turkey-club with bacon and cheese, French fries and catsup, sugary coleslaw and the crusts and malodorous remnants of these meals remained, on a tray shoved against a wall, on the shag carpet behind the darkened TV where a hotel maid would discover it, hours later. Through a crack in the drapes my eyes discerned what appeared to be a moon, a crescent moon, unless it was just a light in the parking lot, on a tall pole. Hungrily I was kissing the man's mouth, that tasted of beer. I was kissing a mouth like Daddy's mouth. The man himself lay sprawled and slovenly in his nakedness amid churned-looking bedclothes. The man was cupping my left breast in his hand, kneading and squeezing, squeezing and releasing in the way that you stroke or caress an animal, to allow the animal to know that you feel affection for it though you can't pay it your fullest attention at just this moment. I was half-crying, suddenly I was stricken with emotion saying, "Oh Aaron, oh God—I forgot what I'd meant to do for her—" and the man said, "'Do for'—who?" and I said, "Jacky DeLucca. I forgot what I'd meant to do," and the man said, "What's that, honey?" and I said, tears streaming down my face, "I meant to bathe her, Aaron! To wash her, to change her bedclothes. That poor woman, I meant to take her address so that I could send money to her," and the man said, laughing, "Jesus Christ, her again! Fuck old Jacky."

"Aaron, you don't mean that."

"No? Why don't I?"

"She has put our souls to rest, Aaron. She needn't have done it, it was an act of kindness."

The man had ceased kneading my breast. Idly he kicked at the bed-clothes that were restricting his leg movements.

"Fuck who's got a soul."

"You have a soul."

I framed the man's face in my hands. I told him he had a soul, I'd seen that soul.

Love had made me speak in such profundities.

Drunk-love, especially. Crazed profundities.

Aaron laughed. Aaron shook off my hands.

I insisted, I said. His soul. I'd seen it, I was the only one.

I was drunk, Aaron said. But he liked me, he said.

Aaron laughed, embarrassed. But also with pleasure. His face was aglow with pleasure. He grabbed me and pulled me down beside him and burrowed his face in my neck, so that I couldn't see his face, as a child might do, to hide. His arms around my naked sides, my back, his hands restless on me, I knew were strong enough to crack my bones. Almost inaudibly he said, "Don't go back. Stay here."

"Stay—where?" I thought he meant the motel.

"Stay with me. Where I live. There's room."

"I can't stay with you. I don't even know you."

"Yes. You know me."

Later: shaking my head, to clear it. Somehow I had fallen asleep beneath the man's heavy arm. And my own arm was twisted beneath me, numbed. I was unaccustomed to drinking anything stronger than white wine, and that only occasionally, and I had never been drunk but I liked being drunk. I had to lift the man's heavy warm arm, that was covered in hairs, to pry myself loose from him. I was uncomfortably warm, over-warm, the nape of my neck felt scalding, rivulets of sweat ran down my naked sides. How my mother would scold: Krista, you smell of your body! For there was nothing more shameful for a girl than to smell of her body. This man's smell was sharp, pungent, unmistakable. It was the male sex-smell, frank and undisguised. And the man took not the slightest care, he lay sprawled in sleep in a luxury of abandon, sleeping so deeply, his mouth part-opened, his breathing loud and wet. I thought *The male has to snore, to frighten away predators.* I laughed, this was a radical new insight perhaps, an entirely new and ingenious sub-theory of evolution. Where Aaron had been kissing me, rubbing his stubbled jaws against me, my skin smarted as if with sunburn. The impracticably soft skin of my small hard breasts, and my stomach, and the insides of my thighs, was reddened and chafed as if with sandpaper. Where he'd entered me, that too was chafed. That too felt raw, appropriated. I thought *No one has ever come so deeply into me. But I can walk away from him even now.*

In a heavy stuporous sleep the man lay on his back, one arm flung above his head in an expression of arrested alarm. His forehead was furrowed, there were creases at the corners of his eyelids, in even this stuporous sleep he was tense, restless. Softly he moaned, he ground his back teeth. On his face that was a coarsened boy's face was a scattering of old scars. On his forearms that were muscular and covered in thick dark hairs were purplish-dark tattoos, their shapes and significance obscure. And on his torso and belly and groin were swirls of dark hair like seaweed. Together we'd grappled underwater. Together we'd struggled in each other's arms. The lengths of our straining bodies, naked and pressed tightly together. Like slithering fish. Like eels. Not just we'd been naked together but there had seemed to be no skin between us, no barrier. Yet now, I was fully awake and aware of him, the sleeping man, as he lay heedless of me. Where I was most alive was inside me, where he'd entered me, his penis, his thrusting penis but also his fingers, he'd pushed his fingers inside me, I'd come close to fainting, the sensation was near-unbearable. There was no part of me the man had not entered, penetrated. There was no part of me he had not appropriated. I thought of neuro-anatomical lesions—a part of the cortex injured, a corresponding sense (sight, smell) appropriated, erased. Yet now I stood alert and apart from the man, above him. Lightly I drew my hand across his chest, I stroked the man's chest, the heat of his coarse skin, the man's breasts hard with a layer of muscle. His skin was the hue of stained parchment and the male nipples small and tight as dried berries. With the palm of my hand I dared to feel the man's heart beating deep inside his chest, a vigorous fist-sized heart, stronger than my own. I thought of the Indian boys in our school who'd played their violent games of lacrosse together, and Aaron Kruller among them, how it was said that no girl could touch a player's stick, if so the stick was defiled, and I thought *This is what I can do that he can't know: touch him.* In a swoon of adoration of the sleeping man I leaned over him, nearly lost my balance touching the side of my face against his chest, the pelt-like hairs were a dazzlement to me, I felt the heart, I heard the heart, astonishing to me, a kind of oblivion swept over me, unspeakable. I was sick with love for the man, I could not bear it. I stroked the more flaccid flesh at his waist, at the small of his back. I smiled to think of these secrets of the sleeping man's body, small pockets of flesh, where once he'd been a thin lanky insolent boy. *Indian-looking Aaron Kruller.* The boy of whom my mother warned *They grow up fast in their way of life. Keep your distance.*

Calmly I drew back, to observe him. The sleeping man oblivious of me. Never again in this man's sleep would I observe him like this. I drew a rumpled sheet to his midriff. Still he slept, oblivious. I had never seen anything so beautiful. You would not have said that the man was beautiful, his face was not beautiful, a hard-chiseled face, a coarse face, a face that could be cruel, a face of obstinacy, male stupidity. Yet it seemed to me a beautiful face, I was lost in wonderment of it. The beauty of the man, the maleness, swept over me leaving me weak, disoriented. I would stay with him in Sparta, if he wished me to stay. I would believe him, that truly he wanted me. I would believe that the man's ravenous sexual hunger was a genuine love, for me. I foresaw our lives together here in Sparta. I would have this man's next child. (Would I? Was that possible?) (Certainly, it was possible! The hot fluid leaping from this man teemed with life ravenous to reproduce itself.) I saw our disparate and unlikely lives conjoined as a single life here in Sparta. For Aaron Kruller and I could have a life together only in Sparta. We were a romance of Sparta, our parents had been born here. We had been born here. My father had died here. Wherever Delray had finally died, Delray had died here in Sparta. I thought *Maybe it hasn't ended. Maybe nothing is ever finished.* I saw that the man was like my father, a predator male. His body was suffused with a powerful sexual restlessness. I would love him, and I could not bear it. Every time we made love, the man's possession of me would grow. I would love him more, as he would love me less. There can never be equality, in sexual love. I would wait for him, nights. I would wait for headlights on a ceiling. As my mother had done. For he must appropriate Krista Diehl, I'd seen the determination in his face, in our booth at the restaurant, in the water-splotched mirror above his aunt's sink, for otherwise Aaron Kruller was repelled by me, my blondness, my small-boned white-girl body. For otherwise he'd have wanted to strangle me, to have done with me. To kill his desire for me. And it was an insult to him, as a girl I'd left Sparta and I'd left *him*; I'd grown into an adult female for whom such words as *paralegal, criminology, subpoena, prosecutorial misconduct* were commonplace. Aaron Kruller would marry me to claim me and appropriate me as a daughter of Sparta, as he was a son of Sparta, the doomed city on the Black River. He would never leave me, probably. His first marriage had ended in wreckage but he would not make the same mistake a second time, his pride would not allow it. He would not leave his family as my father had not left his family but had been made to leave, finally. I foresaw that this man would betray me, for how could Aaron Kruller not betray Krista Diehl?—he was the predator male, by nature he was promiscuous, restless and cruel, he could not help himself. That I was a woman was a challenge to him, and a triumph for him, in the motel bed he'd made me cry out as he'd entered me, but I was not a mate for him, not Aaron Kruller. I knew this, already in high school I'd known this. When he'd closed his big-knuckled hands around my throat, I'd known this. I foresaw the slow wreckage of my life, if I gave in to him. In Peekskill it would be said wonderingly and pityingly of me *Where is Krista Diehl? Why has she moved away? Is it true, Krista is married? To someone she knew in Sparta? When she'd been a girl? And is Sparta where Krista is living, now?*

The remainder of my life, in Sparta on the Black River, Herkimer County, New York.

In the blinding-bright bathroom hurriedly I washed. I washed parts of myself, leaning against the sink on one leg. I was not so drunk now, in a part of my brain the after-pain of drunkenness began to beat, I would deflect it for now swallowing aspirin, rinsing my face, my eyes. I was not sober but I was not swaying-drunk as I'd been. I was not dry-mouthed as I'd been. Quickly and as quietly as I could I washed as homeless persons wash, just crucial parts of the body. The smelliest parts, the telltale parts. To dry these parts—armpits, groin—I did not use the pristine-white terry cloth towels hanging on racks in the bathroom, but wads of tissue. Even now thinking *He would see how slovenly I am like himself, he would be disgusted.* For still I felt the naive female fastidiousness, a kind of horror, that a man, any man, even a man who had lain with me in bed for hours making love with me in an abandonment of drunkenness, even such a man must be spared seeing that I'd left hotel towels in a dirtied and rumpled condition. A second time, I rinsed my mouth. My whiskey mouth that tasted too of the predator's tongue and his saliva. I spat into the sink. I was still dizzy, dazed as in the aftermath of sexual pleasure, that piercing of my lower body that left me stunned and wordless as if an area of my brain had been pierced, that controlled speech. If I shut my eyes and opened them the tile walls of the bathroom began to tilt and lurch, I had to concentrate on a horizon, the edge of the filigree-framed mirror above the sink. (The Formica-sink looked to be made of pink plastic bubbles, like teeming protoplasm.) Of necessity I'd inserted a wad of tissue into my vagina that throbbed and burned, to absorb the man's semen. This semen would leak from me otherwise, it would stain my paralegal-clothes. I'd groped and located these clothes to bring into the bathroom with me. I believed that I had most of my clothing, including my underwear the man had taken from me, fumbling in his impatience, these clothes I managed to put on, with my shaky fingers. What I'd pulled over my head—a white silk top, with long sleeves, small pearl buttons—I did not trouble to determine if it was right-side out, or not; if the front was in the back, or the back in the front; my hair was partly unplaited, my hair too the man had dragged his fingers through, pulling, tugging, my pale-blond hair the man had marveled at crinkling and crushing in his big fingers, disheveled now as poor Jacky DeLucca's silver-wire wig. My face was chafed and swollen-looking and not to be contemplated too closely in any mirror, my mouth was swollen from having been kissed, gnawed-at. I would discover my shoes outside, on the shag carpet. Kicked off on the carpet just inside the door. And my black wool belted coat, part-slid off a chair. There was the man's heavy sheepskin jacket, on the floor. My shoulder bag that was good Italian leather, a friend had bought me for a birthday, a friend whom I no longer saw, whom I had lost. For so many friends, I had lost. So many relatives, I had lost. There was my suitcase, almost I'd forgotten my lightweight Tartan-plaid suitcase on rollers, so practical for one who traveled on commuter planes and shuttles. On the bed the man was still sleeping, snoring wetly, sprawled and slovenly. When I passed by him in the wan light from the bathroom, where I'd left the door ajar, I could scarcely bear to look at him, for fear that I would love him so desperately, I would crawl into the cavernous bed beside him, I would embrace him, I would bury my face in his neck and never leave, not ever. As if sensing this, Aaron reached for me, in his sleep; too sleepy to open his eyes yet Aaron seemed to be seeing me, with a part of his brain. Mumbling, "Come back, c'mon. C'mere." I had to wonder if he could have said my name, just then. If I'd leaned over to kiss his mouth could he have said, "Krista? Come back. . . ."

Krista come back, I love you.

I left the room! Swiftly and unerringly I moved. Wanting to think that I was fully sober now. The throbbing headache had begun, this was full wakefulness, penitence. Pain was something with which I could deal. Pain was a legacy I knew, and accepted. Much of my life—personal and professional—was a strategy for dealing with pain, at this I was practiced.

By my watch I saw that it was 8:10 P.M. The day had lurched drunkenly by. I had paid for my room with my Visa card and so had no need to speak with or even be glimpsed by any desk clerk. Through a side door marked EXIT, I fled. After a few minutes' panicked search I located my car, my secondhand foreign-made car, rolled my suitcase to it, climbed into it and fled. Thinking how wise I'd been, to drive my own car. Not to have succumbed to the man's offer, to ride with him in his. In my car I drove south along route 31. I took care to drive just below the speed limit for I worried that my driving was what might be called *impaired*. I could not risk being stopped by any law enforcement officer, subjected to drunk-detection tests and found to be *impaired*. I would enter the New York State Thruway at the intersection at which, the previous night, I had exited the Thruway closely followed by Aaron Kruller in the vehicle behind me. I would head south, and east. Thruway signs would speak of Utica, Albany, New York City.

Eventually, signs would speak of Peekskill.

As I left Sparta the air was porous and there were patches of fog yet I could see, in the rearview mirror of my car, the lights of Sparta on its several glacial hills glittering and shimmering like a distant galaxy in the nighttime sky until it became occluded in mist, and in distance, and vanished from my sight.